PRAISE FOR THE FEMMES FATALES SERIES

"Delicious examples of the pulp genre, written by women and reissued by the Feminist Press. . . . When people think of pulp they generally conjure up male authors like Dashiell Hammett or Raymond Chandler. But in its heyday women were there alongside the men, sometimes subverting its conventions. . . . These stories moved fast, and they were a guilty pleasure, easy to hide under the mattress." —*New York Times*

"Femmes Fatales offers a window on another time and place. . . . It offers little details, daily dreams often overlooked by history books. . . . Pulp, after all, is about pushing limits, about revealing the edges of a culture we can't quite see. Especially at a moment when society seems to be turning backwards this may help tell us who we are." —*Los Angeles Times*

"Fascinating pulp. . . . A lot of fun to read as well as illuminating sociologically." —**"Fresh Air," National Public Radio**

"Fun sells and these books are both historic and fun. To me, the Femmes Fatales series is genius. It's the kind of thing that's going to take the Feminist Press to the end of the century." —Susan Post, owner, BookWoman, in *Publishers Weekly*

"Each of these rediscovered gems boasts its original, gleefully provocative cover art, with dayglow titles, snappy-looking 'broads' and hilarious taglines. . . . Plus, they've got spiffy new commentaries putting each title into modern perspective. . . . This isn't pulp, it's got permanence." —Caroline Leavitt, *Boston Globe*

"The feminist perspective does give these works an undeniable extra dimension." —*Village Voice*

"When we think of the pulp era today, we tend mainly to think of crime novels and male authors. The folks at the Feminist Press are here to set us straight. Their new reprint series . . . celebrates a group of female authors [who] . . . deserve a second look. . . . Damn were they cool." —Bill Ott, *Booklist*

"Sleazy does it. . . . Complete with vintage noir covers, the books feature the tough men, sex-crazed women, drugs, booze, homosexuality, and other wonderfully sleazy trappings of the genre. . . . So bad, it's good." —*Library Journal*

"While pulp fiction, which peaked from the '30s through the '60s, has been rehabilitated in the past decade, this revival has not benefited the genre's female practitioners. . . . Kudos, then, to the Feminist Press, as it launches the 'Femmes Fatales: Women Write Pulp' series in an effort to spotlight forgotten women writers."
—*Time Out New York*

"There's another kind of woman in pulp noir fiction: the kind bold enough to write it in a man's world. They not only wrote noir thrillers but in the other pulp genres as well — sometimes using male pen names to sell more books. The Feminist Press, like a good private eye, has tracked them down. . . . Check out these queens of pulp." —*Minneapolis Star Tribune*

"[A] great success. . . . The press is crossing the borders of genre, launching an unlikely series of pulp fiction . . . 'set in pivotal moments in history when there was a shift in gender roles.'"
—*Poets and Writers*

PRAISE FOR *NOW, VOYAGER* (1941)

"*Now, Voyager* provides an excellent opportunity for the use of Olive Higgins Prouty's outstanding gift as a novelist—delineation of character. . . . One gets to know and like and believe in these people. As though they were friends, there is both suspense and satisfaction in watching them work out the freedom which is hardest to attain—the freedom of peace with one's self" —*Booklist*

"Mrs. Prouty has to a certain degree repeated the formula which made *Stella Dallas* such a success. She has again done a compassionate and intense study of a woman's mind and heart, made vivid and real by her selection of significant and effective details . . ."
—*Springfield Republican*

NOW, VOYAGER

FEMMES FATALES
WOMEN WRITE PULP

THE GIRLS IN 3-B
Valerie Taylor

SKYSCRAPER
Faith Baldwin

IN A LONELY PLACE
Dorothy B. Hughes

THE BLACKBIRDER
Dorothy B. Hughes

BUNNY LAKE IS MISSING
Evelyn Piper

NOW, VOYAGER
Olive Higgins Prouty

NOW, VOYAGER

OLIVE HIGGINS PROUTY

AFTERWORD BY JUDITH MAYNE

FEMMES FATALES: WOMEN WRITE PULP

THE FEMINIST PRESS
AT THE CITY UNIVERSITY OF NEW YORK
NEW YORK

Published by the Feminist Press at the City University of New York
The Graduate Center, 365 Fifth Avenue
New York, NY 10016, www.feministpress.org

First Feminist Press edition, 2004

09 08 07 06 05 04   5 4 3 2 1

Originally published in 1941 by Houghton Mifflin Co., Boston, Mass.

Library of Congress Cataloging-in-Publication Data

Prouty, Olive Higgins, 1882–1974
  Now, voyager / Olive Higgins Prouty ; afterword by Judith Mayne.— 1st Feminist
Press ed.
      p. cm. — (Femmes fatales : women write pulp)
    ISBN 1-55861-476-1 (pbk. : alk. paper) — ISBN 1-55861-477-X (library cloth :
alk. paper)
  1. Single women—Fiction. 2. Mothers and daughters—Fiction. 3. Self-realiza-
tion—Fiction. 4. Women travelers—Fiction. 5. Boston (Mass.)—Fiction. 6. Cruise
ships—Fiction. 7. Married men—Fiction. 8. Architects—Fiction. I. Title. II.
Series.
  PS3531.R863N69 2004
  813'.52—dc22   2004010066

The Feminist Press is grateful to Sallie Bingham, Laura Brown, Blanche Wiesen
Cook, Lis Driscoll, Barbara Grossman, Nancy Hoffman, Florence Howe, Betty
Prashker, Susan Scanlan, and Donald C. Thomas for their generosity in supporting
the publication of this book.

Text and cover design by Dayna Navaro
Cover photo: from *Now, Voyager* © 1942 Turner Entertainment Co. A Warner Bros.
Entertainment Company. All rights reserved.
Printed on acid-free paper by Transcontinental Printing
Printed in Canada

Women write pulp? It seems like a contradiction in terms, given the tough-guy image of pulp fiction today. This image has been largely shaped by the noir revival of the past decade—by reprints of classics by Jim Thompson and best-sellers by neo-noir writer James Ellroy, the rerelease of classic film noir on video, and the revisioning of the form by Quentin Tarantino. Fans of such works would be hard pressed to name a woman pulp author, or even a character who isn't a menacing femme fatale.

But women did write pulp, in large numbers and in all the classic pulp fiction genres, from hard-boiled noirs to breathless romances to edgy science fiction and taboo lesbian pulps. And while employing the conventions of each genre, women brought a different, gendered perspective to these forms. Women writers of pulp often outpaced their male counterparts in challenging received ideas about gender, race, and class, and in exploring those forbidden territories that were hidden from view off the typed page. They were an important part of a literary phenomenon, grounded in its particular time and place, that had a powerful impact on American popular culture in the middle of the twentieth century, and continues to exert its influence today.

Pulp fiction encompasses a broader array of works, and occupies a more complex place in the literary, social, and commercial culture of its era, than the handful of contemporary revivals and tributes to pulp suggests. Pulp emerged as an alternative format for books in the 1930s, building on the popularity of pulp magazines, which flourished from the

1920s to the 1940s, and drawing on traditions established by the dime novel of the nineteenth and early twentieth centuries. The dime novel had developed the Western, the romance, the sleuth story, and the adventure story as genres, with narratives geared largely to young readers, in particular on the frontier. Pulp magazines, needing to compete with early motion pictures and to connect with an urban audience, offered similar stories with an edge. Grouping fiction or believe-it-or-not fact under themes like crime, horror, and adventure, magazines such as *Black Mask*, *Weird Tales*, and *Dime Adventure* demonstrated the existence of a market for inexpensive and provocative teen and adult reading matter. The move to book-length narratives provided an expanded scope for a voracious literature rooted in American popular culture, reflective of American obsessions, and willing to explore American underworlds.

Printed on wood-grain, or pulp, paper, and cheaply bound, the books were markedly different from hardbound editions. These first modern paperbacks served different purposes, too—entertainment, thrill, or introduction to "serious culture"—and were presumably read differently. Books intended for the pulp lists were undoubtedly produced differently, with less time given to the writing, and less money and status accruing to the authors. As pulp publishers grew in number (Fawcett, Pocketbook, Bantam, Ace, Signet, Dell), economic patterns emerged in the treatment of authors and texts: pulp authors often received one-time payment (no royalties); editors focused on keeping books short, tight, and engrossing; and author identity was often submerged beneath the publisher's pulp brand name and the lurid cover art that sold the books. Some pulp authors used pseudonyms to conceal an everyday identity behind a more saleable one, often of the opposite gender. Georgina Ann Randolph Craig (1908–1957) wrote prolifically as Craig

Rice. Some used several names, each evocative of a genre they wrote in: Velma Young (1913–1997) published lesbian pulp under the name Valerie Taylor, poetry as Nacella Young, and romances as Francine Davenport. Eventually some contemporary authors emerged as brands themselves: a Faith Baldwin romance was a predictable product.

At the same time, classics and contemporary best-sellers were reincarnated as pulp, as the format absorbed and repositioned literature that might otherwise have been inaccessible to working-class readers. Pulp publishers seem to have selected classic fiction with an eye to class politics, favoring, for example, the French Revolution and Dickens. They tended to present science as an arena where good old-fashioned ingenuity and stick-to-itiveness win the day. The life of Marie Curie was a pulp hit. When classics were reprinted in pulp editions—for example, *The Count of Monte Cristo* or *The Origin of the Species*—author identity might move to the fore on covers and in descriptive copy, but in becoming pulp the works acquired a popular aura and gravitated into pulp genres such as adventure and romance. Again, when new titles like William Faulkner's *Sanctuary* or Mary McCarthy's *The Company She Keeps* were issued in pulp editions, the cover art planted the works firmly in pulp categories: ruined woman, Southern variety; the many adventures and many men of a fast city girl. The genre, more than the author's name, was the selling point.

As the stories in pulp magazines were marketed by themes, so book-length tales were distinctively packaged by genre—Dell used a red heart to mark its romance line, for instance. Over time there were Westerns, science fiction, romance, mystery, crime/noir, and various others to choose from. Genres were to a large extent gendered. Crime/noir, for instance, focused on a masculine world of detectives, crooks, femmes fatales (positioned as foils to men), corruption, and violence, all described in hard-boiled prose. Romance focused on women's problems around courtship, virginity, marriage, motherhood, and careers, earnestly or coyly described. Since genres were gendered, the implied assumption was that men wrote and read crime/noir and women wrote and read romances. In fact, this assumption proves largely false.

Because pulp genres tended to rely on formulaic treatments, it was not difficult for writers to learn the ingredients that make up noir or, for that matter, how to write a lesbian love scene. The fact that authorial name and persona were rarely linked to real-life identity further permitted writers to explore transgender, or transgenre, writing. In so doing, they might self-consciously accentuate the gendered elements of a given genre, sometimes approximating parody, or they might attempt to regender a genre—for instance, writing a Western that foregrounds a romance. These freedoms, combined with the willingness of pulp publishers to buy work from anyone with the skill to write, meant that women had the chance to write in modes that were typically considered antithetical to them, and to explore gender across all genres. Leigh Brackett (1915–1978), a premier woman author of pulp, wrote hard-boiled crime books, science fiction, and Westerns, in addition to scripting sharp repartee for Bogart and Bacall in *The Big Sleep* (director Howard Hawks hired her on the basis of her novel *No Good from a Corpse*—assuming she was a man, as did many of her fans). Other women authors wrote whodunnit mysteries with girl heroines, science fiction battles of the sexes, and romances that start with a Reno divorce. Women wrote from male perspectives, narrating from inside the head of a serial killer, a PI, or a small-town pharmacist who happens to know all the town dirt. They also wrote from places where women weren't supposed to go.

Notoriously, pulp explored U.S. subcultures, which then often generated their own pulp subgenres. Where 1930s and 1940s pulp depicted gangster life and small-town chicanery, 1950s and 1960s pulp turned its attention, often with a pseudoanthropological lens, to juvenile delinquents, lesbians (far more than gay men), and beatniks, introducing its readers to such settings as reform schools, women's prisons, and "dangerous" places like Greenwich Village. These books exploited subcultures as suggestive settings for sexuality and nonconformism, often focusing on transgressive women or "bad girls": consider *Farm Hussy* and *Shack Baby* (two of a surprisingly large group in the highly specific rural-white-trash-slut subgenre), *Reefer Girl* (and its competitor, *Marijuana Girl*), *Women's Barracks, Reform School Girl,* and *Hippie Harlot.* Other books posited menaces present in the heart of middle-class life: *Suburbia: Jungle of Sex* and *Shadow on the Hearth.* A growing African American readership generated more new lines, mysteries and romances with black protagonists. Though the numbers of these books were fairly small, their existence is significant. With a few notable exceptions, African Americans were almost never found in pulps written for white readers, except as racially stereotyped stock characters.

While a strengthened Hays Code sanitized movies in 1934, and "legitimate" publishers fought legal battles in order to get *Ulysses* and *Lady Chatterley's Lover* past the censors, pulp fiction, selling at twenty-five cents a book at newsstands, gas stations, and bus terminals, explored the taboo without provoking public outcry, or even dialogue. (Notably, though, pulp avoided the four-letter words that marked works like *Ulysses*, deploying instead hip street lingo to refer to sex, drink and drugs, and guns.) As famed lesbian pulp author Ann Bannon has noted, this "benign neglect provided a much-needed veil behind which we writers could work in peace." Pulp offered readers interracial romances during the segregation era, and blacklisted leftists encoded class struggle between pulp covers. The neglect by censors and critics had to do with the transience of pulp.

Circulating in a manner that matched the increasing mobility of American culture, pulps rarely adorned libraries, private or public. Small, slim, and ultimately disposable, they were meant for the road, or for easy access at home. They could be read furtively, in between household chores or during a lunch break. When finished, they could be left in a train compartment or casually stashed in a work shed. Publishers increasingly emphasized ease of consumption in the packaging of pulp: Ace produced "Ace Doubles," two titles reverse-bound together, so that the reader had only to flip the book over to enjoy a second colorful cover and enticing story; Bantam produced "L.A.s," specially sized to be sold from vending machines, the product's name evoking the mecca of the automobile and interstate highway culture; Fawcett launched a book club for its Gold Medal line, promising home delivery of four new sensational Gold Medal titles a month. To join, one cut out a coupon at the back of a Gold Medal book—clearly, no reluctance to damage a pulp volume would impede owners from acting on the special offer.

The mass appeal of pulp proved uncontainable by print. Characters and stories that originated in pulp soon found their way onto radio airwaves (e.g., *The Shadow*), onto the screen in the form of pre-Code sizzlers, noirs, and adventure films, and into comic books and newspaper comic strips. Through all these media, pulp penetrated the heart of the American popular imagination (and the popular image of America beyond its borders), shaping as well as reflecting the culture that consumed it.

Far more frequently than has been acknowledged, the source of these American icons, story lines, and genres were women, often working-class women who put bread on the table by creating imaginary worlds, or exploring existing but risky or taboo worlds, to fulfill the appetites of readers of both genders. But these writers, and the rich variety of work they produced, are today nearly invisible, despite the pulp revival of the last decade.

This revival has repopularized a hard-boiled, male world of pulp. Today's best-remembered pulp authors are not only male but also unapologetically misogynistic: pulp icon Jim Thompson's *A Hell of a Woman* and *A Swell-Looking Babe* are not untypical of the titles found among the noir classics recently restored to print.

In fact, it is interesting to note, even in a broader survey of the genres, how many male-authored, and presumably male-read, pulps were focused on women (remember *Shack Baby* and *Reefer Girl*)—a phenomenon not found in the highbrow literature of the period. Men even wrote a fair number of lesbian pulps. But more often than not, the women in these books are dangerous and predatory as well as irresistible, exploiting men's desire for their own purposes. Or they are wayward women who either come to a bad end, or come to their senses with the help of a man who sets them straight (in the various senses of the word). Some critics have noted that such female characters proliferated in the immediate post–World War II period, when servicemen were returning to a world in which women had occupied, briefly, a powerful position in the workplace and other areas of the public sphere—a world in which the balance between the genders had been irrevocably altered.

In contrast with these bad girls and femmes fatales were the heroines of traditional romance pulps, most of them relentlessly pretty and spunky girls-next-door. They occupied the centers of their own stories, and navigated sometimes complicated social and emotional terrain, but in the end always seemed to get—or be gotten by—their man.

Given this background, and given the strict generic dictates to which all successful pulp writers were subject, did women working in undeniably male-dominated pulp genres such as crime/noir write differently from their male counterparts? And did women writers of formulaic romances, both heterosexual and lesbian, reveal the genuine conflicts facing real women in their time and explore the limits of female agency? They could hardly fail to do so.

Relatively little scholarship has been done on pulp fiction; less still on women writers of pulp. It is not possible to speculate on the intentions of women pulp authors, and few would suggest that they were undercover feminists seeking to subvert patriarchal culture by embedding radical messages in cheap popular novels. Yet from a contemporary vantage point, some of their work certainly does seem subversive, regardless of the intention behind it.

Women writers provided the first pulps with happy endings for lesbians: Valerie Taylor's *The Girls in 3-B* is a prime example of this suprisingly revolutionary phenomenon, and still more intriguing for its contrast of the different options and obstacles faced by heterosexual and homosexual women in the 1950s (with little doubt as to which looked better to the author). The femme fatale of *In a Lonely Place,* the luscious Laurel Gray, has brains and integrity, as well as curves—and in the end, she is not the one who turns out to be deadly. In fact, Dorothy B. Hughes's bold twist on the noir genre can be seen as addressing the crisis in postwar masculinity, with its backlash taken to the furthest extremes. The protagonist of Faith Baldwin's *Skyscraper* is typically pretty and plucky; she longs for domestic bliss and she loves her man. But she also loves the bustle and buzz of the office where she works, the rows of gleaming desks and file cabinets, the sense of being part of the larger, public world of business—and she epitomizes a new kind of heroine in a new kind of romance plot, a career girl with a wider set of choices to negotiate.

These premier books in the Feminist Press's Femmes Fatales series were selected for their bold and sometimes transgressive uses of genre forms, as well as the richness of their social and historical settings and their lively and skillful writing. We chose books that also seemed to have some impact on public consciousness in their time—in these cases, rather inexactly measured by the fact that they crossed over into different, and even more popular, media: Both _In a Lonely Place_ and _Skyscraper_ were made into films. And we can only speculate whether _The Girls in 3-B_ played any part in inspiring _The Girls in Apartment 3-G,_ the syndicated comic strip about three young working women (heterosexual, of course) living together in New York City, which debuted in 1961.

The enormous popularity of the Femmes Fatales series's first season, in 2003, confirms readers' intense interest in these rediscovered queens of pulp. In 2004, the series expands to include a second book by the incomparable Dorothy B. Hughes: _The Blackbirder_, a World War II espionage novel with a unique hard-boiled heroine. It also includes two books that achieved fame, again, primarily through the films they inspired. _Now, Voyager_, the renowned romantic melodrama that gave Bette Davis her favorite role, deals directly with issues of women's emotional, sexual, and social autonomy. The fascinating psychological thriller _Bunny Lake Is Missing_, made into a supremely creepy (and cult classic) film by Otto Preminger, introduces a hard-boiled mom, who must rapidly transform herself from a handwringer to a gunslinger when her daughter is kidnapped.

In the past three decades, feminist scholars have laid claim to women's popular fiction as a legitimate focus of attention and scholarship, and a rich source of information on women's lives and thought in various eras. Some scholars have in fact questioned the use—and the uses—of the term *popular fiction,* which seems to have been disproportionately applied to the work of women writers, especially those who wrote "women's books." The Feminist Press views the Femmes Fatales series as an important new initiative in this ongoing work of cultural reclamation. As such, it is also a natural expression of the Press's overall mission to ensure that women's voices are fully represented in the public discourse, in the literary "canon," and on bookstore and library shelves.

We leave it to scholars doing groundbreaking new work on women's pulp—including our own afterword writers—to help us fully appreciate all that these works have to offer, both as literary texts and as social documents. And we leave it to our readers to discover for themselves, as we have, all of the entertaining, disturbing, suggestive, and thoroughly fascinating work that can be found behind the juicy covers of women's pulp fiction.

Livia Tenzer, Editorial Director
Jean Casella, Publisher
New York City
July 2004

LIST OF CHAPTERS

CHAPTER ONE:
THE STRANGER

A blizzard was raging in New York, so she had read on the bulletin board before she left the ship. It was difficult to visualize sheets of fine snow driving obliquely against façades, while sitting on an open terrace in the sun gazing at calla lilies in bloom bordered by freesia. It was difficult, too, to believe that the scene before her was reality. It was more like a drop-curtain rolled down between herself and the dull drab facts of her life.

She sat at a small white iron table close to a railing, keenly conscious of the sun beating down on her shoulder blades, of the burnt-nut tang of the black Indian coffee which she was sipping, and the sharp smart of unfamiliar cigarette smoke at the back of her throat. Keenly conscious, too, of the clothes she was wearing, which were not her own. She sat close to the table, knees crossed beneath its top, one foot emerging encased snugly in light amber-colored silk and a navy-blue pump. She flexed the ankle up and down as if to convince herself it was hers. At the same time she raised her hand to the back of her neck. It was as irresistible as exploring the empty space left by a pulled tooth. But she mustn't appear self-conscious when her companion returned. He said he would be gone only long enough to send a cable.

She leaned forward on elbows lightly placed upon the table-top and took several sips of coffee, gazing down reflectively between sips. She must tell him her name and explain why it wasn't on the passenger list. Every time he called her Miss Beauchamp it was a reminder of the difference between herself and the vivid and vivacious Renée. And how Renée Beauchamp would hate it! She returned the cup to its saucer and raised her eyes.

In the foreground there was a luxurious garden with glimpses of steps and portions of balustrade; in the lower left-hand corner the proverbial flower-filled urn with hanging vines; behind the urn a cliff with a cascade of purple bougainvillea falling down its face, and at the top an umbrella pine leaning out against the sky at a spectacular angle. In the distance there was a glimpse of aquamarine blue sea with boats floating on its surface.

The largest boat was hers. It was an ocean liner, with two squat, black-banded funnels amidships, and long festoons of windows, portholes, and deck railings extending from stern to bow. The liner hailed from New York. It was the first time she had dropped anchor since she had backed out of her berth into the Hudson River. It was the first opportunity offered her passengers to feel the pressure of earth beneath their feet.

She had not intended to come ashore at Gibraltar. It was an old story to her. She had been here with her mother many times before. But that morning, looking out of her porthole at the crooked tiers of mellow-toned old buildings crowding down close to the water's edge beneath the jutting rock, her consciousness had been pricked by the realization of her independence. She had never wandered alone all day in any foreign city! She had dressed for the shore with something like excitement. But now she was regretting her decision. She couldn't keep up the false rôle she was playing with this strange man much longer.

She congratulated herself that she had not choked when he lit her cigarette. How surprised he would be if he knew it was the first time in her life anyone had lit her cigarette. The first time in her life she had smoked a cigarette except opposite her own reflection behind closed doors. But no more surprised than Doctor Jaquith, she imagined, if he could have seen her casually flicking ashes over a terrace railing! Doctor Jaquith would consider it a great triumph, she supposed. But she hadn't smoked the cigarette to assert her own personality. On the contrary she'd smoked it to conceal her own personality.

She had been the last passenger to board the last tender scheduled to leave for the shore trip. The tender had in fact been held for her for several minutes. She had selected a seat as far removed as possible from the other passengers, and had kept her eyes steadfastly turned away from any possible contact with another human being—studying the shore-line, following the lazy motions of the overfed Gibraltar seagulls, plainly conveying that she did not wish to be spoken to.

She looked as if she might have been recently ill. She had little natural color, and no artificial color whatsoever. There was something that suggested old ivory about the cast and quality of her skin. Her cheekbones were high and accentuated by hollows in her cheeks. Her brows were black, well-defined, and extraordinarily far apart. Her hair was also black—what could be seen of it. It was cut very short. Her eyes were the somber blue of late-blooming monk's-hood. She was dressed in the conservative good taste that is expensive. A navy-blue costume, very plain and very perfect, with a small snug navy-blue hat on her close-cropped head. Over her shoulders hung the pelts of several little animals, probably Russian sable. She caused much comment among the other passengers because of the incongruity between her distinguished appearance and her wary manner.

Most of the cruise passengers who had signed up for the Gibraltar trip had already left the liner on the earlier tenders. At the dock there had been only a few of the local horse-drawn vehicles left. She had engaged the last one. She was seated on its narrow back seat when the effervescing and ever-present cruise manager, Mr. Thompson, had called out from somewhere behind her, "Oh, Miss Beauchamp!" and a moment later, "Would you be so kind as to share your carriage with Mr. So-and-So?" She didn't catch the name. "He had to go back to

the tender for his guidebook. We'll all be lunching together at
one o'clock. I'll see you both there. Thank you so much. Have
a nice time."

Before she could think of any reason for not sharing her
carriage, Mr. So-and-So was seated by her side and they were
moving up the long pier toward the huddled shopping district.

"I hope you don't mind too much."

"Of course not," she replied, as warmly as she knew how.
("Pull your own weight," Doctor Jaquith had exhorted her
that last day in his office. "We've taught you the proper technique. Now go ahead and practice it on this cruise. Respond!
Take part! Contribute! Be interested in everything and everybody. Forget you're a hidebound New Englander and
unbend. Loosen up. Be nice to every human being who
crosses your path.")

"We've already been introduced, Miss Beauchamp," her
companion informed her. "On deck two days ago, as we were
passing the Azores," and without giving her a chance to reply,
"I've never been in Gibraltar before." If her mother had been
present this statement would instantly have placed him: not
alone the fact of his limited experience, but because he mentioned it. "What an amusing conveyance this is! Built on the
lines of a hansom cab. Female of the species, possibly, with all
this lingerie and lace."

When her companion rejoined her on the terrace, he sat
down opposite her and poured himself a cup of coffee from
the small silver pot, blindingly bright in the sunshine.

"I got the cable off finally," he announced, dropping two
lumps of sugar in the cup, and stirring them vigorously. He
had nice hands, bony and veined, with a scattering of dark
hairs on their backs, and knuckly fingers with close-cut nails.
"So that's one of the umbrella pines! And that's a bougainvillea! And that white stuff in the garden down there is freesia
blooming outdoors in March!" He took off his hat, placed it on

the railing, and lifted his face to the sun. "Isn't this heat simply marvelous!"

Until then she would have said his eyes were brown, but now with the sun shining straight into them she saw that they were blue with brown flecks. The blue was a deep indigo. It reminded her of her fountain-pen ink in its bottle, when looking down its wide-necked top. *Midnight blue-black*, the label said. The most striking feature about him was the difference between his eyebrows and his hair. His hair was thin and turning gray, his eyebrows thick, and a warm sienna brown. His clothes were a nearly an American businessman's uniform as possible—white shirt with soft collar, gray suit with an innocuous stripe, and a plain dark blue tie.

"I hope you've had enough to eat," he said, taking a sip of his coffee. They had been over an hour too late to eat with the cruise passengers. They had lunched alone on hors d'oeuvres, cold cuts, and a bottle of wine, splitting the cost of all but the wine, which he insisted should be his contribution.

"I've had plenty to eat," and she wished she had the confidence to add, *And too much to drink.* She never had wine in the middle of the day. Sometimes a glass of sherry when her mother and she were lunching at the home of one of her sisters-in-law. It always made her sleepy. Moreover, this was the hour she rested, according to her Cascade schedule. Cascade was the name of Doctor Jaquith's sanatorium in Vermont.

It had been a strenuous morning for an invalid. Her companion had been interested in every unusual detail Gibraltar has to offer a first visitor, from its fortress at the top of the rock to its monkeys which occasionally wander down to the town from their caves on the sides of the rock. He had spent over an hour among the shops, frequently consulting a small black leather book which he had produced from his breast pocket. One of his daughters, he explained, wanted a certain brand of perfumery which she'd heard one could get cheap in Gibraltar; and another, a certain kind of English sweater; and he'd also like to find something right for a girl around twelve. He would be grateful to her if she could direct him to the right shops for such articles. She had gone farther. She had helped him select the articles.

"You're not at all what I'd expected you'd be like, Miss Beauchamp," he remarked, draining his cup and pushing it aside.

"As we met for the first time only two days ago, how could you possibly expect what I'd be like?" she asked in that supercilious tone which she had learned to employ to conceal self-consciousness.

"Oh, but I've heard of you! And you're quite different from what I expected."

"Pray how am I different?" she inquired briefly, making her smoke-screen still thicker by a condescending shrug.

"You're so much more comfortable. I mean—" She saw a slight suggestion of dark color beneath the swarthiness of his face. It immediately steadied her. "I mean you're so much easier to talk to," he floundered. "I've heard a lot about your week-ends up there at your farm in Connecticut, and your monologues, and how clever you are. I have a friend who goes to your famous parties sometimes, and he's told me about them. Classmate of mine at college. Frank McIntyre. Have you seen Mack lately?"

"No. Not lately." She paused. "Nor *ever*," she added. "I don't know Mack."

"But he told me—"

"Please listen. I'm not Renée Beauchamp. Renée is out in Arizona somewhere. A few days before this boat sailed she had an invitation from some friend of hers to visit his ranch."

"But the ship's hostess introduced you as Miss Beauchamp. And this morning Thompson—"

"I know. And the headwaiter, and the deck-steward too—they all think I'm Miss Beauchamp. But the purser knows all about it. I took Renée Beauchamp's space at the last moment—too late for my name to appear on the first passenger list printed. Renée was booked only as far as Nice. Naturally if you know anything about Renée Beauchamp, you know she isn't the type to be taking this cruise, or any cruise, if she can help it."

"Oh! Isn't she? I suppose you are getting off at Nice, then?"

"No, I'm taking the whole trip."

"As Miss Beauchamp? Keeping your own identity a secret?"

"That's an idea! But no, the only reason I didn't correct the mistake up there on the deck when we were introduced was because there was such a crowd it would have been awkward."

"Oh, then you *do* remember meeting me on the deck! Let's have a liqueur on the strength of it. What do you say?"

Before she could say anything he had pushed back his chair and had gone in search of a waiter. She remembered perfectly when Miss Demarest, the ship's hostess, had introduced them. It had been her first day on the deck—her first appearance in her borrowed clothes since her transformation that last hurried day in New York.

She had lain in a state of half torpor for the first three days out of port, and for the next two had remained in her stateroom, grateful for disagreeable weather, disagreeable physical symptoms, for anything that provided an excuse for remaining a few days longer in hiding.

She had carefully kept in the background when the other passengers gathered at the deck railing to exclaim on the spectacular sight of the Azores which had appeared at the sunset hour, green as June peas on the pewter-gray sea. They were the first sight of land since the New Jersey coast had disappeared five days ago, and the first clear sunset. She was seated in her steamer chair, or rather in Renée Beauchamp's steamer chair (it still bore her name), when Miss Demarest spied her and exclaimed with a squeal of delight, "Oh Miss Beauchamp! At last! I want to introduce you to these people!" And she had routed her out of the chair, and led her to a group of strangers of which this man had been one. They hadn't exchanged a single word.

"I've ordered two Cointreaus," he announced when he again returned to the sunny table. "I hope that is all right for you. Is that the coast of Africa over there?"

"No, no, no! Spain!" she laughed.

"Bullfights. Matadors. Grilled ironwork. Señoritas," he sighed, gazing wistfully. "That is, if the old traditional Spain is Hemingway and Carmen. I've never been there. The fact is I've never been much of anywhere east of New York," he laughed. "I'd give anything if I could be in your shoes and take the whole cruise."

"Where are you leaving the boat?"

"At Nice, worse luck. I'm on my way to Milan on business. Look here," he broke off, "if you aren't Miss Beauchamp, who are you, please?"

"I'm not quite sure," she said, glancing down at her unfamiliar foot. Not since a specialist in orthopedics had told her mother 20 years ago that she required a certain low-heeled, wide-toed shoe had she worn anything else. Again she wished she dared to reply, *If there's any truth in the adage, "Clothes make the man," then at present I'm my sister-in-law, Lisa.*

"Not quite sure who you are?"

"No. But don't be alarmed. I'm quite harmless."

A waiter approached with two tiny glasses on a tray. The glasses were filled with liquid clear as dewdrops. Her companion raised his glass high, and looking straight into her eyes, exclaimed, "Well, here's how, Stranger."

She was not accustomed to these little playful ceremonies.

But she could at least do as he did. She raised her glass to the same level as his and repeated his words, "Well, here's how, Stranger."

"By the way," he remarked, twirling the slender stem of his empty liqueur glass between his thumb and forefinger, "don't you think I ought to know your name before the day is over?"

"But I don't know yours!"

"You don't! How stupid of me to think you got it when no one ever listens to names. My name is Durrance." He spelled it. "On the passenger list I'm J. D. Durrance, New York City. Now it's your turn."

"My name is Vale." She also spelled it. "If I'm ever on the passenger list, I'll be 'C. Vale, Boston, Mass.'"

"I've heard of Boston." He smiled. "And the name Vale, like Bunker Hill, rings a familiar bell. Are you one of the Vales of Boston?"

"One of the lesser ones."

"Well, which? I don't know yet whether it's Miss or Mrs."

"It's Aunt. I'm the proverbial spinster aunt. Most families have one, you know." Her mouth fell into the lines of the least resistance—a downward curve, with the corners lifted into an ironical smile.

"But aunt *what?*"

She couldn't keep up the persiflage any longer. "My name is Charlotte Vale," she announced flatly, as if she resented the fact. "*Miss* Charlotte Vale."

It was several hours later when they were seated in the tender crossing the harbor to the waiting ocean liner that he produced a small package from his overcoat pocket. It was wrapped in bright pink paper, tied with fine string, strong as dental floss, with a loop so one could carry it dangling on one's finger. He held it up before her by the loop.

"I hope you'll accept a slight offering for being my guide today. I don't know the first thing about perfumery, but the clerk said this was all right. It's a mixture of several kinds of flowers. It's called Quelques Fleurs. I thought that would be safe, as I don't know your preference in flowers." He dropped the little package in her lap.

She was glad it was dusk, for she could feel the color mounting to her cheeks. Ridiculous! At her age! But she couldn't remember that any man had ever gone into a shop and bought a present for her. Except her father. He used to. Her companion mustn't know she didn't use perfumery. Her mother had brought her up to believe it was bad taste. She lifted the little package.

"Thank you ever so much," was all she could manage to say at first. But later she added, "I'll put some on my handkerchief tonight."

"Will you? Good! And let's meet for a cocktail in the bar at a quarter of eight."

CHAPTER TWO:
LIKE CINDERELLA

When Charlotte reached her stateroom she switched on the lights, bolted the door, took off her hat and coat and sat down before the triple-mirrored dressing-table. Glancing into one of the side panels she gazed at her profile in another mirror across the room. The profile was looking away from her which gave her the odd sensation of gazing at someone else. So *that* was how she looked! For years she had avoided all such painful speculation and shunned mirrors, schooling herself never to study her reflection in order to see herself as others saw her.

But today, although her companion had not remarked upon

her appearance, several times she had caught that peculiar expression of approving appraisal which she had observed in other men's eyes directed toward other women. Her borrowed clothes alone couldn't draw forth such a look. Today she had been borrowing more than Lisa's clothes—her manner, posture, many of her gestures. The fact was she had seen Lisa one day last summer dressed in this very same costume, all but the furs, seated at a small iron table on a terrace at her country house, knees crossed, elbows lightly placed upon the table-top, with Barry Firth opposite looking at her, his eyes filled with far more than approval. Lisa was her sister-in-law, the widow of her oldest brother, Rupert, who had died six months ago. For years Charlotte had been observing Lisa enter rooms, preside at tea-tables, rise, sit down, light a cigarette, toss away a match—speculating, with a dull pain of envy, what was the secret of her attraction. She had never attempted to imitate her. Even today her performance had been more the result of absorption than conscious imitation.

She and Lisa didn't look alike. Lisa was fair, with faint, delicately penciled eyebrows, grey eyes, and fawn-colored hair. While she was dark. Spanish blood might have run in her veins. Her skin was dusky where the shadows fell; *sallow* was her own adjective for it. Her brows were black and had always been heavy and straight, nearly touching in the middle. Her hair, too, had always been heavy and straight, and dull and lusterless except on the first day after washing. Now, as she gazed, it was as glossy as a charred log with a wavy grain shining in the sun.

Up to six months ago her figure had been as unlike Lisa's as her coloring—blocky, bulky, uncontrolled by a restricting diet. Her mother disapproved of skinny women, especially of those who starved themselves to keep so. Her mother disapproved of short hair, too. She had never allowed her daughter to cut it. As a child Charlotte had worn it in one long, heavy braid. Later she was taught to wind it into a bun, fastened at the back of her head with sturdy hairpins. Her bun was so heavy it dragged her hair back in an unbecoming fashion, slipping down until it looked as if it were resting on her shoulders, bound in place by cords. But now the cords had been cut. As she gazed at her long neck and the modeled contour of her head, that sensation of detachment from her own personality increased.

She turned away from her profile and, adjusting one of the side mirrors, studied the back of her head. The French coiffeur, into whose hands Lisa had delivered her a few hours before he boat sailed, had made some comments which she had remembered ever since. While busily snipping at the back of her head, after the heaviest locks were cut off, he had exclaimed, "Oh, Mademoiselle, I discover something very valuable, like a nugget of gold buried beneath much earth! A widow's peak behind! So nice a border will it make upon the neck, Mademoiselle must have her hair cut very short, *n'est-ce pas?*"

She had no opinion to offer. Lisa was absent, attending to last-minute details about her wardrobe. Lisa had told her to leave everything to Monsieur Henri. She was glad to do so. She felt little interest in a proceeding which she had consented to simply because she lacked sufficient spirit to combat it. Even during the ordeal of permanent-waving she had made no protest. Physical pain had the advantage of putting mental despair in the background for the time being.

After Monsieur Henri had finished with her that day, she had been transferred to another room, and laid out prone in a low-slung, streamlined dentist's chair. Sheets had been spread over her body. Pads had been placed over her eyes. Steaming hot compresses and ice cold had been applied to her face. Afterward her face underwent such a process of kneading, molding, slapping, rotating, vibrating, and she knew not what else, that it became numb to the various treatments applied. What did she care? Even before her illness her motto for years had been, *Follow the line of least resistance.*

It had been Lisa who had been at the bottom of the plot of her banishment from home to Cascade. Banishment? No, escape rather, as it turned out. Three months of blessed surcease from her mother's taunts that her illness was only imagination. The diagnosis of her "nervous breakdown" had filled her mother with scorn. Charlotte no more had a nervous breakdown than a moulting canary! No one in the Vale family had ever had a nervous breakdown! As to Lisa's proposal that Charlotte go to that place called Cascade, no one in the Vale family had ever been an inmate in a sanatorium or asylum, either!

Her mother was lunching at Lisa's on the day Doctor Warburton, the family doctor, took her in his own car to the train bound for Cascade, and settled her in a drawing-room with a trained nurse. It was the first time she had taken a railroad journey without her mother since her father had died when she was at boarding-school. Each time she had mustered enough courage to attempt to run down to New York, or to run anywhere for a day or two without her mother, it had ended in defeat. If she persisted in any such plan, her mother always had a heart attack, and a daughter cannot abandon a mother in physical distress.

Her mother had been well on in her forties when she had been born. Three boys had preceded her. "The child of my old age," she had often heard herself described when she was small. It had always filled her with a vague sense of shame, as if her existence required an explanation. Or was it that her appearance required an explanation? Several times her mother had laughingly referred to her as "my ugly duckling." She used to wonder if all "children of old age" were ugly ducklings—branded with marks of the advanced years of their parents. Her brothers were all handsome specimens. "An old-fashioned little thing," was another phrase often applied to her when she was a child. She had always felt not only apologetic to her mother, but under deep obligation to make amends for her undesired arrival.

Ever since she was a child she had worn glasses. Steel-bowed spectacles when she went to kindergarten; later, horn-bowed spectacles; rimless eyeglasses at her coming-out party. "You'll never have another pair of eyes," her mother always warned her before ordering her to put on her glasses, if she ever caught her without them. At Cascade Doctor Jaquith had sent her to an oculist, later announcing that glasses were no longer necessary and advising her to discard them entirely. She always felt undressed without her glasses, as if she'd left off her shoes or blouse.

Gazing now in the mirror straight at her unspectacled, unfamiliar face, apprehension about the outcome of this ridiculous camouflage returned to her. The very expression of her face had changed. Lisa herself had been shocked by her altered appearance when she returned to Henri's that last day in New York. Charlotte had overhead her gently expostulating with Monsieur Henri. Why had he been so extreme, she had inquired. It was always safer to cut hair the *first* time a little too long than too short, didn't he think? "But Mademoiselle say to me do as I wish, she do not care," he had protested. "And so nice a shape head she has and two widows' peaks. One in front and one behind."

Lisa had also remonstrated with the young lady who had presided over the streamlined dentist's chair, and less gently. "I said nothing about eyebrows, Célestine. You know very well I never allow you to pluck mine. How did you ever come to do such a thing?" "Because they were terra-ble, Madame. Not like yours. Verree thick and strong, like a man's, and they meet in the middle and make her look always scowling. She say do anything I desire. It was no matter to her. Only in the middle did I pluck much. I make her look so beautiful, *n'est-*

ce pas? She has nice skin." "Well, well, it's done," Lisa had laughed. "It can't be helped now. The eyebrows will grow again. So will her hair in time."

When Lisa had rejoined her in the waiting room, "Have you looked at yourself?" she had asked. She hadn't. She hadn't had the courage yet. "Well, let's wait till we're safely on the boat. It sails in less than an hour. We must hurry. Here's one of those fur-pieces that are simply indispensable on a cruise at this time of year," and she had opened a pasteboard box bearing the name of a well-known Fifth Avenue furrier. "It cost something, I confess, but it's worth it. I hard it charged to Mother Vale."

Mother Vale could well afford the fur-piece. She was one of the wealthiest of the wealthy old ladies in Boston. Charlotte's clothes were still charged to her mother. Charlotte still received the same monthly allowance for "spending money" as had been decided sufficient when she went to boarding-school.

"But what will Mother say?" she had asked Lisa weakly, gazing dubiously at the furs. "You know very well she will think they are too showy for me. And they are! Why, if I should suddenly appear in these even the maids would be shocked. And they look horribly expensive."

"You can rip them apart and wear only one skin when you come home. I'll make my own peace with Grandmother Vale about the expense." And she had placed the four limp skins, dripping with pointed tails, soft paws, and small sharp down-pointing noses, around Charlotte's shoulders. "They simply *make* you, my dear!"

When Lisa had appeared at Cascade with her preposterous proposal about this cruise, Charlotte had protested, at first, but Lisa had an answer to every objection, a way around every obstacle. Moreover Doctor Jaquith was in favor of it. It was futile to combat such a combination.

Several weeks before, Doctor Jaquith had pronounced her well enough to leave Cascade. He was anxious to have her try out her new technique alone, but strongly advised some other environment than home at first. Where she should go when she left Cascade had long been under discussion. Lisa had asked the advice of her friend Renée Beauchamp among others. Renée was widely traveled and well-informed about pleasure-resorts and retreats of various sorts. When Renée telegraphed Lisa that her plans had suddenly changed and her reservations on a cruise ship sailing four days hence were available, Lisa immediately got down her trunk and proceeded to pack it with an appropriate wardrobe for a Mediterranean cruise.

It had been discovered that, since Charlotte's loss of 30 pounds, Lisa's clothes fitted her perfectly. Lisa had already lent her a dress or two for use at Cascade till she was able to re-equip her wardrobe. Lisa was still wearing mourning for Rupert, therefore all her colorful dresses and accessories were useless to her for the time being. Not only her dresses, but even her shoes fitted Charlotte; also belts, gloves, collars— everything, in fact, except hatbands. There was not time enough to buy new hats, Lisa said, when Charlotte feebly suggested it, even if any could be found in the shops large enough to accommodate her heavy head-of-hair. Not was there time to make over the hatbands, even if it wouldn't ruin the style of the hats. "So she calmly made over me!" a sardonic smile curved her lips. "It didn't matter if *my* style was ruined!"

Everyone has a style of one's own which is the result of adaptation to one's physical appearance. Lisa had meant well, of course, but it is extremely unpleasant to be stripped suddenly of one's physical appearance, however unattractive. She had learned to adjust not only her manner but her habits and behavior to it. Now her reflection offered a paradox which was bound to expose her to all sorts of humiliating experiences.

Moreover, what would be the effect of her transformation upon her mother? The plan was for her to go directly home after the cruise. She would be absent less than eight weeks.

Her hair wouldn't grow much in that time. Also what would be the effect of the news of this cruise upon her mother? Her mother had not been consulted about it. Disapproval often caused distress in her mother's chest. Why, it might kill her mother! What putty she had been in the hands of Lisa and Doctor Jaquith! *Putty*, that was the word for her! Putty in the hands of her mother too! Irony deepened to self-contempt. She could feel the familiar pressure of depression closing on her like the jaws of a vise. And she'd got to meet that man for a cocktail at quarter of eight. "I'd rather be murdered," she said out loud.

With a yank she pulled open the door to the small closet where the stewardess had hung her dresses. What had it to offer? That familiar red dinner gown of Lisa's was as good as anything. Lisa had pinned a small paper on the shoulder of the dress which read: *Silver Slippers and silver evening bag will be found in accessory drawer.* Humph! *Suppose Lisa thought I'd wear Oxfords and carry my shopping bag*, thought Charlotte.

She dressed quickly. The red gown was the shade of a scarlet tanager, very plain, with a low square-cut neck in front. She produced the silver bag, selected a handkerchief, and gave it a shake. It puffed out like a spurt of steam. She was about to shove it into her bag when she remembered the perfumery. She opened the pink-wrapped package, unsealed the stopper of the bottle within, and drew out the tiny crystal stiletto. It was dripping with moisture. She wiped it off on her handkerchief, refueled it twice, and thrust it, wet and icicle cold, behind each ear. Then again she searched the closet, this time for an evening wrap.

There was nothing of Lisa's she recognized, but at the back of the closet she caught a glimpse of something else scarlet. It proved to be a long cape wrapped around its hanger, lining side out. Unfolding it she discovered a garment which she had never seen before. It was velvet the tawny yellow of French mustard, with a conventional design painted on it in various shades of brown, with shimmering silver spots here and there. She threw it quickly around her shoulders. It reached to below her knees. She glanced into the mirror for one last quick inspection, then stopped to gaze longer. The stranger who she saw reflected in the startling mustard cape would have made her look twice had she been seated as usual on a wall sofa beside her mother in the Grande Salon. She hadn't been watching the gay galaxy go by all her life without having gained something of the keenness of a critic. This stranger in the mirror lacked something. Her lips should be as scarlet as the glimpse beneath her cape.

She knew how to apply the lipstick. She had never confessed it even to Doctor Jaquith, but occasionally, in the privacy of her own room, she had experimented with cosmetics. Oh, not only had she smoked cigarettes behind those closed doors!

According to Lisa's request Célestine had given her a box equipped with various creams, lotions, and powers. She now took it down from the top shelf of the closet, opened it, discovered a small nickel cylinder within, and applied it to her lips quickly and skillfully.

It was not until she gave that last glance around the room, to be sure she had left nothing of value in sight, that she caught sight of two blue envelopes on the round table fastened to the floor in the middle of the room. She tore them open. The first read: *Have told Mother Vale stop no bad effects stop see it through Lisa.* The second: *Now voyager sail forth stop play the game stop à bas New England conscience Jaquith.*

These phrases in Doctor Jaquith's message were quoted from a poem by Walt Whitman, which he had given her typed on a bit of paper her last day at Cascade. It was in her pocket-book near-by.

She pushed both the radiograms into her evening bag, snapped it shut with a click, snapped off the electric lights with several clicks, and left the room, her silver slippers scuttling along the long narrow corridor with the haste of a Cinderella's. She was already ten minutes late.

CHAPTER THREE: A SECRET SHARED

Charlotte stood in the threshold searching the crowded, smoke-filled room, not sure that she would recognize him among so many. Not sure that he would recognize her. She saw him finally emerging out of the smoke, coming toward her smiling. He had been waiting for her in a distant alcove. He led the way to it. They sat down at a bare table side by side on a straight-backed bench. He was dressed as conventionally as in the afternoon—dinner-coat, black bow-tie, dark mother-of-pearl studs.

"What will you have?"

She had no knowledge of the various names of cocktails. "I'll leave it to you."

"Well, how are Old-fashioneds? Will you have a cigarette?" And he offered her one from a half-package, which he produced from an inner pocket.

She took it, and gave a slight cough when he lit it this time. *I can't keep up this farce much longer*, she said to herself.

"Oh, by the way," he remarked, "I just saw Thompson, and he wanted to know if I'd signed up for Majorca. I hadn't. He said you hadn't either, and asked me if we'd like to sign up to go together. He says they like to have us pair up, or quadruple up, beforehand if possible. You may not be getting off at Majorca. You've been there before probably. And very likely you'd rather leave it to luck whom you get. Or probably you've a friend or some acquaintance on board you'd like to go with."

"I haven't a friend, nor an acquaintance either, on board. I'd like to go with you very much."

They didn't dine together. She sat in her allotted place at a table with five others, and he somewhere on the other side of the dining-room. She was seated in the deserted library after dinner, close to an imitation open fire when they again met.

"Oh, here you are! I've been looking everywhere for you. Do you want to take the automobile trip to some town— Söller, I think it's called—on the other side of the island, or just stay around Palma? Thompson wants to know."

"What do you want to do?" asked Charlotte, secretly preferring to stay around Palma.

"Let's go to Söller. Take in everything there is!"

"All right! Let's!"

"Good! I'll tell Thompson." He drew up a chair beside her. "Don't you love the smell of an open fire?" He rubbed his outstretched hands before the artificial flame.

"Yes, and the crackle, too."

"Might as well try to get milk out of a wooden cow!" He gave an exaggerated shiver. The temperature had been steadily dropping ever since Gibraltar's fringe of lights had disappeared. "Who'd ever believe you and I were sitting on that open terrace in the sun drinking coffee and liqueurs at noon?"

"Nobody!" Also nobody, who knew her, would believe that she was sitting here now with rouge on her lips, and perfumery behind her ears, so much perfumery in fact that this man, sniffing the air, remarked upon it.

"I can smell something much sweeter than burning logs." He glanced around in search of its source. "I wonder what it is."

"It's called Quelques Fleurs," she announced flatly. What a fool! She'd put on too much!

"How awfully nice of you!" He paused, leaned back and gazed at her closely, a whimsical expression in his eyes. "I can't seem to pigeonhole you." His close scrutiny was disconcerting. She drew the cape closer about her as if in protection. "That's a marvelous coat you've got on—wrap, garment, whatever you call it. You made quite an impression up there in the bar as you stood in the doorway looking for me tonight." *Oh, dear*, she thought, *I put on too much lipstick too, probably.* "Whoever designed it knew his entomology mighty well too. I don't pretend to know much, but I recognize the Fritillaries."

"I have no idea what you're talking about," said Charlotte.

"Why, the butterfly design painted on your cape." She looked at him in dumb amazement. "Didn't you know you're a perfect specimen of one of the silver-spotted Fritillaries? I have several Mountain Silver-Spots in my collection. They're Fritillaries, too. I caught my specimens myself one June on Mount Washington."

"Are you an entomologist?"

"No, indeed! Butterflies are just a hobby of mine. Do you mind leaning forward? Those dark lines coming over your shoulder are supposed to be your antennae, I think." He was bending over her now. "I hope you don't mind being examined. Wish I had a magnifying-glass. Hello," he broke off. "What's this?"

"What's what?"

"Something on your cape! Wait a minute! Why, it's pinned on! Somebody has been playing a joke on you, I guess."

"Unpin it, please."

He did so, fumbling so long with the small pin that he couldn't help reading whatever Lisa had written. "Here it is!" he said at last, and passed the paper to her.

In Lisa's clear firm hand Charlotte read: *I had no evening coat that was right, so Renée wants to contribute hers. She says it always makes an impression, and has always given her a good time. She hopes it will do the same for you.*

"Well, this ought to pigeonhole me for you, all right." She gave a short derogatory laugh and passed the paper back to him.

He put on a pair of horn-rimmed glasses and studied it. "What does it mean? I can't make head or tail of it."

"It's perfectly clear. Read it again." She raised her chin, resorting as usual to hauteur to conceal discomfort.

He studied the paper. "I don't get it."

"Why, this cape belongs to your friend Renée Beauchamp. Naturally she had no use for it at a ranch and so lent it to me. I didn't know what design was painted on it, or I assure you I would never have appeared in wings tonight!" she informed him, with all the scorn she could summon.

"Oh, I see!" he exclaimed with delight. "Your wings are borrowed! Well, they suit you mighty well!"

"No, they don't!" she contradicted. "They don't suit me in the least! They're perfectly ridiculous on me! This entire situation is ridiculous!"

She spoke with such indignation that it was his turn now to stare at her in amazement. He sat down again. "What situation? Why is it ridiculous? I'm all in the dark about you."

"I'll enlighten you then. Did you ever read a book when you were a child called *Sara Crewe?*"

"I don't think so, but the name sounds familiar."

"Well, Sara Crewe," she began, picking her words slowly the better to express her self-contempt, "was a poor, pathetic creature who had no friends, and only a few ugly clothes. She lived a dreary existence on a bare garret until a nice, rich, old gentleman came along one day, and took pity on the poor thing." She paused, her lips curving into more of a grimace than a smile. She simply mustn't let that painful red flood of hot blood rise to her face. He would think she had no sense of humor. "Give the paper back to me, please." He did so. She tore it into small bits and shoved them into her bag. Thank goodness, he was getting off at Nice. She needn't see him after tomorrow! "You were quite right when you said someone was playing a joke on me," she went on desperately. "It's a far funnier joke than you realize. Jokes are usually based on the incongruous, you know." She rose, slipping the cape off her shoulders and throwing it over her arm.

"You aren't going, are you?" he said rising too. "Please don't, yet."

Suddenly from the threshold someone called out in a high shrill voice, "Oh, here you are!" It was Miss Demarest, dressed in a black taffeta gown with a voluminous skirt. She approached the fireplace with the bobbing motion of a toy balloon. Such balloons have small mouthpieces attached and when the air escapes a shrill whistle is emitted. When the wearer of the taffeta skirt reached the close vicinity of the fireplace, it emitted a similar shrill squeal.

"O—oh! *Mister* Durrance! *Just* the man I'm looking for! And *Miss* Beauchamp too! How simply *perfect!*" She paused for breath. "We lack one couple for our contract tournament. Will you two be a couple of lambs and join us? It will help me out no end."

"Oh, I'm afraid I'm not good enough."

"Oh, *Mister* Durrance! Don't believe him, Miss Beauchamp! He played the other night and made two little slams. I saw you make one with my own two eyes!" She wagged a playful forefinger at him.

"Yes, I know, but—" He turned to Charlotte. "Do you play cards?"

"I used to play slap-jack when I was a child, and later whist occasionally years and years ago." That would date her, and put an end to this farce she was enacting.

"Oh, *Miss* Beauchamp! I just know you're joking!" Miss Demarest wagged her finger at Charlotte.

Charlotte was speaking the literal truth. Her mother disliked all card games. But her father was an inveterate whist-player, and sometimes she had made a fourth when one of his cronies dropped out. But not until she had gone to

Cascade had she ever made a fourth at a bridge table. However, for the last six weeks she had been playing bridge almost every evening. Everybody at Cascade was supposed to spend the evenings in some form of social intercourse, and contribute something to their small community, even though it was an agreeable facial expression. Charlotte had chosen bridge as the least painful contribution she could make to sociability.

"You can't swear to me you never played a game of bridge in all your life. Now, can you, Miss Beauchamp?" Miss Demarest persisted.

"Well, but I know only the bare rudiments."

"Oh, if you know the rudiments, then let's try it!" exclaimed Durrance. "It will help out Miss Demarest."

Such amiability was a new experience to Charlotte. Her mother's attitude toward all paid hostesses was always chilly. She preferred to make her own social contacts. Charlotte hesitated. *Respond, take part, contribute,* she could hear Doctor Jaquith saying from 3000 miles away. And as she pressed her evening bag closer to her side, she could hear the crackle of his last message, and in her mind's eye see the typed words on the ice-blue paper: *Now, Voyager*—exhorting her to effort and to action.

"I don't know many conventions," she demurred.

"Thank Heaven! Neither do I," said Durrance.

She turned to Miss Demarest. "Do we have to change partners?" Too late she realized that her question implied a preference.

"No. Same partners from start to finish tonight," Miss Demarest assured her.

"Come on, let's try our luck together—Miss Beauchamp," said Durrance, pausing significantly before the *Miss Beauchamp*, his eyes flashing her an intimate look that implied, *We know something this interloper doesn't know, don't we?*

Her heart warmed toward him. She had often seen such signals flashed between others when she was the one excluded. They always made her feel the chill of rejection. There was no reason why he shouldn't have corrected the hostess's mistake about her name. Didn't his not doing so imply that he considered her explanation confidential, and show protection of it? As she returned his intimate look, she felt he would be just as protective of her embarrassments as his partner at the bridge table.

"Well, all right," she acquiesced. "I'll do my best."

Of course, *then* was the moment when she herself should have told the hostess that she was not Miss Beauchamp, but before she could say anything at all, the balloon was exclaiming "Lovely! Perfect! Hurry!"

The sharing of a secret usually spins a binding thread between two people. At the end of every four hands the winning couple moved to the next table, and before the cards were dealt, names were exchanged if the players had not already met. Charlotte had met no one, and Durrance only a few. Taking the initiative as her partner, he introduced her as Miss Beauchamp at each shift—five times in all, and always with a covert twinkle whenever he could catch her glance.

As the evening progressed, she wasn't sure whether his object was so much protection of her as just prankishness. But for her to come out with a bald statement that her name wasn't Beauchamp would be a flat refusal to play any longer the rôle of secret-sharer with him, and snap the fast-growing thread he was spinning. Of course, a woman of experience would have known how to dispose of the situation with a little playful persiflage. But persiflage was something that couldn't very well be practiced alone behind closed doors. It would be ridiculous for her to attempt it for the first time now. As for humor, though she possessed it, it was of the caustic variety, and caustic was the last thing she wanted to be to this kindly-intentioned stranger. So, despising her shyness, she acknowledged the repeated introduction as Miss Beauchamp without a word of remonstrance.

Charlotte needed all the composure she possessed to apply to her bridge game and prayed that nothing would arise to tax it further. But before the tournament was over, something so near a catastrophe occurred that she didn't breathe freely for ten minutes afterward.

At the beginning of the last round of play an elderly woman turned to her and said, "Do you remember me, Renée?"

"I'm afraid not. I—"

"I don't blame you. I would never have recognized you either, but I saw your name on the passenger list. I used to visit in your home when you were a little girl. Before my marriage I was Harriet Parmallee, your mother's best friend at school—'Aunt Hattie' you used to call me." She looked at Charlotte with a sickishly sweet smile, waiting for her outburst of recognition.

Charlotte shot her partner one despairing glance and started to speak. But he cut in first. "Oh, this isn't *Renée* Beauchamp!" obligingly he informed Aunt Hattie. "You've made the same mistake I did! This is"—he paused a moment, then brought out with a perfectly straight face, "this is Camille Beauchamp. Quite a different family, Miss Beauchamp tells me, though distantly related. Such stupid mistakes as they make on passenger lists! But are we playing bridge or not? Whose bid is it, anyway? Oh, mine! I must consider this." In silence he studied his cards for a long quarter minute or more, then glancing up and giving Charlotte a triumphant little wink, "Pass," he said briefly.

At the end of the tournament, after the names of the winning couple had been announced (which were not Miss Beauchamp and Mr. Durrance) and the prize (an aluminum ash-tray with a colored picture of the boat embossed upon it) had been presented, Durrance suggested a nightcap in the bar. "Perhaps our alcove will be empty."

They hadn't been seated over three minutes when the balloon reappeared. "Oh, here are the runaways! I want you to meet the people you're going to share an automobile with tomorrow. Mr. and Mrs. Ricketts of Sioux City, Iowa. Such nice people. And they play bridge, too." She had Mr. and Mrs. Ricketts in tow. Mrs. Ricketts wore an extremely low-cut gown, covered with sequins and a scintillating display of bracelets on her plump wrists. Mr. Ricketts—a small, harried-looking man—hadn't changed for the evening. He wore a business suit, and a red tie. "Mr. and Mrs. Ricketts, Mr. Durrance and Miss Beauchamp," announced Miss Demarest. "And I hope you all have a lovely time together tomorrow. And, by the way, Miss Beauchamp, I have a favor to ask of you. Will you be an angel and take part in our Benefit Concert next week? Somebody told me you do the cleverest monologues!"

Again, before Charlotte could speak her companion leaped to her rescue. "This isn't Renée Beauchamp," again he announced, looking immensely pleased with himself.

CHAPTER FOUR:
MUTUAL RESPONSE

"You're very ingenious," remarked Charlotte dryly, once they were alone again, not at all sure she was enjoying the situation.

He didn't deny it. "But I'm not so quick on the trigger as I seemed with Aunt Hattie. I was prepared for her. I'd been afraid someone who knew Renée might pop up, ever since I began introducing you as Miss Beauchamp."

"But why did you begin?"

"Why, I thought you wanted me to!"

"Why should I want you to?"

"I didn't know *why*, but seeing you didn't tell the Demarest woman that you weren't Miss Beauchamp, I concluded it wasn't up to *me* to let the cat out of the bag, especially after I'd found that paper, and forced you to tell me something you wouldn't have otherwise. Did I do the wrong thing?"

"Well, it doesn't make my situation on this cruise any easier."

"Why didn't you stop me, then, at the first table?"

"Because I haven't enough backbone. I simply lacked the courage," she scoffed.

"Lacked the courage! Why are you in need of so much courage? What is the big mystery anyway? I still don't know. I'm really awfully sorry if I've made things difficult for you. But is it very serious? After I leave the boat at Nice, all you'll need to say is that I was just having a little fun."

"Why did you call me Camille?"

"Oh, it just came to my mind. I thought it was as good a first name to go with Beauchamp as Renée. I considered Fifi, but I didn't think that went with you very well. My knowledge of French names for girls is limited, and the few I know disappeared from my mind completely, except those two. I hope I haven't offended you. The fact is, my knowledge of French literature is limited too. I never read *Camille*. I couldn't say offhand whether it's a play or a novel."

"And yet it went with me!"

"Well, better than Fifi. In that stunning red gown you're sort of like a gorgeous red camellia, I think. Except," he added, leaning nearer and again sniffing the air, his eyes full of merriment, "camellias don't have any such sweet smell."

It was the second time he had referred to her perfumery. She must be reeking with it! At home when one of her tormentors, June or Nichols or any of the older nephews and nieces, made fun of some obvious defect ("razzing Aunt Charlotte," they called it), she was always in mortal terror that one of those humiliating floods of blood would rise up from her depths and dye her face a deep red. Sarcasm had proved the most effective defense against it, so now she resorted to it.

"I suppose that is meant to be funny," she said, conveying by tone and posture all the contempt of which she was capable.

The merriment fled from his eyes as quickly as if she had clapped her hands and frightened away a bird that had perched upon her window sill. He didn't reply immediately. There was a tall glass, half-full of beer, on the table in front of him. He drew it toward him, gazing down into it, turning it slowly round as he spoke.

"Yes," he said quietly. "I think I did intend it as humor. Evidently it struck you as extremely fresh. I'm sorry."

Instantly Charlotte regretted her derision. Oh, she always alienated people. She couldn't keep the goodwill of even a stranger for longer than one day. She longed to burst out, *Forgive me, please. I didn't mean that,* but the words stuck. She was a New Englander and a Vale. She had been taught to conduct herself so that it would never be necessary to say, *Forgive me* (except occasionally to God in the self-respecting privacy of silent prayer). So now she said nothing. There was a tall glass in front of her, identical to her companion's, except the foam was nearer the top. Charlotte hadn't liked her first glass of beer. But she now raised it and took several long swallows of the bitter stuff.

"My wife calls my lighter moods trying to be funny," Durrance went on. "She, also, finds them extremely trying at times. So I can't blame you for feeling the same way." It was the first time he had referred to his wife.

Charlotte wanted to reply, *Your wife sounds as disagreeable as myself*, but instead she changed the subject. "Do you live right in New York?" His reference to his wife implied he was living somewhere in orthodox fashion.

"No. In one of the suburbs."

"Which one?" she pursued, to keep the ball of conversation rolling until she could leave him without adding insult to injury, go to her room, and endure alone the familiar pangs of failure and regret.

"Mount Vernon."

"I know someone who *used* to live in Mount Vernon," eagerly Charlotte informed him. "A girl I knew at boarding-school. But her family has moved further out now, to some place in Connecticut."

"Naturally."

"Why *naturally?*"

"Most people's destination is 'farther out, to some place in Connecticut,' if they once start in that direction. That is, if they've got the gas to get there."

His voice had a mocking intonation. It might easily have been herself speaking, when someone had inadvertently touched a sensitive spot. She leaned across the table. "I didn't mean what you thought I did, a moment ago. I didn't think you were fresh. I like your lighter moods." She stopped abruptly. She had never so completely thrown herself on another person's mercy.

Looking up from the glass which he was still turning, he replied, "You mean you forgive me for acting like such a bull-in-a-china-closet? Making things difficult for you on a cruise? And then trying to be funny?"

"You haven't acted like a bull-in-a-china-closet. You haven't made things difficult! The fact of the matter is I don't know how to take a joke. I was as aware I'd put on far too much of that strong perfume, and was too poor a sport to take a little razzing about it."

"You didn't put on too much for *my* taste. I think it was awfully nice of you to put on *any*. How do you think we got along at bridge?" he broke off amiably. "Was I pretty bad?"

"Bad! You were wonderful!"

"Isobel—my wife, doesn't think I ought to impose my game on anybody but children."

"Is she awfully good?"

"Oh, no. Isobel doesn't play at all. You know I let you down that time that woman told me I ought to have taken you out of your opening bid of two spades."

"It was none of *her* business! You weren't *her* partner!"

"It was mighty nice of you to stick up for me, and tell her you didn't expect me to take you out."

"It was the truth. I didn't expect you to."

And she hadn't. They had already played several hands, and he ignored all conventions with the imperturbability of one so at ease at a dinner table that it didn't embarrass him if he chanced to use the wrong fork. He had what is called instinctive card sense. Also instinctive card manners—playing quickly, quietly, and with no comments. She told him so.

"Well, I certainly wish Isobel could hear you!"

"And I wish Doctor Jaquith could hear me! I am not given to making pretty speeches. I wish he could *see* me too."

"Oh! Doctor Jaquith is the nice rich old gentleman, isn't he? When are you going to tell me the rest of that story about Sara Crewe?"

"Well, not tonight. But Doctor Jaquith is *not* the nice rich old gentleman!"

A waiter approached with a slip of paper. Durrance signed it and gave him a fee. Then, "Where do you live in Boston?" he inquired. "It's all right for me to ask, I hope, seeing you asked me a similar question."

"You're awfully afraid I'll snap at you again, aren't you?"

"No, I'm *not!* Not a bit! Tell me where you live. On the

Hill? In the Back Bay? On the Avenue? On the Esplanade? Or are you a suburbanite like me?"

"I live in the Back Bay. On Marlborough Street. I see you know Boston."

"Well, better than Gibraltar," he acknowledged. "I ought to. I'm a New Englander. Vermont is my native state."

"Are all Vermonters so familiar with Boston?"

"Oh, I'm not really familiar with it. I know Boston only from the Cambridge side."

"I see. Harvard, I suppose."

"Wrong. Sorry. M.I.T. But only for one year." Then abruptly, "I've got an idea!" he announced. "What would you think of letting the Ricketts tie up with someone else tomorrow, and you and I hiring a car of our own, meeting our cruise-mates at Söller for lunch, of course," he hastened to assure her, "but taking our own time about getting there."

"The Ricketts didn't look so very promising, but I was told to be nice to everybody on this cruise who was a human being, so—"

"Well, concentrate on being nice to *this* human being tomorrow."

"Do you dare run the risk? There's no telling how long I can keep up being nice. I have a reputation at home for a sharp tongue. You've had one example of it."

"I'll take the bitter with the sweet."

She glanced at her watch. "Look at the time!" she exclaimed, and stretched out her left hand toward him. He took hold of her wrist as impersonally as if it were made of wood, and drew the watch nearer his eyes.

"Only twelve-thirty! That isn't so bad. Let's look in at the dancers on our way down."

There were only three or four couples in the small cleared space in the center of the Grand Salon when they arrived. The orchestra was playing a vague droning wail in a minor key, accompanied by a monotonous tomtom. They sat down on a sofa just inside the door. The music paused, seemed to take a long breath, and then broke out in a different mood—as refreshing as an east wind at home, thought Charlotte, at the end of a hot spell. The opening measures of a familiar waltz fell upon their ears.

"The 'Vienna Woods,'" Durrance murmured, his face lightening with pleasure. By the time the music had expanded to the full beauty of its theme, the dancing space was crowded with couples swinging and swirling. "Shall we try it?"

"I don't dance," said Charlotte. He caught the bitterness in her tone.

"I'm glad of it. It lets me out. I don't dance either, according to my daughters. Let's take a walk on the deck instead."

Charlotte had one of those uncanny sensations that this had all happened before. The next instant Leslie Trotter flashed before her vision. It *had* happened before!

"No, thanks. I think I won't," she said, her eyes on the dancers.

"Oh, there's Thompson!" exclaimed Durrance. "Guess I'd better speak to him now about our car tomorrow. Back in a minute." He disappeared.

Charlotte continued to keep her eyes on the dancers.

She and her mother had been taking a cruise to Norway and Sweden that summer. Her mother had been confined to her stateroom with a cold the night she met Leslie. Leslie was a young officer on the boat. The young officers were allowed to dance with the young-lady passengers, so as to increase the popularity of cruise travel, her mother said. Her mother highly disapproved of it. Charlotte had been sitting on a sofa, just inside the door of the ballroom in the same location as now, watching the dancing. Alone as now. The sofa was so far away from the dancers that she was in no way a candidate for a partner. When she saw the tall handsome young officer coming straight toward her, she looked away. Experience had taught her that approaching young men were never headed for her, so when the young officer stopped and asked her formally if he could have the pleasure of this dance, she was wholly unprepared. "I don't dance," she had said brusquely.

As a débutante two years before she had not proved successful on the ballroom floor, and had given up struggling with the art. The young officer had suggested that they take a walk on the deck instead, exactly as had this stranger tonight—this man with an odd surname which she'd never heard before—Durrance, J. D. Durrance. She didn't even know what J. D. stood for. Leslie, too, had been a stranger, with an odd surname which she'd never heard before. Why, it was just as if life were repeating an old pattern. She must see to it it didn't repeat the whole pattern!

Leslie had taken her up to the top deck that first night, in search of a breeze, he said. It was a hot night, too hot for dancing. They had sat down in the black shadow of a ventilator. After about 20 minutes, he had casually slipped his arm around her waist. She hadn't objected. She hadn't wanted the young officer to think that she was afraid of a man's arm around her waist, even if she didn't dance. She had suggested that he return to the ballroom and find another partner, but he had said he preferred her company and wasn't going to dance again that evening.

It wasn't often Charlotte could be absent long from her mother without being questioned, or, worse, followed and found. She and Leslie had sat there in the dark for over an hour. He had kissed her finally. Her response had been quite different from what he had expected. Charlotte hadn't been sure what he expected. In the novels she'd read, men didn't like prudes. She wasn't a young girl any more. She had been out two years. Then Leslie had kissed her again. And still again. The third time Charlotte had felt the response which the first time she had only pretended. By the end of the fourth day she was deeply in love with Leslie Trotter.

"Thompson says it's all right. He'll fix it with the Ricketts." Durrance's bright voice exclaimed triumphantly as he sat down on the sofa beside her. "He says we ought to get off by nine-thirty, so if that's not too early for you—"

"O-oh!" It was Miss Demarest's squeal. "I've found you again! Why aren't you dancing, Mr. Durrance? Last night I saw you waltzing simply divinely. And, Miss Beauchamp, why aren't *you* dancing too? Come on and join us."

"Not tonight," said Durrance, rising. "We've decided to call it a day. And by the way about the Ricketts tomorrow. We think that—"

Charlotte glanced toward the door. This was her chance to escape. His back was toward her, the door was close at hand. She had only to step across the threshold.

"O-oh!" another squeal. "Here come the Millers. Such a charming couple. I promised to introduce them to you. Mr. and Mrs. Miller, Mr. Durrance and—why, where's Miss Beauchamp?"

She was halfway down the first flight of stairs. Her room was two decks below. It wasn't until she had reached the hall outside the corridor that led to her room that she heard Durrance's hurrying footsteps behind her. "Wait a minute," he called.

She stopped then and turned around, facing him as he approached. "What is it?" she asked, as if at a loss to know why he had followed her.

"What is it!" he repeated in a tone that reproached, condemned, and sentenced all at once. "What is it! You run off like that without even saying good night, and leave me stranded with Miss Demarest—Miss Damn Pest, I call the woman, and then ask me, What is it? Look here. What do you mean by playing a trick like that on me?"

"Well, I thought—I heard her say you were dancing
divinely last night, and I thought if I just quietly disappeared
that you'd be free to dance tonight, so—"

"I don't want to dance. I told you so."

"Well, it was getting awfully late. It's long after my bed-
time."

"Is it? Have I tired you all out? Please forgive me if I have."
(*Forgive me* caused this New Englander no effort. Nor *I forgive*, either, as his next words proved. Even her unceremoni-
ous departure was already wiped off the slate.) "I've had a
wonderful day, and all due to you," he went on; "you've been
very kind to a boring first tripper."

Such goodwill, so spontaneously and so unstintingly
offered to her, was a new experience to Charlotte. The conta-
gion of goodwill was also a new experience to her.

"You haven't been boring," she heard herself replying.
"You see, I'm a sort of first tripper myself in some ways. The
fact is—I mean—" She stopped, horribly aware of her inade-
quacy. "I've had a wonderful day, too," she finished lamely.

He didn't seem to be aware of her confusion. "Have you?
Really?" he exclaimed eagerly. "Thanks for saying so. Let's
have another wonderful day tomorrow. Remember, nine-
thirty. Good night." He put out his hand. She put hers in it. He
gave it a firm quick shake. Then, still holding it, "Good night,
Camille," he said, his eyes twinkling, his head cocked on one
side. The bird had returned to her window sill again, trusting
and unafraid.

A rush of gratitude welled up in Charlotte, and with it courage
and self-confidence. If she only knew his first name she'd show
him she was not beyond response to such friendliness.

"Good night—" She paused. Well, his initials were less formal
than his surname. "Good night—J.D.," she added, then pulled her
hand free, turned, and hurried down the corridor.

CHAPTER FIVE:
WHAT OUR MEMORIES ARE

Durrance stood staring after Charlotte for at least a half a minute, his face lit up with an expression of surprise and pleasure. He used to be called "J.D." in college. At least by his most intimate friends. It was seldom that he saw any of his old college crowd, except at reunions. He didn't go to reunions often now, but when he did, being called "J.D." warmed his heart more than all the hearty exclamations and vigorous handclasps put together.

In college he had had a knack for dialect—Scotch and Irish, chiefly. At reunions the old crowd were constantly calling for his Harry Lauder stunt, or for his "Mack and Mike." When Buck, who was now a famous surgeon, or Josh, who had become a potentate in the banking world, or Dutch, who had gone to the top as a lawyer, or any of the other top-notchers, put their heads together and sang out in rhythmic unison, over and over again, "We want J.D., we want J.D.," it never failed to leave the barriers between himself and those who had made outstanding successes. It seemed, too, to obliterate the years since they all had been starting at scratch.

As he descended the several flights of stairs to his inside stateroom on Deck E, the glow of pleasure still lingered on his face. He felt 25 years younger! But he didn't look it! Once inside the room he gazed at himself critically in the mirror. Then, with a grimace, "Hell," he murmured and turned away.

He shared his inside stateroom with a married man whose wife and two daughters occupied a room on a deck above. The married man, whose name was Littlejohn, had explained that his family split up this way because he was a heavy breather and kept his wife awake. Mr. Littlejohn was already in bed, and already heavily breathing. The breathing did not disturb Durrance if the air-conditioner was emitting its roaring blast. Mr. Littlejohn found the roaring of the air-conditioner so annoying that he couldn't get to sleep unless it was closed. However, Durrance had discovered that after Mr. Littlejohn began to roar himself he didn't object to it. So now he turned it on, and quickly proceeded to undress.

After clamping his trousers, nicely folded, upside down in the top of the small cupboard door, and stretching his coat on one of the six hangers (from which he had to remove Mr. Littlejohn's overcoat, as he had appropriated more hangers than his share), he slipped into blue chambray pajamas and climbed nimbly into his upper bunk.

No sooner had he arranged himself for sleep in its narrow confines than it occurred to him that he hadn't finished his letter to Isobel. From a rack on the wall he produced a pad and pencil. The first sheet of the pad was covered with his fine writing. He had started a letter to Isobel mid-ocean.

He always found it difficult to write Isobel. He must never say anything to make her feel he was enjoying himself. For she would wonder how it was possible, while she was at home enacting the rôle of a drudge. If he could succeed in giving the impression that he was bored and anxious for the disagreeable ordeal to be terminated, his letter would be a success. Propped against his two pillows he re-read what he had written:

Dear Isobel: So far the trip has been extremely disagreeable. Rain and fog all the time and no interesting people.

I was sorry to leave you with one of your sick headaches coming on. I know you need a change more than I, and realize how much travel means to you. But remember if I can pull off this deal in Milan you and Beatrice and Muriel are just so much nearer your "so-you're-going-to-Southern-Italy" trip. You've done fairly well in checking off your list most of the other "so-you're-going-to" countries over here.

I don't mind my inside stateroom-and-no-bath at all. And nobody else seems to mind it either. Perhaps it hasn't leaked out. At least the waiters have treated me all right so far, and the deck steward deigns to speak when spoken to. By which I do not mean it would do for you and the girls. I know it wouldn't. And that's how Mr. Littlejohn feels too. His wife and daughters occupy an outside cabin two decks above. Mr. Littlejohn is my roommate. He is a Baptist, a Republican, a Rotarian, and a teetotaller. He hasn't got any bad habits that I might pick up, except one—competing with the fog horn—

Here the letter stopped. He studied the last sentence then rubbed it out. Isobel found any attempt at humor irritating, when she was feeling injured. She felt injured most of the time, true, but the degree fluctuated. *Mrs. Littlejohn,* he now continued in pencil, *weighs about 200 pounds, doesn't know how to dress, and, briefly, is an awful frump.* He frowned as he surveyed this sentence. He liked Mrs. Littlejohn. She was so genuine. But derogatory remarks about another woman always had a salutary effect on Isobel's positive self-feeling. So he let it stand. It wouldn't hurt Mrs. Littlejohn any.

The two daughters are replicas of mama. The only time I've graced the ballroom floor was last night when I divided a waltz between them, as they had no partners whatsoever. It was agony for all concerned.

I cabled you from Gibraltar when we arrived this morning. As you told me, Gibraltar has little to offer of worth-while interest. We arrive at Majorca tomorrow. I shall have a look at the cathedral, but I understand there is not much else to see on the island, except scenery. Your advice that I waste no time around Nice, but go straight to Paris and make the most of my ten days doing all the "cultural" sight-seeing I can get in, is sound I guess. But it's pretty late to do much about my culture now. I'll probably never come over again. It's your turn next, Isobel.

Don't tire yourself all out with your church work. Your strength has always been limited, you know, and you must be careful not to overdo. I hope you're having better nights. I know what a hard row you've had to hoe all these years with me, Isobel. I wish it might have been different. Perhaps it will be sometime. I shall do my best to make it so. Much love to all four of my harem. Affectionately, Duveaux.

He had always been "Duveaux" to Isobel. The difference between Isobel's "Duveaux" and the old college crowd's "J.D." was as great as between two contrasting characters in a monologist's repertoire. To the old college crowd J.D. had always been the most straightforward, single-minded fellow in the world—one character under all conditions. But Isobel had developed in him a dual personality. Whenever in her company he was perpetually trying to be, or to appear to be, the kind of man she wished he was. But whenever she was absent, he resumed his instinctive one-tracked personality. At first he had been bothered by the necessity of constantly being a hypocrite, or constantly hurting his wife, but experience had long ago taught him that tact and hypocrisy were first cousins. However, he still drew a line between the two.

For instance, now re-reading his letter, he felt sure it would disappoint Isobel. She yearned for expressions of affection. He added *dear* to the first *Isobel*, then rubbed it out. It rang too false in his conscience. He added instead, *my dear.* There was all the difference.

He also added this postscript: *I was sorry to leave Tina in tears. I know how terribly difficult she is these days, but she is very highstrung, and punishment is not good for her. Be patient with her till I come. I'll drop her a line. D.*

He folded and slipped this letter in an envelope and put it in the rack. On a fresh piece of paper he wrote the following:

Dear Tina, Get out your calendar and put a big circle around May 15th. That's the day you and I start for the woods, with old clothes, two fishing-rods, two painting-kits, and one cooking-kit. My mouth is already watering for fried trout, scrambled eggs, and flapjacks. What about yours? Only a few weeks more and we'll be off for the sticks. Stiff upper lip, Tina old girl. Daddy.

This, too, he folded and slipped into another envelope. Then he proceeded to prepare for one of his chief delights—reading in bed. There was a row of books on an inserted shelf at the head of his bunk—a worn copy of the *Oxford Book of Verse*, two Modern Library volumes, *The Education of Henry Adams*, Conrad's *Victory*, a shabby Baedeker, and a bright-jacketed detective novel. He selected *Henry Adams*, rolled his two pillows into a more compact mass, jammed them behind his head as close to the dim reading-light as possible, wriggled his shoulders down into the correct location, leaned his book against his raised legs and drew in a deep sigh of contentment.

Isobel had never liked to have him read in bed. She couldn't go to sleep until his light was out, even when he covered it with a dark paper and put a screen between their beds. Once or twice he had suggested separate rooms, but each time it had thrown her into one of her injured moods for days. The twin beds had become a symbol to Isobel of their marital relationship to which she clung with fervor. She resented even the screen between their beds, the evening paper if he held it too high, closed doors, or a lowered tone over the telephone. Often, when he hadn't been aware of any recent act of exclusion, she would remark, with that combination of self-pity and condemnation which always filled him with compunction, "I feel just like a widow!"

Again he felt a prick of the old compunction and his face clouded. It didn't seem right for him to be luxuriating in freedom, while Isobel was back there in her old despised rut, imprisoned in the out-of-date house of which she was so ashamed, on the unfashionable street which he had never been able to change for her, and definitely excluded from his activities. Between their beds now there loomed a screen that couldn't be moved—a barrier consisting of wood, steel, a strip of Mediterranean Sea, a bit of Spain, the Rock of Gibraltar, and miles and miles of Atlantic Ocean, against which his compunction was powerless. So he dismissed it, according to the philosophy he applied to all unpleasant emotions which were futile.

He nuzzled his shoulder blades more comfortably into the pillows and opened *Henry Adams*. But he didn't immediately begin to read. Instead he took off his glasses a moment and closed his eyes, to sense more keenly the details of his liberty. Mr. Littlejohn was outdoing the air-conditioner at present. He could hear the throbbing rumbles of the engines, the shrill squeak of a loose joint in the partition beside his pillow, and the vibration down here was terrific. But not one of these features annoyed him, for not one threatened his freedom. In fact they seemed to safeguard it—like a thick pile of sandbags. No telephone bell could get through such a din. He could read in bed all night if he wished. He could smoke in bed all night if he wished. And tomorrow he could explore an unknown island in the middle of the Mediterranean with an unknown lady, if he wished!

He put on his glasses, opened *Henry Adams*, found the place where he had left off on page 203. These words flashed up at him at the beginning of the next paragraph: *Thus he found himself launched on waters he had never meant to sail.*

When Charlotte hurried down the corridor to her room, her expression was too tinged with a glow. When she opened the door and turned on the light, she too surveyed herself critically in the mirror, and though she didn't murmur "Hell," a caustic grimace obliterated the glow. Camille! Picked out of the blue to go with Beauchamp! It no more went with her than Renée's butterfly cape, or those red lips and slender brows. The brows were so far apart that it gave her a young, eager, hopeful look, absolutely out of character with herself—with Charlotte Vale, embittered and resigned. One cannot evade one's personality by running away from it. Not at her age, anyway. She possessed neither the skill nor the resources with which to return the friendliness offered her by her companion today. No children to compare with his, no friends who might prove mutual, no marriage relationship in common. No sorrow even to make her understanding and sympathetic. And only one faded memory of ever having been wanted by a man. And that a bitter memory.

She rose abruptly and prepared for bed, pulling off her dress, her shoes, her stockings, with jerky, impatient motions, and tossing them carelessly aside to give vent to her displeasure. She thought that episode with Leslie had spent its strength. But evidently her system would never be rid of it. Like one of those fevers one sometimes contracts in the tropics, she would always be susceptible to a possible attack, such as had leaped out of the past tonight there in the ballroom. That fortnight with Leslie and the whole horrible summer that had followed was part of her forever. "We are what our memories are."

She slipped her nightgown over her head, her thoughts pursuing old ruts like a flood of water in a dried river bed. Again she fell to visualizing herself with Leslie in their various trysting places on the ship that summer long ago.

Her mother's cold had developed into an attack of the grippe, which had kept her in her stateroom for the first two weeks of the ocean voyage, so drugged most of the time that Charlotte could slip in and out without her mother's keen awareness. Once outside the room discretion had been necessary, however, because of Leslie's position on the ship, and their courtship had been carried on in concealed places which he knew about. Several times they had crawled into a lifeboat covered with canvas, so that Leslie's brass buttons could not be seen in the moonlight. They would sit crouched in the bottom of the boat with their arms around each other. It had all been new to her. She hadn't wanted Leslie to know how new. When he told her he'd rather have her than any girl on board, or any girl he'd ever known, because she was so responsive, she was anxious to live up to his expectations.

There had been a girl from New York on board the boat who had been attracted to Leslie and he to her, before that night he first kissed Charlotte on the deck, but the New York girl's wiles were like a silly schoolgirl's compared to her warm, generous, gorgeous love-making. No man had ever told her such a thing before. She didn't know what he meant by "gorgeous" exactly, but she wanted terribly to deserve his adjective.

One of their favorite trysting places had been on the freight deck among the crates and canvas-covered automobiles. On the fatal night when her mother had appeared with a ship's officer and a flashlight, she and Leslie had been concealed in the shrouds of a Packard limousine. Her mother had had dinner in the dining-salon that night for the first time since her illness. She had retired early, leaving Charlotte in the library to finish a novel with the understanding that she would follow within an hour. Her mother hadn't been gone five minutes when she had missed her glasses. She returned to the library immediately in search of them. Charlotte wasn't there! She couldn't be found anywhere! Her mother sent for an officer finally. Her daughter might have fallen overboard!

Neither Leslie nor she heard the officer and her mother approach. When she saw the outline of her mother's figure above her, silhouetted against the night sky and an instant later felt the stab of the officer's flashlight she was struck dumb. But Leslie had been superb. He had told her mother, then and there, right in front of the other officer, too, that he wished to marry her daughter. He had said that they were already secretly betrothed. It had been the proudest moment of Charlotte's life.

Her mother had sent her off instantly to her room, but that unhesitating declaration of Leslie's had sustained her, kept her eyes dry, and her chin high, not only for that night, but during the ordeal that followed. All her life she had submitted to her mother's opinions, and cowered beneath her will, but Leslie had placed her upon a throne (and before witnesses, too!) such as she had never occupied before. It gave her courage, strength, and confidence, not only in herself, but in Leslie too. His announcement proved how sincere he was, how fine, how brave, how all things admirable. And, above all, how much he loved her! Such had been her thoughts while she was a prisoner in the stateroom, or seated in icy silence beside her mother in their steamer chairs on the promenade deck. She had been filled with fierce tenderness for Leslie, which had grown fiercer with each hour of separation. Her determination to marry him had hardened like cement.

When her mother found that her opposition alone was ineffectual, she had a talk with the captain, delivering the spoils of her interview to Charlotte with the comment that the facts about Leslie would be more effective, perhaps, than her opinion. Leslie had never been to college or to a university. He had never been to an English public school! His parents were people without means or advantages. They lived in some little suburb on the outskirts of Liverpool. When their son became interested in the sea, did he offer his services to the English navy, her mother had demanded. No! Not he! He preferred the ease and luxuries of a commercial ocean liner! And what a name! Trotter. Why, it was simply humorous— Leslie Trotter! Her mother had always made effective use of ridicule.

But nothing her mother did or said had any effect on Charlotte. She had gone on quietly repeating Leslie's statement to her mother, "We are engaged to be married," and quietly adding, "and someday we're going to be married." Nobody could make a dent in her resolve. Nobody, that is, except Leslie. And nobody did. Except Leslie!

CHAPTER SIX:
THE BRIGHT MORNING

She got into bed and turned off the light. She closed her eyes. But sleep would not come to her relief. She and her mother had remained on the ocean liner only three days after the discovery on the freight-deck. When her mother became convinced that her daughter would listen to neither reason nor ridicule, she decided to disembark at the next stop, and spend the summer in England. Her mother hadn't told her of the plan till an hour before the liner docked. She hadn't allowed her to see Leslie, warning her that if she even attempted to do so, it would cost young Trotter (she never referred to him as anything but "young Trotter") his already endangered position on the boat. But Charlotte had managed to write him a hasty good-bye note.

The note began by assuring him that she loved him with all her mind and soul and body. It went on to say they were still engaged, and that she would marry him, in spite of her mother, whenever he said. She enclosed careful instructions as to how he might safely communicate with her during the summer. She and her mother were going first to London. They usually stayed at Almond's or Brown's. Never by any chance at The Savoy. Therefore, he was to write her at The Savoy. When she left London she would instruct the mail-clerk at The Savoy to forward her letters to General Delivery in the various cities where her mother decided to go. She would not return to Boston with her mother in the fall, but would meet him whenever and wherever he said. And again she assured him of her undying love. This letter she had sealed, addressed, and slipped into the steward's hand with a $5 bill when her mother's back was turned.

Leslie had also written a good-bye note. Her mother had delivered it to her in that bleak little hotel in Norway where they had had to wait for three days for a boat to take them back to England. Charlotte could see herself now seated in their bedroom staring out of the window, not speaking unless spoken to, still calm, still tearless, still determined to marry Leslie, still confident that Leslie was determined to marry her. Leslie's letter was unsealed, her mother explaining that it was understood that she should read it first.

Charlotte had never destroyed Leslie's letter. She had hidden it in a deep pocket of her traveling portfolio, and had reread it many times. It was at this moment in the drawer of the writing table across the room, unless someone had emptied the portfolio without her knowledge.

When Lisa had packed her trunk, she had gone to her room on Marlborough Street and collected a few personal articles which she thought would be useful on the cruise. Among them had been the portfolio, still in excellent condition. She had used it only that one summer. Charlotte had run across the portfolio this morning when dressing for shore. She had shoved it into the desk drawer, without giving a thought to the letter buried in one of its pockets.

She now rose, snapped on the light, and procured the portfolio. She shoved her hand down into the deep pocket. Yes, here it was! Written on the ship's stationery in the small, slanting, precise script of the name and address which Leslie had written in her address-book the second day of their courtship. This is what the letter said:

Dear Charlotte, This is to tell you your mother has had a talk with me and I think she is right about you and I. She has told me about your life and family, and I see now we should never of thought of anything serious. The captain has had a talk with me too, and told me I made a great mistake. I want to apologize to everybody for making so much trouble.

You will receive this after you leave the boat. I would like to of seen you, but I have given my promise to your mother and the captain that I will not. Anyway it would only be harder. Also I have promised your mother I will not write to you. Our friendship was very short and now it is quite all over and I am sorry for my mistake. Sincerely yours, John Leslie Trotter.

"Such misuse of words will, I hope, show you how unsuitable young Trotter would have been for you, my dear," her mother had said, as she had sat staring at the letter, offering this comment as a palliating factor. But oh, it hadn't been the words Leslie misused that had struck Charlotte so hard. But the words he omitted. *Love, marriage,* even *engagement,* all were absent. Over and over she had read those few lines, searching for some recognition of his declaration on the freight-deck. It had been like looking for water in an empty river bed when she was very thirsty.

As she stared now at the letter, 10, 12, 15 years later (*No, longer still*), she felt the old anguish, or was it pity, for that defeated, demoted, deserted girl, lying face down on that big ugly double bed in the bedroom in Norway, cut off from her source of supply of courage and confidence, reduced finally to uncontrollable weeping, while her mother, with that patronizing gentleness which always accompanied one of her victories, brought her hot milk and bromides, and laid wet cloths upon her head.

She put the letter back into the portfolio, and the portfolio back in the drawer. Again she got into bed, again she turned out the light. What a little simpleton she had been! At first she had clung to the hope that her mother had forced Leslie to write that note. She had answered it with passionate indignation.

The first time she was able to elude her mother in London, eagerly she had gotten into a taxicab and driven to The Savoy. But there had been no letter for Miss Charlotte Vale. Again and again she had asked the mail-clerk her futile question. All that summer she had called in vain at General Delivery windows in various post offices. But Leslie never sent her a single line, a single signal. Eight weeks in all were somehow endured before her mother and she had finally sailed for Boston in September.

They had spent the last few days in Old Chester, less than 20 miles from Liverpool. The address Leslie had written in her address-book was *Rockledge, Forestbrook Vale, Liverpool, Lancashire, England.* One afternoon her mother had suggested a drive. It wasn't until she told the chauffeur to stop, they would walk from here, that Charlotte asked where they were going. "You'll see!" her mother had replied.

The automobile had left them in the midst of an outcrop of small detached houses, placed close together in long neat rows on parallel streets, suggestive of a market produce garden, planted with rows of vegetables of different varieties. The houses in one patch were all brick, in another all cement, in still another a combination of both brick and cement.

When Charlotte saw the signboard ahead bearing the words *Forestbrook Vale,* she realized her mother's objective. It was a short street with a dead end, lined on both sides by small oblong brick houses, flat-roofed, and all exactly alike. A long fence ran in front of them with cement pilasters at each gateway, bearing impressive titles instead of numbers. Rockledge was the fifth house down on the left. It had orange-colored curtains made of theatrical gauze at its pair of front windows, pink petunias and portulacas of all colors in the window-box outside, and a single monkey pine tree in its small front garden.

"Well, now you see what I've saved you from!" her mother had commented as they paused on the sidewalk opposite. Charlotte had made no reply, choked by an emotion of hatred for her mother and a wave of loyalty to Leslie stronger than ever before.

She had been at home several months before the blow fell that finally destroyed that loyalty. One Sunday morning in December, glancing through the society page of a New York paper she saw the announcement of Leslie's engagement to the New York girl, and the next June she read a description of the wedding at Glen Cove. The article gave a glowing account of Mr. John Leslie-Trotter (hyphenated), of Rockledge, Lancashire, England, and mentioned with pride his interest in shipping, adding that he was to enter the banking firm of his father-in-law after his marriage.

That had been the way the New York girl's parents had met the situation, no more welcome to them, at first, probably, than to her mother. *That* had been the way (it had been borne in upon Charlotte) that Leslie had met the situation! All those weeks and months that she had been calling in vain for letters from him, longing, hoping, refusing to lose faith, he had been consoling himself with another girl! She used to try to get comfort from the thought that at least it had taught her a lesson. Never again would she be so vulnerable. Small comfort! Leslie had been her first and only romance.

Sunlight was shining through the flowered-cretonne window-hangings over her head when she woke up from three solid hours of deep sleep induced by two turquoise-colored capsules to which she had at last resorted. Doctor Jaquith had not taken the capsules away from her. Instead, he had impressed upon her that one's own knowledge of how the nervous system works was the most effective way to treat sleeplessness.

At Cascade Charlotte had spent many hours studying nerves and their functions; instincts and emotions, and their differences; and the effect of all these upon one's mind, body, and behavior. She knew why an evening spent in some form of light amusement prepared the way for peaceful sleep, and why anything emotionally or mentally arousing invited wakefulness. She had also learned at Cascade not to fear sleeplessness—that rest and relaxation even without sleep refreshed the body. To rid oneself of false fears by the intelligent application of one's own knowledge was one of the fundamental principles of Doctor Jaquith's philosophy.

At her first conference with Doctor Jaquith he had told her, with that brusque manner of his, but kindly, in spite of the frequent interpolations of blunt humor, that she was a mature and intelligent human being, equipped with all her five senses, and with what was more of an asset still—free-will. Not to make use of her free-will was like putting a blindfold over the eyes and letting somebody else lead her around. He said he'd gladly help her learn how to use her free-will, but *she'd* got to do the using, and apply it to everything—blue capsules included.

As she gazed at the cretonne curtains, she noticed they were hanging motionless, and at the same moment she became conscious of the exaggerated stillness. There was no murmur, no tremor. The engines were not running. For a moment she lay as still as the ship, like someone waking up free from pain following some physical ordeal, not daring to stir a muscle. For 30 seconds or more she lay inert in a blissful state of half torpor. But she was aware that reality was slowly and surely advancing.

During the peak of her illness waking up in the morning had been like entering the sea when the surf is high on a beach where there is an undertow. Returning consciousness would hit her in a series of waves like breaking combers. After she had managed to pass through those first worst combers of consciousness, the waves did not break often—just rose and fell all day like a sullen sea. But for weeks now she had been spared the choking combers of waking up. Their diminishing size and strength had been one of the indications that proved she would soon be well. But Doctor Jaquith had made a mistake. The combers had returned, and here she was a whole ocean away from Cascade and protection. Oh, she should never have come on this cruise! She must send that man a note that she was ill and unable to take the proposed trip today.

Kneeling on her bed, she pushed back the cretonne curtain and looked out her porthole. The ship was moving! Slipping along as smoothly as a swan. Gulls were rising and falling, stopping in midair without seeming to move their wings, spread out to full capacity, like the petals of some large luxurious flower in full bloom. In the distance she could see a strip of furry land, the blurred gray-green of a mullein leaf.

The land must be one of the Balearic Isles. Majorca probably. As she gazed at the waiting island anchored way out here at sea, for her to take or leave as she chose according to her own free-will, she felt the prick of a sort of obligation, not to that man—but to the slightly known person in herself, using her free-will with no one to say nay, aye, why, or when.

There was, besides, the challenge of Doctor Jaquith's expectations acting like a spur. That poem of Walt Whitman's which he had given her was in her billfold now. She reached for her bag and produced it. It was typed on a blue-lined index card. She held it up above her eyes. The poem was entitled *The Untold Want*. It was only two lines long. It read: *The untold want, by life and land ne'er granted, Now, Voyager, sail thou forth, to seek and find.* Very well! She would! She flung back the bed-clothes and got out of bed.

She had taken the blue capsules so late that she felt drugged, heavy-eyed, and slightly nauseated. Doctor Jaquith's Spartan exhortations recurred to her: *Ignore sensations.*

Discount emotions. Think, act, feel, in this order. Then thumb your nose at what you feel. By no means did Doctor Jaquith confine himself to poetry! She rang for the stewardess and ordered breakfast sent to her room. She must eat, put food in her mouth, chew, swallow. It was simply a matter of determination. She laid out Lisa's tweed suit, and Fabia's thick-soled walking-shoes. Her head was simply splitting. She went into the bathroom, ripped off her nightgown over her head, and took a cold salt shower.

When Durrance joined Charlotte she was standing on the deck gazing at Palma across the bay. The pointed pinnacles of the cathedral loomed up above the heterogeneous mass of buildings surrounding it like the pointed tops of spruce above deciduous trees of various varieties. The buildings crowded down to a string of small boats at the water's edge. The blue bay was full of rippling reflections—sails, roofs, pinnacles, and mountain-tops. The air was full of sunshine, breezes, gulls and gulls' calls. The tenders were already plying between the liner and the shore. Other little boats were chugging here and there, plying through the reflections, trailing long wakes of watered silk.

Charlotte surveyed this scene through clouds of despair and bitterness, continually rising from one source or another in her depths—from the smoldering fires of bitter memories and resentments which she had tried to discard.

"Hello! Here you are! I've been looking everywhere for somebody in dark blue and a lot of soft brown fur. You should have told me what you were going to wear, Camille. Hope you slept well?"

"I managed to pass the night, thank you."

"Thank you *who?* I rather liked the sound of my initials last night." He was in excellent spirits. "I rather like Lisa's tweeds, too," he went on, stepping back and surveying her critically.

"Lisa certainly has quite an eye for color." The tweeds were dusty green, jacket and skirt, with a pale yellow jersey waist. She wore a yellow felt hat, and over her arm carried a Burberry topcoat which matched the suit. "Only I hope I don't mistake you for an olive tree today and lean up against you, or a grapefruit and cut you in two."

"Are you usually so scintillating so early in the morning?"

"No. Not always. Only when I'm about to explore an unknown island with an unknown lady. Guess that extra coat is a good idea. I'll get mine. Wait for me here."

She was thankful to be spared the necessity of making a rejoinder. She was in no mood to respond to his good humor, even if she had the skill. She wished she hadn't worn the green-and-yellow costume. Remarks about her appearance always embarrassed her. That facetious comment about the olive tree and grapefruit was just the kind of arch humor June indulged in frequently at her expense.

June, witty, pretty, and only 18, derived much amusement poking fun at her, and exposing to clearer view her most obvious defect. She would put her head on one side and inquire roguishly, "Isn't that skirt a little too short, Auntie?" when it was painfully too long, or with mock surprise, looking closely at her pale dry lips, "Have you been putting rouge on your lips, you naughty girl?" What remark would June make now, she wondered, to convey to this stranger what a funny dub Aunt Charlotte was?

If June should as much as catch a glimpse of her in the company of this man, she'd never hear the last of it. It was especially tempting to June's sense of humor to imply that poor Aunt Charlotte had an admirer. It had been such a taunt of June's that had snapped Charlotte's endurance finally, on that horrible Sunday afternoon last October, when she had broken down before the whole family and fled from the phalanx of their shocked, staring faces.

She had not seen any of those faces since, except Lisa's and her mother's. But as soon as this cruise was over, she must go home again. Her preordained environment was waiting for her. This cruise was but an interlude, transitory, soon over. It would leave no more trace on her life, once she entered the shadows of the Back Bay Station, than the reflections of Palma on the sea, once the shades of night shut down. The thought of returning to the scene of her ignominious exhibition filled her with revulsion. She felt the physical pressure of rising sobs.

Good Heavens! She must pull herself together. Her companion would be back any moment. She stood up very straight. Think, act, feel. That was the order. Then ignore what you feel. But it was too late now. The tears were already in her eyes. She heard his voice beside her.

"There's the tender coming back for the next load," he remarked cheerfully. "Hadn't we better be going below?"

"I've decided not to go," she managed to quaver.

He looked at her sharply. All he could see was the contour of her averted cheek. "Have I said something? Was I too fresh again?"

She shook her head.

"Yes, I was! I'm sorry."

"No, no! It isn't anything to do with you. It's only—I've been ill. I'm not well yet. I—" She might as well tell him the whole truth, and the sooner the better. "I've been in a sanatorium for the last three months—a place called Cascade." At hearing the announcement for the first time from her own lips, tears of self-pity filled her eyes. "Please leave me."

His answer was to fold his arms upon the deck-railing and move over nearer to her till his shoulder touched hers, then to grasp her wrist with his concealed hand.

"Cascade?" he queried casually. "I couldn't afford to go to Cascade when I was ill." Then, in a lower tone, "I know all about it. I understand now." The firm steadying pressure continued on her arm. There was no suggestion of a caress about it.

She dabbed her eyes with her free hand and blew her nose. "I'm an awful fool!"

"Thank God for that! So was I! Why, it's like discovering we've got a common ancestor, and are cousins or something."

She felt an insane desire to laugh. She blew her nose again.

"I was thinking," he went on, "that the first thing we'd better do when we get on shore is to have a little refreshment of some sort. It's been a long time since I had breakfast, and some good strong black coffee would appeal to me. Then, after a look at the cathedral, I thought we'd get on the road. Of course if you've got anything to suggest I'm willing to listen. I thought perhaps—" Still his hand grasped her wrist.

"I'm better now."

"Sure?"

"Sure." And she gave him a swift glance to prove it.

He let go of her wrist then. "Well, shall we take this tender or wait for the next? Makes no difference to me."

"We'll take this one. And thanks a lot."

Never had she regained her poise so completely after a tailspin like that. Usually when the tears once started, there was no stemming the flood till it had spent its force.

As she followed her companion down the hanging steps attached to the side of the liner, she was filled with one of those waves of elation which frequently mark the last stages of convalescence from an illness such as hers. Perhaps she was going to get well! Perhaps Dr. Jaquith hadn't made a mistake, after all!

At the end of the steps Durrance leaped lightly down into the bobbing tender, then turned and lifted his arms to her, taking both her hands in his and steadying her down into the boat beside him. Just before he let go of her hands, he gave her fingers a squeeze of encouragement, calling out above the confusion of voices and waves and looking straight at her, "All right?"

She returned the squeeze and called back in a strong bright voice, "All right!"

CHAPTER SEVEN:
BIOGRAPHICAL DETAILS

A half-hour later they were walking up the main aisle of Palma's cathedral. Their footsteps on the stone floor rose in tiny sound waves side by side, pushing their way through the floating dust-motes and disappearing in the great empty space above. Their gazes, also side by side, slowly circled the vista of soaring columns, then climbed one of the shafts, wandering off to the faraway regions of the vaulted roof, leaping to the old stained-glass windows, first one, then another.

"Cram's right!" Durrance exclaimed softly. "Marvelous! What can Chartres be like?" His tone was as excited as a boy's.

Later Charlotte looked at him with dawning conviction, as he stood in a shaft of dusty sunlight slanting down through a high open window. One hand was placed on a column in an almost affectionate way. His chin was lifted. On his face there was a rapt expression, not of reverence, but rather of intense interest.

Later, seated on the back seat of the automobile, she remarked, "I think I know what you were doing at M.I.T. Aren't you an architect?"

"No, I'm not, Mrs. Sherlock Holmes. Sorry not to oblige you."

"Weren't you studying architecture at M.I.T.?"

"Possibly. But there's a lot of difference between studying architecture and being an architect. Rodrigo!" (Rodrigo was their driver who had eagerly informed them, "I speak English.") "What is the population of Palma?" And Durrance waved a hand in the direction of the disappearing city.

"Almond trees."

"No! No! Palma. People. *Combien? Nombra populaysiong?*"

"Almonds, olives, oil, oranges, lemons, prunes, grapes, wine."

"Well, if you're not an architect," said Charlotte, "do you mind if I ask what you are?"

"Not a bit! It's just what my daughters ask. And my wife too. She says it's embarrassing when she has to open a new charge account." He paused. "I'm a jobber."

"I've heard of stock jobbers. Investments, I suppose."

"Wrong again! I job brass articles—copper, zinc, tin, some iron, some glass. Just about what the junkman jobs. I'm going to Milan to pick up a little old rubbish there."

Again the note of flippant self-contempt! Again she had touched his sensitive spot! She changed the subject. "I'm afraid Rodrigo didn't understand your Majorcan," she laughed. "Shall I try mine?"

"I used to be an architect," he acknowledged. "But I'm not now. It always irritates me—to have the girls and Isobel—my wife—refer to me as an architect. So to get *their* goat I insist I'm a jobber. But there's no reason in the world to be cantankerous with *you*. I sell electric light fixtures."

"Are you going to get electric light fixtures in Milan?"

"Hope to. One of my old friends is an architect, and a successful one too. He is about to place a big order for some fixtures for an Italian villa he is building for a multi-millionaire out in California. When he was in Italy last year he saw just what he wanted for that villa in an old palace not far from Milan. Somebody had to come over personally and see about it. My friend gave *me* the chance, and is going to get the stuff through our firm."

"I see. I'd like to ask you another personal question if you don't mind."

"Go ahead, if it gives me the right to ask *you* a few."

"What does J.D. stand for?"

"For the gloriously happy young hopeful I was in college. That was what I was called, 'J.D.' And the sound of it last night certainly warmed my heart!"

"I suppose J is for John. John D. Am I right?"

"No! Haven't even *that* claim to fame. J.D. is for Jeremiah Duveaux, after a professor my father admired. Old chap I never even saw, and nobody distinguished. I was called Jerry up to college days. But there was another Jerry in the clubhouse when I arrived, so I was J.D. after that. My wife thinks Jeremiah is impossible. Had her calling cards engraved 'J. Duveaux' from the start. And calls me Duveaux. When she was a child her father had a horse named Jerry. She'd as soon call her husband 'Black Beauty.' By the way, what shoes are you wearing?"

"Fabia's."

"Who is Fabia?"

"My niece. Lisa's oldest daughter. We all three, it appears—Lisa, Fabia, and I—have the same generous-sized feet."

"Let's have a look at them."

She stuck out her foot. The shoes were tan brogans, with perforated trimmings and flapping tongues.

"They'll do! Let's get out and walk into Söller when we get nearer, and send Rodrigo ahead to meet us at the hotel. Are you feeling up to it?"

"For the last two months I've been walking four to five miles daily. Certainly I'm feeling up to it."

Rodrigo dropped them about two miles out of Söller. Soon after he disappeared, a narrow road branching off the main thoroughfare tempted them. The road wound upward and had high walls on both sides. It was like following the dried-up bed of a river which had worn a deep gorge. When rounding one of the curves they were met by an unexpected torrent rushing down the river bed, and, to escape annihilation, hastily climbed the wall nearest at hand, as a herd of sheep undulated down the narrow passageway amidst a din of pattering hoofs, crowding bodies, bleats, and bells.

The wall they climbed had broken bits of glass and sharp stones stuck in its top. It was an uncomfortable perch. When glancing down on its other side they saw a plump little old lady in black, with a white kerchief across her bosom, smiling up at them, she was like a good fairy who had come to their rescue. She not only smiled, but beckoned too, and invited them in Majorcan to come right down into her garden.

They accepted with pleasure. It was a charming garden, no bigger than a tennis court and of the same proportions. There was round bed of white-spotted calla lily leaves in the center, and in the center of the calla lilies a little fountain splashed. At one end and along the back there were walls. At the other end a tiny porch fringed with flowering window-boxes. At the front, blue space, and far away a dim mountainy horizon line.

With more gesticulations the plump lady urged her guests to come and sit down on her porch. Durrance assured her that they would be delighted, but were expected to *mangé, déjeuneé, lunchée, à l' hôtel à Söller*, and must *hurrée*. The plump little lady (who seemed not only to understand him, but to take a great fancy to him too) led him to the edge of her wall and pointed to Söller. Its buildings looked like few crumbs in the bottom of a large gray-green mixing-bowl.

It was decided between the two of them that it was too late to get to the hotel in time for lunch. When Durrance inquired, in his most elegant manner, if she could possibly spare them a few curds and whey to stay the pangs of *mangé*, the little old lady's face broke into countless smile-wrinkles and her body performed a series of short, jerky affirmative bobs.

They ate their eggs, bread, cheese, milk, jam and home-made wine leaning against the sinewy branches of a grapevine that climbed the wall. Countless lizards peered at them with bright birdlike eyes from the cracks and crevices. After they had scraped their plates clean, and emptied the cruet of its rose-red liquid, Durrance hitched his body away from the wall and stretched out flat on the ground, perching one foot upon a raised knee.

He started to shove his hand under his head for a pillow when Charlotte remarked practically, "Here, this will be more comfortable," and slipped her leather shopping-bag under his head.

"Perfect!" he murmured, closed his eyes, and laid his wrist palm-upturned over them as a shield from the sun.

Charlotte tossed off her hat and leaned her head back against the wall. She didn't close her eyes. Instead, she surveyed her companion lying there on the ground—like some great dog, she thought, and as much at ease in her presence.

She, too, was at ease. This sense of quiet enjoyment in the presence of a man had never happened before! While she gazed, his breathing became so measured that she wondered if he had fallen asleep. She had never been in the presence of anyone asleep except her mother. Or at least not since she was very young. There was something about it that gave one a feeling of superiority. Or was it protection?

"Are you asleep?" finally she asked in almost a whisper.

"Good Heavens, no! Just thinking. About *you* chiefly. Putting two and two together. Having difficulty to make four.

But since this morning—since discovering that you and I are sort of cousins, because of our disagreeable relative—you're not quite such a mystery to me. I thought, perhaps, out there on deck this morning that Sara was sort of back in her old garret again."

"She was! Seeing all its terrible details." She paused. "There is a difference between Sara and me. Sara didn't have to go back to her garrett. But I've got to. As soon as this cruise is over."

"Perhaps we've both got garretts we've got to go back to. Some sort of situation or other we've got to stick to—and live with—which no rich old gentleman can do anything about. I think my wrestling about with nerves taught me how to make my garrett more comfortable to live in."

"I can't imagine your ever having anything the matter with your nerves."

"Why not?"

"You don't seem to be the type."

"What seems to be my type may just be my technique. I wouldn't be a bit surprised if you have me labeled wrong. Why don't I seem to be the type?"

"You get such a lot of pleasure out of every little thing."

"I see! A sort of Simple Simon?"

"No, I don't mean that. You're so—so gay, and—and unrepressed." She groped.

"Well, take the steadiest old plug of a horse, and the first time you let him run loose in a pasture, he's apt to kick up his heels. At home, with my wife and daughters, I'm very dignified."

"How old are your daughters?"

"Beatie's twenty-one, and Moonie's two years younger. Both of them too old to be called those baby nicknames, so Isobel says. But I've still got a few years more that I can go on calling Christine, Tina."

"How old is Tina?"

"Only eleven. Isobel calls her the child of her old age."

"The child of her old age! What is she like?"

"Well, Tina is sort of in the awkward age now. Seems as if Tina has been in the awkward age ever since she cut her first tooth. Even before. She wasn't well as a little baby. And now—well, Tina is a nervous, highstrung little kid. The two older girls can pull their weight anywhere. They are both in college now, and doing very well. Wait a minute. I think I have a picture of them here." Without sitting up, he produced a worn leather case, searched its recesses, and pulled out a frayed-edged kodak picture. He passed it back to Charlotte over his head. "There's my harem. All four."

There were two tall, well-developed young women, near enough alike in appearance to be twins. Both looked as if they had just come from under the drier at the hairdresser's, their coiffures molded into the correct fashion of the day. One was standing up against a high privet hedge, the other was seated in front of her on a folding wooden settee beside an older woman who was knitting. Surely not Isobel! Not this man's wife! His mother possibly. She was a small woman, flat-chested, narrow-shouldered, narrow-faced. She wore her hair drawn straight back into a tiny roll in the nape of her neck. Her head was bent, her eyes were upon her knitting, her lips tightly compressed.

"Who is that knitting?"

"That's Isobel. She's always knitting. I asked her to stop just long enough to look into my camera, but she is the kind who knits the way cigarette fiends smoke. That picture isn't very good of Isobel. If she'd only looked up and smiled!"

"Is that Tina sitting on the grass with her legs crossed?"

"Yes. That's Tina. We hope she won't have to wear glasses always. Tina wouldn't smile for me either. She never will when I take her picture. Tina says if you're as homely as she is you look better cross."

Charlotte gazed closely at the square-jawed, square-figured child on the grass, scowling straight into the camera. Scowling, now, straight into her eyes.

"Does Tina know she wasn't wanted?"

"I didn't say she wasn't wanted. But as a matter of fact—" He stopped and decided he'd better start off again. "Tina is our problem child. That's another reason I'm glad I've had the experience of a nervous breakdown. It helps me to understand a girl like Tina better. Tell me about your family. Haven't you got any pictures of them here?"

"I think I have one of my mother in my billfold inside your head-rest." He passed her bag, then got up and sat down beside her, with his back against the wall.

"Here it is. It's a reduced photograph of one of her portraits."

The portrait was by Sargent. He had made her mother look very imperious and regal. She wore her pearl-and-diamond dog-collar and her hair was dressed in a high marcelled pompadour. Durrance looked at the picture in silence for a moment. "She looks like a very strong character," he said.

"She is."

"I bet it isn't easy to put anything over on that grande dame."

"It isn't."

"Where are the rest of your household?"

"There are no 'rest.' My father died the year I went away to boarding-school, and I went home to stay with my mother, so she wouldn't be alone. I had three older brothers, but I was the only girl."

"The adored little sister, I see!"

"Scarcely!" She scoffed. "My brothers were so much older they were extremely embarrassed by the arrival of an infant. The oldest, Rupert, had graduated from college when I was born. I was always a source of deep humiliation to Rupert. Once, when I was about five, my mother asked him to call for me at the dentist's. The dentist thought he was my father and called him, 'your daddy.'" She gave a short, dry laugh. "When we got home I overheard Rupert tell my mother never to ask him to call for 'that child' again, and expose him to such humiliation. I was a terribly plain little rat." Funny to be talking so intimately to this man. It was, of course, because he was a stranger. After tomorrow they would never see each other again.

When she was replacing her mother's picture in its pocket in the billfold, several calling cards, addresses, clippings, and a kodak picture fell out into her lap.

Durrance gathered them together. "May I look at this?" he asked, holding up the picture.

"Certainly. I haven't looked at it myself since the day Lisa gave it to me out at her house. It's one of those awful flash-light family groups taken after a large Thanksgiving dinner."

"Who's that? And that? And that?" Durrance asked, as, heads together, they examined the picture.

"That's my brother Lloyd. That's Rosa, his wife. That's my brother Hilary with the staring eyes, and his wife Justine beside him with her eyes closed. That's Windy. That's Murray. That's Lisa. That's June. That's Nichols down in front. And that's Fabia."

"And who's the fat lady with the heavy brows and all the hair?"

"That's a poor, pathetic spinster aunt."

"Where are *you?*"

She could easily have said, "I was taking the picture," but she didn't. "The name of the spinster aunt is Charlotte."

"You don't mean *that's* Camille!"

"The same! I told you I was just dressed up, playing a part. Come, give me back the picture. You've looked long enough into my garrett."

He did so. "How long since you've been home?"

"Not since my exit last October, which was anything but covered with glory."

"What happened? Tell me about it. Or would you rather not?"

"I'd rather not."

"All right. Perhaps you'd like to hear what the guidebook has to say about Söller." He drew a red volume out of a side pocket. "Lean back and make yourself comfortable. Let's see—here it is: 'Söller. Some three miles inland, 10,000 inhabitants, lying in a beautiful valley, with orange and other groves on every side. The road—'"

CHAPTER EIGHT:
BLOSSOMING OUT

Charlotte closed her eyes. Her companion's voice became a blurred drone. As if she were sitting in a moving-picture theater the scene before her suddenly shifted to Marlborough Street, Boston, and the time to one Sunday last October just before dinner was announced.

The family were all gathered in the big upstairs living-room, overfurnished and overdraped, its dark walls covered with oil paintings in huge gilt frames. The paintings were chiefly landscapes—spectacular mountains, picturesque lakes, and pastoral scenes with grazing cattle and herds of sheep.

There was a large family gathering that Sunday because it was Lloyd's birthday. Barry Firth had been invited to add a note of festivity. Barry Firth was always delighted to accept any invitation if there was a likelihood that Lisa would be present. Barry had been devoted to Lisa for years; in love with her in fact, if she were any judge of the signs. But the family seemed unaware of the fact. Last summer June and Nichols had begun teasing her about Barry Firth—making insinuating remarks about her "boy friend," and exchanging winks and glances.

Her mother took pleasure in giving birthday parties for her adult children. She always dressed up in her best finery, and required Charlotte to follow suit. She had told Charlotte several days before that she was wearing her black chiffon-velvet, and that Charlotte was to wear *her* black chiffon-velvet too. Charlotte had long since found life was more bearable not to disagree with her mother. It was too early in the fall for velvet. No one else would wear long dresses. She and her mother would look like a pair of dowagers. However, she accepted the edict without protest.

When she took her black velvet dress out of the closet on Saturday afternoon, she found the artificial bunch of white roses on the shoulder was falling to pieces. In a moment of misguided judgment she called up a florist and ordered a shoulder bouquet of gardenias. The gardenias were fresh and crisp, and tied with a silver ribbon. They did much to improve the shabby appearance of her dress, she thought. It never occurred to her that the gardenias would be the grist for June's mill.

All the guests had arrived when June first spied the gardenias. "What is it I see?" and making opera-glasses out of her hands she directed them upon Charlotte. "Come here, Nichols, and tell me if *you* see what *I* do. Nobody in *this* family can get away with a thing like that on her shoulder without *some* explanation."

Charlotte was silent. What a fool she'd been!

"Looks sort of suspicious to *me*, Nichols, doesn't it to you?" and June winked at Barry Firth's back across the room.

Barry might turn around at any moment! Barry couldn't help but be aware that her mother had always had designs on him as a son-in-law. Charlotte could feel a hot surging wave of embarrassment mounting up from her depths, spreading to her arms and shoulders, breaking out, probably, on her neck and face in those horrible red splotches, which had been appearing of late.

"Come, don't keep us waiting. 'Fess up," June goaded.

"Do you enjoy being disagreeable?" Charlotte began. "Do you get pleasure out of making others uncomfortable? Do you—"

She stopped abruptly, her voice, her breath, cut off by a flood of rising sobs, as uncontrollable as the splotches on her face, and as unfamiliar to her, up to several weeks ago. She put both her hands up to her mouth to stifle the awful sound they made. Everybody in the room turned and stared at her. She groped her way through a gauntlet of family faces—white, staring, shocked, increased to a multitude by blurring tears.

From that day until she went to Cascade, Charlotte had remained in her bedroom.

The low monotonous drone of her companion's voice ceased. She opened her eyes. "That sounds very interesting," she remarked prosaically. "I guess there's lots to see and do on these islands." A few minutes later: "Do you know the cause of your breakdown? And how long did it last?" she inquired, with the license one feels with another victim of a common malady.

"The underlying cause was a long-drawn-out period of a sense of failure," Durrance replied. "It lasted about eight months. Do you know the cause of your illness, and how long did *it* last?"

"The cause of mine was also a long-drawn-out sense of failure. It has lasted nearly a year so far. At least this attack. I guess I've had other attacks before, but didn't know it. What in particular made you feel your sense of failure?"

"What makes most men feel it—not making good at the chief object of his existence—as a provider, I mean. Strikes pretty deep sometimes. What was the cause of *your* sense of failure?"

"Not very different. A woman has a chief object for existence too, you know. And if she fails to make good at it, why, it, too, can strike pretty deep. Do you remember, when you went to school and studied history, that one of the stock questions was to state the underlying and immediate cause of a war?"

"I remember."

"Well—you've stated the underlying cause of your illness. What was the immediate cause? Or would you rather not speak of it?"

He closed the guidebook and tossed it aside. "The immediate cause was pretty prosaic. It was connected with this little junk business of mine. I went into it when I got out of architecture. A lot of my friends lent me money. When friends who've lent you money ask if they're going to get a dividend pretty soon, it isn't easy to make light of it, and say that you guess they won't get a dividend this year anyway, when you know darn well there isn't the slightest hope for a dividend this year nor next year either, nor God knows when. After a while it gets under your skin if you've got any nervous system at all."

"Why did you get out of architecture?"

"Because grocery bills had to be paid. Isobel has delicate health. Specialists' bills had to be paid too. I was in by myself, then, you see, and the rent of a first-class architect's office and all the overhead expenses mount up. Perhaps if there'd been no World War things would have been different. Maybe I'm rationalizing."

"Were you in the war?"

"Well, I wouldn't go so far as to claim I was actually *in* the war. But I was in a training camp. Never got across, worse luck. Never got a single glimpse at a French cathedral, tower

or spire!" he said flippantly. "Instead, I spent my time outside
Ayer, Massachusetts, learning how to salute an officer, and
bayonet a dummy, and losing what little headway I'd made in
architecture." He picked up a small pebble and flung it off into
space. It disappeared over the low parapet of the retaining
wall. "After the fray was over, the architects who'd stuck
around were the ones who got the contracts. Oh, I made
another stab at it. I tried hard, but it was pretty hard sledding
after the war. It was especially hard sledding for Isobel. Isobel
never had any faith that I'd ever be a White or a Cram or a
Bulfinch, and I guess she was right too." He paused. "For several years the electrical equipment business wasn't so bad," he
went on. "Then gradually— But what am I thinking of, running on about myself like this? I guess it was that wine. Do
you hear that fountain? Let's close our eyes and not say a word
for a minute or two. Just listen, and be aware. That's what Tina
and I do sometimes."

Charlotte leaned her head back against one of the bare arms
of the grapevine, lifted her chin to the sky and closed her eyes.
Trickle of water, splash of birds' feathers, tinkle of bells, pressure of earth, warmth of sun, warmth of companionship. Thus
they sat, both with closed eyes and raised chins, for a minute.
Finally Durrance stood up and walked over to the low wall at the
outer edge of the garden. Placing his elbows on top of the wall,
he looked down at whatever lay below, then turned to Charlotte.

"Come and look," he called.

She obeyed, leaning on the low wall beside him. It was like
looking over the parapet of a high building, she thought. The
series of narrow, terraced gardens were like the mounting stories of a New York skyscraper, one set back of the other. There
was a grove of olive trees in the valley hundreds of feet below,
with some sheep wandering beneath them.

"The sheep look like blobs of yellow foam scattered on the
ground," Charlotte remarked.

"And the olive trees look like a lot of gray-green balloons tethered on the ground," said Durrance. "One of the balloons has broken its rope, I think, and is sailing away with us in its basket looking down over the edge." He paused. "Makes me want to spit," he remarked reminiscently, looking around his shoulder at her impishly to see how she took it. It was the sort of humor he could never indulge in with Isobel.

Charlotte replied prosaically, "Why is the pleasure of spitting from high places supposed to be confined to the male of the species? I always want to."

This remark of Charlotte's filled Durrance with such an ecstatic sense of companionship that he remarked, "I don't really *have* to get off at Nice tomorrow."

Charlotte was silent. Could she play her part another day?

"I'm not due in Milan yet. I'd planned to run up to Paris for a few days, but I think I could persuade the purser to let me keep my bunk a little longer, anyway till Genoa, that is, if you—"

Still Charlotte was silent, feeling shy and inadequate.

"Oh, all right! It was just a passing thought I had. How old do you think those olive trees are down there?"

They returned to the ship on the last trip made by the tender. On the dock there was another little old lady in black with a white kerchief, selling flowers. There wasn't much left in her basket when Durrance made his selection. But there still remained several bunches of freesia—the short-stemmed, lavender-streaked variety. The stems of each bunch were bound closely together by yards of string, compressing the flowers into a solid mass as difficult to carry as a cauliflower. Durrance bought all the freesia that remained and presented them to Charlotte.

On the ocean liner both Mr. Thompson and Miss Demarest were stationed at the top of the hanging steps, checking off the returning cruise passengers, as two sailors hauled them in one by one. Charlotte appeared first in the open space, one of the bunches of freesia clutched under her arm. Durrance followed with the other two bunches, both their topcoats, an umbrella, two guidebooks, and a package containing three jars of jam made by their luncheon hostess.

"Well, well," exclaimed Miss Demarest, "here are the runaways! At last! Where in the world—"

At that moment somebody behind Miss Demarest leaped forward and grasped Durrance's free hand, vigorously pumping his arm up and down. He was a tall, tanned, loose-jointed man, wore a loose-woven, amber-colored tweed suit, and a striking plaid tie of bulky homespun.

"Hello. Hello, J.D.," he grinned.

"Mack!" gasped Durrance, also grinning, also pumping, the two bunches of freesia dropping to the floor, so also the guidebooks and jam. Charlotte leaned and picked them up. "Well, what do you know about this! As I'm alive, Mack!"

"Sure thing! And Deb, too! We've been in Majorca for the last four weeks. Saw your name on the passenger list. What in the devil are you doing over here?"

"Business." He turned to Charlotte. "This is an old friend of mine, Frank McIntyre. Mack, I want you to meet—" For only a second did he hesitate. Miss Demarest was listening in. "I want you to meet Miss Beauchamp. She's been good enough to take me in for the land trip today."

"Miss Beauchamp! Wait a minute." Mack looked puzzled. "I saw her name on the list, too. Are there two Renée Beauchamps?"

"No. Not two Renées. This is Camille. Tell you about it later. Where's Deb?"

"Waiting for us. Man, it's good to see you! Let's go up."

Deb was also tall, tanned, and loose-jointed. Also wore loose-woven tweeds. A rough, faded-looking plaid suit, but smart. Everything about her was smart in a careless, instinctive sort of way. As Charlotte shook hands with her, she blessed Lisa with all her heart. For the first time in her life that swift, appraising first glance of another woman was not followed by discomfort.

Deb also appeared delighted to see J.D. "Been behaving yourself, old dear? How're Isobel and the girls?"

She had a deep voice, and a loud, frequent laugh, both of which were extremely attractive. Her face presented a similar paradox. No one could call it beautiful, yet it was full of beauty. She had a big nose, and eyes so abnormally far apart that she looked absolutely wall-eyed at times. But when she smiled, which was often, her faced glowed and scintillated, and you no more saw its defects than those of a room when logs in the fireplace are radiating light and warmth. Her two outstanding characteristics were self-confidence and candor. The latter sometimes got her into hot water, Durrance later told Charlotte, but the former kept it from scalding her.

"Let's meet for a cocktail," said Deb. "Mack and I did our last lap of tramping today, and need a tub. How is eight o'clock in the bar? And won't you come too, Miss Beauchamp?" she added.

This unmistakable cordiality was so different from the response to which Charlotte was accustomed when standing beside her formidable mother that again she blessed Lisa. Not only for the clothes she wore, but for the situation in which she found herself—alone, among strangers, making her own impression. She had passed muster, evidently! There had been nothing perfunctory about Deb's invitation. But of course she must not accept it. These were old friends.

"How lovely of you!" Charlotte replied, with a fulsomeness which surprised her own ears. "But I think I won't tonight. I'm rather tired."

"Then I won't either!" instantly Durrance announced. "The fact is I've already asked Camille—Miss Beauchamp—for a cocktail and she has accepted," he lied smoothly.

She gave him a helpless glance of uncoagulated reproval, pleasure, and panic. Then turned to Deb, "Well, all right," she acquiesced weakly.

It was after the first round of Martinis that Mack told J.D. that it was a rotten time of year to be going to Paris. The only reasonable thing for him to do, since he'd had the damned good luck to run across Deb and himself, was to enjoy their charming society as long as possible, play around Nice and Monte Carlo with them tomorrow, and proceed as far as Naples, where Deb and he were to board another liner for home. After their departure, he could take in Rome, Florence, and even Venice, and arrive in Milan on the appointed day, with a little of the tan of Italian sunshine on his pate. "Why, damn it, man, nobody goes to Paris this time of year, and alone!"

"Well, it's worth considering," J.D. replied, glancing at Charlotte. But she wouldn't look up. Her eyes were concentrated upon the important business of fitting together the broken pieces of a potato chip. She wore the same dark crimson dress of last night. He noticed that she had pinned a few freesia at its low V. Their lavender white gave her skin the warm rich cast of thick cream.

During the cocktails Mack announced that he'd fixed it up with the headwaiter for a table for four for dinner. Dinner was followed by coffee, cigarettes, and liqueurs in the Grand Salon. Just when Charlotte had decided that at last she could rise and gracefully excuse herself, Mack inquired, raising one eyebrow drolly, "What about a little—?" and pantomimed dealing a pack of cards. "One rubber before by-by."

"Great! Let's take them on!" J.D. exclaimed. "What do you say, Camille?"

To such childlike eagerness, to such urgency in both eyes and voice, what could she say? "Well, all right."

"All right *who?*" he had the boldness to pursue. Right before Mack and Deb! He was evidently in very high spirits. Better not cross him. She really knew nothing of him.

"All right, J.D.," hastily she obliged him, adding, in an aside to Mack, "Isn't he a perfect infant?" A phrase she'd often heard used by her nieces and nephews.

"Yes! Too damned perfect, some of us think." Mack too was in high spirits.

"I hope you don't mind a little profanity, Camille," remarked Deb. "And by the way, I'm Deb to you hereafter," she announced, slipping her hand through Charlotte's arm, as they sat side by side on an upholstered sofa before the low coffee table, the two men opposite in huge armchairs. Charlotte was as unaccustomed to such a friendly gesture as the average kennel dog to a casual pat on the head. She hoped her eyes wouldn't show a similar gratitude. "Mack's profanity is as innocent as 'Fudge' and 'Oh, dear,'" Deb went on to explain. "But if you mind it, I can stop him."

"Oh, no, please don't stop him." The fact that Mack had taken it for granted that she was shock-proof was as gratifying to her as to a child treated like a grown-up by sophisticated elders. "If you had any idea what my life is, you'd know I simply glory in anything that's unrepressed—and native!"

Mack pulled a portion of his six-feet-three out of the soft depths of the upholstered armchair and leaned toward her. "So you're a nature-child, too," he drawled. "Welcome to our city! Shake! Put it there!" And he held out his palm to her. She put her hand in it. "Your name isn't the only thing I like about you, Camille. I guess we all speak the same language."

"No, we don't!" Charlotte denied. "It's because I'm *not* a child of nature that I find anything on the raw side refreshing. I've been wrapped up in cotton wool ever since I was born!

I've drunk nothing but water that's been filtered and milk that's been pasteurized!" she brought out. "Even the facts of life were all sterilized before being mentioned in my presence. I don't speak your language *at all*. So don't try it."

Mack stared at her with a perplexed expression. "Are you trying to take me for a ride, Camille?" And he winked at Charlotte. "Damned if I know."

"No, I'm not. You've already been taken for a ride. A terrible ride, too! I'm just trying to put you on your feet. My name isn't Camille, nor Beauchamp either." She glanced across at Durrance. "Oh, I'm sorry! But I couldn't keep it up any longer. Won't you please tell them about your little joke?"

"On one condition," Durrance replied sternly, "that if I decide to go on with Mack and Deb, you'll be one of our crowd."

Three minutes later Deb was exclaiming, "Vale! Not one of the Boston Vales?"

"Well, I was born and grew up in Boston. I suppose that does make me a Boston Vale, like Oregon apples, or Bermuda potatoes."

Deb gave one of her short, explosive laughs. "I simply love it!" and she squeezed Charlotte's arm. "Now be serious and answer yes or no. Have you a sister-in-law by the name of Lisa?"

"Yes. Lisa is the only contribution I ever made to the family. Rupert never would have met her but for me. I met Lisa at boarding-school."

"At boarding-school!"

"I know. It *does* seem incredible! But I was there for less than a year. It didn't have much effect. I crawled right back into my cotton wool again. The only reason Lisa paid any attention to *me* was because I'd been assigned to her as one of her Raw Recruits. Each of the Seniors had to take on several of the new girls as her special responsibility. And that's what we were called."

"That's what's puzzling me. I spent a week-end with Lisa

during her last year at boarding-school, and met all of her Raw Recruits. One of them was Charlotte Vale. Your sister, perhaps. She wore tortoise-shell glasses, and was a solemn, square-shaped little owl at the time."

"I'm that owl. Just feathered and plucked."

"But I spent another week-end with Lisa in Boston only two years ago, and Charlotte came in to tea one afternoon with her mother. You're not 'Aunt Charlotte.'"

"I'm under the impression I was called that once."

"But you don't even *look* like Aunt Charlotte!"

"I'm aware of it. But these look like her hands." And she lifted them, examining first their palms, then their backs. "All but this pink enamel on the nails."

"You're priceless!" Deb exclaimed.

There was a low knock on Charlotte's cabin about a half-hour after she had closed and bolted it for the night. She had changed her dinner dress for a black kimono, covered with a chaos of snarling dragons. She was busy at the moment attempting to arrange the freesia, which when unbound revealed stems hardly more than crocus length, in two cylinders better suited to gladioli.

At the sound of the knock Charlotte glanced toward the door. *Now* what? Couldn't her inexperience be safe even behind a bolted door? The knock was repeated. She gathered the snarling dragons closer around her and advanced toward the door. Opening it slightly, "Who is it?" she inquired.

CHAPTER NINE:
NOT TO BE HARNESSED

It was ridiculous to have thought that the low knock on the door was cause for accelerated heartbeats. This wasn't a scene in a novel or a play. Charlotte's information, as far as knocks were concerned and what goes on afterward behind closed doors, was confined to the stage, the screen, and the written page.

Charlotte had always been an omnivorous reader of fiction. She never let a novel by Hemingway, D. H. Lawrence, Proust, Somerset Maugham, or Aldous Huxley slip by her unread. A lending library supplied her demand for modern literature. The lending library books were all covered with uniform paper jackets, and it was not difficult to conceal from her mother all those of which she would disapprove. The books which she could not obtain from a lending library she purchased, and, after reading, hid in the dark tunnels behind her sets of approved literature. The prim white bindings of Jane Austen concealed Boccacio's *Decameron* and Flaubert's *Madame Bovary*; Thoreau, in dark green cloth and gold, screened *Ulysses*, and *Sons and Lovers*; and behind the hand-tooled leather backs of Ralph Waldo Emerson crouched Bertrand Russell and Havelock Ellis. But in spite of a broad book knowledge of life, it is not easy to know whether an author is writing for fact or fancy, realism or comedy, if one has had no personal experience. The low knock was only Deb. She flung the door wide.

"I thought I'd drop in and tell you the plan." Charlotte had excused herself at the end of the second rubber, leaving the three old friends alone to discuss the next day's program. "We've got it all worked out. We're going to bring along some evening things when we start tomorrow, so we won't have to come back to the boat to dress. We plan to have dinner at the dear old Café de Paris and go to the Casino afterward. Antibe in the morning, with lunch at a perfectly heavenly place we know about, a Corniche drive in the afternoon. Can you be ready to start at ten o'clock?"

"I think I'll stay here on the ship tomorrow and rest."

Charlotte had made this decision as soon as she had reached the safety of her closed stateroom, and felt the relief of its solitude, like solid ground, beneath her feet.

"But you gave J.D. to understand you'd come!"

"Well, I've been over the Corniche drive a good many times."

"Of course! And Mack and I have too, Heavens knows! But it's J.D.'s first trip over here. It will spoil everything if you don't come. J.D. has taken a great fancy to you and you know it! And does it do my heart good! Why, you're just a godsend! If you knew what that man's life at home is! Now listen to me. I know all about J.D. I've known him ever since he was in college. He's had a terribly tough deal, and I've always felt a little responsible because he met Isobel at our house. Have a cigarette?"

Charlotte took one, struck a match, lit Deb's cigarette, then her own, flicked out the match, tossed it in the wastebasket, as nonchalantly as she'd ever seen it done on the stage. Deb settled herself on the folded blanket at the foot of the turned-down bed. Charlotte stretched out her feet, and leaned back in the low armchair. "I've seen Isobel's picture," she said. "He had a snapshot of his whole family, and seemed to be very proud of them too."

"I never saw such a good sport! Honestly, when I see what a woman like Isobel can do to a man like J.D., it makes me boil. Most men wouldn't stand it."

"Why does he?"

"Because J.D. has been cursed, from the first day he found himself engaged to Isobel, by a ruling passion not to hurt her. Also he doesn't like getting hurt himself, I guess."

"How did they happen to be engaged?"

"Propinquity. *And* propriety. Isobel was one of those pure, high-minded girls who believed a kiss required a proposal of marriage. Isobel came to New York to study the 'piano-forte,' as her mother called it. She had memorized three or four pieces in Syracuse. That's where she lived. And apparently wanted to acquire a few more pieces with which to attack the forte. That was just what her playing was like. She met J.D. at our house on her very first afternoon in the big wicked city, and from that day to this he's had her hung around his neck."

"Was she a friend of yours?"

"Scarcely! Or I wouldn't be talking like this about her. No! Her mother knew mine slightly in college and wrote and asked if Isobel, who was coming to New York to study the piano-forte, could spend the first few nights with us, and did Mother know of a nice place where she would be safe in the big city? There was usually a crowd at our house, and Isobel arrived one Saturday afternoon when we were having tea and drinks. Mother greeted her with great effusion, as she does everybody she doesn't know very well and wants to make feel welcome. Any outsider would have concluded that Isobel was one of our most intimate friends. I know J.D. got that impression. Isobel was quite a pretty little thing in those days. After tea Mother asked her to play for us. When she sat down at the piano, she put on all the airs of a professional. Later, when the question came up as to rooms, J.D. spoke up and said that at the place where he was rooming there were several girls studying music and art. Well, to make it short, Isobel went there. Inside of three months they were engaged."

"What was J.D. doing in New York?"

"Just starting in on his first job in one of the big architects' offices there, and boiling over with enthusiasm. He had nothing but his salary to marry on and they were engaged for three or four years. Isobel, instead of getting a job to add her earnings to J.D.'s, went back to Syracuse 'to wait for him.' But it's getting late. I must go. Say you'll come with us tomorrow."

"Don't go. Have another cigarette. Tell me what happened to make J.D. give up architecture."

"Tell me first what happened to *you*. You're an absolutely different person from the one I saw last."

"It's all Lisa's doings." And she explained briefly but vividly the orgy of her transformation, to the accompaniment of frequent chortles from Deb.

"Imagine the sensation you'll make when you go home! What will your mother say?"

"I'm trying not to think."

"And all your friends?"

"Oh, I haven't any friends."

"You're simply marvelous! It's your absolute honesty I like so. Tell me about Lisa and that man who has been in love with her for so long. Barry Firth. That's his name!"

"Who told you Barry Firth was in love with Lisa?"

"I saw it with my own two eyes when I spent that week-end with her. But I never mentioned it to anyone, and I wouldn't to you now if you hadn't just told me she is a widow. I just wondered if Barry had run to cover, as old admirers have a way of doing when all obstacles are removed."

"No. Barry hasn't run to cover."

"Are they married?"

"Scarcely. Lisa has been a widow only a few months."

"How long will they wait?"

"I haven't discussed it with her. But as long as Mother is living, I don't think Lisa will do anything to shock her. Mother's heart is far from strong. We all have to be careful."

"Lisa told me a lot about your mother. Said she was one of the last of the old Victorian matriarchs in existence, still ruling her family with a rod of iron. And she said you were one of the last members of the Holy Order of Devoted Daughters in existence."

"My presence on this pleasure cruise certainly looks like it!"

"Well, it's none of my business, but it seems to me as if *you* deserve this break as much as J.D. Make the most of it, my dear. Gosh! Look at the time! One-thirty! I'll tell you about the architecture tragedy tomorrow if you'll come with us. I must go now, and let J.D. go to bed. He's waiting. Oh, darn it, I'm no good at diplomacy. Listen, I'm just a messenger sent here by J.D. He is going to start for Paris tomorrow if you don't come with us. I'm to take him your answer before I turn in."

Charlotte and Deb lay stretched out in the sand in one of the sheltered coves of the Cape of Antibe, Charlotte on her side, her head propped up in the palm of her hand, Deb flat on her back, weathered face and browned throat exposed to the full blast of the sun's rays. It was one of the Mediterranean's brightest of blue days. Twenty feet away breaking waves made a ragged edge of white against a pale yellow beach. Thousands of feet away the snow-capped mountains of the Italian Alps made another ragged edge of white against a pale sky. The two men had started out on foot to inspect the town, and to satisfy J.D.'s eager curiosity to have a closer look at the two old square watch-towers.

"His enthusiasm for architecture seems to have persisted," commented Charlotte.

"I know, his other enthusiasms too! You simply wouldn't recognize him for the same man he is at home. We'll get him to tell some of his Scotch and Irish stories tonight at dinner. He can be screaming. He'll never tell them when Isobel's around. She says it's making a buffoon of himself for others' amusement. She stepped on his butterfly collecting, too. Called it a waste of time."

"Why did J.D. give up architecture?"

"For about the same reason he gave up about everything else he liked to do. Isobel seemed to look on his architecture as a sort of hobby. She told me once that she had had to give up being a pianist when she married and had one baby right after another, and she saw no reason why Duveaux should keep on indulging his youthful dreams after he had taken on the responsibility of a wife and children. Isobel has always considered that she has very delicate health as compared to other women. It was a horrible shock to her nervous system when she found she was pregnant two months after she was married. She'd planned not to have a child till J.D. could afford it, *if* then, because of her health. It was a worse shock still when the same thing happened two years later. She considered herself a great martyr. And then proceeded to consider the children great martyrs to have to go to a public school and live in a neighborhood that was all run down. Oh, how she used to run on to me! Both the older girls ought to be earning their own living by this time, but Isobel was bound they should go to college, though neither is a brilliant student. She told me once, with tears in her eyes, that if Duveaux didn't do something more practical, she'd have to pay for their daughters' college education with *her* money."

"Has she money?"

"No. It was just a nasty threat. Her father left her a few thousand dollars when he died. But whether it's much or little it isn't very pleasant for a man to have his wife keep saying, 'Well, if *you* can't afford this or that, I'll get it with *my* money.'"

"Do you live near each other at home?"

"Not now. Mack and I have moved out to Darien. But when we were first married we rented a house in Bronxville. Mother was always at me to be nice to Isobel. I tried to be, but she didn't fit into our crowd. She didn't approve of Mack in the least. Thought he was a bad influence. She disapproves of most of J.D.'s college friends. She used to claim the old crowd met chiefly for the purpose of becoming intoxicated. 'Even,' she told me once in her most injured tone, 'when there are only two of them, and the meeting-place the home of one of the men whose wife and innocent little six-months-old daughter are upstairs in bed!' Buck Mortimer—the surgeon, you know—dropped in on J.D. in Mount Vernon one Saturday while he was interning in a New York hospital and spent the night. Isobel never forgot that he sent her husband upstairs to her in a state of intoxication at three o'clock in the morning, at which hour, unable to endure it any longer, she called down to J.D. Buck never forgot it either. He never dropped in on J.D. in Mount Vernon again! J.D. told Mack about it, and how dreadfully he felt about Buck. J.D. wasn't drunk, he said, but fool enough to talk too much to Isobel when he finally went upstairs, and tell her one of Buck's shady stories. And then on top of that the poor boy had the rotten luck to stumble over a chair. Isobel told me Buck's story was so awful that when Duveaux began bumping into the furniture, she decided to sleep in the room with the baby. For weeks she assumed the tragic rôle of a woman who has discovered her husband is likely to become an alcoholic."

"I suppose," said Charlotte, "she has principles about alcohol. I know the type. There are a few of them still left in Boston."

"Well, it's no type for J.D., or for any normal man, these days. It's perfectly all right not to touch a drop herself. Lots of good sports don't. But Isobel was always in a dither for fear J.D. would touch too much. And she is terribly jealous, too."

"Is there a reason to be jealous?"

"If you mean does J.D. have affairs with other women, no, he doesn't. Not that I know of. But Isobel is jealous of his even *talking* to another woman. At a party, if J.D. appeared to be engrossed in conversation with a woman, Isobel would worm herself across the room somehow, appear at his elbow, and ask roguishly what in the world they were finding so interesting. Of course J.D. does like people and people like him. He has a very strong instinct of gregariousness, but Isobel doesn't do a thing about it."

"What should she do about it?"

"What any sensible woman does with a man, once she finds out what his strong instinct is. Satisfy it, if it isn't downright bad, and I've heard none of our instincts are bad. It's up to a woman with a gregarious husband to provide a few people for him, I think. J.D. loves parties, but Isobel is one of those women who feels she is excused from all social debts and duties because she has three children and only one general-housework girl (and such a poor one) and her church work besides. Isobel's terribly religious. And she's such a devoted mother, to hear her tell it. Oh, I hate a hypocrite!"

"Isn't she *really* a devoted mother?"

"Oh, perhaps, perhaps, to the two older girls. I'm probably horribly unfair to her. Partly envy, I guess," Deb paused. "I never had a baby. We've got three kids, but they're adopted," she tucked in gruffly. "I suppose it's because I know Isobel didn't want any one of those girls before they were born that her sanctimonious maternal attitude gets my goat so. Before Tina was born she tried to get a doctor to say it would be bad for her health to have another child."

"Tell me about Tina."

"I don't know much. She was born after we'd moved out to Darien. But I've seen her. She had awful eczema for the first year, poor kid, and is a terribly plain child now, and a misfit at school, I guess. She doesn't get along with Isobel, and simply worships J.D. The result is Isobel is jealous of the child she never wanted. So you can see J.D.'s home life isn't any spring song. Do give him a good time. He deserves it."

"What sort of architect was he?"

"J.D. did dwelling houses mostly. But he was just on the edge of bigger things—churches, libraries, public buildings. Mack says he just barely missed out on several instances he knew about. Perhaps he was inclined to be a little visionary. One of his pet schemes was to transport the heart of a Vermont village down to Central Park, and set it up. J.D. was born in some little town up in the northern part of Vermont. His father was a country doctor, and he knew just where he could get all the things he wanted for his 'Early American Village,' as he called it. But neither the Art Museum, nor the city, was willing to appropriate anything for the project of 'the fanciful Mr. Durrance'! That's what he was called in a certain editorial. It wasn't long after that editorial that J.D. came to Mack and told him 'the fanciful Mr. Durrance' was getting out of architecture, and could Mack spare any money to buy a few shares in a new electrical supply business? Of course Mack bought some shares. He adores J.D. But the business has never done well. Still J.D. managed to send Isobel and the two older girls to Europe twice! They just love to travel! Gosh!"

Deb stood up. Charlotte glanced at her. She was gazing at the white-tipped Italian Alps far away, a deep scowl between her eyes.

"If there's anything that makes my blood boil," she said, in a tone to match her frown, "it's to see one of our American dogs harnessed and made to draw a cart, even though a child may be driving him. Same with a man. Dogs and men aren't meant to be harnessed in our country. Come on, we'd better be getting back to the car if we are to meet those two boys at three o'clock."

CHAPTER TEN:
THE TWO CRUSOES

Four days later Charlotte and J.D. stood on a dock in Naples waving good-bye to Mack and Deb as their ocean liner slowly nosed her way out of the crowded harbor, music playing, tugboats snorting, seagulls swarming.

Charlotte's cruise boat was to set sail for Alexandria at 12:00 that night.

"There will only be fourteen hours left after Mack and Deb sail at ten for us to do all the things we didn't do in Majorca!" J.D. said to Charlotte the night before, leaning on the deck railing beside her. The cruise boat had just left Genoa. Mack and Deb had gone below to their room, and Charlotte and J.D. had gone above to the highest spot on the boat to gaze upon the little island of Elba, shrouded in darkness.

All the things they hadn't done in Majorca? What did he mean by that, Charlotte had wondered. But she hadn't asked. Nor had she taken the inflection of his voice as anything more than playful masquerading. It no longer embarrassed her.

Three days in the good graces and constant society of Mack and Deb had given her self-confidence. But not to be relied upon, she discovered, when, while still gazing at Elba, the same touch that had steadied her a few days before now unsteadied her. Without warning or provocation, J.D.'s hand had found its way along the rail and clasped her wrist!

Panic-stricken at first, she had not drawn away. She hadn't made a sound or moved a muscle. His fingers had tightened on her wrist, and his grazing shoulder had pressed closer against hers. Thus they had stood for at least three minutes, J.D. as mute, as motionless, as Charlotte. Finally he loosened his fingers, and abruptly moved away.

"Italian spring fever, I guess. Let's walk."

Side by side they tramped several times around the deck, their hands shoved deep in their topcoat pockets, saying little. No reference whatsoever was made to the three poignant minutes by the deck-railing.

That night Charlotte dreamed about Leslie. At first she was standing with him on the freight-deck, leaning on its scarred railing, with his arm around her, when Isobel Durrance appeared at his elbow, and inquired roguishly, "What in the world are you two finding so interesting?" Almost at the same moment her mother loomed up on Charlotte's empty side, and said, in a low voice, "I saved you once. Remember 'Rockledge'!" And instantly the scene shifted to that pathetic little house on the outskirts of Liverpool.

She was inside the house. Leslie had just returned from a sea voyage. They stood in the little front room in a long embrace. Suddenly Leslie stiffened and pointed out the window. There was a woman seated just outside the iron gate, shoulders stooped and head bent. At first Charlotte thought it was the New York girl, but as she gazed she recognized Isobel Durrance, knitting, and beside her sitting cross-legged on the ground was a child. Tina, of course. Looking back at Leslie, she discovered that he was no longer young. There were unfamiliar hollows in his face, his sky-blue eyes were midnight-blue-black, and his corn-colored eyebrows were dark sienna brown. It wasn't Leslie in whose arms she was standing! It was J.D.! The shock woke her up instantly.

Freud would have explained the jumbled events in terms of desires and repressions, but there was no time for Charlotte to reflect upon its significance. The thrill of participation in the day that lay before her, and the unfamiliar joy she felt in reality, were enough to lay the ghosts of any dream. The sun was shining brightly. The Bay of Naples was holding out both her arms in warm welcome, offering her various attractions with the generosity of an abundant supply, while in the background Vesuvius comfortably smoked, like a spent old man on the sidelines.

The quartette had selected the Capri trip. Whatever constraint J.D. felt with Charlotte as the walked on the deck last night had disappeared completely. He seemed even more unrestrained, Charlotte thought, whenever occasion arose to offer her a helping hand up and down unsteady gangplanks, hanging escalators, donkeys' backs, bobbing rowboats, or pitching steamers. He was in such a gay, bantering mood that Deb said she wouldn't be a bit surprised to see him stop and turn a handspring at any moment.

"The old dub's winnings have probably gone to his head," Mack had drawled.

Two nights before at Monte Carlo, J.D. had had one of those phenomenal experiences of beginner's luck. Whether he played red or black, odd or even, the little ivory ball seemed possessed to fall in his favor. He had been conservative at first, but as the evening progressed and his luck held, he took bigger risks and played higher stakes. When the quartette left the casino at midnight, they had all lost except J.D., but to no such extent as he had won. The $500 which the bank presented to J.D. was like a windfall from heaven to him. He insisted on giving a farewell dinner for Mack and Deb, followed by the opera—none other than *Traviata*, triumphantly J.D. had announced after he had secured the tickets. Wasn't it marvelous of the opera company to honor Camille's presence by producing Verdi's version of the character whose name she bore?

After the opera, there was a late supper and much gayety. With their memories refreshed by the opera, J.D. became Armand, and Mack dubbed himself the rakish old count. Everyone was in the best of spirits. Charlotte entered into the merrymaking as heartily as if she were an old hand at it. Good humor ran high.

Charlotte and J.D. didn't wait on the dock till Mack and Deb's ocean liner had disappeared.

"Come," said J.D., slipping an urgent hand beneath Charlotte's elbow. "Giuseppe is waiting for us. We can't afford to waste a minute here with the program I've laid out."

He had studied maps, figured mileage, talked to guides, and made his own arrangements with Giuseppe. J.D. had reserved for this last day alone with Charlotte the little town of Ravello, near Amalfi, and an old Benedictine abbey with a 12th-century cloister near Salerno. Both could be included in a day's trip from Naples. The route he planned made a loop following an inland road from Pompeii to Salerno, then skirted the sea to Amalfi, detoured up to Ravello, descending to follow the famous road to Sorrento. At Sorrento they would eat their last dinner together in state, returning to Naples in the early evening, in good time for Charlotte's midnight sailing.

Giuseppe had assured Durrance that he had often been to the old abbey, and "*Si-si, oui-oui,* okay, Signor," was familiar with the short cut, which J.D. had read was well worth the roughness of the road because of its marvelous views. But Giuseppe must have had in mind some other abbey, and some other short cut, for though the road he took was certainly rough, it dwindled into a twisting cart path which ended finally on a bare uncultivated hilltop.

Charlotte and J.D. did not dine in state at Sorrento that night. Instead they drank café-au-lait and munched hard bread beneath a fragment of tiled roof across the corner of a crumbling wall. Not far away their car lay at the foot of a retaining wall. Luckily it wasn't a high wall, or else when Giuseppe had backed off over its edge, Charlotte and J.D. wouldn't have been able to crawl out one of its windows unhurt, and survey its plight with emotions that provoked laughter instead of tears.

When the catastrophe occurred, it was mid-afternoon, and they were already so far behind their schedule that they had decided to omit Ravello in favor of the abbey. Soon after leaving Pompeii, something wrong had developed with Giuseppe's car. It was unable to make over 20 miles an hour on the level, and crawled up hills with the snail's pace of a tractor.

"Well, at least it's safe! And who wants speed when the views are so glorious?" Charlotte had rationalized, when J.D. began blaming himself for being such an inexperienced traveler as to engage any car he saw on the street, just because its driver had a friendly grin on his face and a collapsible top on his car. Or, at least, he *said* it would collapse. The fact of the matter was, neither Giuseppe nor a brawny mechanic at a gasoline station en route could budge it.

Giuseppe was on the verge of hysterics when Charlotte and J.D. first crawled out of the overturned car. Tears streamed down his face, and he leaned his head against one of its upturned tires and sobbed. J.D. patted his round, shaking shoulders in the hope of calming him so he could listen.

As the car had slowly ascended the rough road a thick white cloud slowly descended, shutting out the surrounding landscape, so that they had soon lost all sense of direction. But Giuseppe would know where lay the last town through which they had passed and could descend on foot by the quickest route, once he became sufficiently calm.

Finally J.D.'s pattings were rewarded by Giuseppe's straightening up, and bursting forth not only into speech, but into action too, his avalanche of words being accompanied by violent gesticulations, by which he conveyed his intention of descending to the valley to get *cavallo-e-corda* while Signor and Signorina remained with the car. *"Cavallo-e-corda, cavallo-e-corda,"* he said again and again.

"Horse and rope, of course!" finally Charlotte exclaimed.

"No! No! Giuseppe!" J.D. remonstrated, "not *cavallo* and *corda!* Not *now*. Not first. First, Giuseppe, go get another automobile and chauffeur. Much money for Giuseppe, *multo lire—multo!* Signorina must go Napoli *immediatement*. Catch big boat. Giuseppe stay here after Signor and Signorina go Naples and *then* Giuseppe go get *cavallo-e-corda* and come Napoli later. *Comprehendare?*"

Giuseppe shook his head, a pained expression in his eyes. So J.D. resorted to a medium Giuseppe *could* understand. From an inside pocket he produced a pencil and the black notebook. On one of its blank pages he sketched an automobile, the figure of a chauffeur bent over the driving-wheel and two windblown passengers behind, holding on to hats and flying scarves. On the opposite page the outline of an ocean liner flowed from the magic pencil-tip. Giuseppe stared fascinated. So also Charlotte.

"What's the word for 'tonight'?" he inquired, his pencil flashing.

"*Stasera,*" Charlotte replied.

The face of a clock appeared over the ocean liner, both hands pointing to 12:00. He tapped the hands. "*Stasera,*" he repeated several times slowly and emphatically. Then tapped the ocean liner. "Big boat go, depart, puff-puff-*puff, stasera.*"

"*Capisco!*" Suddenly Giuseppe exclaimed. "*Si, si, si, si!* Okay! Puff-puff-puff," he mimicked with the delight of a child. "Giuseppe go quick for *altra* automobile. Come back quick! Okay! Fine and dandy!" As elated as a dog who at last understands his master's wishes, he was as eager to be off.

"*Presto! Vivo! Allegro!*" J.D. shouted as he disappeared in the mist, running down the pebbly road as fast as his stubby legs would carry him. It was the last they ever saw of Giuseppe.

The overturned car did not belong to Giuseppe, and it occurred to him as he hurried down the rough hillside that when its owner discovered what had happened to his automobile he would not pat him on the shoulder, however much he sobbed. The automobile was the property of a Neapolitan who was earning a scant living by purchasing old cars and fitting them out for sightseeing service. Giuseppe had been in his employ only a few days. He had come to Naples to make enough money to buy a truck of his own. He was a good truck driver. He had delivered many loads of wine casks to Bari, and even as far as Gallipoli, for his former employer.

The vision of the overturned car returned to Giuseppe like the ghoulish details of some crime he had committed. The instinct to escape from that automobile lying up there like a dead body gripped him like a vise. All the money he had was now strapped to his body in a worn leather wallet. He felt sure his employer would take it all away from him to pay for the damage to his car. How then would he ever get back to his beloved Alberrobello again? Ever since he'd left it, he'd been homesick for his little beehive-shaped *truli* hugging the ground, and for Maria and the *bambini* huddled around the fire in the middle.

Giuseppe decided it would be wise to crawl into some underbrush to wait for darkness to conceal his escape.

"Let's walk along the road and meet Giuseppe," J.D. suggested to Charlotte at the end of the half-hour.

They descended through the dense cloud of mist. They'd gone about a quarter of a mile when they came to a fork in the road. Neither could tell by which prong they'd come.

"If we choose the wrong one, we may land at another cellar hole," said Charlotte.

"And if Giuseppe finds us gone, what then? I think we'd better go back to the spot where he left us. He is sure to be back in an hour."

But he wasn't. At the end of two hours and a half, J.D. proposed that he go in search of help, leaving Charlotte on the hilltop in case Giuseppe arrived in his absence.

"We'll stick together, if you don't mind," said Charlotte. "Even though I may not impress you as the clinging-vine type, I prefer not to be left alone in this God-forsaken spot."

The mist became rain as the afternoon wore on. It was fortunate that they had even a fragment of roof over their heads. The overturned automobile offered impossible quarters. There was a pile of something soft beneath the roof—old straw of some sort. It smelled of autumn woods. Seated upon it side by side they were as dry, at first, as two birds perched behind the overhanging eaves of a building gazing out through a torrent of water. As their hope of rescue diminished, Charlotte's cheeriness increased.

"But what if you lose your boat?"

"Well, I've no one on board who will lie awake worrying."

"What if we have to stay here all night?"

"It won't kill us. There are no man-eating animals up here."

"You are a darned good sport!"

"Nonsense! This is the first thrilling experience I've ever had! Dullness day after day requires a lot more good sportsmanship."

In spite of the laprobe salvaged from the car, they were far from warm. Every little while they stood up, stamped their feet and waved their arms. J.D. had slipped a flask of whisky into his overcoat pocket before starting, but he didn't disturb it. Its warming effect might be needed later.

As the oyster-white shroud enveloping the hilltop turned to slate-gray and night began to fall, J.D. descended to the car to sack it of all it had to offer, calling out to Charlotte, waiting outside, that he felt like a deep-sea diver scuttling a sunken ship. There had followed a variety of articles—rubber floor-mats, linen seat-covers (the seats themselves wouldn't go through the window), several pieces of carpet, a bunch of oily waste, a tool kit, a flashlight that worked, and Giuseppe's lunchpail with a bottle full of café-au-lait and several hunks of bread. Together they transported their plunder to their shelter. It had sprung a leak in their absence. A steady drizzle was falling onto the center of their straw couch.

"Don't worry. I can fix it," said J.D. "I'm a very handy man around the house. Give me one of those rubber mats."

The roof was low. There was a pile of stones beside it and he easily climbed on top. He had laid the mat over the hole, but the wind was blowing a gale now, and it wouldn't stay in place. He returned to the car, the tool kit under his arm, and attacked the locked door of its upturned tail-end, prying it open with a screw-driver and hammer. There was a spare tire and a bagful of chains in its dark interior. The combined weight of these would hold down the rubber mat! He carried them up to the roof. Before he had completed his job, Charlotte's bare head, sleek and wet as a seal's, appeared at the edge of the tiles.

"Hi!" she shouted, for the wind and rain were making a terrific noise now. "Can I help?"

"No thanks. Nearly finished. How's the leak?"

"Not a drop now. Here, I'll hold this edge. She was on top of the roof on her hands and knees beside him now.

"No, no! Get inside and keep dry. Do as I say."

Meekly she obeyed. He joined her a few minutes later, the water running off him in streams. Before going onto the roof he had removed all but his white shirt and underwear. But he hadn't stopped to remove his tie. It was sopping wet now. He stepped up in front of Charlotte, lifted up his chin, and said, "See if you can untie this darned thing."

When she had succeeded, he pulled off his shirt over his head, Charlotte again helping in the process, for it clung to him like a wet handkerchief to a window-pane.

"Use this for a towel," she said, and passed him one of the linen seat-covers.

"Good idea! Say, aren't we a wonderful pair of Robinson Crusoes?" he grunted as he rubbed. Night had fallen rapidly. He was only a splotch in the sea of shifting darkness. "Where's that flashlight?"

She passed it to him, snapping the little button on its shaft. It shed a glow hardly brighter than a firefly's gleam, but strong enough to cast big shadows, and sufficient for J.D. to see his clothes. He pulled on his trousers, tightened his belt, slipped into his coat. It was the first time Charlotte had ever witnessed this automatic series of motions, so familiar to most women, she supposed.

"Supper is on the table," she announced crisply and turned the flashlight full onto the results of her recent activities.

In front of the straw couch, now covered with a rubber mat and a steamer rug, she had placed her small suitcase. Two handkerchiefs served as doilies, on which she had placed the bread, the bottle of coffee, and four graham crackers each.

"Holy smoke! Where did those crackers come from?"

"I learned at Cascade that a sensation of fatigue can often be quieted with a cracker, like a fussy child. So I slipped them in my suitcase this morning."

"In case I tired you? Look here, are you cold?" She had given one or two suspicious jerks.

"I'll be all right when I've eaten something."

"You'd think with a boxful of matches in my pocket and a tankful of gasoline in the car I could think of some way of making a fire, besides burning up the car. If we could only find something in the way of fuel! Hot coffee inside is more warming than cold. Look here! I've a thought!" He picked up the tool kit and turned to go.

"You aren't going to leave me in this place alone, and go hunting for wood, are you?"

"Only as far as the car. Where's Giuseppe's tin pail?" She passed it to him. He held it up under one of the streams of water running down from the roof. "Good! It's tight! At least the bottom. I'll leave it here on the ground, filling up while I'm gone."

"When he returned he had several jagged-edged pieces of boards under his arm. One had been a rack for luggage over the spare tire, and he had discovered more wooden construction on the floor and under the seat. He broke up his loot into small pieces while Charlotte held the flashlight.

"Dry as a chip! How full of water is Giuseppe's pail?"

"As full as it ever will be. It's got a hole quarter way up."

"Well, all we need is enough to act as a bottle-heater for Giuseppe's coffee, so we won't run the risk of losing the precious stuff in the fire."

Squatting down, he began fashioning a small nest, no bigger than the inside of a man's hat, out of the stones near-by. Suddenly the flashlight went out! "Damn!" he muttered. "But our eyes will get used to it. We'll wait a little." They both tilted forward on their knees and sat back on their heels.

CHAPTER ELEVEN:
A FLIRTATION, BY DOCTOR'S ORDERS

"Were you ever a Boy Scout?" Charlotte's voice inquired out of the darkness.

"Good Heavens, no! I belong way back in the Christian Endeavor era. Why?"

"You seem to know a lot about making fires and roughing it."

"Well, Tina and I do a little roughing it once in a while.

Tina loves the woods, and is a great kid in such a setting."

"You seem to be more congenial with Tina than with your other daughters."

"I've seen more of her. I've always felt responsible for Tina's existence, which she never asked for, and which she has found so full of difficulties, poor kid. I look upon Tina as my guilty-conscience child."

"Something like guilty-conscience flowers, I suppose."

"Well, possibly. A little. Not exactly, though. You see—"

"I think I understand."

"No, I don't think you do." She had probably jumped to the conclusion that there had been "another woman" in his life, and that Tina was the unexpected result of an act which relieved suspicions. But such were not the facts. There had never been another woman. Only Isobel's constant fear that there was. And his constant sense of guilt that he aroused such suspicions. He had failed to provide Isobel with either the material or the spiritual things she so desired. Try as he might, he simply couldn't make himself feel that tender devotion for her which shows itself in countless simple, homely ways, so convincing to a woman that she doesn't need avowals of love, or periodic renewals of its ultimate expression as reassurance.

That expression had never been anything that Isobel desired, except as reassurance. And to him, finally, its chief satisfaction was its effect as a sop to his conscience. He wasn't failing Isobel so utterly if he could dispel her suspicions so simply, and make her feel reinstated again. Poor Isobel! He'd been the wrong husband for her. Good Lord, what a train of thoughts that chance remark about Tina had started! Good thing mind-reading was still in the undeveloped stage.

"Tina reminds me a little of myself," Charlotte commented. "What other things does she like to do besides roughing it?"

"She likes to paint. Has a notion she's a budding artist. She has rigged up a studio in the attic. Trouble is Tina neglects her home lessons to paint, so she and I have to keep the studio a secret. She also has a passion for animals, but her mother is allergic to fur, so she can't have as much as a white mouse. However, she usually has several pet worms and a few beetles. Where's that bunch of oily waste?"

She passed it to him. He placed a few shreds in the bottom of the stone nest, on top of it a stick or two of the wood, whittled like a feather on the edge, and struck a match.

Fifteen minutes later, seated on their low couch before the dying embers, they washed down their bread and graham crackers with piping hot coffee. But there wasn't enough of the hot liquid to compete long with the chilling effect of the fast-falling temperature. After their supper things were cleared away, the rain turned to hail, pelting down on their tiled roof with a great clatter. When J.D. returned from an inspection of the elements, he reported that they were surrounded by a sea of ice.

"Look here," he demanded sternly, "is that hail on the roof or your teeth?"

"Hail," Charlotte replied, through jaws tightly clenched.

He reached out, groped for her face in the dark, and placed his fingers on her lips as lightly as a blind mute. She clenched her teeth tighter, but she couldn't control her body.

"This won't do! Let me feel of your feet. Soaking! Take off your shoes and stockings. I'm going to rub your feet." He did so vigorously. "Why didn't you tell me you were cold? Relax. Give me your hands."

She managed somehow to place the jerking members in his. For the last hour her muscles had been threatening her with this trembling state, but not until help was at hand did she lose control of them. She tried to tell him how ashamed she was, but her chattering teeth prevented speech.

"Take off your overcoat. Your suit coat, too. Why, you're soaked to the skin! Look here, I'm going to pound your shoulders till you cry out for mercy." He did so. Then, stopping abruptly, "What have you got in that suitcase?"

"Nothing but a thin silk dress," she replied, "which I put in, in case you gave me a chance to change before dinner," she managed to explain.

"Well, I'll give you a chance *now*. Then you're going to have a stuff drink of whisky. Understand? I'm going to have a drink, too. Afterwards we're going to roll up like a cocoon in the laprobe, pile our overcoats and those strips of carpet on top of us, and pray our two heat units will keep us from freezing to death." He struck a match and raised the cover of the suitcase.

It was a fitted case, a going-away present from Lisa. The silver and crystal of the toilet articles scintillated in the puttering light of J.D.'s match. He examined its meager offering. Black suède pumps, fawn-colored stockings, a cherry-colored print dress, a folded article of tea-rose silk and lace. A slip.

"Take off that wet waist, and put on all this dry stuff," he ordered brusquely, and tossed the articles into her lap.

The match went out. The shift was made in darkness, J.D. assisting with the stockings, slipping them onto her feet like mules and pulling the inverted tubes over her heels. "Stick out your legs."

She obeyed. He wrapped something around them which recalled wool leggings, warmed by a radiator. The leggings were J.D.'s suit coat warmed by his body.

"Here's the whisky; you'll have to drink it straight." Striking another match which he held between his teeth, he poured a generous portion into Giuseppe's empty coffee-bottle, then drank from the flask himself. "Come on, now, we'll wrap up."

Throughout this performance J.D. was as impersonal as if he had been called in to give first aid. As she lay against the warm wall of his chest, she was convinced she was no more to him than an inanimate object which he was patiently holding from flying to pieces. She, too, felt a similar suspension of the personal relationship. He had become simply a source of much-needed heat. As the jerks gradually diminished, she drew in a deep breath, and closed her eyes. A permeating drowsiness stole over her.

The improvised couch ran up into a right-angled corner beneath the roof. J.D. had placed Charlotte's suitcase across the corner. Leaning against this solid support, he helped her firmly and easily. It gave him great satisfaction when he felt her body gradually relaxing. She lay, finally, limp and confiding in his arms. In his mind's eye he could see exactly how those long black lashes of hers looked, folded down on her ivory-smooth cheeks.

She had fallen asleep almost as soon as the twitching had ceased. He didn't, however, loosen his arms. Leaning his head back against the rolled-up seat-covers on top of the suitcase, he closed his eyes, and five minutes later also fell asleep. . . .

Charlotte was the first to awake. Her sensation was of warmth—delicious, luxurious warmth, even to her toes and fingertips; her second, of complete relaxation, no less delicious; and her third, of silence. She could hear no hail, no rain, no blustering wind. She could hear nothing at all but a deep, muffled thud, thud, thud, like a measured drumbeat far away. Never before had she listened to the beating of a heart three inches beneath her ear.

She lay perfectly still, keenly aware of all the details, but, oddly enough, unamazed, unperturbed, as calmly curious as if she were lying in a bed at home reading of this situation in a novel. Her companion was asleep. Both his arms had fallen away from her. Only the laprobe held them together now.

Very cautiously she raised her head and looked around. The sky was filled with scudding clouds through which the moonlight was filtering. It was light enough now to see the outline of her hand. She looked up at J.D. His head was thrown backward and had fallen a little sidewise. His lips were slightly parted. His breathing was that of profound sleep.

For a long minute or more she gazed at him. So *that* was how they looked! So off-their-guard, ungroomed and unaware. His overcoat was pulled grotesquely askew showing his bare, defenseless neck. But he wasn't repulsive to her, not even when he made a little puffing sound occasionally when he let out his breath. He was like a child asleep—like the little boy "Jerry" whom he used to be, she imagined. What presumption! What did she know about a little boy? What manner of woman was she, anyway, to prolong such intimacy a moment longer than was necessary? Now that she was warm and fit again, she should wake him instantly and ask to be released. Instead of which she laid her head back, closed her eyes, and in five minutes was asleep again. And this time dreaming.

When she awoke the second time, his arms were no longer limp and listless. In fact it was their pressure that woke her. She had been dreaming about Leslie again. She did not struggle to escape the unmistakable embrace. Instead one hand groped upward and grasped his shoulder. His arms tightened, and half-sitting up, he leaned down and kissed her! On the lips! As Leslie used to do! She returned it as she used to do, as if there had been no interval between Leslie's last kiss on the deck of a boat, and this next one on the top of a hill.

Afterward he unwound the laprobe that bound them and stood up. Leaning down he arranged it over her, shoved the seat covers beneath her head, and extricated his coat, explaining gently that he would walk up and down outside for a while. No, he wouldn't go far away. She must go to sleep again. Which she actually did!

The next time she awoke, it was to an apricot-tinged sky, and to a cheery voice calling down from the roof, "Morning's here! Time to get up!"

She struggled to a sitting position and swung her feet around to the ground. The patch of hilltop which she could see was yellow-brown. Slowly the events of the night returned to her as she pulled on her heavy shoes and leaned down to tie their stubborn laces.

How much had been dream, how much reality? Had he held her in a tender embrace for five minutes or half an hour? Had he kissed her once, twice, or three times? Had he kissed her at all? She had been dreaming about Leslie. Perhaps Leslie's personality had merged into his, as had happened in her dream two nights ago. But as her consciousness cleared, she knew better. Once fully awake, one knows beyond all shadow of doubt what is dream and what is fact, unless one's mind is deranged. That was one consolation.

These were Charlotte's thoughts as she dragged on her damp skirt and pulled on her coat. J.D. was already dressed, even to the wet tie knotted into the semblance of a four-in-hand. He scanned the surrounding landscape which had emerged. There were olive trees not many feet below the hilltop, here and there the pointed tops of cedars and cypress, and rectangles of cultivated terraces. Walls appeared, terracotta–colored roofs, and chimneys. And finally a chimney with smoke curling out of it!

"I can see the smoke from the fire where our coffee is brewing," he called out gaily. "Nearly ready?"

"Nearly," she called back, drawing the comb through her short black hair, and arranging it in the mirror of her fitted suitcase as best she could.

When finally she joined him, he exclaimed, "How marvelously you look on the 'morning after,' Camille." A flippant remark, as if to imply that whatever had happened in the night, it was not to be taken seriously.

"I was lucky in having my suitcase, Armand! I even put on lipstick!" She could also be flippant.

As they stumbled down the steep road, he carried her suit-case, she his camera and her shopping-bag. Whenever possible they shortened their descent by short cuts. It was rough going; their remarks were brief, and jerky. They stopped at the first habitation and in their best Italian asked for a cup of hot coffee, a pail of hot water, and the privilege of drying their clothes before the kitchen stove.

But there were no such luxuries as hot coffee and kitchen stoves at the first habitation. Instead, they were offered a bowlful of the family's breakfast porridge, and ate it with relish, while a group of black-eyed children stood by and stared. Afterward they were given a jug of hot water and a basin placed on a three-legged stool before a stone hearth with something that looked like roots smoldering on it. Laughingly they took turns putting to good use the oval French soap in the suitcase, also its brush and comb, clothes-brush, and even a nail-file.

By the time they had finished their breakfast and ablutions, and were on their way again, seated in a two-wheeled cart drawn by a donkey, the sun was high and warm, and their clothes were fast drying on their backs. As they joggled along the road, still no reference had been made to the events of the night. It occurred to Charlotte that if *she* had questioned how much had been reality, and how much dream, was it not possible that it *all* had been a dream to J.D.? A dream of which he had no memory as yet? Well, certainly *she* must show no knowledge of it.

When they had stopped the donkey cart and inquired of the driver his destination, he had replied, "Mercato." Neither had heard of Mercato. *"Grande mercato! Molto grande!"* the driver had explained, as they demurred. It must be a town of some importance, then. So they had accepted the seat he offered them on the top of a box in the back of his cart.

There were open cleats on the front of the box through

which glimpses of gray feathers and yellow beaks could be seen. Every little while the driver stopped at a farmyard and disappeared, returning with an armful of feathers, which he shoved into the box through a trapdoor. The meaning of *mercato* finally dawned on J.D. Their drive was going to a market.

"Another jobber," he smiled at Charlotte as they waited outside a farmyard gate. And then abruptly: "How are you standing it? You must be just about all in after last night."

"I don't know why I should be all in. I had several hours' sleep."

"Were you asleep *all* the time?"

"Practically all the time."

"I thought you were probably just dreaming."

"I thought *you* were, too."

He grasped her hand eagerly. "I was! The most beautiful dream! And woke up and found it was true! You *do* remember, then?"

"Vaguely. I don't know what you can think of me. It was because of that strong drink. I'm not accustomed to it."

"Well, I am! I've no such excuse to offer. So what can *you* think of me! Married. Tied hand and foot to a situation I've got to go back to."

"Well, don't let it worry you. I've got a situation I've got to go back to also. I don't see that any harm was done to your situation or to mine either. A kiss or two! Over now. Soon forgotten. In case your conscience may be troubling you, you've probably done me a good turn. Doctor Jaquith once suggested that a flirtation would be excellent for me. It's a very effective measure for pulling one out of a depression." She turned and gave him one of her twisted, sarcastic smiles.

"Don't, please," he said shortly.

Before she could reply, their driver returned, stuffed another squawking contribution into the box, and jumped up onto the narrow board in front.

CHAPTER TWELVE:
ON THE BALCONY

J.D. dropped Charlotte at the Excelsior Hotel in Naples shortly before noon. From the donkey-cart they had transferred to a Salerno-bound bus, from the bus to the most reliable automobile available, and had returned to Naples by the same route they had come, covering the thirty-odd miles speedily and uneventfully.

After dropping Charlotte, J.D. sought the American Express Office, not delaying long enough even to change his clothes and get a much-needed shave. He felt a distinct wave of love for his country when he entered the doors of this American haven-of-hope, and a tall young man with a charming smile asked him if there was any way he could be of use to him.

His story elicited not only the quick interest, but the quick efficiency, too, of the entire office staff. J.D. had taken the number of the overturned car, and was able to draw a fairly accurate map of its present location on the hilltop. The young man said he would take care of all details connected with it; also would inform the cruise ship by cable of Miss Vale's safety. When told she would like to rejoin the cruise, he delved into folders, consulted schedules, and announced that there was a liner due in Naples a week later, sailing straight to Alexandria. It could drop Miss Vale at Alexandria, where her own boat would be lying at dock while its passengers were in Cairo and Luxor. He wasn't sure whether he could obtain space for Miss Vale, but he would look it up immediately and let Durrance know at his hotel.

J.D. called Charlotte on the telephone and reported, adding he would be at her hotel around four o'clock to tell her the result of the young man's investigation.

Charlotte was waiting for him in the lounge, seated at a writing-table by one of the long windows that look out on the Via Partenope that skirts the bay, and she caught a glimpse of him as he drove up to the hotel. He was seated in the back of still another automobile, behind a chauffeur in visored cap and uniform.

She still wore the olive-green suit, but it had been pressed, and the brogans shone like polished copper. She wore a new blouse beneath her suit-coat, new light sheer stockings, new light chamois gloves, and, as a last touch, had added a dash of Quelques Fleurs to her ensemble.

"Good gracious! I don't know you, Camille!" were J.D.'s first words when he found her.

"Same here, Armand." For he, too, had been visiting the shops, and was smart in a fawn-colored gabardine coat and an almost flashy tie.

He drew up one of the big armchairs, and sat down on its extreme edge. "It's all right about your reservation on that boat. I told the American Express chap to go ahead and engage it for you. Then I asked him how he'd advise you to spend the week you've got to hang around in this vicinity. He suggested Ravello. I told him I was an architect and had got to see that abbey for business reasons. He advised a reliable car and driver, and suggested that I take the reverse route this time, via Sorrento and Amalfi. The road to Ravello branches off at Amalfi. It just occurred to me that I could drop you off there. As a usual thing I wouldn't indulge in an automobile, but I've got to spend my Monte Carlo winnings somehow."

Charlotte remarked prosaically, "I'll go halves on the automobile."

"You'll go to Ravello?"

"Well, I've got to kill time somewhere."

"I have the car at the door!"

"You have? Of all the things in the world!"

"And all my stuff is in it! Can you come immediately? Are you packed?"

"Am I packed? No! There are still my two hat-boxes and shoe-trunk to do. But I'll tell my maid to hurry."

"Razz me to your heart's content! I love it! Come on, let's get started. We'll have our dinner party in Sorrento yet!"

The hotel at Sorrento was built on top of a cliff. The windows of the dining-room were almost flush with the cliff. The table they occupied was placed close to the window, so they ate their ravioli and drank their white Orvieto looking out over the edge of a natural sea-wall which fell several hundred feet to the water below.

It wasn't until they were drinking their black coffee that J.D. broached the subject of his own plans for the night. Was there any objection in his putting up in Ravello until morning? Of course he could go to another hotel in Ravello, but it didn't seem to him that anybody could question the propriety of two victims of the same disaster traveling in the same car behind the same chauffeur en route to the same popular resort, and once their signing their own names on the same hotel register.

She demurred in silence

"I promise to sit at a different table in the dining-room," he pursued, "and say, 'Good morning, Miss Vale, I hope you slept well,' so people can hear me and never guess I'm head-over-heels in love with you!"

Banter, of course! His play-instinct was irrepressible! "Honestly, I feel old enough to be your mother sometimes," sighed Charlotte.

"Do you? Well, then, please let me come with you, Mother. Anyway, don't say, 'No.' Say, 'I'll see.'"

"I'll see," she acquiesced with an indulgent smile.

"Adorable Mother! Don't we have fun!"

Darkness had fallen by the time they were again on the road, following its snake-like convolutions cut into the cliffs that bind the scalloped shore-line between Sorrento and Amalfi. They were both too impressed by the unearthly effect of the night-shrouded panorama for continuous conversation on any subject. The young new moon had been shrouded in clouds when they started, but on the first height where they stopped, she emerged from her filmy draperies—nude, luminous, and lovely.

"Like a young girl on the way to her bath," J.D. suggested, as he observed her reflected in the sea. A "suggestive" remark, Isobel would have called it.

Charlotte was silent for a moment, as if reflecting. "No," she said finally. "She is not on the way *to* her bath, but on the way *out* of it. She glistens so."

"You win!" J.D. exclaimed, conscious of another of those thrills of companionship.

It was nearly midnight when they rolled into Ravello's little flat, mesa-like square. It was wrapped in darkness! A sleepy porter appeared at the door of the automobile when it came to a halt, to guide the expected guest to her hotel. No automobile or even horse-drawn vehicle could proceed beyond the square. Narrow passageways with intervals of steep steps led to the houses above. Charlotte's hotel was located near the town's peak. Oh, yes, the porter assured J.D., there was plenty of room at the hotel for the signor too.

The hotel had once been a palace. The contrast between its steep, narrow approach and its spacious tiled vestibule was impressive. Once inside the hall, a smiling little woman, alert as a robin, appeared from somewhere in the rear. She spoke English with a strong Scottish accent. She knew all about the automobile accident and the missed boat. The American Express young man had told her over the 'phone. Such a shame! But she had a lovely room all ready for Miss Vale, and had lit a fire in its grate. Yes, she had other unoccupied rooms. Why, certainly she'd be delighted to accommodate the gentleman too. In fact at this hour of night it would be folly for him to push on. Now if they'd just register.

They mounted a wide stairway, their hostess leading the way, the porter following, their combined footsteps making a great clatter on the marble treads. At the top of the stairs their paths divided. The Scottish lady told the porter to show the gentleman to a certain room to the left, while she conducted Charlotte to a door straight ahead. The door opened into a suite consisting of a vestibule, bedroom, and bath.

"I do hope you'll rest well," the bird-like little woman chirruped. "You'd better take a good hot bath before you get into bed. If you'd like breakfast in bed, just ring for the maid when you want it. Now have a good night."

She was nothing like a hotel proprietress. Far more like some kind little lady in her own home, solicitous for her guest. Charlotte closed and locked the vestibule door with a sigh of relief.

The bedroom was of generous proportions, high and square, with long, faded, figured draperies at the windows. There was a corner fireplace in which glowed a nest of coals; on each side of the fireplace two worn willow armchairs, and a chaise-longue facing the coals. The double bed was also of generous proportions. One corner of the bedclothes was turned down, and an enormous maroon-colored puff was stretched over its wide expanse.

After Charlotte was ready for bed, she turned out all the lights and drew back the draperies. Behind them were long windows opening onto covered balconies. She slipped on her tweed coat and stepped out onto one of the balconies.

The moon had gone behind a cloud. The darkness into which she peered was like a sheet of carbon copying-paper, blue-black with tiny pin-pricks in it. She didn't know whether the pin-pricks were stars or the lights of some far-distant town at first.

There was one pin-prick larger and redder than the others. As outlines began to appear, it looked to her as if the larger pin-prick might be a light attached to a wall of the palace projecting out at right-angles. As she stared, the moon broke through a slit in the clouds. The larger spark was the glow of J.D.'s cigarette! He was standing on a balcony similar to her own about 12 feet away.

He wore a long loose robe drawn in below his waist. His head was bare. His silhouette suggested a priest. His hands were folded on the balustrade in front of him, his chin raised, as if he were contemplating the mysteries of the heavens. The Gothic arch above him completed the resemblance.

Charlotte stepped backward quickly, but at her first motion of withdrawal he said, in a low tone, "Don't go."

She stopped short.

"Step back to where you were."

She obeyed as if she had no will of her own.

He made no further comment. While the silence became prolonged, she glanced over at him. The cigarette spark had disappeared! So also had he! Suddenly she heard a step behind her. She drew in her breath with an audible gasp.

"Oh, I didn't mean to frighten you! I'm sorry." He was standing close beside her! He rested his elbows on the balustrade beside her. "Isn't it beautiful?"

"How did you get here?"

"Through the hall window which is just outside my door. There's only one small light way down at the end of the hall. Everyone has gone to bed."

"So must I."

"Please! Not yet." He reached and took her hand. "Let's talk a little while."

She tried to pull her hand way. His fingers tightened. "Well, I'm certainly not going to wrestle with you," she said.

"That's right," coolly he replied. "No telling what sort of brute qualities you might arouse! Are those the lights of Minori or Maijori down there? Can't tell which is land, which sky, and which sea. Makes me feel woozy. By the way," he broke off, "you're still very puzzling to me."

"I'm not surprised. Any woman of my ripe age and inexperience must be quite a curiosity, I should think."

"If what you say is true about your inexperience anyone would think you'd be chock-full of fears and inhibitions, but you're one of the most fearless, unsqueamish women I ever met. And I'd say you were anything but ignorant about the facts of life."

"Oh, well, naturally I've read a few novels. And then, too," she went on, "there are broad plays and musical shows and moving pictures for giving information to inexperienced but curious spinsters like me." She tried to withdraw her hand.

"Don't talk that way about yourself. I don't like it." There was a long pause when her hand again had given up its struggle apparently. "Thank you for letting me come to Ravello with you," J.D. said gently. "It was glorious of you."

With a sudden turn and twist she jerked her hand free. "Glorious! You're surprised! You mean I *should* have raised an objection. You expected me to."

"No! No! You shouldn't! You did the simple, natural thing. It's wonderful to find a woman of anywhere near *my* era, and a New England woman at that, who is so independent and fearless. Most of them are bound by their own local set of rules even if marooned in the jungle in South Africa."

"You're just saying that to be charitable. This isn't a jungle in South Africa."

"It's the nearest *I'll* ever be to one! The farthest I'll ever get from *my* local set of rules, and from the tyranny of duty," he added with an exaggerated sigh.

"Don't you believe one should be governed by duty?"

"Yes. Governed by it, but not reduced to submission by it, like the victims of a dictator. I heard about somebody who let her duty to her mother assume such power over her that she had no life of her own at all. Couldn't indulge any of her own inclinations, interests, or ambitions. A great pity, I thought." He leaned toward her and added in a lower tone, "Deb told me a lot about you."

"Deb told me a lot about *you*, too," she retorted.

"What did Deb tell you?"

"Oh, various things about your inclinations, interests, and ambitions. People who live in glass houses, you know!"

"I know Deb's opinion of me. I suppose she told you I was a poor, spiritless, faint-hearted creature."

"Chicken-hearted I think was her word."

The tang of her reply sent another sharp sensation of delight in her company tingling through him. "You're wonderful!" And again he possessed himself of her hand.

"I must go. It's disgracefully late."

"Not by your Boston clocks. Let's see, it's only a little before dinnertime in Boston. Let's not say anything for a little while, close our eyes, listen, and be aware, the way we did in that little garden."

For several minutes they neither spoke nor stirred. Opening his eyes, gazing at the vastness above, below, and all around, J.D. inquired, "Do you believe in immortality?" as casually as if inquiring if she believed in free trade.

"I don't know. Do *you?*"

"I don't know either. I want terribly to believe that there's a chance for such happiness as *this* to be carried on somehow, somewhere, if not in this life, then in the next."

"Are you so happy, then?"

"Well, not *completely* happy, but close to it. 'Getting warmer and warmer,' as we used to say when I was a kid, and you got near to the hidden prize. Remember?"

"'Look out or it will burn you,' we used to say," she remarked dryly.

"Are you afraid you may get burned if you and I get too close to happiness?"

"Mercy, no! I'm immune to happiness, therefore safe from burns."

"I think I can prove you aren't immune to happiness."

"You certainly flatter yourself."

"You weren't immune last night!"

"Oh, last night! So that's what you mean by happiness!"

"No. Only part of what I mean. There are other parts of happiness we've sampled, and you aren't immune to those either."

"Such as?"

"Having fun together, getting a kick out of simple little things as well as out of beauty like this, sharing confidences we wouldn't with anybody else in the world, exchanging our honest-to-goodness feelings, too, without soft-pedaling them. Like last night." His tone was wistful. He pulled her hand through his arm and slipped his fingers up to the bare hollow of her elbow. She made no motion of withdrawal. "You *did* respond to those few kisses last night! Won't you be honest enough now to tell me that you feel the happiness, too?"

She was unable to speak. It wasn't only what he had said, but the quality of his voice that sent her defenses flying. Her only answer was to press her shoulder harder against him. His fingers began stroking her arm, and he went on speaking in the same caressing tone.

"You fascinated me the first day I met you. Your sarcasm and self-ridicule didn't frighten me off, as you meant them to. Simply egged me on. And they do still. I can't get you out of my mind. Nor out of my heart either." There was a long pause. "Last night when I kissed you, it was no sudden impulse, Charlotte. You know that already. But what you don't know and what I want you to know is, that if I were free there'd be just one thing I'd want to do—prove that you're not immune to happiness. To the whole of it. *Everything*." Her underlip was clenched beneath her teeth. "Would you want me to prove it, Charlotte? Tell me you would, then I'll go. Speak to me. Why, darling, you're crying!"

His arms were around her instantly. It was the "darling" that finished her. No one had ever called her "darling" before. She buried her face in the merciful refuge of the thick folds of his bath-towel robe.

"Oh, I am such a fool! I am such an old fool!" she said at last when she was able to speak, and grasping frantically at anything shocking in a way of self-ridicule. "These are only tears of gratitude! An old maid's gratitude."

"Stop talking like that."

"An old maid's gratitude for the crumbs offered," she went right on.

"I told you that sort of talk always egged me on," he said, and he kissed her on the lips.

She fought against it at first, but it was useless to resist. Gradually she relaxed, became supple, limp, and returned his kiss. Whether from her own desire, or submission to his, he wasn't sure. Nor was she.

"Let me go," she whispered finally. He dropped his arms. She stepped away from him, and without a word turned, sped swiftly into her room, closed and locked the windows, and drew the draperies tight.

CHAPTER THIRTEEN:
THE LADY OF THE CAMELLIAS

She sank down on the nearest chair at hand and pressed her fingertips hard against her closed lids. This must stop! No woman of refinement allowed a man such intimacies on so short an acquaintance. Far less allowed herself to respond to them! Men felt little respect for such women. That which is easily attained soon loses its desirability. Familiarity breeds contempt.

These and other similar bugaboos of her Victorian bringing-up appeared in the shifting moats behind her pressed eyelids, like a nest of enraged hobgoblins suddenly waked up from their long sleep. And presently behind the bugaboos appeared the two figures she had seen in her dream—the knitting woman and the child sitting cross-legged on the ground beside her. Yes, it must positively stop! Not only because of Isobel, but for the sake of Tina, that other unwanted child of an old age. The Scottish lady had suggested that she breakfast in her room. She would send J.D. a brief note in the morning saying she was ill and bidding him good-bye.

She slipped off the tweed coat and climbed into the big double bed. She lay wrapt in deep dreamless unconsciousness for over eight hours. The hands of her clock were pointing to 9:45 when she woke up. Bells were ringing. It was Sunday. She remembered now.

The bells were of different tones and qualities and came from different directions and distances, as if answering each other. They reminded her of foghorns in a crowded harbor. She lay flat on her back, head and shoulders sunk deep in the pillows, listening to the medley with a faint smile on her lips, tranquil in both body and mind. Sunlight lay across the maroon-colored puff. The bugaboos had disappeared. The picture of the knitting woman and cross-legged child had become dim and indistinct.

Wouldn't it be making too much of the situation to write a note and remain in her room all day pretending illness when she was feeling fit enough to climb a mountain? She had been seeing things all out of proportion last night. Up to her old trick again of disassociating an event from its setting in the general scheme of things. That was how people made mountains out of molehills, Doctor Jaquith said. Remove a molehill from its surroundings, place it on a dinner-plate, and of course it looks enormous. Look at a pimple through a magnifying-glass and nine times out of ten it will make you press it. Another of his similes. Most situations if left alone will take care of themselves, like most pimples. Doctor Jaquith would be proud of her this morning. Here she was alone, making her own decisions, her own mistakes too, perhaps, but afraid of nobody. She leaned and rang for her breakfast tray.

Tucked underneath the plate of fluted butter curls there was a sealed letter addressed *Miss Vale.* If there had been no daylight, no eight hours' refreshing sleep, that letter would have been enough to lay all her ghosts. J.D. certainly possessed what Doctor Jaquith had tried so hard to teach her to acquire, "the light touch." The smile widened, lifting the corners of her mouth, spreading to her eyes as she read the letter, between frequent swallows of coffee and bites of crisp crescent rolls:

Dear Camille, Precious grains of time are running away fast. Please hurry. We've got a lot to do today and ought to get started.

I've been in consultation with Mrs. Scottie and she suggests the Rufolo palace and the something Cimbrone this morning, thinks we'd enjoy a walk to the little town of Scala this afternoon. She says that I can easily run over by car from here

*some afternoon to Vava and see my Abbey and the ruins of
Paestum too. Therefore, please may I follow her excellent
advice and make Ravello my headquarters? I am on tenter-
hooks till I hear you say, "I'll see."*

*You will find me on the terrace underneath one of your bal-
conies—the corner one with the tightly drawn curtains and
locked door. You needn't have locked it! That hurt, until I wondered if possibly it might have been just instinctive, because I
frightened you pink. I promise not to lose control of my temper
again, and do any more caveman stunts. For even a chicken-
hearted worm may turn. Penitently, Jerry.*

Anger? Had he kissed her last night because he was angry?
Egged him on? Had she egged him on? Perhaps that had been
as instinctive as locking her door.

The part of the letter that touched her feelings on the quick
was the signature, *Jerry,* the despised, discarded name of his
boyhood. It had for her something of the same young joyous
quality of the bells which were still intermittently ringing.

A half-hour later they set out on their first tour of inspection
of the town. The sunshine was blindingly bright on the
muskmelon-colored walls, the shadows like silhouettes cut out
of ink-black paper. Apple blossoms were blooming on gnarled
old trees. Voices of bells, clear and full-throated, were issuing
from disintegrating campaniles. Tiny leaves, pink as the fingers
of a newborn baby, were sprouting on the brittle skeletons of
ancient grapevines. Even the garden statues were showing signs
of life, J.D. pointed out to Charlotte, laying his hand on the
thigh of a broken-nosed, armless lady standing in the sunshine.

"It's as warm as human flesh," he remarked. "And as for
this old fossil," he added, tapping himself, "it doesn't feel a
day over twenty-one."

They wandered around and about Ravello for six days, studying the road-map, laying out their route each morning and

tramping to various little towns in the vicinity. Sometimes they picnicked in an olive grove, sometimes had a snack to eat in a shop along the route, often stopped at humble back doors to ask directions, or to beg the privilege of sitting beneath an arbor or against a wall to eat their bread and wine—white Capri the first day, red Chianti the next, sweet muscatel and Asti spumante the third and fourth. Occasionally the chauffeur met them and brought them back to the hotel, weary-bodied and ravenously hungry.

On one afternoon they made a pilgrimage to the abbey; on another, walked down many flights of steps to Minori and called upon an artist from whom Charlotte bought an oil painting of a crumbling Ravello arch. In a shadow behind a pillar of the arch, J.D. had drawn her to him that first Sunday morning and kissed her, because, as he naïvely explained, "he had to."

No Mrs. Grundy appeared upon the scene. No questions were asked. No eyebrows were lifted. Each day's program was unrestricted by discretion, untainted by suspicion. Each evening after dinner they joined the other hotel guests in the main reception room; played bridge with an elderly couple from Glasgow one evening; another evening drank their coffee and smoked their cigarettes with a Harvard professor spending his sabbatical in Europe.

Each night, if later J.D. stood with Charlotte on her balcony, or even sat before her glowing nest of coals in the willow armchair, or in the chaise-longue, no one knew it. Nor observed at what hour he returned to his own room via the balcony. To all appearances they were merely a couple of travelers whom an unfortunate accident had thrown together temporarily. In a few days they were departing in opposite directions.

Both agreed that the fast approaching separation must be final and complete. This agreement was as solemnly made as vows before a witness. It did much to dispel Charlotte's inner vision the haunting picture of Isobel and Tina, and dull her twinges of guilty conscience. There was to follow no exchange of letters, even. Therefore there would be no involving consequence. Their home-settings were separated by 300 miles of space, and circumstances were such that there was practically no danger of unexpected encounters. Neither had had experience with a relationship requiring secrecy, and recoiled from the constant deceit it must involve. It was evident to Charlotte that J.D. had never carried on a clandestine relationship. He was unfamiliar with it devices as presented in fiction. A needy cousin of his wife's was his stenographer. She presided over his office mail. On Charlotte's side her mother presided over all her mail.

The very restrictions that forbade a continuance of their companionship in any form, once they said good-bye, acted as an urge to enjoy their freedom to the full. They didn't consider deserting their home barracks. They had been born with similar traditions, disciplined in similar schools of ethics. Each spelled Duty with a capital D, even though they did fight against its pricks.

Before the six days were over, doubts and fears recurred to Charlotte. The bugaboos returned, but for short periods only— J.D. was so constantly with her. The present was all-consuming. J.D.'s arguments all-convincing. Again and again he reminder her that the number of days together was fixed and unalterable. Repeatedly he assured her that nothing but memories would follow their adventure in intimacy. It was simply a beautiful idyl, injurious to no one, ephemeral, fleeting. Like footprints in the snow, leaving no trace when the snow melts. Like the flowering of a night-blooming cereus, he told her on their last night together, unfolding but once. What a pity to prevent a single petal of so short-lived, so rare and exotic a flower from opening to its full capacity.

When the last day together arrived finally, and the hourglass held only a pitiful pinch more of time together, J.D.'s light touch forsook him. As the end approached, it was Charlotte who attempted gayety to avoid a tragic parting. But it wasn't successful. J.D. wouldn't respond.

They ate their last meal at a shabby restaurant on a low spit of land sticking out into the Bay of Naples several miles north of the city. Somebody had told J.D. the restaurant had a charming location and a lot of atmosphere. The last statement was certainly true. It smelled strongly of a combination of stale tobacco and sour wine.

They talked very little as they sat opposite each other, struggling with their food and a last bottle of wine. But conversation would have been difficult—two powerful baritones with greasy faces and sorrowful expressions, dressed in frayed dress-suits and wilted collars, stood in one corner and split the air with reverberating sound-waves, rendering tragic love-songs, to judge from the sheep's-eyes they made, with voices that throbbed and pulsated.

It wasn't until Jerry performed the simple act of lighting her cigarette when they were sipping their bitter black coffee, that Charlotte lost control of her tears for a moment. It was Jerry's last attempt to perform one of their playful little rituals, trivial in itself, consisting merely in lighting both their cigarettes from one match and then exchanging cigarettes, a ceremony practised, Charlotte had no doubt, by many another pair experimenting with untried intimacies. Or was it one of Jerry's original ideas? She had never read of it in a novel. As Jerry held the flame to the tip of the shaft between her lips she thought, *It's for the last time in our lives,* and the tears had sprung to her eyes, and her throat had been so constricted that it was difficult to draw in enough air to keep the glow of her cigarette alive so as to pass it lit to Jerry.

Charlotte's boat sailed in the late afternoon. She didn't want Jerry on the dock to watch her pull away. It had been decided that after lunch she would return to Naples by taxicab, and he would proceed to Rome in the car. Before lunch Jerry had visited Charlotte's boat, inspected her stateroom and established her scanty baggage in it. He had also presented her with his last gift—two branches of camellias, at least 18 inches in length and covered with crimson blooms. He had bought them from a vendor on the dock.

"For the Lady of Camellias from Armand," he had said with a crooked smile. Had she ever seen so many blossoms on one branch? Camellias lasted a long while. "I'll be with you even in Egypt!" The lighting of their cigarettes was Jerry's last playful speech. To Charlotte, last acts, last words, last moments, became indelibly imprinted on her consciousness.

Their last embrace took place in the dirty hallway outside the restaurant. It was a bare carpetless corridor with a ground-glass window at one end, and two doors with ground-glass panels at the other end. When Jerry's arms were around her a man had burst out of one of the doors, then had quickly withdrawn again. They were so unmistakably a pair of lovers! Charlotte had stiffened. Jerry had dropped his arms. They had stepped apart quickly, their last kiss crudely interrupted—spoiled, unfinished. Afterward they walked out to their waiting cars. Jerry escorted Charlotte to the door of her taxicab. She got in. He slammed the door. They shook hands stiffly through the open window.

"Well, good-bye."

"Good-bye." Charlotte kept her hand out of the window, steadily waving, and her eyes steadily upon him as he stood there with bared head and upraised arm until her car turned a corner and he was lost to view.

When she reached her stateroom she sent for a deeper vase for the camellia branches. The next morning the first thing her eyes sought were their crimson blooms. At the sight that met her eyes she sat up straight, and stared. Every one of the blossoms was hanging down, limp and shriveled! She got out of bed and examined them closely. Jerry had been deceived. The flowers hadn't bloomed on the branches. Each one had been pierced through the calyx by a wire and skillfully attached. Poor Jerry! She was glad he didn't know. And need never know. She removed all the flowers, drew out the wires, twisted them together, and put the coil into her jewel box.

CHAPTER FOURTEEN: WELCOME HOME!

When Charlotte rejoined the cruise ship at Alexandria, she found herself very much in the limelight. Such a shame for her to have missed Egypt! Had her car really gone down the bank at one of those awful hairpin turns? Hadn't she been injured at all? And where was that nice Mr. Durrance? In Milan, Rome, or Genoa, she thought. She didn't appear to know definitely. The mistake about her name simply added an element of interest. The captain wrote her a personal note, and asked her to fill a vacancy at his table.

Mack and Deb had introduced her to some friends of theirs, who had boarded the cruise ship at Nice—the Devereaux and the Montagues. They asked her to join them for cocktails the first night after she joined the ship. Such a shame she was sitting at the captain's table! The captain's table was such a bore usually. They'd love to have had her at their table. She could have made an even six. At Shepheard's they'd run across Hamilton Hunneker. They hadn't planned to return to New York on a cruise ship, but its remaining itinerary was so unique—Crete, Sicily, two days at Algiers, and a week at

Casablanca—that they had decided to endure the disadvantages. Of course they made all the land trips independently, and took no part in any of the ship's social activities. She probably never traveled on a cruise ship before, or she wouldn't have signed up for the bridge tournament tonight.

"Oh, yes, I would. Mrs. Littlejohn's husband doesn't play, and she asked me to be her partner. I started from New York with the cruise," she added, as if proud of the fact. "I came over on the *Mayflower*, you see."

"Who's Mrs. Littlejohn?"

"Somebody else who came over on the *Mayflower!*"

The fact was that the kindness extended by the Littlejohns warmed Charlotte's heart just as much as that from Mack and Deb's friends. In fact, she was more eager to respond to a smile or to any gesture of friendliness from someone whose appearance or bearing recalled her own feelings of self-consciousness or inferiority.

By the time the cruise ship started on its last lap across the Atlantic, it was no novelty to Charlotte to be sought by various groups and individuals. Everybody felt kindly toward her, from the Ricketts and the Littlejohns to the Devereaux, the Montagues, and Hamilton Hunneker.

Hamilton Hunneker was an ex-polo player, an ex-steeple-chaser, and ex-husband three times over. He was a well-known figure, not only at all the notable rendezvous of gentlemen-sportsmen in his own country, but all the similarly notable hotels all over the world—Shepheard's in Cairo, the Taj Mahal in Bombay, the Ritz in Paris, Claridge's in London. Sunken-cheeked, droop-lidded, lopsided, stiff-kneed in one leg since he'd taken a header two years ago, still he was good-looking in his own way—virile, magnetic, and as used to homage as to the air he breathed.

Charlotte did not make a propitious start with Hamilton Hunneker. Her first few caustic remarks made him jump like a horse dug by a spur. When he told her that the Vales of Boston were well known to him, in fact that he was a member of the same club at Harvard to which her brothers belonged, she had shrugged and said, "What a pity!"

"How's that?" It was a very executive club.

"I know the mold so well. It doesn't interest me." She had turned her back square on him.

From that moment Hamilton Hunneker laid himself out to prove that he could be of interest to this female, who scoffed at *all* established institutions, no doubt, and disagreed with all popular opinions simply because they *were* established and popular. They did it to sound original and cause a sensation. It never occurred to him that the caustic remarks and turned back were due to shyness and fear.

It was this sophisticated type of man before whom Charlotte always was dumb. Mrs. Devereaux had already mentioned his several divorces and his many other *affaires* with ladies. Such a man would be too keen a judge of women's charms and devices not to see how utterly lacking she was in both. The quicker the painful period of inspection was over the better.

The back Charlotte had turned on Hamilton Hunneker tweaked his memory. It was covered by a yellow velvet cape with brown markings and silver splotches. It looked like one of those hand-painted things from Taormina. He'd bought one of them once himself—a negligee for Bernice, his second wife. Paid $250 for it. She'd wheedled it out of him, the little golddigger, after she'd already made up her own mind to get a divorce.

Later in the evening, after he'd had a whisky-and-soda or two, he confided to Charlotte he'd once known a lady extremely well, with whose same brown streaks and silver splotches on her yellow velvet negligee, and his drooping lids drooped more. It was the sort of remark, accompanied by the sort of look, which filled her with panic. Not because her sense of propriety was offended, but because suggestive language was often just an attempt of the sophisticated to "shock" her. If she didn't get rid of this man he'd simply ruin the rest of the trip.

"Did the yellow negligee you refer to belong to one of your wives?" she inquired witheringly, "or to one of those who decided not to go as far as the altar?"

It sounded worse than she thought it would. She immediately regretted the speech. Especially as Hamilton Hunneker didn't strike back with a parry equally insulting.

Instead, winking very fast, the color mounting to his face, he murmured, "Gad!" Then, leaning toward her so that his face was very close, "Why is it you've got it in for me?"

There was something about him that reminded her of J.D.! The mounting color? That surprised, hurt look? Or was it simply the close proximity of his masculinity that made her feel kindly disposed? Charlotte had yet to discover that loving one man intimately, or one child, as a matter of fact, any creature, results in kindly feelings toward the species, individually and as a whole.

"I haven't it in for you! It was a horrid thing to say! I was trying to be funny."

"I see. Just a bit of pretty wit," he said, and he gave a forced haw-haw.

She caught a whiff of the familiar smell of stale tobacco on his breath, which J.D., who loved his pipe, occasionally had, too, though he never knew it. How alike men probably were! No doubt they were all just J.D.'s, just Jerrys, with slightly different physiognomies, and slightly different developed characteristics. Now *that* was a discovery! If she could just remember it, then she need never feel panicky with one of the sex again. All this flashed over her as Hunneker leaned toward her, blinking, a little sorry for himself, and a little intoxicated!

She patted him lightly on the arm, as she would have Jerry. "Forget it, please. I'm sorry."

After that Ham Hunneker became her devoted slave. Whatever land trip she decided to take, he decided to take, too, whether the rest of the sextette (as they called themselves) came or not. He followed her down the gangplank in the morning, hovered in her vicinity all day, followed her up the gangplank at night close in her wake. During the long days at sea he sat on the footrest of her steamer-chair much of the time, and covered many miles walking with her on the deck.

Lisa was on the pier to meet Charlotte when she returned from her cruise. So also was June. Even Lisa was unprepared for so great a change in Charlotte, and June was struck too dumb for the first half-hour to make a single quip. June had accompanied her mother to the pier from a generous instinct. Her mother was always urging all the children to be nice to Aunt Charlotte. June knew Aunt Charlotte had lost pounds of weight and that she'd had her hair cut just before sailing, so her mother's hatbands would fit. But she hadn't tried to think what she would look like.

Neither Lisa nor June caught a single glimpse of her on the decks before the passengers began streaming out. Charlotte saw them, however. Lisa was standing beside a gray cement pillar, tall, quiet, pale, dressed in black. June was flashing from spot to spot. Never still, cherry-cheeked, cherry-lipped, dressed in red. How unchanged they both were!

How unchanged everything was—the low New Jersey coast with glimpses of small farm houses; the distant strip of Staten Island with more houses, mere specks; the brawny Statue of Liberty, with her black-flamed torch; the first head-on view of New York's famous skyline (which was never as impressive to her as she thought it ought to be); the dwarfed Aquarium; the lumbering ferryboats; the stolid docks fringing the Hudson River; the bullet-shaped top of the Empire State Building, everything just the same; as if time had been standing still since she had been away. Surely she could not have changed much either.

When she came down the gangplank, Hamilton Hunneker followed close behind her, carrying her suitcase, Lisa's topcoat, his own overcoat, and a huge copper brazier she had picked up at Marakesch to give Rosa for a bird bath in her summer rosegarden. She herself coped with a gaudy-colored basket as large as a clothes hamper for Justine's sunroom. No wonder neither Lisa nor June saw her till she stood in front of them.

"Well, here I am!" She lowered the hamper. "This is Mr. Hunneker. Two more Vales for you, Ham—Mrs. and Miss. How's Mother?" She and Lisa kissed. "Hello, June!" And *they* kissed. "Yes, splendid crossing. I got your cable, 'All's well,' yesterday. No bad news since, I hope!"

Before Lisa could reply, someone interrupted—Henry Montague—smooth-skinned, black-browed, every hair crisp and well-groomed. "Oh, here are you two beggars!" Montie exclaimed. "I've got to hurry along. Man waiting in the office. Leaving Iris to get through customs as best she can. *Au revoir,* Camille. Don't forget about our reunion at Glen Cove week-end of the boat race. Be good, Ham. Say your prayers, Camille." Charlotte introduced June. "Delighted! Camille— Miss Vale, that is—has been a great addition to our little group. Before he got any further, there was another interruption—the Devereaux this time.

In fact there were a constant succession of interruptions around the clothes hamper. They continued even after Charlotte was standing in her proper section beneath a large printed V. It was here that the Littlejohns bade her good-bye. Also Mr. Thompson and Miss Demarest, the latter bursting out to June that there was no one on the cruise more popular than her sister! Close upon the departing heels of Miss Demarest, Mrs. Ricketts appeared, accompanied by a tall young man.

"I want you to meet our boy, Miss Vale—Jim, you know—the one I told you about. In Yale."

Charlotte looked up into the smiling countenance of a veritable Adonis, and felt her extended hand gripped in a grasp that hurt. She introduced the Ricketts to Lisa and June.

"Pleased to meet you, I'm sure," said Mrs. Ricketts. "If you've made friends with somebody on a cruise it's nice to meet their folks, I think. Well good-bye, Miss Vale. Be sure and look us up when you come to Sioux City.

There were similar "be-sures," "look-ups," "good-byes," and "don't-forgets," taking place beneath all the letters of the alphabet, while customs officers proceeded with their task. The majority of these passengers had been sharing the same fortunes for nearly two months. This last meeting before they scattered to the four winds was something like the last collation of a college graduating class.

If the scene had been prearranged for Charlotte, the lines and action written and rehearsed, the effect on Lisa and June could not have been more dramatic. Not only was June struck dumb temporarily, but it acted something like a sedative on her restlessness. She was held spellbound as she stared at Aunt Charlotte.

It was time for lunch by the time Charlotte's baggage, also the hamper and brazier, were properly chalked by the customs officer. Hamilton Hunneker didn't make his exit from the stage of her first performance in America in her new rôle till he'd put her in a taxicab and slammed the door upon her, shutting out Camille—shutting *in* Aunt Charlotte, it flashed over Charlotte with a sinking feeling as she watched Ham limping away in the distance. There went the last member of her supporting cast! It was over! One can't go on acting a part all alone, with no stage, no scenery, and no one to give or answer cues. Or can one?

CHAPTER FIFTEEN:
SPEAKING OF SECOND MARRIAGES

Charlotte, Lisa, and June lunched at a small dimly lighted French restaurant somewhere in the East Sixtieths. Henry Montague had told Charlotte about the restaurant. Lisa and Charlotte sat side by side on a low-cushioned sofa seat upholstered in oyster-white leather piped in red. June sat opposite. By this time June had recovered her wits sufficiently to make a few remarks.

June's wit was often so pointed that it pierced deeper than she intended, but there was nothing malicious about June. Her object was simply amusement. No doubt the right way to take her was to treat her as one would a terrier keen for a romp, but Charlotte had always acted on the theory that terriers turn elsewhere for their sport if one appears indifferent to their advances. Ever since landing, she had been dreading this first opportunity for June's comments and questions. She knew they were coming from that way she had of tilting her head on one side and looking at her closely.

"You could knock me over with a feather! Honestly! You look younger than Mona!" June had a nickname for everybody. Her mother's was Mona.

"As it happens she *is* younger by several years," Lisa remarked.

"Well, at the rate she's going she'll be back in the cradle in a few weeks! I don't know when I've had such a shock."

"Perhaps a cocktail might help you," Charlotte suggested.

June's jaw fell. Charlotte motioned to the waiter. She could feel the old familiar discomfort as June continued her penetrating gaze. But there was no reason to be afraid of June, She was a young, inexperienced chit of a girl. June had never been loved deeply. There had never been a Jerry in her life, to soften her and sober her. Jerry! In the same longitude now. Same latitude. Same time of day. Same temperature. Same weather. Same city. Sitting in a restaurant, probably, not many blocks away. "Oh, it's simply wonderful to be here!" suddenly she burst out. "There's no city in the world like New York! No country like the U.S.A.!" Such a wave of patriotism she had never felt before. She gazed around the restaurant. It was lined with mirrors. She caught reflections of herself from various angles. They were all extremely reassuring. She was still in costume! The stage was still set. She knew her lines too!

"Daiquiri for me, please, waiter. What do you want? This is my party, by the way."

June had never seen Charlotte take even a glass of Dubonnet. Her eyes glittered like a champion's when challenged.

"Old-fashioned for me!" she said, and produced a cigarette-case from her bag, selected one, tapped it on the table, and passed the case to her mother. Lisa shook her head. Then to Charlotte. Charlotte took one. June struck a match and held it up. "They've got cork tips. Be sure you get the right end, Auntie."

"Thanks for the instructions, Roly-Poly," replied Charlotte.

June had been a plump baby. The nickname, as well as the plumpness, had persisted so long that she'd finally refused to answer to Roly-Poly.

Lisa broke into a low, amused laugh. "Good for you, Charlotte!"

"I'll say so too!" June agreed, as sporting was her reputation.

Charlotte felt a flash of liking for June, and June for Charlotte. Neither was aware that they had any characteristics in common. But the fact was that Charlotte's sarcasm and ironic comments, and June's wisecracks and teasing were both expressions of a similar tendency for perceiving the incongruous. Both possessed a keen eye for the foibles and frailties of human nature, a faculty which, when shared, is very conducive to companionship.

"In other words you think little Roly-Poly is disgustingly fat!" June demanded with a disarming sigh of despair.

"No just plump and juicy."

"You're right, I *am* too fat. Put on ten pounds since spring. What's the use of dieting? If I ate nothing but cabbage I'd still be the shape of one. Tell us *your* secret. How have you lost all *your* pounds, Rawbones?"

Charlotte again motioned to the waiter. "The à-la-carte card, please," she said, pushing aside the table-d'hôte menu as if beneath her notice. "I'll keep your figure in mind when I order lunch, Roly-P— I mean June, dear."

"Look here!" said June, "what's happened to you, anyway? Have you been having monkey-gland injections on the quiet?"

"Not on the *quiet*. It's become quite the thing in certain parts of the world. There's a doctor in Fez who is very clever at it. Most of his patients are the wives of rich men with harems. It's making a good deal of trouble among the younger wives." She made this speech with a perfectly straight face.

"And where did you get your face lifted, Auntie, dear?" June inquired.

"Oh, I had that done in Naples, Roly, darling, by a surgeon known all over Europe for his success in that field."

"I see! Mother told us you missed your cruise boat in Naples. But the truth *will* out! So that's what you were up to!"

"That, among other things. The Naples surgeon was so skilful I wasn't in the hospital long. Even so soon the scar is invisible to the naked eye."

"Extraordinary!" murmured June.

Still neither betrayed by either voice or expression the slightest indication of levity. It was Lisa who broke the spell.

"What perfect nonsense! You two!" Inwardly, she was not only surprised but delighted that Charlotte could parry with June for even a brief period. Of course she couldn't keep up her end long. She decided she'd better come to her help before it was necessary. "Come, let's be sensible now. Your letters have been so vague, Charlotte. I'd like a few *facts*. When you cabled that you'd missed the cruise boat out of Naples, I was afraid you might take the next liner for home. I don't know to this day what you did all the time you were waiting around for another boat. It must have been lonely."

"Not so bad. I hired a car and chauffeur and took a little side-trip on my own. You'll find Fabia's walking shoes in bad shape. But let's see what we'll have to eat."

She became engrossed in the bill-of-fare. For the last few weeks she had been listening to Henry Montague ordering meals for the sextette in various restaurants and cafés.

Charlotte again motioned to the waiter. "No soup. Not for lunch," she murmured, remembering Monty. "I'll not forget about the calories, June," she tucked in. "We'll start with the flaked fresh crab meat waiter, à la Canaille. Then cuisses de grenouille Provencal, but please omit the garlic. Then, let's see. How are the artichokes? Very well. Artichokes, with Hollandaise, for two. The young lady does not care for Hollandaise. Avocado and grapefruit salad for two. For the young lady, plain lettuce, no dressing, just a slice of lemon. And for dessert—well, what do you say, Lisa, you and I try their crêpes suzettes? Two crêpes suzettes, flambée, waiter. An orange ice for the young lady." She laid down the menu card.

June reached across the table and gave Charlotte's wrist a savage shake. "You heartless brute!" she hissed. No ill-feeling whatsoever. However, June was not yet defeated.

After June had scraped her frog's legs as close as possible to the marrow, dipped the last blade of her artichoke into a glob of velvety Hollandaise on the side of her plate (nothing

fattening in Hollandaise—just a little egg and lemon-juice),
she launched her next attack: "Tell us about your boy-friend,
Auntie."

"Which one, Roly?" asked Charlotte, wincing inwardly.

"Hamilton Hunneker. I recognized him instantly. His picture was in last month's *Spur*. You know who he is, don't you,
Mona? Lives in a swell penthouse here in New York on top of
a skyscraper he owns. Got a big estate in Aiken and a marvelous stable. And out in Far Hills something he calls a shack
that looks to me, from the picture, more like a stone castle on
the Rhine. Our Charlotte is stepping out some. Cavorting
around with Hamilton Hunneker! What do you think, Mona?
Doesn't it look a little suspicious to you?"

There was as little foundation for June's implication about
Ham, as there had been for her similar innuendoes last fall about
Barry. But no hot wave of embarrassment followed Charlotte's
first wince. Again Jerry came to her rescue. Jerry had found her
desirable. She must never claim it, never speak of it, no one
must ever know of it. But her own secret knowledge of the fact
divested June's insinuations of their sting. June often teased her
mother in similar vein. Lisa always took such teasing with
amused tolerance. Well, now that Jerry had brought Charlotte
inside the pale, she too could be amused and tolerant.

"Well, we're waiting," June pursued. "Do let us into your
secret, you sly puss. We won't tell." Words, voice, manner,
almost identical to those that had sent her stumbling out of the
room in humiliating tears last October. "Am I going to have an
Uncle Ham some day? Are you going to be Mrs. Hamilton
Hunneker the fourth?"

"I haven't made up my mind yet," Charlotte replied. "Ham
has his points. Good-hearted. Kind to animals; and you'd simply love to ride his horses if you should visit us at Aiken. But
he's got that game leg, and is a little too old for me, I'm
afraid."

"I didn't know you had this side in you!" June exclaimed. "Perhaps there really *is* something between you and Hamilton Hunneker. Why did they call you Camille?"

"I'm afraid you're too young to be told. Your mamma has never allowed you to read the novel, *Camille*, I expect. Tell me about Fabia, Lisa," she said, changing the subject.

Fabia was Lisa's oldest daughter. She was in a New York hospital training to become a nurse. She had left home a year and a half ago, just before the news of her father's financial ruin became public, ostensibly to take up nursing in order to become self-supporting. Only her mother and a few members of the family knew that her object was to escape from the vicinity of Dan Regan. Fabia was still engrossed by her nursing, Lisa told Charlotte, and seemed to be very happy. "She's gotten over Dan entirely apparently."

"All but the memory," Charlotte said reflectively. "Fabia will never get over that. Dan will always be part of her. 'We are what our memories are.'" She paused, taking a sip of her coffee. *Jerry will always be a part of me, too,* she thought, her face suffused with a softness of expression Lisa had never seen there before.

June had an early afternoon appointment and left her mother and Charlotte still sipping coffee. "I know you're dying to have me go, Mona," she said as she rose, "so you can set off your own little bomb without any witnesses."

"What did she mean by that?" asked Charlotte.

Lisa pushed aside her coffee-cup, folded her hands on the tabletop, and announced quietly, "Barry Firth and I are going to be married."

"I'm not surprised."

"We are going to be married tomorrow afternoon."

"So soon?"

"Yes. We've cared for each other for years. Barry has waited for a long while. I know, according to convention, it is too soon for me to marry again. But you know my age. A younger woman can afford to consider convention. I can't." Her voice had become earnest, and, for Lisa, extremely tense. "You're such a straight thinker, Charlotte, I thought I would tell *you*, and you can tell the rest of the family, that if Barry and I should have a child I should be very very happy."

"I suppose," said Charlotte, "having a child does make a woman very very happy."

"In *this* case, yes. It would be a reward for waiting—for refusing to give Barry secretly what I couldn't publicly."

"Why did you refuse if you didn't love Rupert, and, of course, it's been clear to me you didn't."

"Barry's wife was living at first. They weren't suited, but it didn't seem fair to her."

Charlotte winced.

"And then, too, I had the children. My children were Vales, and *I* was a Vale then, too. I was brought up to believe one shouldn't involve one's children, and their family name as well, in anything that might cause shame, just because of a personal matter of one's own. And then there was Rupert—so proud, and in many ways so fine. I want to tell you something, Charlotte, that Rupert did before he died, something that was very wonderful—very big. Ever since I've known about it, something of the same feeling I had for him before has come back to me."

"Good Heavens, I can't imagine what he did! He was always just a self-opinionated figurehead, according to my opinion, with very little of the milk of human kindness in his veins."

"Sisters are a man's severest critics sometimes."

"Rupert never seemed like a brother to me. He was always ashamed of me. I never could understand what *you* saw in him. What in the world did he do that was so big and so wonderful?"

"He wrote a letter to Barry to be read after his death."

"What did the letter say?"

"That he had known that Barry and I cared for each other ever since that first year when Barry came down from Canada to go into the Boston office with Rupert. He just waited. When he became convinced that I had no intention of disregarding my responsibilities to him, he decided never to refer to it. He wrote Barry he thought it was wiser to spare the relationship between us all the stain of such a discussion, and kinder to protect my pride and dignity by saying nothing about it."

"Incidentally he was protecting his own pride and dignity, you realize," Charlotte remarked with a flash of old irony.

"That's not just to Rupert," Lisa remonstrated. "For at the end of the letter he ignores his own pride completely. He tells Barry not only that he approves of our marriage after his death, but of our *speedy* marriage, and to allow no conventional notions as to proper respect to *him* to delay the step. Rupert's financial losses changed him in many ways. He became gentler. And his illness brought out still more gentleness. Doctor Warburton once said he wouldn't deprive any man or woman of the opportunities of a long-drawn-out last sickness. I know what he meant now. It was a second chance for us all—for me, for each of the children, and for Rupert too."

"What does Mother think of the marriage?"

"I haven't told her yet. I thought your return was enough for her to take at one time. But I've written her a letter which I'm going to ask you to give her when it's wise."

"And none of the rest of the family know about it either?"

"Oh yes, I told Lloyd and Hilary night before last. They are greatly upset. They like Barry, but they think the interval of only eight months is unpardonable—'indecent' was Lloyd's word. And being married by a justice of the peace in a New York lawyer's office—'second rate' and 'sensational' were

Hilary's adjectives. Lloyd said no member of a large and important family like the Vales has the right to act as irresponsibly as I'm doing."

"Oh, isn't that a typical Vale remark! Thank goodness you've got the guts to stand up to them. What is your own children's attitude?"

"Typical of most children their age. They've all always liked Barry. But much prefer the relationship of family friend to stepfather, although they're being very nice about it. However, even if they weren't nice I'd marry Barry anyhow now. It won't make any difference to my providing a home for the children. We're going to open up the closed rooms, and the old house is going to come alive again. All four of the children are going to be here tomorrow afternoon. I want you, too. We'll have a little celebration before Barry and I sail for Bermuda at midnight."

"But won't Mother expect me to come directly home?"

"Oh, I've paved the way for that. I told her that Doctor Jaquith wished to see you, which is true, here in his New York office, and I've made an appointment for day after tomorrow morning."

"You're simply wonderful! I cabled Doctor Jaquith myself in hopes he'd be in town, and could give me half an hour."

"Also I made an appointment for you at Henri's. But I can see that was unnecessary. You're looking marvelous. I'll cancel that."

"No, you won't. And if you've got any time to spare this afternoon you'll go shopping with me. For I suppose you'll be wanting what's left of your wardrobe now."

"No. I'm starting from scratch again. Barry wanted me to."

"Oh, I can see, then, you're far too busy to shop with me!"

"No, I'm not. My trunk is locked and ready to go to the boat this minute. I hoped you'd want me to shop with you. Mother Vale has asked all the clan for dinner day after tomorrow

night, and you must have a lovely dress. My, but I'd give a lot
to be there."

CHAPTER SIXTEEN:
A REMINDER OF JOY

Whenever Charlotte approached Boston after a long absence,
she was conscious of a hollow sensation which increased as
she drew nearer to the brownstone steps which mounted to the
door of her birthplace in the long row of brick and brownstone
façades on Marlborough Street. There was a portico over the
door upheld by four brownstone pillars with Ionic capitals.
When she was a little girl she could tell from across the street
which tier of steps was hers by the clenched fists at the top of
the pillars.

The hollow sensation could not be attributed to dread of
returning to her mother's domination, because her mother
always accompanied her on a journey. It was due to the
realization of her lack of friends and contacts in the city
where she had been born and had always lived. She was
indigenous to the soil, yet somehow her roots had failed to
take hold in it.

Whenever she rumbled into any one of Boston's railroad
stations, she was bitterly aware that not a single one of the
city's 700,000 odd was anticipating her return. Not one of its
many organizations, institutions, clubs, or groups had as much
as noted her absence. She used to feel a secret hatred for
Boston. But it wasn't the city's fault. Even at boarding school,
she had lived the same solitary, desultory existence.

This time the old hollow sensation was submerged by anxiety, and a disturbing sense of excitement. It wasn't so much
fear of her mother as fear of herself, which filled her with
alarm. Would she prove worthy of Doctor Jaquith's, "Well

done! I'm proud of you," and show her mettle in the important
encounter awaiting her at home?

During the five-hour journey from New York, there had
been little opportunity to dwell on the approaching encounter.
June was with her, and kept up a lively conversation from
125th Street to the outskirts of Providence, when one of her
many young men admirers discovered her and asked her into
the club car for a drink. He asked Charlotte, too, but she
refused, leaning back in her chair from sheer exhaustion.

There was no one besides William at the station to meet
Charlotte. June asked to be left at the Ritz. The high, old-fashioned limousine stopped in front of the entrance opposite the
Public Garden. The trees were in fresh young leaf now, the
tulips in full glory. The round beds were like huge whirling
pinwheels of color. The Public Garden had been Charlotte's
playground when she was a little girl. It was as familiar to her
as if the raked paths, the clipped edges, and the glimpse of
water in the distance were all part of her father's private estate.

In less than five minutes after leaving the Ritz, William
drew up in front of the brown steps. He descended from his
chauffeur's seat, opened the enclosed quarters behind, and
escorted Charlotte up to the heavy double oak doors, carrying
her hand-baggage.

She rang the bell. It was answered almost instantly by a
stranger—a young woman in a long dark coat and a sailor hat.
Charlotte recognized her from Lisa's description as the trained nurse
now in attendance upon her mother. There had been a string of
nurses since Charlotte's departure. The present nurse was a treasure,
Lisa said. Although Mother Vale had dismissed her already twice,
the nurse had treated it as just a whim and still remained.

"Mercy!" she exclaimed. "I tried to get down before you
rang! I'm the nurse. Pickford is my name. Dora, not Mary.
Come in here a minute." She led the way into the reception-
room.

"Is something wrong with Mother?"

"Mercy, no! She's fit as a fiddle." She had a broad, pleasant face. Charlotte liked her instantly. "But she's got ears sharp as a cat's, and heard the doorbell sure as preaching. Now listen, I'm dismissed. I'm paid off, said good-bye and everything. But if you should need me I'll be on the floor above your mother's room, armed to the teeth. She's been complaining all day of a pain in her chest. You know how it is with the funny old dears. My Grandma Pickford was just like her. She's crazy to go to the party she's putting on for you tonight, so she won't let her pain get very bad. But in case she needs to be told that her heart, and all the works, are steady as a clock, why, I'll be on tap. She's all ready for the party except her dress, sitting up in her chair all dressed up in her best negli*jee*, looking as cute as a little red wagon. Now hurry and go up to her."

Charlotte found her mother seated in her high-backed Martha Washington armchair, resembling a dowager queen seated in state on her throne. Lavender ostrich plumes covered the top of her body. A gorgeous white robe that looked like bleached caracul fur was spread over her knees. Her transformation, pure white and glossy as spun glass, rested on her head like a crown. She wore her pearl and diamond dog-collar around her neck, and in her ears pearl and diamond earrings. On her hands, resting on the short arms of the chair, large diamonds, set in gold, scintillated. In contrast to all this brilliance, her skin looked dull. It had a brownish cast, and hung limp and lifeless. But there was nothing limp or lifeless about her eyes. They were steely blue, bright, and piercing.

"Well, Mother, hello!" Charlotte crossed the room, leaned down and kissed the surface of the transformation. "You're looking wonderful. What a marvelous slumber-robe!" she went on, standing so close to her mother's chair that the piercing blue eyes could scrutinize only the material of her skirt.

"Lisa says you've been very well. No colds all spring, and free from the old pain. I'm so glad."

"Lisa knows nothing about me! Step over here so I can see you."

Charlotte obeyed.

Her mother lifted her tortoise-shell lorgnettes. She was silent for at least 30 seconds. "Turn around," she said in an icy tone. "Walk up and down. Sit down. Take off your hat."

Charlotte complied, trying to stifle the old self-consciousness. "It's worse than Lisa led me to suppose," her mother announced. "Much worse! Much! Much! Smelling-salts, please."

Charlotte found the familiar, squat, dark-green bottle in the adjoining bathroom. She removed the glass stopper and held the bottle at just the right distance from her mother's nose. With lips and eyes tightly compressed, her mother inhaled slowly and deeply.

"It's passing," she whispered. "That will do. Go and sit down." She took the bottle herself and Charlotte returned to her chair. "I must pull myself together," she murmured. "It's getting near dinnertime, and I have things to say to you. I've asked a number of the family to dinner at seven-thirty—Lloyd-and-Rosa, Hilary-and-Justine, Uncle Herbert and Hester, also Nichols and June."

"Yes, Lisa told me. That's very nice of you, Mother."

"Wait! Listen, please! There'll be twelve in all. I'm wearing my white lace. I'd like you to wear your black-and-white foulard."

"But, Mother, it won't fit. I've lost over twenty-five pounds."

"Oh, yes, it will. I've had Miss Till here for the last week. Hilda, the new waitress, is just Liza's size. We've fitted all your dresses to her. Have you rouge on your lips?"

"A little."

"Have you enamel on your nails?"

"A little."

"What's happened to your eyebrows?"

"Surely you can see," said Charlotte, starting toward the door.

"Wait a minute. I've something else to say to you. Now that you are cured of whatever ailed you, and come home to take up your duties as daughter again, I have dismissed the last nurse. I have become used to having someone occupy your father's room on the same floor with me. You will occupy your father's room from now on. I had William move all your things down yesterday."

The color mounted to Charlotte's face. She had left for Cascade so unexpectedly last fall that she had failed to remove a number of articles from the dark tunnels behind her books—cigarettes, three reclining bottles of medicated sherry, so bitter she'd never been able to consume but half of one bottle, a pink tin make-up box, and all that literature which her mother considered indecent. Her bookshelves had never been disturbed since she could remember. She had felt no anxiety that these pitiful evidences of her vices would be discovered.

"You had no right to move my things, Mother," she murmured.

"No right in my house to move what I see fit? I'm not surprised you blush! I was in your room when William took your books down, and let me say what we found hidden there was a very great shock. No wonder my old pain started up again. Now, on top of it, comes the very great shock of seeing your appearance!" She wafted the smelling-salts beneath her nostrils. "Why, Charlotte, you'll be the laughing-stock of the whole city if you go around looking the way you do now. Worse than that, you'll be pitied and avoided."

"Well, I've always been pitied and avoided in this city, so I shan't mind it," retorted Charlotte, in an attempt at levity.

"When an unmarried woman of your age begins trying to look like a girl, it's obvious to everybody that she's trying to catch a man. And if she has spent months in a sanatorium, and hides such things behind her books as I found yesterday!—If I were in *your* place I'd do all I could not to arouse any more suspicions about myself. Remember Stephanie Stebbins."

Another wave of color surged to Charlotte's face. "Your mother can't hurt you," Doctor Jaquith told her. "Don't let her frighten you." Well, but what if her mother were right? What if she would appear like one of those pathological cases of a spinster masquerading as an irresistible young girl? Stephanie Stebbins she used to see in the Public Gardens when she was a child. She belonged to an old proud Boston family who were able to afford an attendant. They humored her hallucination to the extent of allowing her to dress in her absurdly youthful costumes.

"But there were other members of the Stebbins family who were queer, Mother," said Charlotte. "The queerness broke out in Stephanie when she was only fourteen. I'm past the age."

"Humph! There's no age limit for women making fools of themselves, and an old fool is more ridiculous than a young one, to my way of thinking. I've seen many a woman old enough to have grandchildren suddenly begin dressing like a young chicken. They deceive nobody but themselves."

Still another hot wave surged up. Was it possible that the favorable impression she thought she had made on the cruise was self-deception? And the conviction that Jerry loved her a delusion—anyway, tainted by delusion, because she *wanted* to be loved so? The hills of Italy seemed very far away. Ravello, the balcony, the little pocket of glowing coals in the corner of the dark room—It was all more like a dream now than reality—one of those pernicious daydreams, largely a fabrication of one's own imagination. An idyl, Jerry had called it, footprints in the snow, letters traced by an airplane in the sky.

What a fool to be treasuring melted footprints, dissipated puffs of vapor, the dead petals of the flower of a night-blooming cereus! What romantic sentimentality! The mantle of self-contempt fell upon her shoulders. She drooped perceptibly beneath its weight.

"I think if you wear your glasses tonight," dimly she heard her mother saying, "you'll be less of a shock to the others. Also leave off whatever you've got on your face. As to your hair and eyebrows, you can say that often, after severe sickness, one loses one's hair, and that you are letting yours grow as soon as possible." Charlotte made no comment, and her mother added, in a kinder tone, "Don't feel too badly. I'll do all I can to help the situation."

Still Charlotte was silent. As she sat staring out at the street, the same similarities of its details recurred to her. The mounting doorsteps looked like a row of back yard bulkheads from this angle, the chimneys and ventilators like stalactites sticking up along the regular roofline. How they endured! They were facts. Her relationship to Jerry existed only in thought. It had no substance—no reality except in that invisible stream-of-consciousness Doctor Jaquith talked about. By now, perhaps, she had ceased to exist in Jerry's consciousness, except as an occasional fleeting memory of a brief episode.

She rose. "I think I'll go to my room," she remarked in her old listless tone.

She crossed the hall. She wouldn't have known her father's room from hers just above first glance. Everything was placed exactly as it had been, even to the pictures on the walls—a photogravure in green and white of the Coliseum by moonlight, another photogravure in color of the pigeons in Saint Mark's Square. There was also an engraving of a woman with long crimpy hair kneeling before a cross, and several of Aunt Lizzie's watercolors of Gloucester sea-scenes in narrow gold frames.

Most of the articles in the room had been selected by her mother. The "set" of mahogany furniture her mother had given her when she was 21. It consisted of a swell-front bureau and a swell-front chiffonier, two chairs, and twin beds, so that when she married no new bedroom furniture would be necessary. She gazed at the long-resented objects. These, too, were facts—solid and inescapable.

The black-and-white foulard dress was stretched out on the foot of one of the beds. She held it up to her. It smelled strongly of some cleansing fluid. Quelques Fleurs would clash with such an odor. Everything on the cruise would clash with her life here.

There was a knock on the door. It was Hilda, the new parlor-maid.

"This just came by express for you," she announced, and passed Charlotte a box, wrapped in brown paper. There was a white address tag on the box with the name of a New York florist on it, and beneath it her name and address written in ink.

It was Jerry's handwriting! There, right before her eyes, was her name inscribed by a pen Jerry had guided, as unquestionably a fact as her girlhood furniture or the brick façades. Her reaction was like that of a thirsty traveler on a desert when he discovers that the water, palms, and shade, which he feared were a mirage, are a real oasis.

She placed the box on the foot of the bed, removed the brown paper, the several layers of newspapers beneath, raised the cover and lifted out a cotton-batting-wrapped bundle. There was no card. She unbuttoned the cotton batting. Three fresh, crisp, crimson camellias! Arranged in a cluster all ready to wear. Exact replicas of the camellias Jerry had given her the last day in Naples!

It was the first signal she had received from him. Both had abided by their solemn agreement so far. Even now Jerry had not broken any of its specified terms, but he had ignored its underlying principle for the first time. Probably for the last time, too. But God bless him for this once!

The camellias assured her that their brief relationship was still existing in his consciousness too. They were proof that she was not a victim of delusion, or self-deception either. Courage and self-confidence gushed back into her depleted reservoir, welling up in her like water quickly rising in a pool when a strong stream beneath its surface rushes in. She wouldn't wear the foulard tonight! And she wouldn't occupy this room!

It required two trips to transfer all her baggage to the room above. She accomplished it without her mother's knowledge, each time carefully stepping over a certain well-remembered creak in the stairs. The room was unsettled. There was a pile of pictures in one corner. In front of the grill-covered fireplace several pairs of chairs were stacked—seat to seat, bare legs sticking up, undersides exposed, like a dog on his back waiting to be scratched. The rugs were rolled up. The marble mantel was bare. But the important pieces of furniture were in place. The bed was set up and had a mattress on it. It was an enormous black-walnut turreted affair.

She proceeded to unpack. She shook out the gown which she was going to wear tonight. She hung it up in the empty closet—blissfully empty, it struck her. Blissfully empty, too, the walls of the room bearing only a faint pattern now of the stodgy pictures that had crowded so close around her night and day. It was as if the room had been purged! She would never allow them to return! Unwittingly her mother released her from their incubus.

CHAPTER SEVENTEEN:
A REBEL INDEED

She procured sheets, blankets, and pillow-cases from the linen-closet. She was stretching the bottom sheet over the yellowed blue-and-white ticking when she heard a warning creak on the stairs. She stood up straight and faced the door. Her mother opened it, without knocking, as usual.

She wasn't a tall woman and had always been thin. She looked like an emaciated bird of some exotic species, as she stood there on the threshold, head held high, her eyes flashing beneath the white topknot—a bird that was moulting from the breast down, for the negligee proved to be a bed-jacket. Beneath it she was dressed in her austere underclothes—plain corset-cover and straight white skirt reaching a little below her knees. She wore white stockings and her evening silver slippers with low French heels.

"What are you doing in this room?"

"Getting ready to sleep here."

"Didn't you understand I wish someone to sleep on the same floor with me?"

"Yes, I did."

"And who do you think is going to do it?"

"We'll ask one of the maids, or get the nurse to come back."

"We! We! So long as I pay the bills *I'm* running this house. Please remember you are my guest, Charlotte."

"Then please treat me like one. Your guest prefers to sleep in this room if you don't mind." Her tone was playfully cajoling.

"This is no time for humor! And as it happens I *do* mind. Where did those come from?" She had spied the red camellias on the white marble mantel.

"From New York."

"Who sent them?"

"I forget the name of the florist. Here's the tag." Charlotte picked up the precious justification for her self-confidence, crossed the room, and offered it to her mother.

Her mother waved it aside. "I've seen it. I heard the bell and had the box brought to me first. You know perfectly well what I mean. What *person* sent you the flowers?"

"There was no card. Perhaps Lisa sent them because she can't be here herself."

"In other words, you don't intend to tell me."

"Mother, I don't want to be unkind or disagreeable. I've come home to live with you again, here in the same house, but it can't be in the same way. I've been living my own life, making my own decisions for a long while now. It's impossible to go back to being treated like a child again. I don't think I shall do anything of importance that will displease you. But, Mother, from now on you must give me complete freedom as to my personal habits, and tastes—where I sleep, what I read, what I wear."

"I must, must I?" Her mother's right hand was resting against the door casing, and Charlotte observed the fingers begin a characteristic tapping. To Charlotte the tapping was like the rumble of distant thunder when storm is brewing.

"Mother, please be fair, and meet me halfway."

"Be fair! Meet you halfway! So this is my reward!"

This phrase was as familiar to Charlotte as a Bible text heard many times before, and she knew well the sermon that would follow. It dwelt chiefly upon the sacrifices of mothers and the ingratitude of children—of daughters especially, more especially of only daughters who arrive late in the child-bearing period.

"They told me before you were born that my recompense for a late child would be the comfort the child would be to me in my old age, especially if it was a girl. And on your first day at home you act like this! Comfort? No, Charlotte. Sorrow, grief." She leaned her head against the door casing, closed her eyes, and drew in a deep breath, letting it out cautiously, at the same time pressing her hand against her left breast.

Always before, compunction had stirred Charlotte at the sight of these gestures of distress. But now she made no motion toward her mother, expressed no sympathy or alarm. Finally her mother opened her eyes, and murmured, her hand still pressing her side, "Have you tried on the foulard?"

"No, I'm not wearing the foulard."

"You mean to disregard my wishes on your first night at home?"

"I'm sorry, but I'm wearing a dress Lisa and I bought in New York yesterday."

Her mother stood up straight, clutching both her breasts now. "Oh, the pain! the pain!" she moaned, staggered toward the stairs, groped for the banisters, and hobbled down.

She wasn't used to banisters, or to hobbling, or to French heels. On the third step from the bottom one of the French heels caught on a loose edge of the stair carpet, and she tilted forward, falling in a heap at the foot of the stairs on the thick red Turkish rug at the bottom.

Charlotte stared down from above, aghast at the crumpled little pile of lavender and white, lying there like broken doll with no wig, for the transformation had fallen off. *Oh, what if I have killed her!* She started down the stairs.

"Coming!" a bright voice called out. Charlotte glanced up, and saw a vision in white—like a shining angel above her. "Here I am! I heard it all. Don't go near her. Let *me!*" Charlotte stepped back and Miss Pickford, in starched cap and uniform, came tripping down the stairs. "Don't worry," she whispered. "So long as she can moan like that she's good and alive."

Charlotte called up Doctor Warburton, who lived next door. He wasn't in, but his assistant Doctor Regan would come right over. A half an hour later Charlotte's mother was ensconced in her bed, her transformation redressed and replaced, her lavender bed-jacket exchanged for her orchid pan-velvet-and-écru-lace, her left ankle, strapped and bandaged, enthroned on a pile of pillows.

Dan Regan told Charlotte that her mother had only torn a ligament, he thought. But it would probably swell and discolor. She mustn't walk on it. Her heart? No, she had referred to no pain in the vicinity of her heart. Probably the fall had acted like an antidote, he smiled. Certainly, go right ahead with the dinner plan.

"In fact, the old lady—excuse me—Mrs. Vale is looking forward to the excitement she is going to cause. I've told her she can have her guests come up and see her, one or two at a time. By the way, Miss Vale, it looks as if your cruise was a great success." He paused. "I supposed you stopped over in New York." Charlotte nodded. "And saw Fabia."

"Yes, Dan." All she could do in way of comfort was to make her tone kind. "Fabia is in the operating-room now, and is fascinated by your profession."

"Well, I must go along. I've left some sleeping-powders with the nurse for your mother."

Her mother's enforced absence from the dinner party released Charlotte from many restrictions which Doctor Jaquith had advised her to observe at first. He was a strong supporter of the Commandment which prescribed honoring one's parents. Honor was usually just a matter of consideration. He believed it was possible to be both considerate and courageous. It would be considerate to avoid surprising her mother with changes for which she had not been mentally prepared. "For instance, I wouldn't wield a lighted cigarette in her presence till you've told her you've taken up smoking," he suggested. "I myself prefer a doctor who says, 'This will hurt a little,' to one who makes me jump. Don't make her jump any more than you have to."

But he hadn't advised her not to make the others jump. Charlotte was aware of a streak of deviltry breaking out in her as she dabbed her skin with foundation cream, vigorously rubbing it in, later, generously coating her cream-colored neck and arms with Henri's finest ivory-tinted powder, dexterously applying the crimson tube to her lips, and, as a last touch, thrusting the crystal stiletto dripping with Quelques Fleurs behind each ear. Just before she left her room to go downstairs, she pinned at the bottom of the low V of her gown Jerry's three camellias. *My amulet,* she thought.

The family were all assembled in the living-room, when Charlotte appeared five minutes after the appointed hour. No one was ever late to any event at the Marlborough Street house if he wanted to keep in good favor with Grandmother Vale.

"Hello, everybody," said Charlotte from the threshold, in a voice which she forced to sound casual.

They all stared at her in silence for a moment. She was dressed in a long clinging gown the color of hothouse violets, with not so much as a rhinestone clip in way of decoration. Her only ornament was the red camellias. *She made me think of one of those bunches of violets florists make up with a red rose in the center,* June wrote Mona that night.

June was the first one in the room to move or speak. She rushed up to Charlotte as if proud of her prerogative, and slipped an arm through hers. "You're gorgeous!" she exclaimed. "I simply love your dress," and led her into the room.

The family swarmed about her, shaking hands, pecking her on the cheek, then withdrawing to survey her from a distance. She had a hysterical impulse to laugh when she caught the dazed expression on Rosa's face. Rosa, high-pompadoured and high-busted, looking down her long prominent nose at

Charlotte, was utterly unable to speak at first. Again she wanted to laugh when Justine, flat-chested and flat-haired, flushed to the top of her high bulging forehead, when Charlotte accepted the cigarette June offered her. Lloyd and Hilary were both extremely ill at ease, at a loss to know what to say at first. She gloried in their discomfort.

On the way out to the dining-room June glanced down at the camellias. "Ham Hunneker, I suppose," she twinkled, and squeezed her arm.

"No, Roly-Poly," Charlotte twinkled back. "Guess again."

It was a cool night. The living-room was chilly. They were having after-dinner coffee, when Charlotte, glancing down at the white paper fans, yellowed with age, spread out beneath the logs in the fireplace struck a match and exclaimed, "Let's have a fire, girls!"

"A fire!" ejaculated Rosa.

"You don't mean an open fire!" exclaimed Justine, aghast.

"No, no, Charlotte! Mother won't like it," warned Hilary.

"It's never been lit!" Lloyd called out.

"High time it was, then!" said Charlotte as the flames leaped up.

At ten o'clock the party began to break up. Nichols and June had to leave early to attend a dance on the North Shore, and Uncle Herbert and Aunt Hester, who had motored in from Groton, wanted to get onto the road as soon as possible. There remained seven guests, one short for two tables of bridge. "Unfortunately," Rosa had sighed. "Unless," she added, gazing down her nose at Charlotte's half-burned cigarette, "you've taken up bridge as well as smoking."

"Well, I learned not to trump my partner's trick."

Rosa looked skeptical. She turned to her husband. "We don't mind taking her on at our table, do we, Lloyd? Just for one rubber?"

"No. Not at all. I'll even take her on as my partner," he acceded generously.

Lloyd had the reputation of being one of the best bridge-players at his club. Since leaving Alexandria, Charlotte had been playing almost every night with Reginald Devereaux as her partner. Reggie also had the reputation of being one of the best players in his club.

It was after midnight before the bridge players at Charlotte's table finished their last rubber. Charlotte was standing with her back to the little pile of dead ashes in the fireplace when Rosa capped the climax of the evening. Rosa had donned her black velvet evening coat and a white Liberty scarf.

"Are you doing anything Wednesday for lunch and the afternoon, Charlotte?" she asked.

"Of course not, Rosa. Why?"

"Well, I thought, perhaps seeing Mother Vale can't go out anyway, she might not feel hurt if— On Wednesday I'm hav-ing— But probably Grandmother Vale wouldn't like it, seeing you've just come home." It was well understood that Grandmother Vale resented being omitted from any invitation which included Charlotte.

"What are you having on Wednesday?" asked Charlotte.

"My bridge club, and I'm short a player. We lunch first, and then play serious bridge. You're really awfully good, Charlotte. Far better than Lisa. She's a member, too. Do you think you could manage to leave Mother Vale on Wednesday?"

"I *know* I could! I'd love to come, Rosa—that is, if I play well enough, and if you think I'd fit in with the others." She stopped abruptly, aware of threatening tears. *For goodness' sake, pull yourself together! Don't be a fool! It's only Rosa for which you've always felt contempt.*

"I think you'll fit in with the others very well, indeed, Charlotte," Rosa replied, almost warmly. Nice old Rosa whom she'd never liked—nice, generous, old Rosa! She gripped her underlip with her teeth. *If I cry it will spoil everything!* "Well, am I to count on you Wednesday, or am I not?" Rosa pursued.

Charlotte looked down. Three crimson camellias looked up! Her amulet! She released her lower lip. She raised her chin. "You are to count on me, Rosa, and thank you ever so much!" she said, without a quaver or a tear.

CHAPTER EIGHTEEN:
A LUCKY BREAK FOR CHARLOTTE

Five minutes later, Charlotte turned out all the lights, first in the living-room, then in the lower hall and vestibule, and mounted the stairs. Halfway up the second flight a moth-like creature emerged from the region above—Miss Pickford, in a dark flannel wrapper and low noiseless slippers.

"She's waiting to see you!" she said, in a whisper. "She's had two hours' sound sleep and is as bright as a button. I know it's going on toward one o'clock, but it won't hurt her. She can sleep all day tomorrow. She's got something on her chest she wants to get off, poor dear."

"Do you know what it is?"

"No. But I know she's good and mad. When she woke up around ten, she smelled that open fire first thing, and sent for Hilda to find out who lit it. You'd better let her blow off some of her steam tonight. It can't blow for long, because the minute the last guest left I gave her her hot toddy—a special tomato soup I make. Tonight, besides two tablespoons of sherry and a pinch of cayenne, I slipped in a sleeping-powder. It will begin to work in about twenty minutes."

"I'll go up and put on a kimono and be right down," said Charlotte. "You're a treasure, Miss Pickford."

"Call me Dora. Everybody does, Queen Elizabeth included. I call your mother 'Queen Elizabeth,' when I don't call her 'Gramma' or 'Dearie,' or 'Naughty girl.' Don't wait for the kimono. Queen Elizabeth hates to be kept waiting."

"But she'll hate worse to see this dress."

"Guess you're right. Just slip the kimono over it, then. Now hustle."

Her mother was in bed lying flat on her back, the bed-clothes pulled up to her chin, her elevated foot making a towering mound under the cover. Her mother's head lay in the dark shadow cast by the high floorboard, but Charlotte could see outlined on the pillow the transformation, and beneath it the two phosphorescent sparks of her eyes.

"How is the ankle, Mother?"

"Extremely painful."

"I'm so sorry. But it's splendid you have had some good sleep."

"I haven't. I've had my eyes closed, but I haven't lost consciousness once. I've been doing some thinking—as I've been lying here in pain, listening to you all having a good time downstairs. Some pretty clear thinking. I see you've taken off the dress you and Lisa bought in New York."

"I'll show it to you in the morning."

"I don't care to see it. Sit down." Charlotte did so, drawing up a straight-backed chair close to the bedside. "How much did the dress cost?"

"It was frightfully expensive. I'll tell you in the morning."

"To whom did you charge it?"

"To whom I've always charged my clothes, Mother."

"And do you expect me to pay for articles charged to me of which I do not approve?"

"For years I've hated the system. But I've worn the dress, so I can't return it. I'll pay for it out of my own account."

"Your own account! All the money you have in the world is

that legacy of $3000 from Aunt Maria."

"It's over 5000 now, Mother, with the interest, and with what I've been adding to it from my monthly allowance for the last 20 years and more."

Ever since Charlotte had come home from boarding-school, she had received on the first of each month $65, for expenditures that couldn't be charged to her mother—fares, library fees, gifts, amusements, and other small personal items. It had seemed a generous amount then. She had never needed any more money. Not until her illness. Then she had been too deeply immersed in despair to be aware of her need. Yesterday she had learned from Lisa that her mother had refused to pay for either Cascade or the cruise. It had been Lloyd and Hilary who had risen to the occasion.

"$5000 won't last long," her mother retorted. "Especially, if your monthly allowance should be discontinued."

Oh, so that was what she wanted "to get off her chest"!

"I've wanted to talk to you for a long while, Mother," Charlotte began in an ingenuous tone, "about my financial situation. The boys all have independent incomes from Father's estate. Why didn't Father leave me anything in his will?"

"Your father left nothing to the boys in his will, so you've nothing to complain of. You don't know anything about financial matters, but I'll try to explain. Your father divided his property before he died. He made four trusts, if you know what those are, naming me as sole beneficiary of one, and each of the boys of the others."

"But why didn't he make a trust for me, too?"

"Because you were a mere child. Your father left it to the discretion of your own mother to provide for *you*. My trust is many times larger than the boys'. I am sure you've always had everything in the world you want."

"I haven't had independence."

"That's it! That's just what I want to talk about!

Independence—to buy what you choose, wear what you choose, sleep where you choose, put paint on your face if you choose, and light fires in my fireplace if you choose! Independence! That's what you mean by it, isn't it?"

"No. Doctor Jaquith says independence is freedom from subjection, and reliance upon one's own will and judgment."

"Jaquith! So he's the snake-in-the-grass! I thought so! I never approved of your going to him. I have no use whatsoever for any of those new-fangled alienists and psychoanalysts. They do more harm than good."

"Doctor Jaquith is neither an alienist nor psychoanalyst. He's a psychiatrist."

"Don't split hairs. Whatever you call him he's been filling you up with poison. He has turned a daughter's devotion to her mother into defiance and disregard of her simplest wishes. I'm glad to give a devoted daughter a home and pay all her expenses, but not if she scorns my authority. I am willing that you occupy your old room until I dismiss the nurse. She will occupy your father's room for the time being and perform a daughter's duties as well as a nurse's. That will give you a good chance to think over what I've said, and consider how you would like earning your own living."

"I think I could do it, if I had to."

"How? A woman of your age and inexperience?"

"I've often thought about it. I think I'd make a very good head-waitress in a restaurant. I'm good height, and older. Or I might get onto the newsstand in one of the railroad stations. Or sit in a cage and take cash in the subway. Or run an elevator in an office building, or be a saleslady in a department store. Oh, there are so many opportunities, if you're willing to do *anything!*"

"And where would you propose to sleep and board?"

"Oh, at the YWCA, or the Franklin Square House, or—"

"That would be nice for the family's reputation here in Boston, wouldn't it?"

"Well, if it would make less gossip I could go to New York!" (New York, and be in the same city with Jerry! She drew the kimono closer around her, pressing the camellias hard against her chest.)

"You may think it's all very funny now, but I guess you'd be laughing out the other side of your face if you found I actually did carry out my suggestion."

"No, I don't think I would. I'm not afraid." She stopped abruptly. What had she said? She repeated it. "I'm not afraid," and then again wonderingly, "I'm not afraid, Mother!" and paused, gazing at the dim outline of her mother's face, and the mound of her body. *I see what Doctor Jaquith means now! She cannot hurt me. She's just a little shrunken old lady who loves authority with only her money to wield it. She has no power over my integrity and my decisions. I see now! I see!*

When she spoke next there was a sort of radiance in her tone. "It might be good for me to have to earn my own living, then I wouldn't be afraid of it. It would be one less fear on my list. Some fears slough off. Some have to be grappled with," she quoted from Doctor Jaquith and paused again. Her mother made no reply. "Fear is the deadliest enemy there is to success and happiness," Charlotte went on reflectively. "Doctor Jaquith says it tends to put an end to both mental and physical activity. That phrase, 'frozen with fear,' has a sound scientific foundation, he says." There was another long pause. "Are you hearing me, Mother?" An audible indrawn breath was her answer. She stood up.

"Where are you going?" her mother demanded sharply.

"You were asleep, Mother. We'll wait until morning."

"We'll do no such thing! And I wasn't asleep. I heard every word you said. I haven't finished yet. Sit down. I want you to know something I've never told you before. It's about my will.

You'll be the most powerful and wealthiest member of the Vale family some day, if I don't change my mind."

"Is that a threat?"

"Call it what you like. It's something else for you to think over up there in your room."

"Oh, but you wouldn't want a daughter of yours to be bought over with a pot of gold, would you, Mother?" asked Charlotte, with playful reproach.

"Well, I advise you to think it over. Where's Dora? I want Dora." She knocked rapidly on the headboard. Almost instantly Dora Pickford appeared. "I want the back of my head rubbed, and my ankle rebandaged, and my pillows fixed, and another cup of that hot soup."

"Which first, Queen Elizabeth?"

"Head rubbed." Dora Pickford leaned, slipped her hands under the nape of her neck, and began rotating the muscles at the base of the brain. "That's good. Don't stop. You're a good girl, Dora. Guess *you* wouldn't stick up your nose at a pot of gold, would you, Dora?" Her voice was thick with sleep now.

"You're groggy, Gramma dear, and talking perfect nonsense. Nobody's listening." She winked one eye at Charlotte, and nodded toward the door.

Charlotte waited until the third day after her return before telling her mother about Lisa's marriage to Barry. It became necessary then because the news was to be announced in the papers that evening. Lisa had thoughtfully arranged that the announcement should be delayed for several days after Charlotte's return, so that Mother Vale would be spared two shocks at once.

Her mother took the news about Lisa calmly. But Dora explained it. "It's just another example of the effect of a counter-irritant. You're like a mustard plaster on the poor dear's feelings, burning her so she can't feel much of anything else."

Of course her mother denounced Lisa and in no uncertain terms. She accused her of bad taste, lack of respect for Rupert's memory, and lack of consideration for the name her children bore. "But it's of no great importance to me what Lisa does, now. Rupert's gone. She hasn't even any of the Vale money since Rupert lost all his share. And *now* she won't get any! So let her go her own way! She's no longer one of us. But," she added, "I should think it might make *you* feel humiliated to have Barry Firth snap her up the first minute she's free, while all these years *you've* been available, and right under his nose."

Once such a remark would have made Charlotte smart for hours, but now, like bird-shot that has missed its goal, it fell harmlessly. "Lisa is welcome to Barry!" she retorted gaily.

This scene took place in her mother's bedroom. It was a bower of flowers. There was also a plate of hothouse grapes, a bottle of old Madeira, two boxes of her favorite candy, and two new bed-jackets still in their tissue-paper-lined boxes. Every adult member of the Vale family had sent Grandmother Vale some sort of tribute. It was very unusual for her to be confined to her room. She had always assumed the Spartan attitude of not giving in to her feelings, however badly she felt. She had always considered bed a concession to weakness. But now it was with difficulty that Dora Pickford got her out of bed.

It was Dan Regan who actually accomplished the feat, slipping his arms under her knees and around her body, remarking casually, "Can't afford to let you get pneumonia! Hang on to my neck tight."

She had taken a fancy to Dan Regan the first time he had picked her up from the floor at the foot of the stairs and laid her on her bed. When Doctor Warburton dropped in the next morning, she had refused to see him, announcing that Dan Regan was to continue with her case. "George Warburton is getting deaf and short-breathed," she scoffed. "That old man couldn't carry me around to save his life—or *my* life either. Why, the very muscles of that young giant's neck gave me a feeling of confidence in him."

She basked in all the attentions showered upon her by the family, and gloried in the impression which her ankle made on those privileged to see it. She was very proud of the shapeless, shiny mass of angry-colored flesh—black, blue, catawba red, with lurid blotches of yellow. She enjoyed the obvious authenticity of her affliction as much as that of her diamonds. More, in fact, because her diamonds brought out only admiration, while her ankle elicited sympathy. And gradually, concern and consultation. It appeared that the cause of the swelling might be more serious than a torn ligament.

At the end of the fifth day Dan Regan again picked up the little old lady's 105 pounds, carried her down two flights of stairs, out her front door into Doctor Warburton's, to a rear room where there was an X-ray apparatus.

The developed film of Grandmother Vale's skeleton ankle revealed a blurred streak where there shouldn't be one. Buried way down underneath the colorful mass of water-filled flesh there was a tiny crack in one of the brittle bones. Grandmother Vale had broken her ankle!

CHAPTER NINETEEN: A GIRLHOOD FRIEND

Her mother's confinement to the house, and to one room in the house until she acquired her wheel-chair, spared Charlotte many a diatribe, and side-stepped many a conflict and dead-end issue. Once beyond her mother's threshold, she was free as that summer years ago when her mother had been confined to her stateroom. Moreover, her mother's dependence on Dora Pickford and preference for Dora's skilful ministrations saved Charlotte from that sense of failure and inadequate devotion which any ailment of her mother's always aroused.

Dora became a fixture in the household. The broken ankle took on as much importance as a newborn infant. In fact, Dora referred to it as "our baby." "Time for his bath!" she'd sing out. "Time to dress him and make him look pretty!" "My, he's a naughty boy to keep his mumsie awake all night."

Dora didn't confine these remarks to the sick-room. "Mother and child both doing well," she would announce to Lloyd, much to his embarrassment, when he dropped in to inquire for his mother's health. Dora felt no more in awe of Lloyd than of "Gramma" herself. The girl was utterly without respect, Lloyd said. But also without disrespect, all the family conceded. The family never had seen anyone quite like Dora before. She treated them as if they and she were on exactly the same level. It didn't seem to occur to Dora that there was any reason for her to feel inferior to anybody in the world. Her good-humor flowed out unobstructed by envy or self-consciousness. To Charlotte Dora was a living example of the kind of nature which Doctor Jaquith had been holding up to her as a desirable pattern.

Charlotte lived up to the impression she had made on the family the first night. The change in her appearance caused no such avalanche of comment and speculation as her mother predicted. The Vales' affairs were not of as much concern to outsiders as they imagined she had suffered far more from self-consciousness and fear of ridicule during her first début in Boston than her second. For that was what the following fall and winter became, to Charlotte, a second début.

The first events started in June. A few days after her appearance at Rosa's luncheon, Charlotte was asked to become a permanent member of the bridge club. At the next meeting one of the bridge-club members invited Charlotte to a dinner-followed-by-bridge. At the dinner one of the guests inquired if anyone present could lend her a helping hand at a rummage sale. At the rummage sale one of the committee asked for a volunteer with a car to deliver what rummage was left to the Salvation Army.

Charlotte jumped at each chance, grasped every opportunity. *I'm like somebody climbing up the face of a cliff,* she wrote Doctor Jaquith, *grabbing at every branch or twig I can get hold of to pull myself up out of the slough I was in. It's pathetic, the thrill I feel over every single friendly gesture I get here in my native city.*

Not so pathetic as not getting any friendly gestures in your native city, Doctor Jaquith replied. *Keep on grabbing!*

Every summer in mid-June it was the custom of Charlotte and her mother to go to Maine and remain until September in the Vale cottage, situated on the coast overlooking a bay. The Vale cottage was a huge pseudo-Georgian mansion, painted yellow. It had some 20-odd rooms, three porte-cocheres, and many spreading porches with railings topped with flower boxes filled with geraniums, ageratum and Vinca vines.

The 20 rooms were usually filled with Grandmother Vale's visiting children and grandchildren, of late grandchildren chiefly, their parents preferring a holiday elsewhere. They were free from all anxiety as to the children's safety, for Charlotte would be in charge. Charlotte could be counted on to act calmly and with intelligence in case of sickness or an emergency, and she never had any plans of her own cropping up inconveniently. What a wonderful opportunity it was for an unmarried woman no longer young to be a temporary mother to her nephews and nieces!

This year, to the family's dismay, Charlotte calmly announced that she was spending a fortnight in July at some club on the shores of Lake Huron with some people named Devereaux; and casually referred to a possible cruise in August on Hamilton Hunneker's yacht *Spindrift*. It necessitated sending no less than three of the clan's children to summer camps.

Charlotte and her mother made the yearly migration to Maine usually by automobile, stopping off at Rockland for a night en route, to break the trip. But this year the journey was made by train. The precarious transportation was much discussed and elaborately prepared for. All of which Mother Vale greatly enjoyed. The drawing-room in the Pullman was engaged days ahead, the bed made up with her own linen and blankets in advance of her arrival. She took keen delight in all the "carries" from house to automobile, automobile to wheel-chair, and wheel-chair to drawing-room. She reveled in the distinction her wheel-chair gave her. Conductors cleared the platform, porters leaped to offer helping hands, solicitous family members followed her with various comforts for the trip.

When she arrived at the steps of the Pullman, Dan Regan was waiting for her. She had insisted that he make the journey with her. He told the family it was quite unnecessary, but complied when they also insisted. Throughout the journey, while Dan and Dora played attendance upon the queen, Charlotte remained unsent for, unnecessary, but well-content.

There was no declared state-of-war between Charlotte and her mother. The amenities were observed, good-mornings exchanged, conversations carried on, none of the threats carried out. Charlotte's allowance continued to arrive as always, on the first of each month, mailed by the bank. When new articles for her wardrobe became necessary, Charlotte charged her purchases to her mother's account as usual. As far as she knew they were settled promptly.

The bills that Charlotte charged didn't come directly to her mother's notice. For years one of Lloyd's secretaries had paid all the household expenses, rendering frequent reports to her mother, which she claimed she examined with care, but which were usually placed on file for a later time. Her mother loved the power which money gave her, but she disliked all the details of its care. A trust company managed her investments. However, the trust company could do nothing about reducing the old lady's enormous income tax. She refused to consider any proposed scheme which required division of her property and therefore her power.

But, although Charlotte's allowance continued, so also did her mother's threats about it. And also her threats about her will. "Ignore them." Doctor Jaquith advised. "It relieves your mother of a lot of emotional steam. I've found in my practice the patients who continually threaten suicide seldom commit it. However, there are exceptions. Don't call her bluff. Be affable. Be diplomatic. In short, stick to your guns, but don't shoot."

This was exactly what Charlotte did. She pursued her own way all summer, casually and cheerfully. She carried out each day's program without consulting her mother, continued the new habits she had acquired with no attempt at concealment, even smoking a cigarette occasionally in her mother's presence, taking no notice of the hostility it kindled. Beneath her mother's frowns and grumblings, it was apparent that she was keenly interested, curious to see the contents of every box that arrived, thoroughly enjoying the trying-on process, though her comments were always adverse and cryptic. She was also eager to be told about every invitation Charlotte received.

Charlotte's skill at bridge had been soon discovered by the summer colony, also the fact that an invitation to Charlotte didn't require including her mother, now confined to a wheelchair. Charlotte Vale became quite the fashion that summer. Her mother thrived on the new vitality that seeped into the house. *And what's more,* she wrote Doctor Jaquith, *I have a notion she is relishing a little spunk in her daughter.*

Charlotte's thoughts turned often to J.D. But the three camellias were followed by no other message from him. She had replied to the camellias. But so cautiously that her signal might have missed fire. Any message mailed to his office was out of the question because of Isobel's cousin. She considered a telegram or a person-to-person telephone call, but for all she knew the cousin might be seated at J.D.'s elbow. For days she had searched for a signal sufficiently disguised.

One day, gazing into the window of an antique shop, her eyes had fallen on some old flower prints. Among them was a crimson camellia. She bought it. The thin parchment-like paper was yellowed with age, but the flower itself was brilliantly glowing.

She dared not mail the camellia to J.D. anonymously. It reeked with the romantic sentimentality of the age it had been printed. She was about to abandon her idea when she thought of Deb McIntyre. She had mailed frequent postcards all along the route of the cruise. She had written her at length about the overturned car, and told her how wonderful J.D. had been about engaging passage for her on another boat and acting the part of the good Samaritan generally. Before J.D. and she had separated, they had agreed on what story to tell Mack and Deb so as to tell the same one.

Charlotte cut the camellia print down to postcard size, slipped it into a government envelope addressed to Deb, and enclosed a note asking her please to give the enclosed to J.D. next time she saw him. In view of the absurd name he had christened her, she couldn't resist sending him her photograph. How was J.D., anyway? She hadn't received even a postcard from him since she last saw him in Naples. And how was she herself, and dear old Mack?

For several weeks she looked for some sort of response from J.D.—another anonymous flower, a picture postcard, a book, anything addressed by his pen. Nothing came. Well, probably it was better so. It was truer to their pact.

His lack of response did not make her feel bitter. She interpreted it as a firm resolve of J.D.'s to step out of her picture completely and spare her all future suffering. She had nursed the camellias till they drooped, then had pressed a few of their petals and laid them away with a coil of wire, an empty perfumery bottle, a letter signed *Jerry*, and a florist's tag with her address on it—all she possessed in the way of material evidence that her path and J.D's had ever met and become one.

It wasn't until the following winter that Charlotte learned that J.D. never recognized her signal. Not for a full 12 months later did Deb find Charlotte's unopened letter in its government envelope in the pocket of a discarded raincoat of Mack's. Mack often stopped for the mail on his way out from town and sometimes forgot to deliver it.

It was September that Charlotte met Elliot Livingston again. She had met him first at dancing-school years ago. Charlotte had come down from the cottage in Maine in advance of her mother and Dora to superintend the annual autumn unswathing of the Marlborough Street house. She was staying with Lisa and Barry.

Lisa called up Elliot Livingston on the morning of Charlotte's arrival and asked him to drop in for dinner that night and to make a fourth at bridge afterward. Elliot was an old friend of Lisa's, and a near one. His 50 acres bordered on the Vale's 12 to which Rupert had brought Lisa as a bride. All Lisa's children had been born in the big rambling country-club–like house built by Rupert's father.

Lisa's children were all there that night for cocktails except Fabia. June, lipsticked and enameled a raspberry red, awaiting the arrival of a brand-new beau who was taking her dancing; Windy, weathered and burned after his summer as a counselor at a boys' camp, in spite of his crutch; Murray, small and spectacled, pale as a toadstool in comparison, not saying much as he held his stemmed glass filled with orange juice, and nibbled an olive. A year and a half ago Windy had infantile paralysis, but now, leaning nonchalantly on his crutch, radiating good-nature and good-fellowship, he still outshone Murray, like the sun a candle-flame.

As Charlotte shook hands with Elliot, she thought, *How little he's changed!* His hair was still black, still curly, though very close-cropped to conceal the fact. He still wore it brushed straight back from his forehead.

"Funny we've never met before," he said, after the first banalities.

"The world is a small place, but Boston is a big one!" Charlotte replied.

"That's a remark to make one think twice," said Barry.

"I think I see what you mean, Miss Vale. Take us—our families—the Livingstons and Vales are old friends, but I can't remember ever seeing *you*. And if I had I'm sure I would remember it!"

Still the same charm! Still the same instinctive courtliness, thought Charlotte, as she sipped a Martini.

She had been 12 years old and Elliot 13 when she first met him. Though both had attended the same dancing-school, they were in different classes. Charlotte was in the Wednesdays; Elliot was in the Thursdays. The Wednesdays were having a cotillion and several of the boys in the other classes were invited to attend. Among these was Elliot Livingston. The dancing-master had announced the names of the guests to the girls *en masse*, explaining that now they were all introduced, and would the young gentlemen now select partners for the grand march.

Charlotte had been well concealed behind Elaine Lovell's mass of spun-sugar–like hair. Elliot hadn't as much as seen her. But later she had danced with him! Every little while the dancing-master blew a shrill whistle and ordered a grand right and left. Everyone flocked to the center of the hall and formed a circle. Charlotte had weaved her way halfway around the circle when the music stopped, and Elliot was holding her hand!

Elliot was one of the best dancers in his class. Just the awareness of her partner's skill always turned Charlotte's body into wood. She had stumbled over Elliot's feet once or twice.

"I don't know how to Boston," she had said, bearing down heavier on his blue serge-covered shoulder.

"This isn't a waltz. It's a two-step. Just limber up. You're doing fine." He had been very kind.

When the ordeal was over, he had offered her his arm, and gallantly conducted her across the shiny floor to the girls' side of the hall. And after she had sat down, he had placed his hand on his chest and bowed, as all the boys had to do. But his bow had been different; not just a jerky duck of the head followed by a swift turn and hasty retreat. But slow and courtly. She might have been the prettiest girl there.

He hadn't asked her to dance again, of course. And not for anything in the world would she have asked *him*, when it came to the girls' turn to favor the boys. Whenever Charlotte had to ask a boy to dance, she always chose the most unattractive, thus avoiding the torture of that pained look which popular boys were so apt to show when she approached. As she had watched Elliot later making the same slow bow with which he had honored her, he became her idea of one of Arthur's Knights of the Round Table.

The girl before whom Elliot had most often bowed that afternoon had been Elaine Lovell. She was very blond and pretty and that day was dressed all in white. It had flashed over Charlotte that Tennyson had described her perfectly—*Elaine the fair, the lovable, the lily maid of Astolat.* Ten years later, Elliot Livingston married Elaine Lovell.

They were still discussing her last remark about Boston when Charlotte drained her cocktail glass, dragged her attention way from the past, and listened.

June had the floor at the moment. "In this burg," she was saying, "who your pals are depends on *when* you were born, quite as much as *where* and of *whom*. Two or three years' difference in age and two people may never meet, even though their mothers and fathers do go to the same dinner-parties. A girl's partners at dancing-school when she's a mere infant will be her partners at her coming-out dance and usually her ushers at her wedding, too. Darn stupid, I call it."

"That explains it, I guess," laughed Elliot Livingston. "I'm too old ever to have crossed your path, Miss Vale. The difference between a Harvard sophomore and a Harvard senior is at least ten years. When I was a sophomore going to débutante parties, you were still going to sub-deb dances—or more likely, in the nursery sound asleep."

"Scarcely!" Charlotte laughed back. "But thank you, just the same."

Charlotte had now learned that it was more gracious to accept with thanks a well-intended compliment, however obviously it stretched the truth, than to scoff at it. In this case the fact was that Elliot Livingston had been invited to usher at her coming-out dance but he hadn't even come.

Elliot Livingston had been selective. He had attended only the parties for girls whom he knew well, and whom he well knew were attractive, and consented to assist only at parties of relatives, or of sisters of intimate club-mates. By the end of his junior year he unusually refused even those.

June's escort for the evening appeared at this juncture. There was another round of cocktails. Charlotte allowed her thoughts to drift back to the past again.

The second time she had met Elliot Livingston had been

when he stood in his wedding-line and gave her hand a brief shake, unaware of her identity. Later, hidden in a corner, eating melted café-parfait, she had watched him pick up Elaine's long trailing wedding-veil, throw it over his arm, and follow her upstairs. And she had thought, *He'll really kiss her, now, in some dark corner up there.*

The marriage had proved to be one of those perfect ones, "made in heaven." But as if Nature begrudged such perfection on earth, it had intervened. Elliot Livingston had been a widower for four years now.

CHAPTER TWENTY:
A QUESTION OF TABOOS

After dinner, when about to sit down at the card table, Barry casually suggested that Lisa and he "take on" Charlotte and Elliot. And thus began a prolonged tournament between the two couples, which lasted until after midnight and was resumed a week later. And again two weeks later. And so on throughout the fall and winter. Each contest was preceded by dinner, Charlotte not returning to town until the next morning. It soon became the custom for Elliot to stop at the Marlborough Street house in the late afternoon, take her out in his car, and in the morning to drop her at her door on his way in to his office.

In the morning Charlotte usually strolled through the gap in the low stone wall dividing the two estates, and when Elliot came out he would find Charlotte already seated in her place beside him on the front seat. Once he was delayed, and asked her to come in and join him with a second cup of coffee. At the next meeting of the bridge tournament, Elliot was the host.

It was the first time since Elaine had died that he had given a party of any sort in the house which he and Elaine had planned, built, and vitalized together. It was cause for much excitement and rejoicing among the servants. They deplored their young master's prolonged mourning, the empty rooms, the empty flower vases, the unused china, glass, and linen. Their mistress gave beautiful parties. Every detail, from the combination of the hors d'oeuvres with the cocktails to the species of floating flower or sweet-smelling sprig in the finger bowls, she decided. Elliot had kept all expression of her art concealed since her death—almost as if one should seal up inside the tomb of a dead painter all his pictures. He would have abandoned the house altogether, he once told Lisa, if it had not been his two boys—10 and 12 when their mother died. Both the boys were at Groton now.

One afternoon in February, when Elliot was driving Charlotte out to spend the night with Lisa, he asked her to marry him. He hadn't planned to do so on that particular afternoon. The weather was responsible. For many weeks Boston had been encrusted in black ice and covered with splotches resembling mold, when one of its typical midwinter thaws arrived.

The days had begun to grow longer. When Charlotte took her place in the car beside Elliot at five o'clock, the dove-gray sky over Marlborough Street was tinged pink. They drove straight into a glowing red sunset as they left the city behind. On either side of the road there were jagged walls of grimy snow piled high by the plows which kept the surface of the main highways scraped smooth. Except for the sunset there was no more color in the landscape than in a pencil sketch. Yet spring was undeniably in the air. The warm breeze that blew through the open car-window seemed to smell of running sap, swelling buds, and growing roots.

"Spring will soon be here," said Elliot, while stopping at a red traffic light. The tone was charged with joy.

"Yes," Charlotte agreed, "just smell it!"

"Are you going anywhere this spring?"

"No. Are you?"

"I suppose not. I've been looking up California and Honolulu—but it's not much fun traveling alone. It would be different if—well, if you happened to be along." Charlotte glanced at him. His eyes were fastened on the back of the next car ahead. "These early false alarms of spring always make me restless."

"I know. Same here."

They rode in silence till the next red light. "If we did happen to be on the same trip together," he went on, "do you think it would be successful?" And before she could answer, "This isn't a sudden idea of mine," he said. "I've thought a good deal about it. I mean about you and me." The light flashed green. He slipped in the clutch, shifted the gears, they sped smoothly along. "How do *you* feel about us? People are beginning to ask questions, you know, and wonder."

"Are they? In this city people ask questions and wonder if you as much as have lunch at the Ritz with a man, I'm told," laughed Charlotte.

Elliot ignored the laugh. "My mother thinks you've saved me from becoming a confirmed recluse," he said gravely. "I must say you've made me very happy this fall and winter."

"Have I? Really?"

"The question is have I made *you* happy?"

"Yes, you have. I might easily become a confirmed recluse myself."

"Do you think I could go on making you happy?"

"What is it you're trying to say?" she laughed gently.

"Something I'm making an awful mess of! It's supposed to be a proposal of marriage."

"I thought so, but I wanted to be sure."

"I've probably been in too much of a hurry, rushed it, failed to prepare you. If I've made a mistake, I'm sorry."

"Don't be sorry. You haven't made a mistake."

"Then you think you *can* be happy with me!"

"It wouldn't be your fault, Elliot, if I couldn't."

"Is that a way of saying you can't?"

"No! I didn't mean that! I'd just like to think about it a little while. It's my very first proposal of marriage, you see." By this time she had told him about their early meetings at dancing-school, but little else about herself. "Though I was engaged once, many years ago, for about five days. At least I considered myself engaged." She spoke in that self-belittling way she had which he found so baffling in a woman with her background and brains. "But there was no proposal." She gave a short flouting laugh. "It was one of those violent affairs with no preliminaries at all."

"There shall be all the preliminaries you want this time, Charlotte. Nothing will be hurried. Nothing. I shall be very careful of you."

"I know you will! I've always thought of you as a sort of Sir Galahad." She paused. "It isn't always easy to make a Sir Galahad happy. They have such high ideals about women. Of course, if a woman is an Elaine—"

"I want to speak of Elaine. I understand how you may feel. I plan to put all Elaine's things in storage for the boys, and to do the house all over as you'd like it. I want it to be *your* home."

"That's lovely of you, but Elaine was always so kind to me I don't think I'd resent her things. Once when we were both at one of those sub-deb dances she saw I had no supper partner. She shared her partner—Johnny Wilder—you remember him. She made him sit between us and get ice cream for us both. Elaine was *actually* as good and kind as people *said* she was."

"That's true. I'm glad you knew her."

"She must have whispered in Johnny's ear and told him to ask me to dance when she left, for when the music started and several boys dashed up to ask Elaine, Johnny got up and asked *me*. Do you ever have patterns like that repeat themselves in your life, Elliot?"

"I don't think I know what you mean. I'm not awfully quick at getting your hidden meanings sometimes, Charlotte."

"Well, don't you see, it is a little as if Elaine had whispered in your ear?"

"No, no, she hasn't," he assured her earnestly. "I don't believe in any of those communication ideas. You need never be afraid Elaine will ever come back in any way. It doesn't hurt me any more to think of Elaine, or to speak of her. She's just a beautiful memory now, like—like—"

"Like a beautiful idyl," she finished for him. "Like foot-prints in the snow." She stopped abruptly. "No, not in the snow," she corrected, "but in the sand that's hardened and holds the impression, for you have her two sons, Elliot!" She paused. "And, oh, so much else besides. Countless objects that she's touched and are a part of her." Her tone was wistful, so too her expression, as she thought of her meager store—dried petals, a coil of wire, an empty perfumery bottle, a few words on paper. And she couldn't even speak his name!

Elliot misinterpreted the cause of the wistfulness. "Don't let anything that is finished disturb you, Charlotte. I'm not good at expressing myself. All I want to impress on you is, my life with Elaine is over, ended. I shall begin a new life with you, and *for* you."

"You couldn't say it any better, Elliot, and I think you're a perfectly lovely person!"

"I don't deserve any credit. It was my mother and sisters who told me how hard it would be for you, or for any woman to live in Elaine's house with Elaine's things."

"Have you discussed me with your mother and sisters?"

They, like Elaine, also deserved their pedestals. That explained his chivalry.

"Yes, I have discussed you with them. And with my sons, too. Do you mind?"

"No, no! I'm honored. I'm pleased—terribly pleased."

"Everything has been done, except speaking to you."

And except making love to me, it flashed over Charlotte. He had never kissed her. According to Elliot's standards the honorable and honoring approach to marriage was to wait until after one's intentions were declared before indulging in kissing or love-making.

When he dropped Charlotte at Lisa's house, the stars were out, the doorway was shrouded in black shadows. But Charlotte had not committed herself, and Elliot's last gesture was simply a longer pressure of her hand as he bade her good night.

There was to be no game of bridge on this occasion. Nor was she to return to town with Elliot in the morning. She was remaining until after lunch. She was spending the night with Lisa, on Barry's request. He had to be in New York. Lisa would be alone except for the servants. There was no cause for anxiety, Barry said, but he'd feel better if Charlotte would come out.

Ever since Lisa had told Barry that her daydream was no longer a mere castle-in-the-air, he treated her like a piece of blown glass as fragile as a soap-bubble. The fact that she had had five children without any complications had little effect on him. His attitude toward the approaching event was a painful combination of alternating periods of bright hope and black fear, while Lisa sailed the familiar course serenely.

Charlotte found Lisa on a couch in her upstairs sitting-room, prosaically paying bills. She joined her with her crocheting—a blue-and-white afghan, which she was making for the "belated kiddie," as Lisa called the awaited child, after Hunt's picture entitled "The Belated Kid." One day Barry had brought her a postcard print of he painting. It showed a shepherdess returning from the field with a limp baby lamb in her arms. The tired mother followed close beside the shepherdess, head uplifted toward a small dangling paw, eyes filled with anxiety.

Although Lisa showed no "holy attitude," she announced that Barry's child was to bear all the marks, stamps, tags and badges of his English-born father that she could "pin on him." His name was to be Christopher, after Barry's father and older brother, recently deceased. Barry now was the eldest son, and Barry's son, if any, would some day inherit the 15th-century manor-house in southern England, and whatever else was left of the depleted Firth possessions. Yesterday a package had arrived from England, from Barry's aged father, containing a pair of silver porringers bearing the Firth crest, hall-marked 1670. There they were, on the mantel.

It wasn't until after Charlotte had properly admired the porringers, that she was allowed to return to her crocheting.

Lisa pushed the bills aside and reached for a ball of pink wool with two knitting needles stuck through it. "Did Elliot bring you out as usual?" she inquired, drawing out the needles.

"Yes." Then, after a pause, she said quietly, "Lisa, Elliot has asked me to marry him."

"I'm not in the least surprised, and I'm awfully glad! You'll be my next-door neighbor! What fun we'll have—we four! And what a feather in the family's cap a Livingston will be! I can say that to you, Charlotte, for you're able to get outside your family and smile at it. You certainly deserve this!"

"But I haven't said I'd marry him yet."

"What are you waiting for? Just to worry him a little? Don't keep it up too long. He's such a dear."

"Yes—but isn't he a little—well, a little like Elaine? He's so fine, I mean so sort of pure. Even his mind and imagination seem pure, and I'm wondering—"

"I know what you mean. He *is* sort of a puritan, I admit. But he's so decent. He's like lots of people in this city—awfully kind down underneath the inherent taboos of their background."

"Inherent taboos," Charlotte repeated reflectively. "That explains it, I guess. Last week at the bridge club when we were discussing Steinbeck at lunch, I wondered what was the matter with me not to be shocked in the least by certain details Steinbeck describes, which are absolutely repulsive to most of them there. I don't like being too different. I wonder why it is I lack the inherent taboos of my background."

"Because your background wasn't very kind to you, and you revolted against it. You're the straightest thinker and freest spirit in the Vale family. Even when you were so dominated by Mother Vale you *imagined* what you pleased, and read what you pleased. By the way, do you realize that we haven't yet mentioned how your mother will feel about Elliot? It's simply amazing to me, Charlotte, how completely emancipated you are."

"Yes, but it may cost me a pretty penny," laughed Charlotte wryly. "Mother keeps right on threatening me about her will. The labor of her song now is that no doubt Dan Regan could make good use of what property she doesn't leave Dora. She insists that Dan come and see her twice a day now." (The ankle had not progressed as it should. There had been more X-ray pictures in the fall, with Dan Regan lifting the little old lady in and out of her wheel-chair, and holding her hand throughout the process.) "Dora says Mother has a crush on Dan. It certainly would be funny if Mother should leave Dan Regan her money after fighting against him tooth and nail when he wanted to marry Fabia."

"Not so very funny for *you*, I should think," said Lisa.

"I'd better tell Elliot he may have asked a pauper to marry him."

"That won't make any difference to Elliot. He's already

told me how he feels about you. The man is in love with you, Charlotte!"

"And you don't think anything I could tell him about myself or my past would make any difference to his—being in love?"

"I've been wondering a little, lately," she began, "about your past, as you call it. You don't need to tell me, Charlotte, but I've been wondering if there wasn't somebody on the cruise, whom you haven't mentioned, who has made you so much nicer to men. I don't think it could be Ham Hunneker."

"No, it isn't Ham."

"Well, it's your own affair. Probably I'd mention it to Elliot if I were you, but in no such way as to let it loom up and spoil things; that is, if it's finished and over with."

"It is."

"Well, then, don't be in doubt about Elliot. He has all the requisites to make you happy."

"Even if I don't love him?"

"Certainly. Loving a man is only one of the reasons a woman marries for. Anyway, a woman of our age."

"What are the other reasons?"

"For a home of her own, a child of her own, and a man of her own."

"Do you think I really might have a child?" Charlotte asked.

"Why, of course you can have a child!" said Lisa brusquely. "Why not? Look at me! If you don't wait too long, our two belated kiddies will be playing ball together some day."

CHAPTER TWENTY-ONE:
J.D. AGAIN

When Charlotte reached home, it was late afternoon. Her mother wished to see her immediately in her room. There was a huge vase full of American beauty roses standing beside her chair.

"What do these mean?" her mother demanded. "They arrived at ten o'clock this morning. The card is in that sealed envelope on my bureau. I've been answering the telephone today. And you've had four calls already from Elliot Livingston."

"Oh! That's a shame. I told him I'd be home for lunch."

"What does it all mean?"

"He's asked me to marry him, Mother."

"He has, has he? So your bait worked? You got your fish!"

"But I haven't given him my answer yet."

"Why not?"

"Well, I'd like to know how *you* feel about it."

"You know as well as I do that it doesn't make a bit of difference to you how I feel about it. You'll do exactly as you please, anyway."

"Well, but what about living arrangements? I don't think Elliot would like occupying the fourth-floor suite here with me. That's always been your plan if I should marry."

"Well, then," her mother flashed, "you can tell your Elliot I will come and occupy a suite in his house, if he prefers." The corners of her mouth were twitching uncontrollably, but not with anger.

"Mother, you're glad! You're pleased!"

"I'm no such thing! Glad to be deserted by my only daughter, pleased to be left in this great big house all alone with only servants?"

"I'll come in every day to see you, that is, if I decide to marry Elliot. I'm not sure I shall yet."

"You'll be an awful fool if you don't."

"Well, then, if you really do approve—Mother, dear—"

"Better save all that soft talk for your Elliot."

"There's no one like you, Mother! And all these years I haven't given you any sort of a game."

"The roses are beautiful, Elliot," said Charlotte, after he had shaken hands with her. The handshake had been brief and formal, but his eyes had a searching intentness that left Charlotte in no doubt as to his earnestness. He had succeeded in reaching her by telephone, finally, and had humbly asked if she would see him for a few minutes before he went home.

The maid had shown him into the reception-room at the left of the front door. The white walls had panels of silk brocade with borders of shells and scrolls and cupids. There were long lace curtains at the front windows, and a pair of lingerie lampshades trimmed with yellowed Valenciennes lace on the mantel, each side of the gilt and crystal French clock. It was not a room conducive to conversation on any intimate subject.

"Let's sit down over here." Charlotte led the way to a silk brocade sofa. She sat down on it.

Elliot picked up a small gilt chair with toothpick-like legs, placed it opposite her and sat down. "I don't want to hurry you," he began in a voice that was a little tremulous, "but I'm very anxious to know whether you're thinking favorably or unfavorably about my suggestion."

"Favorably," smiled Charlotte.

He drew in a deep breath, let it out slowly, and said, "When—when do you think we can tell people?"

"Oh, not until we're sure ourselves. That's what I want to talk about. We don't know yet how we feel about each other."

"I know how *I* feel about *you!* But I can wait. Don't be afraid, I shan't hurry you."

"There are certain things I think you should know about me."

"I know everything I need to know."

"Mother is threatening to disinherit me."

"That doesn't matter. I have enough. There's something I want to say to *you* too. I thought of it in the night. If you prefer a house of your own, there are fifty acres—we can build a new one."

"I never knew anyone like you, Elliot!" Charlotte exclaimed. He hadn't touched her yet, but every word he spoke was a fresh declaration of devotion. "There's something else I want you to know," she went on. "Yesterday I told you I'd been engaged only once, years ago, for about five days. Literally that's true, but I've cared for somebody since then. He was married. I haven't seen him since. It's all over. He belongs to another existence, just as you told me Elaine belongs to another existence. But I wanted you to know about it."

"I didn't need to. Do you think—would you prefer to go somewhere else instead of Honolulu? To southern France, or Italy, perhaps? And what about the ring? I want it to be the most beautiful ring there is."

"Oh, there mustn't be a ring *yet.* Nor any plans. I want to get a little more used to the idea. Now you go on home. It's after six. You'll be late for dinner."

He stood up. She did, too. There was a long gilt-framed mirror over a console table in an alcove opposite them, lit by wall-candelabra on either side. For a long moment they gazed in silence at their reflection. Elliot was several inches taller—a commanding figure. *We certainly look well together*, thought Charlotte.

"Look at those two people in there," she said lightly. "He's really far too good-looking for her, I think, and too young, too. She's getting on, you know. A man of his age should choose someone at least ten years younger. And what's more, he's far too dark for that woman. That man should marry a blonde."

"You are the only one I want to marry," he said.

"But Elliot," she laughed, "just look at us. If we should have a child he'd look like a regular little dago."

"A child?"

Oh, dear. I've shocked him! thought Charlotte; *I've touched one of those inherent taboos.* "Yes, a child!" she repeated, with a defiant toss of her head. "It's one of the chief reasons I shall marry you for, if I do."

"You wouldn't be afraid to have a child?"

"Of course not!"

"Oh, Charlotte"—he was deeply impressed. He put his arms around her then, leaned and kissed her on the lips—gently, in an awed worshipful way, new and strange to her.

She had now learned, from her limited experience, not to take the initiative. Her lips were quiescent, there was no stiffening of her muscles, from either resentment or desire. Elliot's arms tightened around her relaxed body, and he kissed her again. She closed her eyes and drew in a deep breath of fragrant mixture of fresh tobacco, recent soap, and woollen cloth. As definitely as the air which she had sniffed yesterday had been laden with spring, so now this deep breath was impregnated with the peculiar male element so reminiscent of Jerry that it made her suddenly feel tender toward Elliot. Surely, in time she could love him. Wasn't it possible to love the same qualities which two men might have in common, separated from their individual entities? Or was such a line of reasoning a cowardly attempt to evade the unpleasant evidence that she was made of common clay—carnal clay, her mother would have called it?

Charlotte had been engaged to Elliot Livingston several weeks when Elliot's sister, Gracia, gave a dinner-party followed by the theater. No one present knew of the engagement, though by this time many of the guests invited had their suspicions. George Weston, Gracia's husband, came from the middle West. "But he's a very decent chap," Elliot told Charlotte. He was a manufacturer. Had a factory up toward Lowell somewhere, filled with enormous presses that transformed pieces of sheet metal into all sorts and varieties of articles from steel hubcaps to electric-light fixtures.

The electric-light fixtures stuck in Charlotte's mind, so when she entered Gracia's drawing-room that night, and saw J.D. talking to a couple of pretty women, she immediately put two and two together. The room was crowded with a dozen guests, a butler with the cocktail tray, and two maids passing hors d'oeuvres. Therefore Charlotte had plenty of time to say to George Weston, "I think I know that man talking to Hortense and Barbara. I think he crossed on a boat with me once."

"Who? J.D.? That's what we called him at college. Durrance is his name. Nice chap. We were in the same fraternity. He lives in New York, but he's been in several times this winter on business. We sell him goods. Last night when Gracia told me she needed a single man for tonight, I remembered that J.D. had an appointment with me today. I've been urging him all winter to come to dinner sometime, so I gave him a ring, told him to put a dinner-coat into his bag, and come tonight. Shall I tell him your name or let him guess?"

"Let him guess."

"Here's somebody who thinks she's met you before, J.D.," said George, when there was an opportunity.

When J.D. turned and faced Charlotte, his face was set in a formal smile, his expression as concealing as a mask. It underwent one of those complete changes, portrayed in a close-up at the cinema. But neither his manner nor voice betrayed any of the emotions which Charlotte saw registered on his face.

"Why, yes, of course!" he said, shaking hands. "You do look familiar. Don't tell me her name, George. I've got it. Beauchamp, isn't it? Camille Beauchamp. Am I right?"

Dear Jerry! How thin he looked! Dear, ingenious, nimble-witted Jerry! And how pale! And not so tall as she remembered him.

"Sorry, J.D.," laughed George Weston. "That's the time you *didn't* fall on your feet, old chap. This is not the same lady—"

"Vale is my name," said Charlotte, and their eyes met and clung for three seconds, nobody knowing. "I met you crossing the ocean once."

"Oh, yes, Miss Vale. I hope you'll forgive me. I'm sure I—"

"I'll leave it to you, J.D., to make your own peace," said George.

They were not alone until after dinner, and then only for a short time with neighbors near-by. Yet J.D. dared interpolate a few sentences, now and then, for Charlotte's ears alone.

"Yes, I've been in Boston several times this winter. (You're looking simply glorious!) George Weston and I have business dealings. (I've wanted horribly to call you up!) Well, yes, I know Boston fairly well. Chiefly from the Cambridge side. (I've walked by your house on Marlborough Street.) No, Miss Vale, I'm not an architect. I'm a jobber. (Once I almost rang the bell.) Mack and Deb McIntyre? They're both in fine feather last time I saw them. Tina? Well, Tina—" His face clouded.

"Tell me about it."

"She won't eat. I'm afraid we've got to send her away somewhere. The doctor thinks she shouldn't be with her mother. I took her to talk to Doctor Jaquith. Doctor Jaquith was highly recommended to me by this Camille Beauchamp I mistook you for. (Oh, Camille, Camille! It's so good to see you! I'm still horribly in love!)"

"Come on, everybody. Time to get ready for the theater," sang out Gracia.

At the theater Charlotte was seated between Elliot and J.D. J.D. had no idea that she was engaged to be married. There had been no opportunity to tell him. The possibility of sitting beside J.D. at the theater had occurred to Charlotte at dinner (at which he was seated at the opposite end of the table), but the hope was slight. They were a party of twelve.

The instantaneous flash of response that she felt to the first slight touch of his grazing arm startled her. His close proximity caused a recurrence of that flooding sense of elation which she had felt in New York. She sat quietly, not speaking a word, scarcely stirring a muscle, staring straight ahead at the lighted stage. But the performance meant little more than a conglomeration of unintelligible sounds, sights, shapes, and colors.

J.D., too, would have been unable to give an account of events across the footlights. However, he was not tortured by any such revelation as the evening was unfolding to Charlotte. The response that should be flowing toward Elliot was running, unstemmed, in the other direction and with increasing strength.

"I've got to see you," J.D. murmured into her ear at the end of the first act, as he leaned to pick up his program. At the end of the second act: "I've got to leave for New York on the morning train. May I come to your house tonight? I won't stay but ten minutes. I must talk to you."

"Yes, come," said Charlotte.

When Elliot let Charlotte into her door at 11:30, he stepped into the hall after her as usual.

"I'm a little tired. Please don't stay tonight, Elliot."

"Of course not, dear. Is anything the matter?"

"No, Elliot. Just tired. I'll be all right in the morning."

CHAPTER TWENTY-TWO:
AN UGLY WORD

She dropped her evening coat on a chair in the hall and went into the unlighted reception-room. She pulled aside the heavy draperies, raised the window-shade, and watched for J.D. through the long lace curtains. She let him in at quarter of twelve.

When the crystal clock on the mantel began striking twelve, she said to herself, *I must tell him. I must tell him.* After its last stroke had died away, she said out loud, "I've got something to tell you, Jerry."

But even to her own ears her voice sounded faint and far away, drowned by the roaring tumult of her feelings. Jerry apparently didn't hear her at all.

When the crystal clock struck 12:30, she cried out, "Jerry, this must stop!" And too desperate to consider a kinder way to tell the ghastly truth, "I'm engaged to be married to Elliot Livingston."

They were on the sofa. His arms were around her. They dropped away. "You're what?"

She repeated it. He moved away from her, so that not even their knees were touching, and the outline of his taut, straightened shoulders was eloquent. "I ought to have told you the minute you opened the door. I meant to, but—. Oh, I was so glad to see you. It was so good to be with you again."

"Do you love Livingston?"

"Not as we do. Not like us. No! No! I thought in time it might come, or something like it. I thought I was getting over you, Jerry. You were fading a little as you said you would. I didn't think I'd ever see you again. We made our pact, and you were keeping it to the letter. I sent you the picture of the camellia, and when you didn't reply, I thought—"

"I never got your picture. But never mind about that now. What sort of man is this Livingston?"

"An awfully nice man. Like you in lots of ways. Not your sense of humor, nor sense of beauty, nor sense of play, and I'd never think of telling him, as I did you on one of our first days together, about all those little vices of mine I used to hide behind my books. But he likes to play bridge, and to travel, and has two grown-up sons who seem to like me, and besides I'm not too old to have a child of my own." J.D. stood up abruptly. "Most every woman wants a child, Jerry."

"Of course. I know. I understand. I'll go. I ought never to have come. I didn't know. I just didn't know!" He walked over to the chair where he had laid his hat and overcoat.

"Don't go yet," said Charlotte. "Don't leave me this way. This is awful. Let's separate as friends, anyway."

He put on his overcoat.

"Are you angry with me, Jerry?"

"No. With myself. I had no business to come here. I'm sorry. I've got to go back to Isobel and Tina and stick to my job for the rest of my life. The word 'cad' is about the right one for a man who makes a woman like you love him, and then runs off and leaves her to get over it the best she can. It was inexcusable enough of me last spring. But now, when you were well on the way of getting over it, and engaged to be married to a fine fellow like Livingston, well—I liked Livingston. I want you to marry him, and have a child. I want you to," he repeated as if to convince himself. "Good night and good-bye." He gave her hand a squeeze and left her quickly.

He was staying at the Statler. The next morning at 7:30, Charlotte crept out into the back hall and called Jerry up. His train, he said, left at ten o'clock.

"I've got to see you."

"What for? It's better that we don't meet again."

"I shall see you if I have to go to New York on the train with you."

"No. No. Weston is going to be on the train."

"Then I'll come over to your hotel." She had no false pride, no fear apparently of his opinion of her. Only a firm determination to see him.

She arrived a little before nine o'clock. Their conversation took place in the gallery overlooking the lobby.

Charlotte was now as grim in manner and speech as J.D. had been when he left her last night. "There's something I want to straighten out before you go."

As he sat down on the edge of the upholstered armchair opposite, again she was struck with how thin and pale he looked; also, in this light, there were lines on his face which she had never noticed before. The difference between Elliot's crisp thick hair, smooth ruddy face, and Jerry's frail appearance was striking. Jerry wore the same gray suit which had traveled over many miles with her, his tie was one of the gay ones he'd bought in Naples, and the Gladstone bag, which he had placed beside the chair, had been her footstool often when seated beside him in the back of an automobile.

"I don't believe you've slept well, Jerry," she remarked.

"Not so very," he confessed. "What is it you want to straighten out?"

"A wrong impression you've got. I don't know whether I shall marry Elliot Livingston or not, but in any case—"

"But I want you to! If you don't I shall never forgive myself."

"The wrong impression has nothing to do with Elliot. It's a wrong impression about yourself. Whether I marry Elliot or not, I want you to take back the word 'cad,' Jerry."

"I can't do that. I've been thinking about it all night. We

care for each other, don't we?" She nodded. "Well, I can't do anything, not a damned thing, about it," he said brusquely. "Isobel has lost what little money she had, and is even more dependent on me. She's not strong and has given up most of her church work. And then there's Tina. She'll be waiting for me at the end of the train-shed in New York. She's got some sort of phobia that I'm going to die or run off and leave her. No man in my position had any right to get into any such tangle as I did with you."

"It isn't a tangle."

"When I assured you it would be just an episode, soon over, and completely over, I was fooling myself. I knew I was getting in pretty deep, but other men seem to get over such things. I can't. It has been nearly a year, but I can't forget you, Charlotte. I shouldn't have gone to your house last night," and he repeated practically the same speech he had made before. "A man who lets himself love a woman, and lets her love him, and knows all the time he can't follow it up, is what I call a 'cad.'" He wouldn't look at her.

"What is the feminine for cad?" Charlotte inquired. "According to you that's what I am, and with more reason. For you were already married, and I knew it. I walked right into your married life, with my eyes wide open."

He turned and looked at her. "Yes," he said, his voice gentle for the first time, "you walked into it and out, and made it a happier marriage for Isobel, as well as for me. I'm nicer to Isobel now, Charlotte. She says so herself. I can accept her without feeling so much resentment. Now, every time I feel the old bitterness rising up in me, I think, 'Well, she hasn't prevented you from realizing one of your dreams,' and instantly I'm kinder. The fact is, ever since the brief interlude of heaven which the fates granted me with you, Charlotte, I've felt less resentment toward life generally. So never, never blame yourself."

"Then why should *you* blame yourself?"

"It's different."

"It's not! I've listened to you, now you listen to *me*. Do you remember the story I told you once about Sara Crewe?" He nodded. "And you asked who was the nice rich old gentleman in my life, who was making my garret beautiful? Well—*you* are, though you're neither rich nor old."

"I don't quite get it, but your voice sounds kind."

"You're the person who is the most responsible for making my dreary existence beautiful. You're the one who furnished my bare, dreary garrett with lovely things. Why, the very first day you met me, you gave me a little bottle of perfumery, and made me feel important, and as if I wasn't so 'god-awful' after all. But for you, I'd never have dared to play bridge on the cruise. You were my first friend. I owe you Mack and Deb too. But most important of all, that man you call a 'cad' gave me the confidence that comes from being loved by a man like him. So fine, so splendid, that I felt proud every time I thought of him. And oh, how I needed something to feel proud about when I first came home! Why, when your camellias arrived, I could have walked into a den of lions and held my chin up. In fact, I did! And the lions didn't hurt me. The camellias were like an amulet. So, indirectly, I owe you Elliot too. So you can just take back that word you called yourself!"

"In the book what became of that nice rich old gentleman who furnished Sara's garret?"

"I don't remember. It isn't important. He performed a miracle, and so have you. Oh, isn't it wonderful to *talk* again, Jerry?"

"I'll tell you what probably became of him. Being old he conveniently died, of course, and so Sara was free to marry some young Lochinvar out of the west."

Charlotte looked at J.D. sharply. "I hate that kind of humor. How much weight have you lost lately? Last night I noticed you didn't take a cocktail. Why not?"

"We don't own any scales, and I didn't take a cocktail because I'd had a highball. I'm perfectly well, but if—if I weren't, would you care?"

"Oh, no! I wouldn't care a bit if the most beautiful thing in my life existed only in my own mind, and I was left all alone remembering and longing—utterly separated from you by your non-existence."

"But we've got to be separated, anyway."

"Only geographically. And not by so very many miles. When it snows or rains in New York, it usually does here too, and our consciousnesses can share the same weather, the same full moons, the same seasons, and the same holidays, too. We can think about each other, and hope for each other's safety and happiness, and be glad each other is alive, knowing it's still possible to enter a drawing-room, or turn a street corner, and meet each other. Even if we never do meet, the *hope* we may is something, isn't it?"

"Yes. It's a lot! And I'll always be looking for you around every corner," he smiled.

"And you take back that word?"

He rose. Charlotte rose too. "You said last night you wanted a child," he said quietly. "You said that almost every woman does. If I could believe that I'd done anything to make you love someone enough to have what will evidently make you so happy, *then* I'll take back the word 'cad,' *then* I won't regret anything. You'll surely marry Livingston, won't you, Charlotte?"

"I'll try, Jerry."

He took her hand and held it. "All our kisses must be imagined ones from now on," he said wistfully, and looked deep into her pupils for a half a dozen seconds. Then, "Good-bye, darling," he murmured.

"Good-bye, darling," she replied.

As she watched him walking swiftly toward the stairs, it flashed over her, *This has all happened before. Of course in Naples! Another of those repeated patterns.* Oh, would he complete it? Add the last foil! Would he? *No! Yes! Yes!* On the third step down the stairs he stopped, turned his white face toward her, raised his hat high, arm straight up like a mast, and sank from sight.

CHAPTER TWENTY-THREE: THE KNELL OF FOREVER

As Charlotte walked back to Marlborough Street she held her head high, and her step was buoyant. She was filled with an exalted fervor, which she had never experienced before, due partly to the fresh proof that Jerry loved her, and partly to the quality of that love. He still desired her, but he desired her happiness even more. An element of worship had entered into her feeling for Jerry. His will was stronger than hers, his foresight clearer, his love on a higher plane.

Every time she recalled the earnestness of his voice urging her to marry Elliot, she was impressed by his unselfish desire for her happiness. She had been disturbed by a niggling fear that it might hurt Jerry. How fortunate this second appearance! The fresh proof of his love would shine like a benediction on her every day. And perhaps the knowledge that she still loved him would make his lot more endurable.

As she skirted the Public Garden—now dull green and brown—she was filled with a bright confidence. She was going to have a full, rich, happy life, in spite of her belated start, also in spite of the fact that she could not marry the man to whom she was instinctively attracted.

An instinctive attraction between two people with high ideals does not necessarily forbid all communication, does it? If both Jerry and she applied their intelligence to the instinctive attraction, perhaps they could meet sometimes—openly, casually, with no harm to others. Why, just talking to Jerry, just sitting there together in the hotel two feet apart, had given Charlotte that sense of complete companionship which to her was the acme of joy. When she was safely anchored by marriage, and Jerry could no longer blame himself, surely they could be friends! The possibility quickened her pace.

Had the second meeting with Jerry terminated at the Westons' house there would have been no serious consequences. Not for several days did Charlotte realize the effect of the torrent that had rushed out toward Jerry in the theater, and later in the reception-room. Not until she saw Elliot the next time (which was nearly a week later, for he had been called out of town on business) did she discover that it was as impossible to will her former tenderness to flow toward Elliot as to make water run uphill.

At first she made light of it to herself. In time the impression of this second meeting with Jerry would wear away as had the first. Every time she relived the precious moments of their brief reunion, she could feel again waves of inordinate joy filling her like strong music vibrating. No wonder Elliot couldn't drown such music secretly heard. No man could drown it. She must use her intelligence, and turn her thoughts away from Jerry.

Elliot observed no change in her at first. She never allowed herself to withdraw from his arms. She always responded in act to his gentle caresses. Somewhere she had read, *act an emotion, and you'll be more likely to feel it.* But some emotions, like some horses, you can lead to water day after day, but you cannot make them drink. Her tender emotion for Elliot would not drink.

Acting an emotion for the brief duration of a kiss, she did not find as difficult as the protracted periods of sitting in close proximity to Elliot. In the automobile, at the theater, wherever possible, he always established some physical contact. Her impulse to disconnect it became a gnawing desire after the first few minutes.

Elliot liked to interlock his fingers through hers and sit listening to the radio for an hour at a stretch. He preferred interlocked fingers to holding her hand relaxed in the hollow of his. She wished he knew how to break through her thickening armor of ice, and by whatever means, fair or foul, prove she was not incapable of a response to him.

One Sunday afternoon, several weeks after J.D.'s reappearance, they were sitting on the davenport in the living-room of the Marlborough Street house listening to the radio. Charlotte had just withdrawn her locked fingers from Elliot's, in order to rearrange a lock of her hair. She didn't replace her fingers.

"You don't like to have your hand held, do you, dear?"

"Oh, yes, I do, Elliot!"—and instantly shoved her fingers through his again.

"I've noticed lately you usually draw your hand away after the first few minutes."

"I won't again! I'm just not used to it. You must remember I'm an old maid, Elliot." She tried to make her voice light and playful. "You've got to teach me to be loving and affectionate. *Make* me be!" She moved closer. Elliot put his arm around her.

Pretend he's Jerry. Close your eyes and breathe deep, smell Jerry, imagine Jerry, feel Jerry. This man is just as fine, just as desirable! Now stop being stubborn and love him. Love him! But she might as well have tried to will a sluggish salmon lying in the bed of a pool to action. Elliot released her hand to turn off the radio, then interlocked his fingers through hers again, put his arm around her waist, and began patting her side gently. Patting was another of Elliot's habits.

"Do you know, dear, what we'll be doing six weeks from today?" asked Elliot. "We'll be on the ocean. And two weeks from today everybody will know our news! I've disliked this secrecy. I'm so glad it won't be necessary much longer."

Charlotte sat up straight, drew her hand away and folded her arms. "Two weeks is terribly soon! In Boston an engagement is just like a marriage. I do want to be sure. Do you know what I'd like?"

"No, dear. Tell me."

"I'd like you to take me out some night to dinner this week, to some Bohemian place, and give me a very gay time—cocktails, and champagne, and then make violent love to me." She caught a glimpse of his puzzled expression. "What I mean is, if I could only get rid of some of my inhibitions, just for once, I might be able to—to have more confidence."

"You don't need to become intoxicated to have confidence. I understand about your fears. I shall be patient."

"No, Elliot. That is not what I mean."

"What do you mean?"

"I don't know that I can tell you. But—well, I read about a woman, in a novel—a sort of cold woman who was in an automobile accident with a man. It was a very cold night, and they had to sit wrapped up in a robe all night to keep warm. Just before they wrapped up, they both took a strong drink, and she fell in love with him because she lost her inhibitions for a while. She was just—natural. You see—" Now there was disapproval in Elliot's expression. She could feel one of those familiar blushes of shame creeping up her face. "Oh, it sounds sort of depraved, I'm afraid, Elliot."

"It certainly does! We're not that kind of people." He paused. "I sometimes wonder about the books you read. Why do you enjoy reading that sort of stuff?"

"It's life, Elliot. It's about human beings."

"Not the kind of life that I admire. Nor the kind of human

beings I find pleasant to read about. Getting drunk and wrapping up in a laprobe!"

"Oh, Elliot, I don't believe I can ever live up to your ideals! I'm not a bit like your lovely mother, nor Elaine, nor like my own family. You see, I rebelled, and have gotten all twisted into a horrid ugly shape of my own. I don't believe I can ever get back. I do think you are one of the kindest, finest men in the world, and I would simply love a home and a child and I would certainly be awfully proud of you, but I—I'm so afraid it won't work."

"You're tired tonight, dear. Everything will be all right after we're married. It's a well-known fact that the engagement-period is difficult. I shan't hurry you into anything till you're ready for it."

"But what if I'm always a frigid woman to you?"

He winced at the term. "Well, I made Elaine happy," he said.

"You don't deserve two women like that!"

"Must we discuss these things, Charlotte?"

"No, Elliot. No. Not again."

"That's right. Let's turn on the radio." He did so, then again interlocked his fingers with hers, patted her knee with his other hand, leaned his head back and closed his eyes. "This is all I ask."

She offered no more drastic suggestions to Elliot, sought no more remedies for the tender emotion he once had evoked. She accepted the verdict that its malady was incurable unless a miracle intervened. To this slender hope she clung for weeks.

It was due to Elliot's kindness that the ordeal was protracted into late spring. When she told him, apologetically, that she didn't see how she could possibly face the announcement of an engagement ten days hence, he neither reproached nor blamed.

"Well, our wedding is to be so quiet you don't have to face any announcement of engagement, if you don't want to, dear. We don't sail for Honolulu till the last of April."

"Oh, I don't deserve you! But, oh, Elliot, the last of April seems terribly soon too."

"Well, all right, then," he said quietly. "I told you I could wait. I noticed you've seemed fearful and nervous lately. We can give up Honolulu. Perhaps you'd rather postpone everything till June, and go to England next summer? Would you?"

"Oh, yes, I would." And she clung to him, welcoming his arms around her. "Oh, Elliot, I think I'll be all right by June!" she said, something warm and reassuring welling up in her.

But it was only gratitude. Gratitude, like morphine, can deaden aversion for a little while, but when the effect of it wears off, and aversion returns, the pain is apt to be more acute, for there is added to it a sense of obligation. Often one feels resentment toward one's benefactor.

At times the state of Charlotte's emotions was so painful that she considered telling Elliot about J.D., thereby shattering his ideal of her so that he would not want to marry her. But she couldn't expose herself without exposing J.D. too. Only her silence could protect J.D.

March melted into April, April blew into May, May flowered into June, and still Charlotte's and Elliot's engagement survived. It died hard, like a victim of certain slowly progressive diseases. First one and then another part of the body and mind ceases to function, until finally all that remains is the automatic breathing and the mechanical beat of the heart.

The end would have come quicker if it had been the winter season. Elliot was an enthusiastic golfer and horseman, and Charlotte could join him in neither sport. Also he always spent a fortnight in Maine fishing as soon as the ice was out. It was shortly after his return from Maine that the engagement was broken. By that time Elliot's kisses had become brief and per-

functory, and he no longer sought to interlock his fingers
through hers. His love for Charlotte had undergone a definite
change too, and ceased to function spontaneously.

The end came as a relief to them both, one late afternoon in
the Marlborough Street living-room. As with natural deaths,
there was a certain dignity about the final moments. Afterward
Charlotte was glad that she had not hastened the end. Nature's
less violent methods are usually more merciful. They were
both prepared.

"I've been talking to the travel agent today about the reservations I made for our ocean crossing in July. I realize you're
still not ready."

"I'm terribly sorry."

"I exchanged the reservations I'd made for two, to three.
The two boys have never been to England. I can take them
instead."

"Oh, could you? Would you?"

"I've been thinking about us, Charlotte."

"Yes."

"Perhaps you're right. Perhaps we wouldn't be happy."

"Well, I don't believe I would be so very companionable,
Elliot. You see I don't know how to ride, or shoot, or play golf
or tennis, or ski or skate, or any of those things which you
enjoy so much. I do think you ought to marry somebody who
enjoys what you enjoy. And somebody younger, too, who can
be like a sort of older sister to your boys, and join them in
sports too."

"The mere fact you aren't an athlete wouldn't have mat-
tered if I could have made you love me. But obviously I can't.
It's the first time in my life I've failed in something I set out
to do."

"Well, it isn't your fault. I can't explain, but it positively
isn't your fault! And, Elliot, please don't think it's been all
wasted effort. You've made me very important in the eyes of

the family, and it's the only thing that has *ever* happened to me which has made Mother proud. You've made *me* proud too, Elliot," she added. He said nothing. They were standing side by side looking out onto the street. There was his long, black, expensive car drawn up close to the yellow line in front of her door—for the last time as prospectively hers, it occurred to her.

"Of course, Elliot, on your side of the score there isn't so much to show for your effort. I realize that."

"Well, you've shown me I can still care for somebody deeply."

"Oh, Elliot, if only I could feel I'd been a bridge to you!"

"A bridge?"

"Yes, which you passed over, from your grieving about Elaine, to being happy with somebody else. Perhaps on the boat—or over in England—you'll meet somebody, and you'll be all ready for her—the bridge crossed, and everything."

"And I suppose you'll meet somebody sometime who you'll be more ready for."

"No, I don't think I shall ever marry. Some women aren't the marrying kind. But thank you ever so much for asking me. I've got that on my record, anyway!" She smiled in an attempt to relieve the solemnity.

"What will you be doing this summer and afterward?"

"Oh, closing the house, going to Maine, coming back, opening the house, taking care of Mother, same old job. I'm awfully glad there's no ring to give back to you, Elliot."

"When shall I tell my mother and sisters?"

"Tonight. I'll tell my family tonight, too."

There was a pause. "Shall I kiss you good-bye?"

"Oh, let's not. It really isn't good-bye. For we'll be seeing each other next fall. We'll still be friends, won't we?"

"Of course. Well, good-bye till we meet again."

"Good-bye, Elliot, till we meet again."

A moment later she heard him going down the stairs, and then the muffled thud of the front door as it closed. It had never been his custom to turn and wave nor hers to follow him out of sight with her gaze, but this time steadfastly she watched him cross the sidewalk, get into the car, and close the door. It moved away. As if she was performing a last rite she kept her eyes upon the car as it grew smaller and smaller and disappeared.

That last long gesture of Elliot's was something like the last long breath which her father had drawn when he had disappeared into the cosmos of shifting identities. There had been no gasping, no struggle. He had simply taken an extra long intake of air into his lungs and seemed to straighten out his body a little. She had thought at first that he was holding his breath, and had looked questioningly at the nurse. The nurse had nodded and smiled at her, withdrew her fingers from his wrist, glanced at her watch, and said quietly, "Five-twenty-three." Now Charlotte glanced at her watch. "Five-fifty-five." A blur of tears filled her eyes.

She had missed the sound of her father's labored breathing in the house terribly at first. For weeks it had been as incessant as a tide upon the shore. Now she would miss the labored efforts of her engagement to Elliot. No longer would there be any necessity to adjust to its complaints. No longer any brief flashes of false hope. It was over, finished, ended forever.

She went upstairs to her room, stealthily climbing the three flights so that her mother would not hear her.

She would never have a child of her own now. She would never have a home of her own. She would never have a man of her own. She would never have even a friend to whom she was important. She was no longer young. Such relationships must be started in one's youth. *Oh, Jerry, Jerry, where are you? I need you so.* She lay upon the bed and wept.

CHAPTER TWENTY-FOUR:
THE HEIRESS

It was a bitter disappointment to Charlotte's mother when she heard of the broken engagement. She highly approved of Elliot Livingston as a husband for her daughter. For years her tyranny had vented itself on Charlotte, selfishly and cruelly, it may have seemed, but she had a strong maternal instinct.

Charlotte ate dinner alone that night, then went upstairs to her mother's room. She was seated in her wheel-chair in the bay window. Charlotte sat down opposite in a low rocker.

"What was Elliot's hurry this afternoon?" crisply her mother demanded. "He was here less than half an hour."

"Mother, Elliot and I have broken our engagement."

Her mother was leaning back in the chair. Her body stiffened as if a charge of electricity had passed through it. "Why have you done that?"

"Because I'm not in love with him," she replied, rocking gently back and forth.

"Hmph! 'Not in love with him'! At your age such talk is just sentimental foolishness."

Charlotte made no comment.

"What do you intend to do with your life, anyway?"

"Get a cat and a parrot and enjoy single blessedness," Charlotte replied airily.

"Without any means of support?"

"I've already told you I'm not afraid of that."

"I sometimes wonder how you can be a child of mine! Haven't you any ambition at all? Here you've got a chance to join our name, Vale, with the name of one of the finest families in this city, Livingston, and you come in here and tell me you're not 'in love'! You talk like a romantic young girl of sixteen."

"I've no doubt of it," Charlotte agreed calmly, but the old smoldering bitterness was very near the surface.

Her apparent composure was infuriating to her mother. "Stop rocking," she commanded. Charlotte obeyed. "You've never done anything to make your mother proud. Not a single thing. Nor to make yourself proud, either. Why, I should think you'd be ashamed to be born and live all your life as just Charlotte Vale—*Miss* Charlotte Vale."

"I never wanted to be born," Charlotte retorted, the bitterness bursting into flame now. "And you never wanted me to be born either! It's been a calamity on both sides!"

Her mother's eyes flashed. She looked as fierce as an enraged eagle. She opened her mouth to speak, then closed it, pressing her lips tightly together as if to get herself under better control. A sort of spasm contracted the muscles of her face for an instant.

"Oh, Mother, don't let's quarrel. We've been getting along so well together lately."

Again her mother tried to speak and failed. Again there was a muscular contraction.

"That was a horrid thing for me to say. I didn't mean it. I'm sorry, Mother."

But Charlotte's contrition came too late. Her mother's hands were gripping the chair arms. Without further warning, or another spoken word, one of her mother's hands loosened its hold and fell down at the side of the chair. At the same time her body slumped, listing to one side like a rammed ship.

Charlotte stepped to the door. "Dora! Dora!" she called.

By the time Dora had helped Charlotte raise the crumpled body into a sitting position again, one corner of her mother's mouth was pulled down, her face contorted, and she was making strange gurgling sounds.

Once more Dan Regan lifted the shrunken little old body in his arms. "Hold on tight now," cheerfully he sang out. She seemed to understand him. Her good left arm clutched his neck. "Now let go." Again her left arm obeyed his command.

Dan laid her down gently in the middle of the wide bed. Dora pulled down her thick cotton nightgown, and spread the sheet over her tenderly, then the warm blankets, patting and stroking it, murmuring, "There! There, Gramma! Dora is here. So is Dan. Dora and Dan understand. Don't worry, darling."

Her mother tried to speak, but only unintelligible sounds came forth. Her tongue had apparently become as useless as the dangling right arm. Charlotte turned away from the sight. There was nothing for her to do. She went downstairs and waited in the living-room. Another nurse arrived a half-hour later.

"Has anything happened to excite her today?" asked Dan when finally he and Dora joined Charlotte in the living-room.

"Not that I know of," said Dora.

"Yes, there has, too," contradicted Charlotte. "I'm to blame for this. Mother and I quarreled. I did it."

"Oh, I don't believe so, Miss Vale. This often happens to old people without any provocation whatsoever."

"You're trying to let me out, Dan. That's kind of you, but I did it," Charlotte insisted. "I said something simply awful to my mother."

"Well, even so, it isn't likely that the effect could follow so closely upon what you fear may be the cause. It was just a coincidence."

"No, I saw it happen. I know. I did it. I did it."

Five days later, Dora stole into Charlotte's room early one morning and said gently, "Isn't it nice for Gramma? When I went to see if she was all right, I found she'd gone to sleep forever."

"I did it. I did it, Dora," again Charlotte repeated.

On the morning of the funeral Charlotte stole into her mother's darkened room. She was lying on her bed covered with its lace spread. She was all dressed up in her best black velvet, ready to go downstairs to play the grand dame at her last party. Charlotte stood and gazed at her long and silently.

Strange, she thought, *how death repairs, restores, and even beautifies. Or more likely the undertaker,* she concluded, with that relentless honesty of hers. There was no indication of her mother's last sickness. The muscles of her face no longer sagged. Her mouth was no longer drawn down. To all appearances the afflicted right arm had been healed. Both her hands, ringless now except for the wide gold wedding ring, were crossed on her chest, wrists and fingers gracefully flexed. Both her eyes were closed as in sleep. Many of the wrinkles on her face had disappeared. There was no trace of anger, or disapproval, no suggestion of their last quarrel, and yet, as Charlotte gazed, dry-eyed, she was tortured by two refrains: *You've never done anything to make your mother proud* and *I did it. I did it.*

Lloyd told Charlotte about her mother's will in the late afternoon on the day of the funeral. There was no formal ceremony. Besides Charlotte only Lloyd and Rosa, Hilary and Justine were present, all dressed in black, seated in the living-room. Lloyd, as eldest son and one of the executors of the will, assumed the position of master of ceremonies. He produced the important document from his breast pocket and stretched out its long, thin, typewritten pages. They crackled like fresh tissue paper.

"Mother has left a will we shall all feel very proud of, when it is published in the papers," he began. "She has made many public bequests, not as large as I think they should have been in view of the size of her property, but they will be considered generous." He put on his glasses and glanced down. "All the best known charities are included in the list, several hospitals, the Art Museum, the Boston Symphony Orchestra, the Audubon Society, and so forth, to the amount of some $250,000 in all. Also there are many personal bequests. I won't read them all at present. However, the following may interest you." He turned a page, and cleared his throat. "I give to my daughter-in-law Rosa, wife of my son Lloyd, the sum of $25,000. To my daughter-in-law Justine, wife of my son Hilary, the sum of $25,000. To each of my grandchildren, born at date of my signature, the sum of $5000. I give to my faithful chauffeur, William McGinnis, the sum of $10,000; to each of my other servants who has served in my employ for the period of three years prior to my death, the sum of $300 for each year in my service. I give to my devoted nurse, Dora Pickford, the sum of $5000. To my devoted doctor, Daniel Regan, the sum of $5000." Lloyd cleared his throat. "All the rest, residue, and remainder of my estate, real, personal, or mixed, of whatever nature and wherever situated, I give, devise, and bequeath to my beloved daughter, Charlotte Vale."

Nobody said anything for a moment, and then, chiefly to relieve the tension, Hilary inquired, "Doesn't she bequeath anything to either of her beloved sons?"

"Not a red cent."

"Mother told me that Father had already given you and Lloyd your property," said Charlotte. "But if you think you ought to have some more, Hilary, then let's fix it right."

"Good Heavens, Charlotte," Lloyd exclaimed, "if you're going to be any such easy mark as that you don't deserve to be in charge of any such amount of money. Even after you pay your taxes, it's going to be a disgraceful lot."

"Hasn't Mother left anything to Lisa?" asked Charlotte.

"No. Lisa isn't mentioned."

"Nor to little Christopher?"

"Naturally not. The child wasn't born."

"But Mother knew! Please see that both Lisa and Christopher are treated like the other members of our family, Lloyd."

"But they aren't members of our family, Charlotte. We all felt very strongly that out of respect to Rupert, Lisa should not have considered marriage for at least two years."

"*I* didn't feel that way."

"Possibly not. But this isn't *your* will, my dear."

"But it's my money, isn't it?"

"Not yet. But in time—in time, yes," he acknowledged grudgingly.

"Well, then, as soon as it is mine, Lisa and Christopher will receive the same amounts as the others," Charlotte announced.

Lloyd's face twitched. "I hope you aren't going to be difficult, Charlotte. For many years I have been Mother's adviser about all her financial affairs. You know nothing about such matters."

"Then I must learn."

Again Lloyd's face twitched. It was an inherited trait. "Charlotte, Mother has committed to you a grave responsibility. I do not feel this large estate is yours to spend and distribute as you wish. I look upon you simply as the custodian of our family property. It is my sincere hope—the sincere hope of us all—you'll be a wise custodian."

"Well, you're surely very lucky, Charlotte," said Justine, when she rose to go.

"I hope you'll be willing to make a nice large subscription to our new Foundling's Home," said Rosa, "and perhaps come on to our board sometime."

Oh, dear, I wish it made me happier, thought Charlotte that night during the long stretch between one and five when she couldn't sleep. *But all the money in the world won't let me call up Jerry and tell him I've broken my engagement to Elliot and killed my mother and am all alone in the world.*

Marlborough Street in late July presents somewhat the same aspect as a summer amusement boulevard in late September. Some of the houses showed signs of life within, but intermittent and languishing. Many front doors were shuttered. Many windows boarded. There was still a good deal of traffic, however, especially in the morning and late afternoon. The suburbanites still traveled in and out of town along their favorite routes. But there were few pedestrians. Charlotte could walk a whole block or more without meeting anyone.

She didn't open the Maine cottage. There was no reason to now. There was no reason to do anything now. She decided to remain in town for the summer. All the servants, except William and the cook, felt they must get away from the heat of the city. Charlotte didn't try to dissuade them. In view of the *For Sale* sign, which she had attached to one of the brownstone pillars, it was wiser for them to place themselves in permanent positions as soon as possible.

Dora, of course, had taken another case. There were no more calls from Dan Regan. The telephone scarcely ever rang. There were few people left in town who might ask her for an occasional game of bridge. The various members of the family had all departed to their respective summer retreats. June was in Europe with Fabia, who had been granted a two months' leave of absence. Her sisters-in-law, all three, extended cordial invitations to Charlotte for a visit, but she shrank from the effort.

The one activity she indulged in was driving her own car. During the spring she had learned to operate an automobile. The only purchase of importance which she had made since her mother's death was a Lincoln roadster. Every hot evening she would run out into the country to escape, not only the heat of the city streets, but their loneliness. She felt her desolation less keenly speeding by the green lawns and unclosed houses and the hills and meadows farther out. Sometimes she left her car on the roadside, and strolled in the fields and meadows, or sat down against a stone wall and read, or tried to read. She was finding it more and more difficult to feel interest in a printed page.

That lack of interest in reading had been one of the definite symptoms of her last illness. Other definite symptoms intruded themselves upon her—periods of extreme fatigue without any cause, sleepless nights, a sensation of impending calamity, and all those inexplicable sensations too. Most recovered victims of a nervous breakdown fear the possibility of its return for several years after recovery, Doctor Jaquith had warned her. "But fear is nothing to be ashamed of. It's what you do about fear that determines whether you're weak or strong. If there's something you can do to get rid of your fear, do it, or else your fear may become an anxiety, and that's harder to deal with."

Charlotte called up Doctor Jaquith one morning in early August, and made an appointment with him.

CHAPTER TWENTY-FIVE: CONSULTATION

Charlotte arrived in New York on the afternoon before her appointment. It was a forbidding day of fog and drizzling rain. She did not go to an uptown hotel. Either the Roosevelt or Biltmore required less effort. The old pall of lassitude was becoming thicker and thicker.

A bellboy showed her into a musty bedroom on the 20th floor. It was elaborate and perfectly equipped, but about as alive as a dressed-up dummy in a showcase. After the bellboy had left, Charlotte went to the window and gazed out into the limitless expanse of dense gray murk.

She took off her hat and coat, and sat down on the edge of the crotch walnut bed, covered with rose-colored moiré trimmed with gilt braid. It was only four o'clock. What was she to do, closed up in this sealed cube of dead air, nearer the clouds than the ground, till tomorrow morning at ten o'clock?

Suddenly the telephone bell ripped through the still staleness like a streak of serpentine lightning. She took off the receiver and held it to her ear.

"Hello, Babs," a vibrant male voice called.

Charlotte was silent.

"It's Mike, Babs! Missed you at the train. Be up in a jiffy."

"You have the wrong number," said Charlotte and hung up the receiver.

That joyous welcome was not meant for her! The fresh, crisp sound of it increased her pangs of loneliness—like food in a baker's window the pangs of hunger of a half-starved child.

As she gazed at the telephone with a mixture of reproach, envy, and self-pity, an old temptation returned. A person-to-person call. She need only to say that she was at such and such a number, and would he please call her up on a matter of business in the next hour or two. His office wasn't six blocks away. Possibly, perhaps, they might meet for a few innocent minutes! They might even have an early dinner together!

She took down the receiver, but when the girl at the switchboard answered, she hung it up again. Perhaps she'd better call Deb McIntyre instead. Deb would ask her to come out to Darien for the night, perhaps, and they could talk about J.D. But the McIntyres were in Nantucket, the telephone girl informed her. Well, if the Montagues knew she were here, they'd insist that she come out to Glen Cove. After a 20-

minute wait the telephone girl reported that there was no answer. With the determination of despair she looked up Ham Hunneker's penthouse number, and put in the call herself. A Japanese voice informed her that "Mees-ter Hun-na-ka sail lass week for Eu-rup." She had exhausted her resources!

She got up and walked to the window. The mist was not so thick but that she could see the flat tops of the low buildings surrounding the hotel, and between them, far below, the streets filled with traffic—small, moving spots from here.

She wondered, as she gazed, if she could spring over the stream of traffic just below and land on the roof across the street, or if gravitation would pull her body straight down. She would hold up traffic for a while! And a group of those spots down there would leap aside to avoid her, and tonight at various dinner-tables the incident would be described with all its details.

She had no intention of jumping. She contemplated it simply to relieve her suffocating ennui. It was just a ghoulish form of daydreaming, in which she had often indulged before her illness. Daydreaming was a pernicious habit. Action, of almost any kind, was preferable.

She turned away from the window, walked back to the telephone, and put in a person-to-person call for J. D. Durrance. As she waited, she could feel her heart thumping. Finally, "Mr. Durrance has just left his office for the day," the report came back.

Jerry had just left his office! Probably he was on his way to the train for Mount Vernon. It was now after five. Coming nearer and nearer to her every second! It could do nobody any harm if they should chance to run across each other in the Grand Central Station.

She put on her hat and coat and descended to the street. At the Information Booth she asked about the trains to Mount Vernon. There was one that left in five minutes and others later. She hovered in the vicinity of the gate through which

Jerry must pass with as much excitement as if they had an appointment.

He didn't take the first train. Well, she'd wait for one more. She waited for three more. She didn't feel that it was wasted effort. Her pall of lassitude had dropped away.

She recognized him from a long way off when finally she was rewarded, though he was neither strikingly tall nor short, and wore today an unfamiliar stiff straw hat. He walked briskly, as always, though laden with various bundles, a hat-box among them, and a leather businessman's bag.

He was not alone. There was a woman following along several steps behind. She was dressed in dark shapeless clothes, and there was no buoyancy in her step. Charlotte felt sure it was Isobel even before she had come near enough to recognize her from the kodak picture. Half a step behind Jerry on his other side were two young women, also carrying packages, the two older daughters. They had been in town shopping for the day evidently.

Charlotte stepped behind a concealing post. There was Jerry, dragging along his whole domestic load, except the youngest child. Charlotte was reminded of what Deb had said once, that J.D. was like a dog between shafts pulling a cart. As Jerry passed close by Charlotte, she saw that his forehead was shining with a light coating of perspiration. He looked tired and anxious. She was filled with compassion and admiration.

When she returned to her 20th-story room her sense of des-olation had disappeared. Jerry hadn't seen her. He hadn't known she had seen him. But she knew now she was not alone in her unhappiness. Lack of sympathetic companionship was his lot, too. Tonight the same storm that beat her window-pane was beating against Jerry's a few miles away. She wondered if he slept, and wondering, fell asleep.

Doctor Jaquith's New York office was as unconventional as he himself. It was in an old dwelling house with a brownstone front located west of Fifth Avenue. It was as far removed from the "right" district of doctors' offices as west is from east, when the dividing line is Fifth Avenue. Doctor Jaquith had inherited the house. And when, in response to the increasing demands of his patients, he consented to spend one day a week in New York, it seemed sensible to put the empty old house to use again. However, he put far less thought into his house than into his patients, and the house showed it. Its high-studded walls were bare, its heavy marble mantels empty, its windows innocent of draperies. There were no books, no plants, no flowers; but it had a certain homely charm, and struck one as genuine as the man who had been born in it.

Doctor Jaquith saw his patients in the long narrow room at the right of the front door. The walls were a mottled red. One day he had given a boiled lobster-shell and a Paisley shawl to a local house painter, and told him to mix a color for the walls the nearest he could get to a cross-breed of the two, and paint all the woodwork black. It reminded Charlotte of the inside of an old Chinese lacquer box.

It was the most unusual doctor's office she had ever been in. Whatever Doctor Jaquith's interests and hobbies were, there was no trace of them here. Whether he was married or not, had children or not, liked music, art, antiques, ships, fishing, or not, the room gave no indication. Was it, perhaps, because of the impression it gave of Doctor Jaquith's detachment from his own personal life that made confidences run so freely inside the red-lacquered box?

The room lacked even the tags of his profession. There was no flat-topped desk before which he was seated like a king on a throne. There was no upholstered armchair facing him in which one sat and looked up. There was no desk at all. There was no upholstered armchair at all. There was no doctor at all, when one first entered the room. The only articles of furniture that Charlotte could recall after her first visit were two East

Indian cane armchairs, a faded-faced banjo clock and an enormous Bokhara rug of the texture of velvet, and of the tones of a wild hydrangea leaf.

It was still raining and as cold as October when Charlotte kept her appointment. She caught the fragrance of a cannel-coal fire the minute she entered. Flames were leaping in the open grate in the room when she crossed the threshold, filling the space from floor to ceiling with crackle, shadows, and warmth. It drew one toward it, like a bonfire at night.

Doctor Jaquith had something of the same magnetic quality as the fire. His motions were also quick and alert. When he shook hands his fingers were virile to their very tips. His eyebrows and hair were as black as coal, his black eyes as scintillating as the high-lights on the curves of the black marble mantel. One would say offhand he was a man of about 50, but he could easily have been either 40 or 60. He was as clean-shaven as was possible. The lower part of his face was a dusky purple compared to his ruddy cheeks and high white forehead. He was neither tall nor short. "Wiry" described his figure.

After shaking hands and a few sentences in way of greeting he asked Charlotte to be seated in the chair with its back to the windows, thus removing at least one well-known cause for self-consciousness, offered her a cigarette, held a lighted match to it, lit a cigarette for himself, then sat down in a chair identical to hers, facing the windows.

From behind a thick smoke-screen, "Well, let's get down to business," he said in his bluff, blunt manner, as free from any display of his profession as his consultation-room.

His speech, whether conversing with an old friend or a new patient, was always filled with homely similes, and frequently emphasized by rugged terms. This was due to his two outstanding characteristics—he liked people, he disliked pomp.

There was no telephone in the room. Doctor Jaquith never allowed an appointment to be interrupted, except in an emergency, nor an appointment of one patient to trespass on that of the next. He produced no formidable history of Charlotte's case, he took down notes as she talked. All he did now was to cross his legs, fold his arms, gaze down into the flaming coals, ask an occasional question, and listen.

This was Charlotte's first interview with Doctor Jaquith since J.D.'s reappearance. She had written Doctor Jaquith about Elliot Livingston and later of the broken engagement, giving as an explanation that she found she simply didn't have the "right feeling" for Elliot. Also she had written him briefly of her mother's death. She had never written him or told him about J.D. At the interview immediately after her return from the cruise she had referred to "an awfully nice man" who had put her on her feet at the start of the voyage. She hadn't mentioned his name.

"We poor psychiatrists are always wishing for 'an awfully nice man' to put a patient on her feet when we send her on a voyage, and then clear out," he had replied. "But they're scarce as hens' teeth. Usually the patient reports the people were dull and stodgy, or else loud and common, and the whole experience turns out a dismal failure. You're lucky."

Today his first question after getting down to business was, "How's the troupe been behaving?" He referred to her troupe of instincts and emotions.

"I'm afraid I'm in another breakdown, Doctor Jaquith," she said.

"Oh, I don't think so," he replied instantly, his keen eyes observing her closely. "But let's hear about false symptoms anyway."

For the next half-hour Charlotte did most of the talking. Usually 10 or 15 minutes before the end of an appointment, Doctor Jaquith rose and took the floor. Sometimes he walked up and down the room. Sometimes he stood with his back to the fire as he held forth. Today he chose to warm his back, thumbs in trousers pockets, fingers spread.

"Well, I'm still of the same opinion about the breakdown," he began. "But I must say it looks to me as if several members of your cast has gotten pretty well out of hand lately. Why all this remorse about your mother's death? I thought I relegated remorse, compunction, New England conscience, et cetera, backstage left and right. I'm surprised at you! You've let 'em sneak up to center and front."

"Have I?" meekly Charlotte inquired.

"And look here," he went on, "to what obscure corner have you consigned intelligence? Why, you're no more to blame for your mother's death than for an electric light bulb, nearly worn out, going black just after you happened to turn on the switch. Any feeling of guilt on that score I shall have to ascribe to sentimental emotionalism. Also in the same category is that sense-of-failure you say you've felt ever since your mother said you'd never done anything to make her proud. You know as well as I you had about as much chance to make your mother proud as a baby in a perambulator. You also know as well as I that she got a big kick out of you, since she discovered you'd got it in you to stand on your own two feet."

"Possibly. But my mother's very last intelligible words to me were spoken in rage. I feel as if I don't deserve her money or want it."

"Nonsense! The very last words spoken by a wise man are of little significance. That last scene with your mother is of no more importance than a fly-speck on the window-pane. Stop riveting your eyes on the fly-speck, and look at the view. You did a swell job when you broke away from your mother. You did it kindly too. You didn't tramp rough-shod over her feelings, and you controlled your own. You had your cast under darned good control. You're the stage manager, you know," he smiled. "I'm just the director—ex-director. It's really up to you to keep the troupe in shape now."

He glanced up at the banjo clock. Three minutes had ticked away since he had risen. He now clasped his hands behind his back.

"Now I want to say something about this marriage question. You say you'll never marry. Well, maybe not. I won't question that. But what I do intend to quarrel with you about are your conclusions. You say you'll never marry, *therefore* will never have a home of your own, a child of your own, or a man of your own. Good Lord! What are you going to do with all that money of yours? Why, you can have a home of your own, which all your brothers and sisters, nieces and nephews, and friends, and friends' friends will flock to in hordes, if you *want* to. No man is necessary for that in your case. As for a child of your own, the maternal instinct can be satisfied by a child you didn't happen to bear. It doesn't make any difference to a hen whether she hatched her own eggs or not. As for a man of your own, if it's the masculine point-of-view you want, no unmarried woman with brains needs to feel any impoverishment on that score. If it's male companionship and male admiration you enjoy (and God pity the woman who doesn't), an unattached lady can have as many male companions as she has capacity for, and with no objections from a possessive husband. But some satisfactory substitute must be found for her sex instinct. In this age and part of the world incontinence usually leads to nothing but misery. It isn't a good idea either to have a lot of repressed energy bottled up inside us. We must find some worth-while activity on which you can expend effort freely and with benefit to yourself and others. The first thing to do is to consider what you have a talent for."

"I see what you're suggesting. Sublimation. I have no talent for anything except possibly for bridge. Perhaps I could give bridge lessons and donate the proceeds to an orphans' home and so pacify my feminine craving! Oh, that sounds horribly sarcastic, I'm afraid. I'm sorry, but I'm one who prefers to face facts to being deceived by a false pacifier called sublimation."

"Wait a minute! How much do you know about sublimation?"

"Not much!" she shrugged. "All I know is it's something false and artificial instead of the real thing."

"Ever study chemistry?"

She shook her head.

"Well, there's nothing false or artificial about the process of sublimation in the chemical laboratory, I assure you. When a substance passes from one solid state into another, it is as definitely a fact as any of nature's processes. So also in the mental laboratory. When a source of energy, denied normal and healthy expression, is diverted to an activity on a high ethical plane, there's nothing to suggest a pacifier in the definite effect it has on an individual's life and happiness. I speak from personal experience." He paused a moment. "I've never married. There were reasons why I felt I shouldn't."

Charlotte was aware that there was some taint in his inheritance, of which he bore no trace, but which could be passed on. She had heard that it accounted for his interest in medicine, and that he had chosen psychiatry because of his personal experience with fears, and his own excellent adaptation to his fate.

"I was convinced," he went on, "that I ought never to have a child, and I made up my mind I would never ask any woman to share that sacrifice with me. Of course now that I'm older I might perfectly well marry some woman also older with children of her own, but my substitutes for marriage were so satisfying and have become so engrossing that I feel little sense of loss, no self-pity, and no sense whatsoever of having been deceived by a false pacifier. I have in fact had a bully good time in life."

"Your case is different. You always wanted to be a doctor. It wasn't a makeshift. You had a motive for it, and a strong driving motive too."

"Motives, like muscles, have to be exercised to become strong and driving."

"Besides, you had a high-minded and altruistic reason for not marrying. The reason I shall never marry anybody now is because the only man I care for in that way is already married."

"I call that a mighty high-minded and altruistic reason!"

She ignored his comment. "Oh, there's nothing to be done about me. There's nothing I want to do, nothing I'm interested in. All effort seems utterly futile. Now that Mother is dead, I haven't even my freedom to struggle for any more. I have no duty toward anybody, and no obligation."

"What about that pile of money in your possession? Some wealthy philanthropist once said, 'Every possession is a duty, every opportunity an obligation.' It may sound preachy, but it's good talk."

"What I long for most," Charlotte said, in a tone of despair, "is a state of unconsciousness, but I haven't the courage to put an end to things myself, because of the sneaking fear it might not be the end."

"That's a sneaking fear I'd respect. Seems possible to me that suicide might prove to be a case of jumping out of the frying-pan into the fire, judging from the way Nature usually reacts when anyone tries breaking one of her fundamental laws. She has methods of enforcing them that are often harder to take than the law itself. Besides—" He paused.

"I know what you're going to say." Charlotte interrupted with one of her sardonic smiles. "'Besides, suicide is so cowardly,'" she mimicked.

"No, I wasn't going to refer to cowardice. What I was going to say was, that a man contemplating suicide should bear in mind that his act is usually paid for by others. It is not just his personal affair. Everyone who takes his or her own life increases the fear in all his progeny of committing the same act during a period of depression. In fact, every blood relation he possesses gets a drop of the same poison. Nice parting gift. Suicide is not inherited, but the tendency to give in to it seems to run in families. Mighty bad example to set for one's friends and associates, too. Look here," he broke off, "I have a suggestion. Is there any reason why you can't get into your car tomorrow or the next day and run up to Cascade for a week or ten days?"

"I'm giving my chauffeur a two weeks' vacation, but when he comes back I suppose I can have him drive me to Cascade."

"Why bring the chauffeur?"

"I've only just learned to drive. Cascade is over three hundred miles. Those ghastly attacks of weakness have come back again."

"Well, if you feel too weak to sit up and steer, just stop off at a hotel anywhere en route, hire a room, and lie down."

"But I don't know the road. And I might get a flat tire."

"That won't hurt you. In fact, often, when I advise a patient to take an automobile trip alone, I rather hope he does get a flat tire or have some difficulty to get out of himself."

"Very well. I'll come alone," she said with dignity.

"Good! That's the stuff! If you upset there'll be no Italian chauffeur to blame for it anyhow, and," he added casually, but looking at her sharply, "no companion to help you out of one difficulty or another."

Charlotte returned the sharp look, then glanced away. She had referred to the overturned car to Doctor Jaquith several times, but never had spoken of her companion.

"You never told me you had psychic power."

"I haven't. But I'm a fairly good mathematician." He smiled and glanced up at the clock. Three minutes after eleven. "Well, time's up." He stepped up to Charlotte and shook hands. She had to stand up out of courtesy. In a moment he would disappear through the double doors through which he had entered.

"Oh, I do wish we might talk ten minutes longer!" said Charlotte. "There's so much I want to say, especially *now*."

"Well, if you want to wait two hours, I can give you ten minutes, but my advice is, save it till you come to Cascade."

CHAPTER TWENTY-SIX: A TALL DARK LADY

Cascade was not confined to one building or to one group of buildings. It was dotted here and there all over the little town, upon which the two farmhouses where Doctor Jaquith housed his "guests" looked down from their hill. The two farmhouses were both painted white with green blinds, had fan-topped doorways and small-paned windows, in fact they were as alike as a pair of identical twins.

One was called Oldways and was built in 1825, the other Newways and was built in 1925. They were connected by a woodshed filled with logs and kindling, chopped and piled by the guests. At one side of the farmhouses there was a huge red barn and behind there were apple orchards, hay fields, pastures, stone walls, and 100 acres of woods. There were two ponds in the woods, three brooks, and a 50-foot precipice. At the top of the precipice the three brooks joined forces and fell down its face in countless slender, white ribbons raveled at the ends, many disappearing into mist before reaching the bottom. Therefore the name *Cascade*.

The twin farmhouses did not suggest a sanatorium. There were no doctors' offices on the premises, no business office, no weaving or workshops. All these were located in the town on the other side of a river. The guests walked across a trestle-bridge and down the village Main Street to keep their doctor's appointments, or to go to their various places of work. This enforced a brisk ten-minute walk several times a day with a definite goal at each end.

Doctor Jaquith advocated goals even for a walk. Also he believed any conditions, obliging his guests to carry out a daily program similar to that of an average healthy human being, were an advantage. He was in favor of separating the place where one worked from the place where one lived. The journey between the two enforced periods of reflection—"swinging on the gate," as he called it. According to Doctor Jaquith, far better off the commuter than he whose job is just across the street.

When there had been only one white farmhouse Doctor Jaquith had had only one colleague to assist him. Now there were four doctors on his staff. However, Doctor Jaquith made it his business to acquaint himself personally with everyone he accepted at Cascade. Each newcomer was assigned to one of the young doctors for the daily talks and check-ups, but there were always occasional conferences with Doctor Jaquith too.

The younger doctors' offices were located in a remodeled dwelling house on Main Street, but Doctor Jaquith had never moved from his original location, "up over" the First National Bank next door. It was a brick building with granite stops and granite pillars upholding a portico. It resembled a small Greek temple.

Three days after her appointment in New York, Charlotte arrived at Cascade alone in her car, after an all-day run. The trip had so replenished her self-confidence that she felt equal to driving to the west coast alone, and it had reduced her fears of a recurrence of a nervous breakdown to mere shadows. She was tired, but she had reason to be, and welcomed it.

The reception given her when she entered the hall of Oldways made her heart glow. The 30-odd guests were about to go in to dinner. Most of them were strangers to her, but there were a few familiar faces—a few returning graduates, like herself, who greeted her warmly. It was a little like returning to one's club or fraternity in college. The servants knew her and smiled, other staff members came up and shook hands, and Miss Trask, who played the rôle of chief steward (as well as chief warden when necessary), fairly pounced upon her, giving her one of those breezy familiar welcomes of hers that used to increase her sense of isolation horribly when she was a novice.

The dining-room at Cascade was a low-studded, ell-shaped room finished and furnished in old pine, with an uneven floor made of wide boards. For dinner its old pine tables, of various sizes and shapes, were lit by candles in old pewter and brass holders.

Miss Trask seated Charlotte at one of the round tables for eight, introducing her dinner companions so rapidly that she got only a name or two.

She had finished her soup before she glanced around the table to take an account of stock.

Halfway round her eyes came to a stop. Almost opposite there was a pair of eyes that met hers which reminded her of J.D.'s! So dark that they looked black, and with those same striking, sienna-brown brows. The eyes were those of a very thin young girl with hair cut like a page's, only longer. It reached to the bottom of her long thin neck, and was straight and flat. Her bangs nearly touched her eyebrows. Her posture was poor—shoulders stooped, chin lifted, as if crouching and looking up.

Charlotte took a drink of water to steady herself. J.D. had said he had consulted Doctor Jaquith about Tina. Could this piteously emaciated child be that stolid little girl in the kodak picture? This child wore no spectacles, but Doctor Jaquith might have found glasses unnecessary. J.D. had said Tina wouldn't eat. This child wasn't eating. Just going through the motions. She spoke only when spoken to, which was seldom. Evidently her table companions had given up trying to bring her into the conversation. Sometimes it is kinder not to try.

Charlotte knew from her own experience that often well-intentioned attempts at friendliness only make one's incompetence more conspicuous. There were no other young people at the table. That, too, was kinder. Charlotte had often wondered what her life would have been if Doctor Jaquith had introduced her to his principles of self-reliance and adaptation when she was in her teens.

Charlotte conversed with her near neighbors at the table, but her attention was concentrated on the silent figure opposite. Frequently she glanced at her, and almost every time the big eyes were fastened upon her, or in the act of quick retreat. Probably just a curiosity. But it was a relief when the child, during dessert, turned to Miss Barnwell, one of the assistants, murmured, "Excuse me, please," and left the room.

Coffee at Cascade was always served in the living-room. As Charlotte sipped, she searched for the haunting eyes. Groups were forming for various activities—pingpong, bridge, Chinese checkers. A dozen or more were going to a moving-picture in the town. Charlotte was asked to join them, and also received an urgent request to make a fourth at contract. She begged off from all invitations, pleading physical weariness.

When she had finished her coffee, she strolled into the hall, glanced into the library, then drifted into the glassed-in sun porch. There she found the child!

She was seated alone at one of the card tables which were usually set up there, covered with half-finished jigsaw puzzles. She was gazing down, her elbows placed upon the table, her chin in her palms. Her long hair hung down on either side

of her face like a pair of curtains, concealing all but the tip of
her nose. Unobserved, Charlotte watched her from the threshold. She didn't touch a single piece of the puzzle—just sat
there staring down. Charlotte made a noise so as not to startle
her—then approached the table.

"How's it coming?" she inquired casually.

"All right."

Charlotte put her head on one side and studied the portions
of the picture already fitted together—a bit of blue sky here, a
patch of green grass there, a man's face, a girl's foot in a slipper. "What's it supposed to be?"

"I don't know."

"Here's the girls' other slipper! Mind if I join you?" She
drew up a chair and sat down opposite. "What's the title of the
picture?" She reached for the box cover near-by. "It says, 'The
Proposal.' I think the girl is in pink. Isn't that the edge of her
dress above the slipper? I'll collect all the pink pieces, unless
you'd rather I wouldn't. Sometimes it's more fun to do a puzzle alone."

The child raised her eyes, but not her chin and looked at
Charlotte.

"I know who you are," she said in a low tone.

Charlotte was startled. "You do! Who am I?"

"You're my new nurse."

So that was why she had shown such curiosity at the table!
"No, I'm not. You're wrong."

"Well, companion then. You can't fool me. I know why you
followed me out here—to make sure I wasn't going to run
away from this place again."

"Did you run away from this place once? I didn't know it.
What's your name, by the way?"

"Oh, you know my name, all right. And you know, too, just
how much I ate for dinner and just how much I talked and
everything. I saw you staring at me all through the meal."

"Did you? How rude of me! But it was only because you reminded me of somebody."

"Who?"

Charlotte hesitated. "Well, if you must know—in lots of ways, of myself."

"Humph! You're just saying that!"

"No. Truly. I mean when I was your age, of course. Aren't you about fourteen?"

She remembered how it used to please her at that age to be thought older than she was.

"I'm twelve, nearly thirteen."

"So this is where you are!" Miss Trask approached the table. "What are you doing out here, Christine?"

"A picture puzzle called 'The Proposal.'"

"But your schedule says you are to spend your evenings with the young people."

"They're older than I am. They don't want me."

"Of course they want you! But naturally they'd want you more if you'd make a little effort yourself. Doctor Brine has already told you about pulling your own weight, hasn't he?"

"Yes."

"Well, then, go ahead and do it now. I've got a pingpong game all fixed up for you."

"Oh, not pingpong! They all play better than I do."

"If you wait till you're the best in everything, my dear child, you'll never do anything but picture puzzles all your life."

"But I'm feeling sick to my stomach tonight."

"Well, then, a little exercise will be good for you. You're to play doubles. Barbara and Betty against you and Bob Borst."

"But he's the best player here!"

"Well, that's why you're to be his partner, so as to make it an even match."

"Oh, but I'll be the worst one! I'll die! Oh, I'll just *die!*"

"You'll do nothing of the sort. Don't dramatize, Christine."

"Oh, please, please, please!" She looked up at Miss Trask with a terror-stricken expression. "Don't make me, don't make me, don't make me," she beseeched.

"No, don't make her," Charlotte exclaimed.

Miss Trask turned and looked at Charlotte in blank amazement. No one ever interfered with her authority. "I realize your intentions are kind," she said, "but we know what is best for Christine. It isn't good for her to sit here alone doing jigsaw puzzles all by herself in the evening. You know, as well as I do, that it is against the principles of Cascade."

"But we're doing the puzzle together."

"The doctors want Christine to have some form of exercise in the evening. I'm sorry, but I'm here to carry out the doctors' wishes."

"I'll see that she has some exercise. I was going to ask her if she'd go down to the town with me later. I want to leave my car at a garage and get it washed. We'll walk back, or *run* back, if you say so. That is, if Christine will be so kind as to go with me. Will you, Christine?"

She nodded violently. "Yes, yes, yes, yes, yes!" The breathy repetition sounded like a valve letting off surplus steam.

Miss Trask addressed Charlotte. "I thought I heard you say you were too tired to do anything tonight but to crawl into bed," she remarked dryly.

"Cascade must have performed a miracle on me," Charlotte replied, also dryly.

"Oh, please let me go with this lady," Christine burst out. "I'll promise to drink all my cocoa tonight, if you will. Upon my word of honor. Oh, please let me, please be kind to me, just this once. Please—"

"For goodness' sake, stop dramatizing, Christine!" Miss Trask interrupted, and paused, looking down at the imploring eyes, the imploring hands, too, clasped tightly on the table top, the arms stretched toward her. Then abruptly, "Go and get your hat and coat," she said.

Christine shot out of the room without a backward glance, like a bird out of a cage.

"It's the first time that child has wanted to do anything with anybody else since she has been here," Miss Trask told Charlotte when they were alone. "That's why I'm letting her go. But I must tell you a few things about her first. She tried to run away a few days ago, so you mustn't let her out of your sight. She's going to have a nurse within a day or two, but, in the meanwhile, she is my responsibility."

"I'll look out for her. You can trust me."

"I know I can, knowing you. She's not at all adjusted here yet. She's full of complexes and defenses of all sorts. All her life she has depended on an overindulgent father. We've got to wean her and set her on her own feet. By the way, she's in Room 16 in Oldways. You're in 18, and share the same bathroom. Don't be disturbed if you hear her crying. The last person in 18 said she has spells of it. Just ignore it. It's one of her little tyrannies—like not eating. Ignore that, too. But if you can manage it, get some food into her tonight—ice cream soda, or sweet chocolate. She eats practically nothing at the table. Here she comes."

A half-hour later Charlotte and Christine were seated at a small table with a black enamel top in a drugstore, both drinking chocolate ice-cream soda and eating fig-newtons.

"How long have you been here at Cascade?" asked Charlotte.

"Ten days—nearly eleven."

"You don't like it much, do you?"

"No."

"Neither did I at the end of ten days. But the first two weeks are the worst."

"I shall never like it. And if they keep me here I shall die. Then they'll be satisfied."

"Who are 'they'?"

"My mother and sisters."

"Haven't you a father?"

"Yes. The reason I said I'd come here was because of my father. The doctor said it would help him. But I hate it here! I hate it here! I hate it, hate it, hate it!"

"Do you want to go home?"

"No."

"Where do you want to go?"

"I don't know. There's no place I want to go. My mother doesn't want me at home, that's why it's helping Father for me to be here."

"Where were you headed when you tried to run away?"

"For a telephone-booth in the town to put in a reverse call to my father."

"To ask him to come and get you?"

"No. I promised him I'd stay here for two weeks. I just wanted to hear Daddy's voice. I—" She stopped, pushed aside the ice-cream soda, only half-finished, and looked down at the table top, the curtains of hair falling forward concealing her face. "I'm almost sure my father is dying," she murmured.

"Is he sick?"

"They won't let me speak to him so I don't know."

"Doesn't he write to you?"

"I can't be sure from his letters. He wouldn't write me anything to worry me. I want to speak to him, I want to hear his voice, then I'll *know*. But they won't let me! When I told Miss Trask I was afraid my father was dying, she said I was dramatizing and to trot along and forget it."

"And did you ask your doctor?"

"Yes. He said I mustn't let a fear lead me around by the nose, and that I had to wait till Saturday night before speaking to my father. That's four days more. He may be dead by then." She lowered her head. Several tears dropped on the table top.

"Listen, Christine, there's a telephone-booth in the corner, and here's my purse full of change. Will your father be at home tonight, do you think?"

"You mean I can call Daddy now?"

"Certainly that's what I mean. I'll wait for you here.

When she came back to the table, her eyes were shining, her cheeks flushed. She looked almost pretty. "He's all right! He answered the telephone himself. Mother was out at church. He's not sick! He played some chords on the piano so I'd know he was downstairs, and not answering the telephone by his bed. It was lucky Mother was out, or he mightn't have played the chords. Mother thinks he spoils me. Oh, thank you for letting me speak to him. Thank you, thank you! I'd like to finish my ice cream soda now."

"Let's have a fresh one. It's almost gone."

"But I'll owe you so much! My father said I am to pay you back the money. He wanted to know who was letting me call him. All I could say was, 'a tall dark lady,' and that I'd write tomorrow and tell him your name. What is your name, please?"

"Don't you think secrets rather fun? Let's not tell your father my name for a while. Just refer to me as the 'tall, dark lady.' It sounds so mysterious. And, look here, I don't believe I'd say anything to Miss Trask about this telephone call. It might put me in a little wrong."

"Of course not! Nor Doctor Brine nor Doctor Jaquith. I won't tell a single living soul! I'd sooner die than put you in wrong." Her eyes flashed. Her tone was fierce.

It became necessary for Charlotte now to lower her eyes. Never before had anyone expressed such loyalty on her behalf. "Tell me about yourself," she said, changing the subject. "Where do you go to school? What class are you in? And what subjects do you like best? And what do you like to do?" She remembered various details which J.D. had told her about this problem child of his—her love of camping and out-of-doors, her love of animals, her flair for art.

"I don't like anything at school. Both my sisters always got A's and B's. I get C's and D's, and sometimes E's. I used to like to paint, but not any more."

"Why not?"

"Because they found I did it when I ought to be studying algebra and Latin. I had a little secret studio up under then eaves, with a skylight in it, off my bedroom on the third floor. One of my sisters sneaked and peeked on me, and told my mother I was spending most of my time in one of my closets, afternoons when I was supposed to be studying, and one morning, when I was at school, my mother got into my studio and took away my paintings, and my easel, and all my tubes and brushes, and locked the door."

"And your father let her?"

"My father was in Italy, on a business trip. When he got home he told Mother to give me back my things and my studio key. But it was too late. I don't want to be an artist any more. They're always queer, my sisters say. I want to be like other girls now, and swim and skate and ski, and play tennis and pingpong. But it's too late for that, too, so—"

"No, it isn't, Tina. It isn't too late for anything. Tell me what you'd like most to do."

"You called me 'Tina'!"

"Did I? How stupid! But isn't it a nickname for Christine?"

"Yes, but nobody calls me that except my father."

"Well, then, I won't."

"No! Please. I want you to!"

CHAPTER TWENTY-SEVEN:
IN PLACE OF A NURSE

Charlotte surreptitiously indulged in a hot bath that night after all the guests' lights were supposed to be out. She had finished and was ready for bed when she heard the unmistakable sound of muffled sobbing in the adjoining room. She had left Tina smiling only half an hour ago outside her bedroom door. The sobbing was not loud, but the repeated cycles of sound were regular and continuous, and seemed likely to continue.

Charlotte cautiously turned the knob of the door. It was not locked. She opened it. The room was dark. The sobbing came from the direction of the bed. At first glance it appeared empty. Both the pillows were undisturbed, the turned-down bedclothes smooth. But there was a slight mound in the middle of the bed. Tina had crawled down under the blankets, and was lying curled up face down.

Charlotte sat down on the edge of the bed and placed her hand on the jerking mound. Instantly it became motionless, all sound ceased, and the body stiffened. *Oh, dear, I've frightened her,* thought Charlotte.

"It's I. The tall dark lady, Tina. Don't be afraid," she said, leaning over the mound and speaking distinctly. "Tell me what's the matter."

Charlotte was unprepared for what happened. Tina wriggled out of her cave, half-sat up, and stared at Charlotte in the semi-darkness of the moonlit room, and, when convinced of her identity, cast herself upon her, burying her head in her lap, clinging to her with both arms, and began sobbing again.

Charlotte put her arms around the jerking body—terribly thin, like a skeleton covered with skin, and, pushing it over a little, slipped into the bed beside Tina. She held her, firmly and so close to her that her own body jerked a little too with each sob at first. She didn't say anything—just lay there in the dark, waiting for the sobs to quiet, but she was keenly aware. "This is Jerry's child in my arms," she thought. "This is Jerry's child clinging to me."

Gradually the convulsive intakes of breath grew farther and farther apart, the outlets of sound less violent. Finally speech was possible.

"Don't leave me," were Tina's first words.

"I won't till you're asleep."

"No, I mean don't leave me here in this place. Something terrible has happened."

"What's happened?"

"After you left me, that awful Miss"—one of the automatic jerks interrupted—"Trask came to my room—"

"And you had to tell her about the telephone call? Never mind. The truth is better. I'll explain it was my fault."

"No, no. I didn't tell her. I told her we just had an ice-cream soda. The terrible thing is what she told me. She told me my new nurse will be here tomorrow night!"

"Well, you may like her."

"No, I shan't! I shall hate and loathe and despise her! She'll club with Miss Trask and the doctors. You know she will. And what will I do next time when I *have* to speak to my father? Why must I have a nurse? Nobody my age has a nurse. I'll be so ashamed. It will be worse than playing pingpong. Oh, must I? Must I, must I?" Another jerk shivered her body, and a few seconds later still another. The sobbing was beginning again.

"Listen, Tina. Listen to me. Hold your breath, if you can, and listen. I know Doctor Jaquith. I'll talk to him tomorrow. I'll ask him to give you another trial without a nurse. I don't think you ought to have a nurse. I'll tell him so."

"You will? You dare to?"

"Certainly I will. Certainly I dare to. You leave it to me."

"All right. Why are you so good to me?"

"Lots of reasons. But one is enough. I'm trying to pay back a debt I owe. There was someone who was good to me once when things were looking black. Did you ever read a book called *Sara Crewe*?"

"No."

"Well, if you'll close your eyes and make your muscles all go limp, I'll tell it to you. That's better. Now pretend you're a little girl, for the story may be too young for you. Once upon a time—" . . .

Charlotte didn't lose consciousness until after one o'clock. She was afraid she'd wake Tina if she shifted her position, and didn't want to cut short by even a minute the probably never-to-be-repeated experience of holding Jerry's sleeping child in her arms.

Finally Tina stirred, lifted her head from Charlotte's shoulder, sat up, and gazed in silence at her face on the pillow.

"Hello! Know me?" Charlotte asked. Tina nodded emphatically. "You've had a fine sleep. If you'll let me get my arm out from under you, I'll go to my own room now."

"Oh, please don't go yet—" and as Charlotte made no move, "Let's lie spoon-fashion," Tina suggested and turned over, cuddling her back into Charlotte's warm curves, drawing Charlotte's arm beneath hers, across the shaft of her body. "This is the way Daddy and I used to lie when he'd put me to sleep when I was little. I'm too old for it now, Mother says. She says I'm too old to call him Daddy, too."

Doctor Jaquith's office over the First National Bank on Main Street had many features in common with his office in the old brown-stone-front dwelling house on Fiftieth Street in New York. Both locations had been selected because they were available at the time and convenient, and both had continued to meet his requirements. There were two rooms over the bank. The front one, in which Doctor Jaquith talked with his patients, closely resembled the mid-Victorian front parlor on Fiftieth Street. Its walls had been painted with the same mixture of Paisley shawl and lobster red, the New York housepainter having sent on all he had left of it.

At Cascade as in New York there was always a channel-coal fire burning in an open grate, whenever the weather permitted, not beneath a black marble mantel, however, but instead in a Franklin stove, with polished brass balls and trimmings.

This time, when Doctor Jaquith entered the room to shake hands with Charlotte, he came from the room behind as in New York. Again he drew up two chairs on either side of the open grate—a pair of slender-legged, short-armed Windsors painted black. The temperature outdoors was over eighty in the shade. There were no leaping flames on red walls today. The chairs faced instead a low-humming electric fan placed on the flat top of the stove between two large brass balls. Slowly, rhythmically, it turned its face from left to right, from right to left, dispensing its merciful breezes, *like some big fat squat idol with gold decorations sitting there,* thought Charlotte.

"Well, how did it go? Any flat tires? Any dented mudguards? Any overturned car? Any companion? And how many stops at hotels for rests en route?"

"None to everything. You're right. I'm not having a nervous breakdown, I guess, so, if you don't mind, I want to speak to you first about a matter which has nothing to do with my problem at all."

"Good! Guess you must have been looking out beyond that fly-speck since last we met. Tell me what you've been seeing out there on the horizon?"

"It isn't out on the horizon. It's right before my nose and it was shoved there. At dinner last night I was seated at the same table with a young girl by the name of Christine Durrance"—

and Charlotte described her. "I couldn't help but notice the child, she was so thin and ate so little, so after dinner—" And Charlotte related briefly the events that led up to Miss Trask's permission that Christine accompany her to the town. At that point she stopped. "Will you tell me about the child, please?"

"What shall I tell you?"

"All that you can. The child is terribly unhappy here and I don't think she's being treated wisely," she announced flatly.

"Nothing wrong with your courage now, I should say!"

Charlotte didn't even flush. "I suppose I do sound presuming. I'm sorry but the time is so short that I can't stop to be tactful. I might as well confess, first as last, that I'm even worse than I sound. Last night I deliberately ignored the doctor's orders for the child."

"That sounds serious." But his eyes were twinkling. "What order did you ignore?"

"I let her telephone her father. She hasn't been here long enough to lay down an ironclad rule like that! And the same applies to forcing her to play pingpong so soon. A game you can't play well can simply be torture. I was a child something like that myself once, so I understand her better, perhaps, than doctors and nurses who have only book knowledge."

"You do, do you?" Doctor Jaquith sat up straight. "Repeat that last sentence, please." She did so. "There's a lot in what you say," he said, his eyes shining, but with earnestness, not merriment now. "We haven't been very successful so far with Christine, I admit. Cascade isn't the right place for her at present, but we ought to make it the right place for her, or for any child who needs help in adjusting. We need someone with your experience *and* courage, to stand up to us and tell us a few things that aren't in the books. If you're ever hunting for a job—"

"Well, I'm not today, and my appointment with you this morning is for only a half-hour."

Doctor Jaquith ignored this remark. "Look here, I've got an idea! For a long time I've wanted to start a special foundation for children here at Cascade. It suddenly occurs to me that one way for you to distribute a little of that fortune of yours, now lying fallow, might be to help a lot of unhappy children out of a slough which you know something about yourself."

"Possibly," Charlotte replied, "but just now I'm interested in helping *one* child out of a slough, and I've got to talk fast. I'm here for just one purpose, which I haven't mentioned yet. Christine doesn't want a nurse, and I promised her I'd see if you would give her another chance. I've talked to Miss Trask and I fully realize your responsibility. I have a proposition to make. As you know, I haven't anything exactly pressing to take me home immediately. I wondered if *I* might not do instead of a nurse. I'll be responsible for her, and I'll promise not to break any more rules, without getting permission first. Oh, I suppose it's unusual and sounds impractical, but I thought perhaps you'd give it a trial—" She stopped, aware that her voice sounded far too earnest —almost entreating, in fact. She gave a short laugh as if amused at herself. "You see," she explained, "I happened to be assigned to the room next to Christine's," and in a deprecatory tone she told how she had chanced to hear the child sobbing in the night and had done her best to stop it. "So naturally," she shrugged, flushing slightly, for Doctor Jaquith was observing her with that piercing expression of his that saw straight through one's rationalizations, "and so naturally, I have become interested in the child."

"You don't have to tell me *why* you're interested in her. It's enough that you *are!* Go ahead. Try it. I'll cancel the nurse. Why, this is a wonderful stroke of good luck for Christine! She's sadly in need of something to make her feel important. One reason she won't eat is because it makes her an object of interest. You may get enough of it in two days, but even a short period of a friendship of her own with a distinguished ex-guest who blows in on her own power for a brief sojourn will do a lot for her positive self-feeling."

"If I'm to treat her intelligently, shouldn't I know some facts about her? I realize talking to one patient about another isn't done, but—"

"But when you cease to be a patient and become a member of my staff, it's different," he smiled. "Well, Miss Vale," he said in a professional tone, "there's nothing pathologically wrong with your patient. She's just one of those victims of unfortunate environment and bad habits of thought and action. We can't change the environment, but we hope to change the habits in time. The child's environment is controlled by a mother who has a closed mind toward all our theories here: I talked with her once. But she is ready to accept any plan we suggest which relieves her of the child, who has always been a thorn in her flesh, though the lady would strongly protest if she heard me say so."

"And the father? Should I know his attitude toward Christine?"

"Sympathetic and protective: probably too protective for Christine's good. But he speaks our language and will cooperate in every way. He's had some experience with nerves himself. The child is one of three girls. Much younger. Not well as a baby, extremely troublesome. Result, resentment felt not only by the mother, but by the older sisters who had to help take care of her. Result, the father has always defended the child against her sisters and her mother and world generally. Result, the child has developed an abnormal devotion for the father. Result, the mother has developed jealousy of the child. Result, the child's absence from home becomes desirable for all concerned. Result, I take the child here. It's not the right place for her, but it's not so bad as leaving her under the same roof with her mother. That should positively be avoided.

Anything you can do to give your patient self-confidence, Miss Vale, is desirable. If you can make her feel the pride of a friendship of her own, it will be of great value. I will make an appointment with Doctor Brine for you this afternoon and he will give you what other facts about the case he thinks necessary, and tell you what he'd like your attitude to be. And, by the way, *you* tell *him* a few things too. Pitch into him the way you did into me," he said, dropping his mock professional attitude and standing up. "Now let's talk about *you*. What sort of night did you have after your long journey?"

"I had an excellent night."

"In spite of being disturbed by Christine?"

"Oh, I didn't mind that," she replied, with exaggerated indifference, and stopped abruptly, flushing slightly, for he was observing her with such a quizzical expression. She decided to get down to the root of his suspicions, or knowledge, whichever it was. "There are some questions I'd like to ask *you*," she said.

"Fire away."

"How much do you know about Italy?"

"Not a great deal. I understand Mussolini has done away with the beggars," he parried.

"You know what I mean. How much do you know about my automobile accident in Italy and the man who was with me?"

"Not much."

"In New York you said he helped me out of one difficulty into another."

"That was just a guess of mine."

"And you don't know whether or not we ever met after the accident?"

"I rather thought you had."

"Why?"

"Well, a patient of mine who has a phobia about high places was arguing with me one day that it was a reasonable fear because cars did sometimes go over the edge, and she cited the example of such an accident happening to a man and woman who were in Ravello when she was there. They were stopping at another hotel near-by, and if I doubted her statement she knew the woman's name, though not the man's. In fact she told me the woman's name before I could stop her."

"And who told you the man's name?"

"Nobody. I don't know his name."

"You didn't know that Christine's father and I had met before?"

"No, I didn't know it." Though his brief statement was enough to convince Charlotte of its truth, his expression was added evidence, and the immediate change in his tone and manner proved he was completely taken by surprise, and far from pleasantly so. "If I had known it, I certainly wouldn't have advised you to come to Cascade at present. I had no idea you had ever met Durrance!" Charlotte had never heard his tone so hostile before. He walked up the room and down again in frowning silence. "Well, this puts a different light on the situation," he said, coming to a standstill in front of Charlotte.

"You mean you're not going to cancel the nurse?"

"I mean," he said in a crisp, clipped tone, "that I have taken on the child as my responsibility. *She* is my patient at present. Not *you*. You're cured. I must consider Christine's welfare."

"I'll do anything in the world for Christine's welfare," said Charlotte, standing up now, "and I'll leave it all to you to decide what is for her welfare."

"What might be for her *immediate* welfare might be anything but desirable for her ultimate good. I don't know anything about your relationship to Durrance." His voice was still stern "I don't know how emotionally involved you are with him. I can't work in the dark when there's a child in the picture."

"You won't have to. I'll tell you everything."

"Our time is up. I'll have to think it over. Come back tomorrow."

"But you'll cancel the nurse for tonight, won't you? Christine is waiting for me this minute outside, closed up in my car back of the bank, hoping with all the intensity of her age and nature and sickness that I'll bring her good news. If I succeed in my mission, we're going off in my car together to some little near-by town for lunch. If I fail, she'll have hysterics again—and eat no lunch and no supper either. You told me to speak out my opinion. Well, my opinion is, it would be cruelty not to cancel the nurse, and if you're thinking of Christine's welfare—" She stopped abruptly. Her voice was not only earnest, but fervent, and trembled a little.

The stern expression on Doctor Jaquith's face softened as he stood before Charlotte, seeing and hearing. He smiled. "Can this be the woman who only one week ago said to me in my New York office, 'Nothing interests me, all effort seems futile'? I'll cancel the nurse. You're accepted instead. But on probation."

CHAPTER TWENTY-EIGHT: THE DAUGHTER

When Charlotte left Cascade two weeks later, she did not return directly to Boston, but turned her car north. She was not alone this time. Tina was beside her, flush-cheeked, bright-eyed, sitting up very straight and feeling important. A group of a dozen or more stood on the porch and bade them good-bye.

At first the other guests at Cascade attributed Charlotte's attentions to Christine to pity, but when it became known that she had invited the child to take a trip with her in her car to the mountains and Canada, then they remarked upon it to Christine. "Did you know Miss Vale before?" "Aren't you a lucky girl?" For the first time in her life, Christine became an object of envy. She was going to do something somebody else would like to do!

The plan had been worked out under Doctor Jaquith's supervision. The edicts of good form had been strictly observed. Doctor Jaquith had written to Christine's father approving the plan; Charlotte had written to Christine's mother saying that it would give her great pleasure if her daughter, etc., etc.; Christine's father had replied that any plan for Christine approved by Doctor Jaquith he fully endorsed. He appreciated deeply Miss Vale's kindness, and enclosed was a check to cover Christine's expenses for the proposed tour.

Christine's mother replied to Charlotte, saying that it was very hard to be separated for so long from her little daughter, and especially difficult to entrust the child, who was "her baby," to a stranger, but self-sacrifice for one's children was a woman's first duty, and if Christine wanted to go she hadn't it in her heart to deny her little girl the pleasure.

There were no letters exchanged between Charlotte and J.D., although the identity of "the tall dark lady" had not long continued a mystery to him. There were no words exchanged either, although Christine talked with her father almost daily, at first, and with the doctor's consent. Charlotte was usually standing at her elbow, or waiting just outside the booth. J.D. knew she was near-by. Tina told him so. But never once did he ask to speak with her. He seemed to sense the fact that the resumption of their relationship on another basis depended on ignoring the first one.

The privilege of just standing by and catching occasional words and phrases as J.D. talked to Tina appeased Charlotte's gnawing craving to speak to him herself, and every time the wish to see him—to look deep into his eyes—started to rise up in her like a pain, she had only to look into Tina's eyes to get relief. If only she could keep Tina with her long enough, her longings for Jerry, flowing out like blood from a wound, might be absorbed by his child, and the flow stemmed finally.

At Charlotte's last conference with Doctor Jaquith, he had reminded her that she was still on probation. "And you'll continue to be, too, as long as I entrust you to a responsibility that is mine. I'm giving you the child, so long as I think it's good for her, but if for any reason I don't think it's the right environment for her—" He stopped. "Remember what it says in the Bible: 'The Lord giveth, the Lord taketh away,'" he warned, fastening her with his sharp drilling eyes.

"I'll remember. How does it feel to be the Lord?" Charlotte had asked him, with a smile.

"Not so very wonderful since the free-will bill was passed." Quick as a flash he replied. "Too little power."

The tour was a great success. Tina's improvement was marked and steady. She took to the mountain trails like the gangling moose-calf which she and Charlotte saw one day in the wild region north of Katahdin, running up the steep path in front of them, following close after its mother. Charlotte took to the trails too, following their blazed curves with something of the same delight as the steep paths winding over the hills around Ravello.

One day, seated in a sheltered spot on a bed of deer-moss just beneath the top of Mansfield (the first mountain they climbed), eagerly eating their midday lunch of thick sandwiches and common rat-cheese, Tina said, "You aren't old enough to be my mother, are you?"

"Good Heavens, Tina, of course I am! Why?"

"You don't act like it. You don't tell me what to do and what not to do, all the time. Yet a lady at the hotel last night thought you were my mother. I told her you weren't, but it's kind of hard to explain. I wish I didn't have to call you Miss Vale. It sounds funny—as if we didn't know each other very well."

She took a large bite of her ham sandwich. While she was still in the process of chewing it, Charlotte asked, "How would you like to call me some nickname, or special name of our own, as if we were sort of chums?"

"I'd love it! What special name?"

"My first name, Charlotte, has all sorts of abbreviations. You might call me Carlotta or Charlie or—a name I was called once in fun—Camille. Or, if you'd rather, Auntie or Tante, or even Aunt Charlotte. Think it over."

When Charlotte and Tina left Cascade, vague hopes and plans for the future were drifting through Charlotte's mind constantly, as unformed and shifting and shapeless as masses of mist at first. They didn't form into anything definite until after she had told Tina about the preposterous possibility which had occurred to her. It hadn't struck Tina as preposterous. It had started one of those rare displays of joy upon her face, like the northern lights Charlotte had thought, as she watched her cheeks flush pink and the happiness shoot upward to her eyes.

Not until their car had passed the line into Canada did Charlotte commit her project to paper. One evening, about two weeks after her embarkation on this second voyage of hers upon strange waters, seated in the writing-room of the Chateau Frontenac in Quebec, while Tina lay sound asleep in their bedroom above, she wrote to Doctor Jaquith and submitted her proposition.

It was a businesslike letter, formal, and free from sentiment. She had already suggested that Christine visit her in Boston for a few days upon their return. But now she proposed that she remain indefinitely or as long as her improvement continued.

Inasmuch as the child will be benefitting me, she continued, *by relieving the solitude of my life at present, I shall renumerate her very real services as my companion by paying her expenses, including the completion of her interrupted education, when she is physically fit to continue it. In fact, on no other basis am I willing to accept her services.* All matters affecting her welfare were to be under the supervision of Doctor Jaquith. Christine was to visit her parents whenever she felt inclined and to return home permanently at any time she desired. Doctor Jaquith was to submit the proposition to the parents, and act as arbiter if occasion arose. She herself was to continue to be "on probation."

The letter was as official as she knew how to make it, except for the very last word. She signed herself, *Sincerely, Charlotte Vale, Voyager.* Only Doctor Jaquith would get the full meaning of that last word and surmise her "untold want." Would he grant it? She awaited his reply with tremulous anxiety.

When Charlotte returned to Boston in late September with a tall, lanky 13-year-old girl in tow, it created much discussion. She announced to the family that the child was to remain with her indefinitely. She had run across her last summer. She was a protégée of Doctor Jaquith's. Her name was Christine Durrance.

Durrance? An odd name. Not even to be found in the Boston telephone directory! An odd proceeding too. Very odd, indeed! The child was not attractive. No one would take on so unpromising a specimen unless there was some good reason for it, according, at least, to the opinion of a certain lady who lived opposite the Vale house on Marlborough Street.

This lady had had a chat with Christine one day on the sidewalk. She had asked her her name, where her home was, and casually her age. That night she had unearthed an old Line-a-Day diary of hers, and had found it was 13 years ago that the

Vale house was closed for six months, while Charlotte and her mother were absent, taking a world cruise, presumably. This lady confided her discovery to a small luncheon-group of eight friends of hers. Of course they all flouted this scandalous implication. "Well, such things *do* happen in Boston sometimes."

This rumor reached Charlotte's ears finally. Rosa was the bearer of it. It didn't seem to disturb Charlotte in the least, Rosa reported. "So they say Tina is my own child, whom I've been hiding all these years!" Charlotte had remarked, and added with an exaggerated sigh, "Oh, if it were only true!" That kind of humor of Charlotte's, Rosa found extremely offensive.

Charlotte nipped the rumor in the bud by producing Christine's mother and sister. They appeared in November in response to Charlotte's invitation to Mrs. Durrance to come to Boston and inspect "her little daughter's" new quarters. She didn't include Mr. Durrance in the invitation because, she explained, it didn't seem wise yet to run the risk of retarding Christine's excellent progress in independence of her father. Charlotte asked a few people in to tea to meet Christine's mother and sister. Mrs. Grundy lost interest and looked to other fields.

The *For Sale* sign was removed from the Marlborough Street house soon after Charlotte's return from Canada. She coolly informed Lloyd that she had decided not to sell it at present. Much to her surprise, Tina had taken a fancy to it. Its pretentious grandeur—high ceilings, carved woodwork, stained-glass window on the landing, dark-oak dining-room with the built-in sideboard, even its heavy velvets and brocades, and oil paintings in wide gold frames, all appealed to Tina. "Oh my! What a simply wonderful house to live in!" she had sighed in admiration after her first tour of inspection.

"Would you rather live here than in a sweet little house in the country?"

"Oh, yes! I've always lived in the country, or sort of in the back yard of the country. I'd simply love to live in a great big elegant city house like this! I'd feel like a heroine in a book! And I've found a darling little room on the fifth floor in the back with a north window and a skylight that's perfect for a studio. It's full of trunks and boxes now, but I wouldn't mind those."

Doctor Jaquith said it was more desirable to feed Tina's starved sense-of-importance than her starved body, at present. If the Marlborough Street house made Tina feel like a heroine, then it must be retained. Her mother's former bedroom became Tina's. Charlotte stripped it and had it done over according to Tina's ideas. Light sky-blue walls, pale salmon-pink curtains made of stuff taffeta, very full and beruffled. There was a dressing-table with a full, beruffled skirt to match the curtains, and on the dressing-table a blue-enamel toilet-set, each piece embossed with Tina's monogram.

Charlotte moved down to the room across the hall, willingly enough now, which also she rehabilitated. Charlotte's old room above became June's. The friendship between Charlotte and June was resumed with fresh vigor in the fall. June had long wanted to have a room in town so as to be near her work. Incidentally, near her play too. June had a paying job in a Newbury Street gown shop; and frequent dates in the evening with young men from across the Charles River.

The Marlborough Street house underwent almost as great a change as Charlotte. Not only in appearance, but in nature and habits too. From a silent, gloomy introvert, preferring its own company, it became amiable, people-loving and extremely popular among all the younger members of the family; generous with its latchkeys, tolerant to tardy guests, hospitable to all who entered its doors, even the alley-cats and various friends of Tina's dogs who occasionally dropped in. It developed new habits, gave forth new sounds—jazz, giggling, laughing, barking of dogs, the rattling of a cocktail shaker. It emitted new smells—boiling fudge, burning logs, cigarette smoke, and something far less pleasant soon after one of Tina's white mice couldn't be found.

On a certain Saturday morning in early January, Charlotte was seated at her desk in her room between 9:00 and 9:30 in the morning, disposing of various routine tasks before starting out on the program of the day. She was sitting in a favorite position of hers, never allowed by her mother because unladylike—crossed legs, exposed ankles, also exposed knees in the narrow tailored skirt she was wearing this morning.

But Charlotte's ankles and knees could stand the test. Charlotte hadn't taken on an extra ounce more of the discarded layers of either cloth or flesh. Nor an extra ounce more of hair. She still wore it extremely close-cut, in spite of the tendency toward curls and covered ears. Her black sleek head, black far-separated brows, ivory-colored complexion with changing shadows in the hollows beneath her high cheekbones, and brilliant red lips, made her stand out in any group. She dressed extremely well. She had always been a severe critic of other women's clothes, and now that she could buy what she chose and pay what she chose, she applied the same severity to herself, patronizing only experts whose advice she could rely upon.

She reached for her Phillips Brooks engagement calendar now, and studied its crowded squares. Several unanswered invitations lay on the desk beside her. She'd have to regret the tea on the 16th, as it conflicted with a lecture given by the Parents' League which she'd just joined; she couldn't accept bridge on the 17th, for Tina had a private dancing-lesson in the early afternoon; and she'd have to decline even the regular meeting of the lunch-club next time. It was Tina's birthday. She had invited two little girls for luncheon and the matinée.

She turned the calendar to the week following. On the 18th she was giving a dinner and theater party to June and a list of her friends. On the 20th another dinner for Elliot and Lucy Prentice, Elliot's fiancée, a nice girl from Baltimore, around 30, good-looking, good family, fond of golf, and never guilty of saying anything shocking or original. In the space following the dinner for Elliot, Doctor Jaquith's name appeared, followed by the words: *Dinner and Night.*

This would be Doctor Jaquith's third Dinner-and-Night with Charlotte since she had made her contribution to Cascade for a separate building for children. The building was to be located beyond the big red barn around a curve in the road. In appearance it was to be an exact replica of Oldways and Newways. It was to be called Fairways.

On his previous visit Doctor Jaquith had brought large rolls of blueprints to discuss with Charlotte. The value of her gift was greatly increased by her interest and personal suggestions, he said. He had already asked her to be a trustee of the New Foundation. He also solicited Tina's suggestions. There should be animals in the big red barn, Tina said— horses, rabbits, sheep, cats, lots and lots of dogs, and accommodations for one's own dog if one had one. The plans were nearly completed now. Ground was to be broken as soon as the frost was out.

Charlotte laid down the engagement calendar and reached for the telephone. She must make an appointment for Tina with the dentist. Just as she lifted the receiver from its hook, the bell rang.

"Hello," she replied. "Yes, this is Kenmore 6611." Then almost instantly she heard J.D.'s voice, clear-cut, and vibrant, speaking straight into her ear.

"Hello, Miss Vale. Durrance speaking, J.D.—Christine's father. How is Tina?" It was the third time in the last few weeks he had called at this hour and gotten her personally. It was the one half-hour in the day when she always answered the telephone herself.

"Tina is very well. Upstairs at present in her studio. But I can call her."

"No necessity. Just tell her I called, as she hasn't called me for so long. And oh, by the way, I've just been talking to Jaquith. He thinks it's all right for me to drop in and see Tina any time now if I don't stay too long. So I thought I might fly up on a late afternoon plane some day, have dinner, and come back on the midnight train." Charlotte said nothing. "That is if *you* approve." Still she was silent. "Do you approve?"

"When did you think you'd come?"

"Well, down here in New York it looks like glorious flying weather today. How does it look up there?"

"It looks glorious up here, too!"

"That's great! What time do you have dinner?"

"Do you really mean you'll be here for dinner tonight?"

"Well, that was in my mind. Jaquith says it's all right," he repeated. "But if you'd rather I didn't—"

"Dinner will be at seven," she cut him off. "We'll expect you here at the house as soon as you can get here after landing. I'll tell Tina. Good-bye."

Charlotte's impulse was to rush upstairs to Tina immediately, announce her news, and squeeze her tight. It was Saturday and there was no tutor to witness her exuberance. Tina would be alone in her studio, busily occupied with her brushes, palette, and paints. But Charlotte controlled her impulse, and searched her mind for some casual excuse for interrupting the burning of genius. Tina had decided that the kind of heroine living in a grand city house she would most like to be was a budding young Rosa Bonheur. She was at present at work on a life-sized portrait of Hans, posed in a reclining position on one of the brocade-covered chairs moved up from the reception-room. Hans was Tina's amber-colored dachshund.

Charlotte had decided to go up with some puppy biscuit for
Hans when she heard familiar sounds on the back-hall stairs
announcing Tina's descent—the blurred pattering, like hail-
stones on hard ground, of Tina's two cocker spaniels, accompanied by the clatter of Tina's own hurrying footsteps on the
bare stairs.

"Came-eel!" she called, halting in the hall. "Came-eel!
Where are you? Upstairs or down?"

"In my own room," Charlotte called back.

A moment later Tina appeared, covered from her chin to her
knees in a chicory-blue artist's smock. She was still thin, but
no longer emaciated. She no longer wore bangs to her eyebrows, nor side-curtains to her collar-bone. Her hair was
brushed softly off her forehead, and fell in pretty curves
against her cheeks, barely covering the lobes of her ears. She
held Hans in her arms, like a baby, on his back, paws up.

"Hans has been sick to his stomach again! All over that
brocade chair! I'll clean it up. But he can't sit for his portrait
any more today, poor sweet darling baby. Can he stay with you
for a while?"

"Certainly. But I think he'll be happier down cellar by the
furnace in case he feels sick again. He's such a sensitive little
fellow it frightens him to be rushed out in a hurry." Tina
agreed and started for the cellar. "When you come back, I
want to speak to you," Charlotte added.

Five minutes later Charlotte announced, "Your father called
up this morning. He said he was fine. He thought he might fly
on and have dinner with us tonight."

Across Tina's face there passed a series of expressions in
this order—pleasure, perplexity, suspicion, and finally terror.

"What's the matter, Tina?"

"Why is my father coming?"

"Just to have dinner and see what sort of place you are staying in."

"Then why didn't he say so in his last letter? I know why he's coming! I know! He's going to take me home!" She threw herself down in the big chair near-by, and burst into violent crying for the first time in many weeks. "Oh, don't make me go! Don't make me! Don't make me!"

As Charlotte held Tina in her arms, reassuring and comforting her, she thought, *She wants to stay with me! By her own choice, Tina's mine. She's mine! She's Jerry's and mine!*

CHAPTER TWENTY-NINE: THE CRUCIAL TEST

By the time J.D. arrived at six o'clock Charlotte had quieted Tina's fears, dressed her with painstaking care in her sienna-brown velvet dress, and persuaded her hair into its prettiest curves and curls. Tina ran into his arms, so excited at first that she was unconscious of her hair, her dress, her pumps with "grown-up" heels, and her long, sheer silk stockings. But when her father held her at arm's length and exclaimed, struggling with a lump in his throat, "Well, well, can this be Tina?" she flushed with pleasure.

"Do I look nice?"

"You look lovely!" Why, Tina was pretty!

"Do you really like me?" Tina turned around slowly for him to see.

Looking over her head straight into Charlotte's eyes, "I love you," he said, through a blur of tears beyond his control.

Charlotte left them alone then. "Show him everything, Tina, from Hans's portrait to Hans himself, and your mice and the cats, and put on a record later and ask him to dance. I'm going to my room to rest for the next hour. Cocktails at seven, Mr. Durrance."

"Thank you, Miss Vale," formally the "Mr. Durrance" whom she addressed replied to his hostess, while Jerry added in a lower tone, discarding all disguise, "Thank you! Thank you! Thank you!"

Tina always had dinner with Charlotte and June, unless there was a dinner-party. There was no party tonight, but half a dozen sat down at the table. Charlotte had expected only June, but at three minutes before seven Nichols called up from Cambridge and asked if it would be all right if he should drop in for a bite. He'd just called the mater, and she was having one of her formal dinner-parties tonight. His car was at the door. He could be there in ten minutes if it was all right. Nichols' ten minutes, Charlotte well knew, meant nearer half an hour, and she had wanted everything to be especially nice tonight. "Of course it's all right, Nichols," she replied.

"If there's enough grub I might bring Chad along." Chad was his roommate.

"Of course there's enough grub." There was only one extra squab. She'd have to tell the cook to cut it in two.

So Tina sat between her two gods-among-men that night at dinner. The first time Nichols saw Tina, he had taken pains to be nice to the poor scrawny lame duck which Charlotte had picked up somewhere and brought in out of the wet. All the nephews and nieces had followed suit.

Nichols had continued to be more than just nice to Tina. He found it amusing to treat her as a bona-fide young-lady-friend of his for whom he had a decided penchant. Tina realized it was all a sort of game, but that a grown-up Harvard graduate would condescend even to notice her was enough to place him on a pedestal. Next to her father, Nichols was her ideal, Tina had recently confided to Charlotte.

Tina's expression was radiant tonight. So, too, was Jerry's, Charlotte noticed in swift, passing glances. His face had that same peculiar scintillating quality that it used to have in Italy.

Tonight there was nothing about him to suggest a dog between shafts pulling a cart.

Jerry and Nichols found much in common. J.D.'s voice was as animated as his expression, as he and Nichols leaned toward each other discussing the effect of the steel age on architecture. June also was obviously making an effort to appear intelligent to this attractive father of Tina's. Charlotte said little, just sat there quietly basking in the glow of the present moment, as proud of the impression Jerry was making on these two super-critical members of the family as if he belonged to her. Well, those three words he had just said over the top of Tina's head vested in her a right to some of the joys of ownership.

After dinner several of June's friends dropped in, and Charlotte withdrew to the library across the hall with J.D. and Tina. Her mother had always kept the library closed in the winter, because it was difficult to heat, but now a crackling cannel-coal fire burned in the iron grate which Charlotte had installed in the fireplace.

Tina usually went to bed at nine o'clock. Tonight it was nearly ten when Charlotte noticed her nodding, and remarked that she thought it was time for Hans, who Tina held in her arms, to be tucked in. Tina kissed her father good night and good-bye without tears and went upstairs, still holding the quivering Hans, followed by the two spaniels, and Charlotte in the rear.

"I always go up and get her started when I'm home," Charlotte had explained when she rose. "I hope you don't think I'm spoiling her, Mr. Durrance."

"Of course not, Miss Vale. But don't stay too long. I've ordered my taxi for eleven and I have several business matters to discuss with you."

"How long are you going to call her Miss Vale, Daddy?"

"What should I call her?"

"I don't know." She considered it for a moment, then appealed to Charlotte. "Would it sound funny if Daddy should call you my name for you, Camille?"

"I think it would sound very nice, indeed," laughed Charlotte, flushing as genuinely as if J.D. were as new an acquaintance as he appeared.

"All right," instantly he responded. "Don't stay upstairs too long, Camille."

When Charlotte returned, J.D. was standing by the mantel looking down into the fire. She stopped outside the door a moment and watched him unobserved. His face had lost its animation; the anxious lines had returned. The sinuous melody of a tango was issuing from the living-room now, muffled by shuffling feet. Without saying a word, Charlotte approached the mantel, coming to a standstill at the other side of the fireplace from J.D. He raised his head and looked at her, the anxious lines disappearing into the tender smile which stole across his features.

He shook his head slowly. "You've done a wonderful job for Tina," he said, sighing deeply.

"Why so sad about it?"

"Do you remember the last time we met, you referred to Sara Crewe?" Charlotte nodded. "And you said I was the nice rich old gentleman, though I was neither rich nor old?" Again Charlotte nodded. "Well, now *you're* the nice rich old gentleman, though you're neither old nor a gentleman." He paused and again smiled. "Indeed, you're young and lovely and a woman in the prime of life."

"What are you getting at?"

"Your job with Tina is finished. It's time for Tina to go home now."

"To go home! What do you mean? Doctor Jaquith says it would be the worst thing in the world for Tina to go home now."

"Well, it's time for her to leave here. She can't lean on you always."

"Oh, you think I'm too indulgent? I don't intend to keep it up. I've talked it over with Doctor Jaquith. Please sit down." He obeyed. Charlotte also sat down, facing him. "I know all these special tutors and special privileges aren't good preparation for life. But it's only for this year. Next fall I hope Tina can attend some day-school, and later go away to school where she will get good training in art. She has real talent you know. Surely Doctor Jaquith told you we're only waiting till Tina is physically stronger to begin treating her like a normal girl? He doesn't think she'll be firmly established until next fall. Didn't he tell you my plan to take her to Europe for six months?"

"Yes, he mentioned it."

"Listen, Jerry." She lowered her voice to a confidential pitch and leaned toward him, her eyes shining. "I want to start in March and take the southern route, stop off at Gibraltar, drop in at Majorca and climb up some of those darling little hanging gardens, have dinner at the Café de Paris at Monte Carlo, then go on down to Italy, take a car and spend a week or so in the vicinity of Ravello. I thought we'd do a lot of tramping. There's an old Benedictine abbey I'd love to show her not far from Ravello—"

"But, Charlotte—"

"I won't neglect the sights she ought to see—cathedrals, museums, and picture galleries, if that's an objection you're going to make."

"It isn't! Listen to me, Charlotte, please. The fact of the matter is, things have gotten pretty bad with me lately financially. Even Beatrice and Muriel have had to take jobs that are uncongenial."

"Why, I thought you understood! I thought Doctor Jaquith had made the business basis of our arrangement clear to you."

"Yes, he did, but that was only till next summer. No self-respecting man could allow such generosity to go on indefinitely."

"That's the most conventional, pretentious, pious speech I ever heard you make in your life, Jerry!" exclaimed Charlotte, her cheeks flushed. "Why, I simply don't know you!"

Jerry leaned forward, elbows on his knees, hands clasped. "But I can't go on forever taking, taking, taking from you, and giving nothing, darling," he pleaded.

Her anger vanished. "Oh, I know! Forgive me, Jerry. It's your pride, that's all." Her voice was as tender as if he were a little boy. "Just your silly, foolish pride. Let me explain. You *will* be giving. Don't you know that 'to take' is a way 'to give' sometimes—the most beautiful way in the world if two people love each other? Besides, Jerry, you'll be giving me Tina. Every single day *I'll* be taking, taking, taking and *you'll* be giving, unless of course, you let your precious little false god Pride interfere."

"But, Charlotte, the chief reason that looms before me why Tina shouldn't stay has nothing to do with my earning power and my pride, which," he added gently, "you so beautifully protect."

"Has Isobel begun to resent me?"

"Oh, no! Isobel blesses you every day of her life. You've lifted an enormous burden from Isobel's shoulders. In fact, Isobel believes you actually are an answer to prayer, sent by God Himself in response to her fervent pleadings when Tina first went to Cascade."

"Is it because of something Tina has said, then? Don't you think she's happy here?"

"Happy! I've never seen such a demonstration of happiness in my life, and as to what she said to me—she confessed to me upstairs that she thought she loved you almost as much as she did *me!*"

"Then what is the reason?"

"*You* are! Until today I didn't realize how much of yourself you're giving Tina. Here you are, a lovely woman in the prime of life, as I said, being monopolized by a child. Why didn't you marry Livingston?" he broke off. "I'll tell you why. I came along and ruined him for you, and now my child comes along and claims all your attention, when you ought to be giving it to friends of your own age, and so perhaps run across some man, some day, who will make you happy."

"So that's it!" Charlotte exclaimed, in a low tone charged with reproach. "That's it! 'Some man who will make me happy'!" she repeated with all the scorn of which she was capable. "Well, I certainly have made a great mistake! Here I have been laboring under the delusion that we were so in sympathy—so *one*—that you knew without being told what would make me happy. And you come up here and talk about 'some man'! And how too bad it is that your child should monopolize my time! Evidently you don't know anything at all about how a woman feels, or anyhow how *this* woman feels! Apparently you haven't the slightest conception what torture it is to love a man, as I've loved you," she brought out shamelessly, "and to be shut out—barred out—from all the things in his life important enough to worry him or to make him suffer! To be forever just and outsider and an *extra!*"

He started to speak, but she went right on. "When I thought there was a chance for me to squeeze into your real life, and be able to talk to you occasionally on some allowable basis, I was terribly happy, and fool enough to think you were happy too." Again he started to speak. "No; wait till you hear what a still bigger fool I was. Why, when Tina wanted to come home with me and stay, it was like a miracle happening—like my having your child; and I allowed myself to indulge in the fancy that both of us loving her, and doing what was best for her together, would make her seem actually like our child after a while. But no such fancy has occurred to you, I see! Again I've been just a great big sentimental fool! It's a tendency I have!"

She shrugged, her lips curling in self-derision, rose, and began attacking the open fire, thrusting the poker viciously into the smoldering hunks of coal, making new cracks and fissures out of which fresh flames spurted and sputtered. When she straightened and turned around, Jerry was standing facing her. She started to speak again.

"Wait a minute," he interrupted, and he took hold of both her arms just above her elbows. Pinioning them to her sides he held her straight in front of him an arm's length way. His strength had often been a source of surprise to Charlotte. Never had Elliot held her helpless.

Jerry was not angry, simply very much in earnest. "Now I know!" he said, looking straight into her eyes. For a moment she thought he was angry because she had hurled such reproaches at him. But she was mistaken. "Now I know you care," he said. "I wasn't sure why you were doing all this for Tina. I was afraid it might have been out of pity, or compassion, or for some high altruistic principle of Jaquith's. But there was no note of pity in your ridicule of me just now, thank God, nor compassion, nor altruism. You spoke from the depths of your own outraged feelings, and now I know you care. You care! You still care!" he reiterated. "I need no other proof than your scorn and derision—your sharp claws digging into me, trying to hurt me because I'd hurt you. So genuine! So like you! So like the wildcat in you I know and love and adore. Oh, everything shall be as you wish about Tina, and everything else too, for now I know, I know!"

Charlotte's indignation died down almost as quickly as it had burst into flame.

"Forgive me, forgive me, Jerry," she said, "for now *I* know, too." The proof of her knowledge was not alone his assurance about Tina, but his obvious joy. His voice, eyes, and whole expression were exultant. As she gazed back at him, a film of something like adoration replaced the sparks of anger that had flown up and flashed in her eyes. "Please let me go now," she said gently.

But he didn't let her go nor relax his stiffened wrists. Even the muscles of his face and neck were taut, as if it required all the strength he possessed to hold her way from him.

"It won't die—that something between us," he said. "Do what we will—ignore it, neglect it, starve it—it just won't die. Its resolve to live is stronger than the strength of either of us— than both of us put together. It's impossible to kill it. O Charlotte—" He slipped his hands slowly down her ams to her wrists.

June and her friends were still dancing in the living-room, they had changed the tango record. Now the primitive rhythm of a rumba filtered through the half-open door. As Charlotte gazed at Jerry, she saw that indescribable change come over his face which had always filled her with a sense of joy. His expression lost its tenderness, his mouth its gentle lines. She felt again the old sense of joy. But she mustn't give in to it. The beat of the rumba grew louder. Jerry leaned nearer. If she let him kiss her now, all her resolutions would be swept away. Her breakwaters were not yet strong enough to withstand any such wave as she knew was rising in them both. "Let go of me," she said, her voice a command now, pulling away with all her strength and twisting her wrists this way and that. There was a brief struggle.

Then suddenly Jerry dropped her hands. "Oh, all right, all right," he murmured, turned on his heel abruptly and crossed the room, halting before the booklined wall. He stood there with lifted head as if studying the titles of the books on a shelf a little above his eyes.

After a moment Charlotte followed him. "Listen, Jerry," she said earnestly addressing his back. "Doctor Jaquith knows about us. When he let me take Tina he said, 'You're on probation.' Don't you know what he means? I'm on probation because of you and me. He allowed this visit of yours, but it's a test. If I can't stand such tests, I'll lose Tina in time. And we'll lose each other. Don't you see? O Jerry, please help me."

He didn't turn or reply. She walked back to the fire and waited, gazing at his back. His shoulders were squared, his chin was up, and she knew he was getting his disrupted emotions into line and under control again. They did not speak for several minutes, but the protracted silence was veiled by music. Neither tango nor rumba now, nor the syncopated beat of jazz. June and her friends had stopped dancing. The pure exalted strains of Wagner's Prelude to *Lohengrin,* flowed into the room now, calming and uplifting.

When its last bars had disappeared into the void, Jerry turned and walked back to Charlotte. She glanced up at him. The tenderness of his expression was reinstated. Also there appeared on his face all those little indefinite lines, lights, and shadows of that unquenchable sense of play of his, which had the power to divest the most heartrending scenes of tragedy.

"What a woman! What a woman!" he said, shaking his head at her disparagingly. "She has an idea she can make a Galahad out of a Lancelot!" He gave a deep shrug. "Well, perhaps she can. Who knows? I'm putty in her hands. Perhaps she can. Anyhow, I'm going to let her try!"

This was the mood which Charlotte had known first and had always loved. "Oh, let's have a cigarette!" she exclaimed and passed him an open box.

He took one of the white shafts and placed it between his lips. She struck a match and held it to its tip, gave him the lighted match, and they repeated the intimate little ceremony that had broken down her self-control in that grubby restaurant outside Naples. Trivial as it was, and trite, again it struck down into the very core of Charlotte's emotions.

"O Jerry, isn't it simply wonderful to light each other's cigarettes from the same flame again?" she exclaimed. He didn't reply, just kept on shaking his head slowly back and forth, but looking at her so fondly that the negative gesture was another avowal. "And just think it isn't for this time only!" she went on; "that is, if you'll help me to keep what we have, if we both try hard to protect the little strip of territory that has been granted us. Any two people who share an important responsibility have to consult about it occasionally. Don't you see there'll be lots of problems that obviously I ought to talk over with you about your child?"

He stopped shaking his head then. "Our child," he corrected, with a whimsical smile.

She drew in her breath sharply as if he had touched a nerve. "O Jerry," she said when she could trust her voice. "Don't let's ask for the moon! We have the stars!"

A cursory outline of Olive Higgins Prouty's 1941 novel, *Now, Voyager*, suggests a fairly typical romantic melodrama. Charlotte Vale, homely and unhappy woman of unspecified "middle age," controlled by her wealthy and domineering mother, suffers a nervous breakdown. Through psychiatric care as well as a remarkable physical transformation, she begins a new life on a European cruise arranged by her sister-in-law, Lisa, where she both falls in love with a shipmate Jerry Durrance, and becomes the kind of sociable creature she has never been. Although Jerry is unhappily married, he is loyal to his wife, and their daughters, particularly the youngest, Tina, who adores her father and is resented by her mother (who evokes Charlotte's own mother). After the cruise, the two separate, agreeing that they will not see each other again, but will hold onto the memories of their love affair.

After she has returned to her hometown of Boston as a changed woman, and taken up her duties again as her mother's companion, Charlotte has the opportunity to marry. Now at this point, the reader would expect one of several developments: that Charlotte's shipboard romance has prepared her for this, the "real thing," a true love that will last forever, or that Charlotte knows she will never love anyone but Jerry, and his wife conveniently dies, leaving Jerry and Charlotte to raise Tina in a loving and supportive home. Charlotte does indeed end her engagement, for she prefers the memory of Jerry to the living reality of a man she does not really love. But ultimately what Charlotte chooses is her own freedom and autonomy.

Striking coincidences occur in the novel, but they do not facilitate the predictable "man and woman walk off together into the sunset" conclusion of much romantic fiction. After

Charlotte's imperious mother dies during a bitter argument with her daughter, Charlotte seeks refuge at Cascade, the same sanitarium where her transformation began under the care of Dr. Jaquith. There she meets Jerry's daughter Tina, also a patient at the facility, and she becomes her counselor, her nurse, and her "chum." In the end, Charlotte brings Tina to live with her. Jerry comes to see his daughter at Charlotte's house, and Charlotte insists to Jerry that they can never be romantically involved, but will always have a connection based on their devotion to the welfare of Tina. The story ends with one of the most memorable declarations of love and loss ever uttered: "Don't let's ask for the moon!" Charlotte says to Jerry in the last lines of the novel. "We have the stars!"

Many readers of the Feminist Press edition of *Now, Voyager* will likely come to the novel through the 1942 film adaptation, starring Bette Davis in one of the greatest roles of her career (and one of her favorites, as well). For these readers, it may be a surprise to learn how closely the film follows the novel, from the concluding words cited above, to large portions of dialogue, to the "two on a match" cigarette-lighting ritual that Paul Henreid (as Jerry) and Davis share. But for those familiar with the film version, as well as those who are discovering Charlotte Vale and Olive Higgins Prouty's story for the first time, *Now, Voyager* offers more than an ugly duckling tale or a heterosexual romance or a story of surrogate motherhood.

There is a paradox at the center of the novel, in that it simultaneously elevates and undercuts stereotypes about women's desires. On the one hand, *Now, Voyager* seems to offer up many clichés about femininity, the family, and heterosexual romance that have long been criticized by feminists. For example: Only with physical transformation—weight loss, make-up, a new hairdo, and fancy clothes—does Charlotte become desirable, and only when others respond positively to her does she begin to value herself. When mothers wield too much power (i.e., in the absence of the father, as in the case of Charlotte's mother, or with an indulgent father, in the case of Jerry's wife), their children have nervous breakdowns. Only when Charlotte achieves a break with her mother's authority, by falling in love with a man, is her transformation seemingly complete. Most of these clichés are stock elements of what has always been known derogatorily as "women's fiction"—narratives written for a female audience, and built upon "feminine" themes of beauty, love, and self-sacrifice.

An entire generation of feminist critics has challenged the bad reputation that women's fiction and its cinematic corollary, the "woman's film," have acquired. Within the romance and the self-sacrifice, beneath the emotion and the tears, there are powerful explorations, in these much-maligned genres, of women's understandings of who they are and who they want to be. From Tania Modleski's demonstration that women's fiction "contain(s) elements of protest and resistance underneath highly 'orthodox' plots (25)," to E. Ann Kaplan's definition of the "woman's film" as a genre that "addresses female spectators and resists dominant ideology (124)," feminist film and literary critics have demonstrated that women's fiction—most of it written by women, for women—deserves serious feminist attention.

And indeed, *Now, Voyager* reads much more convincingly as a story about self-discovery and awareness than as a conventional love story. Yes, Charlotte undergoes a physical transformation, but in the course of the novel, less and less attention is paid to her physical beauty and more is paid to her developing consciousness of the world around her. Yes, mothers are bitter and mean-spirited in the novel, but they are surrounded by other kinds of models of female support and nurturance—that between sisters (or sisters-in-law, as is the case with Charlotte and Lisa, the widow of Charlotte's brother, who scandalizes the family in her own way by marrying "too soon" after the death of her husband) and between friends (Charlotte and Deb, the friend she makes on the ship). While Charlotte's "mothering" of Tina certainly makes her a better mother than either Mrs. Vale or Isobel Durrance, the connection between Charlotte and Tina is built upon friendship and companionship, with the strong implication that this is an alternative to, not a substitute for, the mother-daughter relationship. The new Vale household includes not only Charlotte and Tina, but June, Charlotte's niece, who was once Charlotte's tormentor but finds in her transformed aunt a supportive and unique companion as well. And yes, Charlotte's love affair is transformative, but Jerry is hardly the romantic hero who is such a stock figure in so many romantic novels—he himself has had a nervous breakdown (a fact eliminated from the screen version), and he is of a distinctly lower social class than the upper-class Charlotte.

Now, Voyager was originally published in 1941 in both hardcover and paperback editions. The Feminist Press edition replicates the slightly abridged Dell pulp, as this was the version most widely (and perhaps avidly) read in the 1940s. *Now, Voyager* is the third of Prouty's five novels devoted to the Vale family of Boston (the others are *White Fawn* [1931], *Lisa Vale* [1938], *Home Port* [1947] and *Fabia* [1951]). Olive Higgins Prouty (1882–1974) was, at the time of the publication of *Now, Voyager*, a well-established, bestselling novelist. Prouty was a woman of privilege who married well. Throughout her adult life, Prouty struggled to fulfill her creative desires as a writer as well as her family responsibilities as a wife and mother. In Prouty's autobiography, *Pencil Shavings*, one of the manifestations of that conflict is how she views her writing in terms of gender. Shortly after her marriage to Lewis Prouty, she meets the editor of *American Magazine* where she will eventually publish a number of short stories. In response to the editor's query about what kind of stories she writes, Prouty replies: "Nothing requiring great knowledge. . . . Just little domestic things that I know all about" (126). Thirty pages later, Prouty quotes herself telling another editor: "There are two things I want to avoid in my writing—sentimentality and melodrama" (154). Prouty is self-deprecating when she makes this statement ("no doubt it sounded painfully priggish"), but these two citations suggest that Prouty was very much torn between two kinds of self-definition: a "writer" (i.e., serious and literary) or a "woman writer" (domestic and sentimental).

To most reviewers of Prouty's work, the "woman writer" was more visible than the "writer." The reviews of *Now, Voyager* were generally positive, except for a particularly negative review in the *New York Times*. The reviewer accuses Prouty of having written bad women's fiction, from its "genteel, gingerly smiling nicety," to its "pretentiousness," to the back-handed compliment that Prouty excels at describing Charlotte's clothes—"an important point which will reconcile many of her female readers" (Hauser 1941). This review was not typical, but even the positive reviews of the novel contain an implicit reference to what are presumed to be the limitations of "women's fiction." One reviewer calls the book "pleasantly substantial," as if this were a surprise (Ross 1941), while another notes that "Young people and women will like it" (Van Dyne 1941).

Some readers may be familiar with Prouty because of her patronage of Sylvia Plath. Prouty attended Smith College (1900–04), and she was the benefactress of a scholarship awarded to Plath in 1950. Prouty also provided financial and emotional support when Plath attempted suicide. Prouty financed Plath's stay at a psychiatric institution, and visited her often; she also took an active role in Plath's treatment ("Prouty was a meddler, but an informed meddler . . ." [Beam 154]). Unfortunately, whatever Plath's disposition was to her benefactress, she mocked Prouty in her autobiographical novel *The Bell Jar*, through the thinly disguised character of Philomena Guinea. Early on in the novel, Ms. Guinea's patronage leads Esther Greenwood (Plath's alter ego) to read one of her books in the town library (she notes, disingenuously, that "the college library didn't stock them for some reason"), and to mock her writing style (33). Not only, then, did Prouty herself struggle with her identity as a (woman) writer; readers of Prouty's fiction must also struggle with the crude image of a wealthy but untalented writer, put forth in one of the works most influential on generations of feminist readers. But Plath and Prouty had more in common than the scornful portrait of Philomena Guinea suggests, for Prouty too wrestled with demons and sought psychiatric care. Indeed, *Now, Voyager*'s exploration of breakdown and recovery stems at least in part from Prouty's own experiences.

Now, Voyager opens as Charlotte Vale, voyager, is exposed to one of her first tests. She is having lunch with Jerry, another passenger from the ship, during a day trip to Gibraltar. Jerry has left the table momentarily to send a cable. The day trip marks the first time that Charlotte has ventured out into the social world of the ship. The opening paragraph of the novel tells us what Charlotte sees and imagines, for she has read that there is snow in New York City. "It was difficult to visualize sheets of fine snow driving obliquely against façades, while sitting on an open terrace in the sun gazing at calla lilies in bloom bordered by freesia" (1). The description of Charlotte's appearance emphasizes that she wears her identity like her new clothes: "She sat close to the table, knees crossed beneath its top, one foot emerging encased snugly in light amber-colored silk and a navy-blue pump. She flexed the ankle up and down as if to convince herself it was hers" (1). This use of free indirect style—the capture of Charlotte's consciousness from both the "outside" and the "inside," thus demonstrating awareness of how she "looks," in both senses of the word—is one of the distinctive features of *Now, Voyager*. Throughout the novel, Charlotte is observed as she observes the world around her.

Immediately, Charlotte's conception of the weather difference between here and there, between North America and this sunny scene on the Mediterranean, acquires a particular form, that of a "drop-curtain", which not only allows Charlotte to distance herself from her surroundings, but also separates and shields her from who she was and who she is becoming: "It was difficult, too, to believe that the scene before her was reality. It was more like a drop-curtain rolled down between herself and the dull drab facts of her life" (1). The use of this image (in the first few sentences of the novel, no less) provides Charlotte with both protection and a means to understand herself. The theatricality of the curtain image evokes in the reader the sense of Charlotte as a player in a drama, pulling back the curtain to reveal different scenes from her past. For here, as throughout the novel, flashbacks are always introduced by way of an association, a connection, with what is happening in the present.

Through flashbacks in early chapters of the novel, we learn about Charlotte's domineering mother and about Dr. Jaquith's role in Charlotte's recovery. In particular we learn about the one love affair Charlotte ever had. As a young woman, on a boat cruise with her mother, Charlotte fell in love with Leslie Trotter, a ship's officer. Charlotte's mother disapproves, and convinces Leslie to end the relationship. In order to make her point, Charlotte's mother, at the end of their trip, insists on taking Charlotte to the neighborhood where Leslie's family lives, as if to rub her daughter's nose in the reality of the inferior social class with which she has dared to mingle.

While the flashbacks have an expository function, they also serve to underscore the links between the past and the present. For if Jerry is the obvious substitute for Leslie Trotter, complete with inferior class credentials (Charlotte notes early on that her mother would disapprove of Jerry), he is also a kindred spirit to Charlotte. After an evening spent together, Jerry returns to his stateroom (a shared, inside stateroom that emphasizes the class difference) and Charlotte to hers. A description of Jerry's unhappy life with an unpleasant wife (also in free indirect style) is followed by the continuation of Charlotte's flashback to Leslie, suggesting the common bond between Charlotte and Jerry as observers of their lives.

The epigram to *Now, Voyager* is from Walt Whitman: "The untold want, by life and land ne'er granted, / Now, Voyager, sail thou forth, to seek and find." Dr. Jaquith has given Charlotte the poem typed on an index card, and she reads it in chapter six, when the painful conclusion of her affair with Leslie Trotter is presented to the reader. Interestingly, in the preceding chapter—when we begin to discover the common bonds between Jerry and Charlotte—he too is defined as a voyager. Jerry is reading *The Education of Henry Adams*, and when, in his stateroom, he finds his place: "These words flashed up at him at the beginning of the next paragraph: 'Thus he found himself launched on waters he had never meant to sail'" (42). In the space of two chapters, then, the flashback to Charlotte's past with Leslie Trotter creates a connection between Charlotte and Jerry that is far more complex than simple romantic attraction. Jerry is not just a replacement for Leslie Trotter; he is also a voyager like Charlotte. And then, when Charlotte tells Jerry about her time spent at Cascade, another connection between the two is revealed: he tells her that he, too, had a nervous breakdown (though he couldn't afford to go to Cascade).

Much of Charlotte's growing awareness is conveyed to the reader by references in the novel to Charlotte's time at Cascade, but especially to the wisdom and caring of Dr. Jaquith. While Dr. Jaquith is not a psychoanalyst and not a

Freudian, he is a psychiatrist. His central role in the novel might well evoke the feminist critique of psychoanalysis that emphasizes the extent to which the central relationship of psychoanalysis, between (male) doctor and (female) patient, reproduces gendered power relationships, as well as the tendency of psychoanalysis to reproduce normative notions of femininity. Dr. Jaquith is the "good father" who takes the place of the "evil mother." Yet the cure initiated by Dr. Jaquith is a far cry from the stereotypical image of an all-knowing doctor who forces the female patient into the socialized mold of femininity. Throughout the novel, Dr. Jaquith's plan of treatment is defined as a combination of several important principles: He believes in the conscious exercise of free will ("He said he'd gladly help her learn how to use her free-will [it would require some study], but *she'd* got to do the using, and apply it to everything" [51]). He urges his patients to trust in actions (*"Ignore sensations. Discount emotions. Think, act, feel, in this order. Then thumb your nose at what you feel."* [52–53]). And he views independence as a vital goal of treatment ("Dr. Jaquith would be proud of her this morning. Here she was alone, making her own decisions, her own mistakes too, perhaps, but afraid of nobody" [117]).

The most dramatic and succinct definition of Dr. Jaquith's philosophy comes late in the novel, when Charlotte visits the doctor in New York City after she has experienced a recurrence of the symptoms that led to her initial breakdown. The timing of this encounter is quite interesting, for Charlotte fantasizes about calling Jerry before her appointment with Dr. Jaquith, and when she does call Jerry's office, she discovers that he has just left. Charlotte goes to the train station, hoping for a chance encounter. Jerry does indeed appear, with his family in tow, and Charlotte observes them from a distance; the scene embodies Charlotte's own perception of herself as a complete outsider to this scene of family life (if not wedded bliss).

How appropriate, then, that when Charlotte meets the doctor—the other man in her life—he challenges her assumptions about family and marriage, in what is one of the most remarkable feminist statements in the novel: "You say you'll never marry, *therefore* will never have a home of your own, a child of your own, or a man of your own. Good Lord! What are you going to do with all that money of yours? Why, you can have a home of your own, which all your brothers and sisters, and nieces and nephews, and friends, and friends' friends will flock to in hordes, if you *want* to. No man is necessary for that in your case" (218). Dr. Jaquith continues to enumerate the ways in which a man is just not necessary in Charlotte's life. But, he says, "some satisfactory substitute" must be found for the single woman's "sex instinct" (218). Charlotte contemptuously refers to "sublimation" as repulsive, as "something false and artificial instead of the real thing" (219). For Dr. Jaquith, such an assumption about sublimation is as ridiculous as Charlotte's notions about the importance of a man in her life, and he proceeds to tell her that he actually prefers his single life, and his attendant devotion to his work. To follow the novel's own conclusion, the stars are not necessarily a (poor) substitute for the moon; they may well be desirable in their own right.

It is tempting, perhaps, to dismiss Dr. Jaquith and his sound, proto-feminist advice, as pure fantasy. Here it is useful to look at the connection between the novel and the life of its author. Autobiography may only go so far in "explaining" a novel, but in the case of Dr. Jaquith and Cascade, there is a direct correlation between Olive Higgins Prouty's experiences and those of Charlotte. Prouty gave birth to four children, two of whom died at young ages, and eventually, in the late 1920s, Prouty had what she herself calls a "nervous breakdown," her second (as a young child she was also diagnosed as having had a "nervous breakdown"). As she describes in her memoir,

Pencil Shavings, Prouty spent time at an institution similar to Cascade, under the care of a psychiatrist, Dr. Riggs, who evokes Dr. Jaquith.

Interestingly, Prouty had to contend with the conflicting opinions of two psychiatrists. One, recommended by her family doctor, insisted that the cause of the "breakdown" was the deaths of the two children at very young ages (even though, as Prouty herself pointed out, nearly two years had passed since the death of the second child when she had her breakdown [179]). This psychiatrist advised Prouty to regard her writing as a pastime, and suggested that she stop writing for a period of time (180). In other words, this man's solution for Prouty confirms the worst stereotypes of psychiatric care: be a wife and a mother, not a writer.

In contrast, Dr. Riggs told Prouty to get back into writing immediately, and to find the proverbial "room of her own"—a rented room away from the family home where she could write five days a week, three or four hours a day (181). Now it will come as no surprise that a psychiatrist in early twentieth-century America would downplay Prouty's writing career for the sake of what was presumably her first responsibility, her home. What is surprising is the advice of Dr. Riggs—not to mention the fact that despite her feelings of guilt about her writing, Prouty took his advice. After describing a number of the rooms in which she pursued her writing, from a hotel room to a clubhouse to a beachside inn, Prouty says that after an hour or so, "there would steal over me that feeling of detachment from my own personality and my own problems, so conducive to writing about another's personality and problems" (183).

This description of the connections between physical separation, solitude, detachment, and the process of writing, also seems an appropriate description of Charlotte Vale. Of course Charlotte does not become a writer, but she becomes a thoughtful observer of her own life and of those around her.

Charlotte's growing awareness offers a deeply moving portrait of a woman who experiences the various ramifications of socially acceptable femininity from a critical vantage point. Charlotte is defined by her developing perception of the world, by how she "reads" the life going on within and around her. Early in the novel, after her first encounter with Jerry, Charlotte sits at her dressing table and looks at her profile as it is reflected in another mirror across the room: "The profile was looking away from her which gave her the odd sensation of gazing at someone else. So *that* was how she looked! For years she had avoided all such painful speculation and shunned mirrors" (10). In looking at herself, Charlotte may well see the transformed woman she has become, but Charlotte's gaze never detaches completely from that sense of stealthy observation that comes from years of watching others. Charlotte is always conscious of herself as playing a part, trying hard to do what she has observed others doing. This is a strategy of fitting in, but it is also a way of calling attention to the fact that appropriately feminine, social behavior is indeed a part one learns to play. Gradually, as per Dr. Jaquith's instructions, Charlotte not only "performs," but becomes the stage manager of her own life (late in the novel Dr. Jaquith tells her the she is the stage manager, and he has been the director—and is now the ex-director [218]).

Charlotte is an avid reader. (One of the symptoms of her first nervous breakdown was a lack of interest in reading). When Charlotte hears a knock on her stateroom door on board the ship, we are told that her knowledge of knocks "was confined to the stage, the screen, and the written page" (78). This provides the occasion for a description of Charlotte's reading habits, which are sophisticated and far-ranging (Flaubert, Boccacio, Bertrand Russell, and Havelock Ellis). But Charlotte's readerly activities are not always indicative of the gap between hands-on, experiential knowledge and "book" knowledge. When she awakens after the night spent with Jerry, aware of what a new experience this is for her (while it is obvious that Charlotte and Jerry are lovers, sexual encounters are never directly presented in the novel), we are told: "She lay perfectly still, keenly aware of all the details, but, oddly enough, unamazed, unperturbed, as calmly curious as if she were lying in bed at home reading of this situation in a novel" (101). As with looks and performances, Charlotte's voracious reading comes to represent not her exclusion from the world, but rather her unique perspective on it as she becomes the narrator of her own life. Indeed, throughout the novel, what is most striking about Charlotte's journey is her desire—her sexual desire, certainly, but also to tell her story, to see herself clearly, to observe herself and the world around her. Yes, love and romance are catalysts, but ultimately it is Charlotte's story, and hers alone, that is central.

While Charlotte's independence and autonomy are remarkable, this is not to say that there are no limitations to this view of liberation. Charlotte is wealthy, a child of privilege, and if both Leslie Trotter and Jerry Durrance are seen as her class inferiors, it is worth pointing out that they are middle-class; only in an aristocratic context could they be seen as social pariahs. The risk of making Charlotte's developing consciousness the center of the novel is that the world created in *Now, Voyager* is ultimately a very insular one—wealthy and white. Charlotte's dealings are largely with the members of her family or those of her social class, and during the ship voyage, "locals" are for the most part either invisible or supposedly comic ethnic clichés, like the chauffeur who leaves Charlotte and Jerry stranded in a wrecked car. There is the odd reference to the gathering crisis in Europe (the novel was first published in 1941, and appears to be set just a few years earlier), but these references are peculiar and few and far between. One, which appears in the hardcover edition, when Charlotte and

Jerry talk with two Germans in Italy ("Nazis they called themselves" [151]), is excised in the pulp edition.

Because of this insularity, the few occasions when Charlotte does take notice of those who are not a part of her world are notable but fleeting. Yet there is one figure of another class who does function more centrally, and that is Dora Pickford, the nurse hired to take care of Mrs. Vale in Charlotte's absence. Dora has a quick wit and she treats Mrs. Vale as a specimen she knows all too well. Charlotte comes to respect and admire Dora, and at one point sees her as a model worth emulating: "The family never had seen anyone quite like Dora before. She treated them as if they and she were on exactly the same level. It didn't seem to occur to Dora that there was any reason for her to feel inferior to anybody in the world. Her good-humor flowed out unobstructed by envy or self-consciousness. To Charlotte Dora was a living example of the kind of nature which Doctor Jaquith had been holding up to her as a desirable pattern" (163). This mention of Dora may well be yet another manifestation of class privilege (an aristocrat's bemused observation of a competent professional who doesn't know she is a social inferior).

On the one hand, appearances of women from other social classes are very brief, and thus they could be seen merely as contrasts that serve ultimately to accentuate the world of privilege of the novel. But on the other hand, the fact that these women appear at all in the novel allows—however briefly—a sense of another world beyond the Vale universe. If I find Dora a magnificent character, it is perhaps largely because she was played in the film by one of the great character actresses in Hollywood, Mary Wickes, in the kind of role for which she was well known—the smart, sassy, "homely" (by Hollywood standards) sidekick, truth-teller, best friend, or school principal. My admiration for Mary Wickes and Dora notwithstanding, I came to the reading of Prouty's novel through the film adaptation, but this does not mean (to follow a tired cliché) that "the novel (or the film, for that matter) is better." The morphing of Dora and Mary Wickes may well be a function of the film adaptation, but it may well also be the case that Prouty's novel and the Hollywood "woman's film" provide an opportunity to read across media in productive and interesting ways. As I've noted, those familiar with the film will perhaps be surprised at how much dialogue was lifted directly from the novel. Although the narrative structure of the novel and the film are different, and there are some other significant changes (Jerry's business failures and his mental breakdown are erased from the film; the class differences between Charlotte and Jerry are downplayed; the cruise is set in Latin America and not in Europe, which was by then at war), in general, the film follows the novel very closely.

Prouty's best-known novels, *Now, Voyager* and *Stella Dallas,* are those that were adapted to the screen. Prouty was suspicious of adaptation, as are many writers, but she also objected to any kind of publicity, perhaps fearing it might jeopardize the delicate balance she attempted to maintain between work and home. Prouty's professional writing career began with short stories published in *American Magazine,* and her first novel, *Bobbie, General Manager* (1913), was based on a collection of those stories. The publisher planned lavish publicity, including the appearance of the name of the author and the novel in electric lights in New York City. Prouty objected to the tactic. Yet her greatest difficulty was with the many adaptations that were made of her 1923 novel, *Stella Dallas* (which was serialized in *American Magazine*). First the novel became a stage play, in which Prouty was actively and not particularly happily involved; then, a silent film, which she disliked, then a sound film (starring Barbara Stanwyck), which she also disliked. Finally, without her permission or her knowledge, the novel became a radio soap opera, and eventually a "sequel" was created for the radio, which she did not write and which she detested. Prouty would have undoubtedly disliked the 1990 adaptation, *Stella*, starring Bette Midler.

Warner Brothers bought the movie rights to *Now, Voyager* within a month of its publication (Allen 17–18). Prouty was far more satisfied with the adaptation of *Now, Voyager* than with the various adaptations of *Stella Dallas* some years before, though she still declined the offer to go to Hollywood for the premier of the film. Prouty had proposed some of her own ideas as to how the novel should be adapted to the screen, including the use of silent, black-and-white scenes for the flashbacks and Technicolor for the present-tense scenes: "The action of the talking picture would pause, the scene would fade, and Charlotte's memory would be portrayed by a silent picture scene" (cited in Behlmer 166). Producer Hal Wallis said that Prouty's suggestions gave him "visions of the entire audience moving quite rapidly into the street" (104). The adaptation was assigned to Casey Robinson and Prouty was invited to comment on his script. Prouty describes covering all available space on the script with comments and suggestions. While most of her suggestions were unheeded, she recalls, in her autobiography, was particularly satisfied with how she aided the portrayal of Claude Rains as Dr. Jacquith, and she noted that the character of Tina "coincided with my conception of the character" (Prouty 198).

An odd detail is singled out by Prouty for particular mention as a violation of her novel. The film opens with exterior shots of the Vale home, and we see the name "Vale" on a brass plaque. About this detail, Prouty said: "No such residence with pillars exists on Marlboro Street in Boston, and names on brass plaques are confined chiefly to doctors" (198). Much to her disappointment, the brass plaque remained in the film. This seems a silly detail, but it speaks to the dislike and distrust Prouty had, not only of the "adaptation" of her novels to other media, but also, and perhaps especially, to their popularization. In upper-class society, everyone would have known who the Vales were; there would be no need for such a vulgar display as a name plate. That this is such a small detail—merely a pragmatic device to announce the Vale name to the viewer—is precisely the point; Prouty was suspicious of anything that suggested her work was being "popularized." Prouty's anger at the vulgar display of the brass name plate in the film suggests her own snobbery, her annoyance at those so unfamiliar with the world of privilege that they require bold announcements that would never be tolerated among the wealthy. Prouty's snobbery is further suggested by her description of the sales of *Now, Voyager* as respectable (though not as strong as for her previous novel, *Lisa Vale*), until she realized that more than half of the copies sold were the Dell edition—"those paper-covered books sold in drugstores and railroad stations at 25 cents a copy" (199). "No wonder my sails hung limp," she concludes. This is a curious paradox; Prouty was a bestselling novelist, yet she objects to the popularizing of her work in any form.

However closely the film follows the novel, what the film version brings to the novel is Bette Davis's incarnation of Charlotte Vale. The film retains the emphasis on Charlotte's transformation. Paul Henreid, as Jerry, is a romantic lead, but there is no question but that this is Charlotte's—and Bette Davis's—film. Our first view of Davis in the film is as a pre-transformation Charlotte, and thus the film engages the spectator in a before and after game, where the heroine not only becomes beautiful, but becomes *Bette Davis*. The question of beauty is a bit complicated in the film by Davis's screen persona, for she was never considered a "typical" Hollywood glamour queen. In other words, Davis brought a certain authenticity to the role, emphasized by the parallels between the actress and the character of Charlotte Vale. Producer Hal

Wallis noted in his autobiography that "she had been an awkward, shy girl who broke free of a dominating mother and a strait-laced background to become an attractive and appealing woman" (104). In a more general sense, the complex and multifaceted star image of Bette Davis, as constructed through publicity, fan magazines, and biographies, inflects the character of Charlotte Vale. If Bette Davis "is" Charlotte Vale, the connection is created not only through performance but through the pre-existing star image.

Charlotte's voyage of self-discovery in the film is shaped by Bette Davis's reputation as an independent star and an unconventional woman (see Mayne 1993, chapter 6). *Now, Voyager* is a classic in feminist film studies, and feminist discussions of the film have examined the ways in which female stars can be seen as "authors" of their own images, the capacity for the "woman's picture" to suggest feminist possibilities, and the various means by which Hollywood cinema speaks to women's desires in contradictory ways. Lea Jacobs speaks eloquently to the appeal of the film for feminist audiences: "Tina, the stars, they all serve as replacements for the man, yet the fact remains that Charlotte refuses the man. In a gloriously perverse gesture the narrative does not bring Charlotte's desire to fruition and an even more perverse sub-text would lead one to suspect that she likes it that way" (103). At the same time, Bette Davis's star image, and in particular her activities on behalf of the war effort, can work to deemphasize the themes of autonomy in the film. The film is as removed from the context of World War II as the novel is, but Bette Davis's activities on behalf of the war effort at the time of the release of *Now, Voyager* can be seen to underscore the theme of self-sacrifice expected from women at the time. Erin Meyers notes that Davis sponsored a contest for readers of the fan magazine *Photoplay-Movie Mirror* in which they were asked to submit stories about the sacrifices women make during the war. The winning responses were published in the November 1942 issue, accompanied by a photograph of Davis that appears to be from *Now, Voyager*. The story contest served as publicity for the film, and "recuperates Davis's independent woman image into standard modes of femininity" (12).

Through the persona of Bette Davis, the film offers contradictory ways of understanding a woman's desire for independence, and the novel—whether read through the film or for the first time—offers a vivid portrait of a woman struggling to live her own life. Charlotte Vale learns how to "play the part" of an attractive woman, but she also learns how to tell her own story, and how to embrace the multitude of stars instead of the single entity of the moon.

Judith Mayne
The Ohio State University
June 2004

Notes

Thanks to my research assistant, Clarissa Moore; and to Terry Moore. Thanks also to Jean Casella for her thoughtful editing.

1. Influential feminist analyses of the film include those by Britton, Doane, Jacobs, Kaplan 1992, LaPlace, and White.

Works Cited

Allen, Jeanne Thomas, Editor. *Now, Voyager*. Wisconsin/Warner Brothers Screenplay Series. Ed. Tino Balio. Madison, Wisconsin and London, England: University of Wisconsin Press, 1984.

Beam, Alex. *Gracefully Insane: Life and Death Inside America's Premier Mental Hospital*. New York, N.Y.: PublicAffairs, 2001; rpt. 2003.

Behlmer, Rudy. *Inside Warner Brothers (1935–1951)*. New York: Viking Penguin, 1985.

Britton, Andrew. "A New Servitude: Bette Davis, *Now, Voyager*, and the Radicalism of the Woman's Film." *CineAction* 26/27 (1992): 32–59.

Doane, Mary Ann. *The Desire to Desire: The Woman's Film of the 1940s*.

Bloomington: Indiana University Press, 1987.

Hauser, Marianne. "Fortunate Cruise." Book Review. *New York Times Book Review* [New York] 30 November 1941: 32, 34.

Jacobs, Lea. "*Now, Voyager:* Some Problems of Enunciation and Sexual Difference." *Camera Obscura* 7 (1981): 89–109.

Kaplan, E. Ann. *Motherhood and Representation: The Mother in Popular Culture and Melodrama.* London and New York: Routledge, 1992.

———. "Mothering, Feminism and Representation: The Maternal Melodrama and the Woman's Film 1910-1940." *Home Is Where the Heart Is: Studies in Melodrama and the Woman's Film.* Ed. Christine Gledhill. London: British Film Institute, 1987. 113–37.

LaPlace, Maria. "Producing and Consuming the Woman's Film: Discursive Struggle in *Now, Voyager.*" *Home Is Where the Heart Is: Studies in Melodrama and the Woman's Film.* Ed. Christine Gledhill. London: British Film Institute, 1987. 138–66.

Mayne, Judith. *Cinema and Spectatorship.* New York and London: Routledge, 1993.

Meyers, Erin. "How to Get Bette Davis Eyes: Star Performance and the Construction of FemininitY." Seminar paper. Dept. of Women's Studies, Ohio State University, 2004.

Modleski, Tania. *Loving with a Vengeance: Mass-Produced Fantasies for Women.* New York: Methuen, 1982; rpt. 1984.

Plath, Sylvia. *The Bell Jar.* New York: Bantam Books, 1971; rpt. 1972.

Prouty, Olive Higgins. *Pencil Shavings.* Worcester, Mass.: Commonwealth Press and The Friends of the Goddard Library, 1961; rpt. 1985.

Ross, Mary. "Fiction of the Winter Season." Book Review. *New York Herald Tribune* [New York] 26 October 1941: Books: 8.

Van Dyne, Catharine. "*Now, Voyager.*" *Library Journal* 66 (1 October 1941): 841.

Wallis, Hal, and and Charles Higham. *Starmaker: The Autobiography of Hal Wallis.* New York: Macmillan, 1980.

White, Patricia. *Uninvited: Classical Hollywood Cinema and Lesbian Representability.* Bloomington: Indiana University Press, 1999.

A daring new series uncovers the forgotten queens of pulp—and subversive new viewpoints on American culture

Femmes Fatales: Women Write Pulp celebrates women's writing in all the classic pulp fiction genres—from hard-boiled noirs and fiery romances to edgy science fiction and taboo lesbian pulps.

Beneath the surface of pulp's juicy plots were many subversive elements that helped to provide American popular culture with a whole new set of markers. Much more than bad girls or hacks, women authors of pulp fiction were bold, talented writers, charting the cultural netherworlds of America in the 1930s, 1940s, 1950s, and 1960s, where the dominant idiom was still largely male, white, and heterosexual.

The pulp fiction revival of the last decade has almost entirely ignored women writers. Yet these women were sometimes far ahead of their male counterparts in pushing the boundaries of acceptability, confronting conventional ideas about gender, race, and class—exploring forbidden territories that were hidden from view off the typed page. The novels in the Femmes Fatales series offer the page-turning plots and sensational story lines typical of pulp fiction. But embedded in these stories are explorations of such vital themes as urbanization and class mobility, women in the workplace, misogyny and the crisis of postwar masculinity, racial tensions and civil rights, drug use and Beat culture, and shakeups in the strict codes of sexual conduct.

The Feminist Press at the City University of New York is proud to restore to print these forgotten queens of pulp, whose books offer subversive new perspectives on the heart of the American century.

For more information or to order books, call 212-817-7925.

A double romance—
with the boy next door and the career in the gleaming tower

SKYSCRAPER
Faith Baldwin

288 pp., $14.95 paperback, ISBN 1-55861-457-5

◆ ◆ ◆

A tale of terror and treachery as a mother searches for her daughter

BUNNY LAKE IS MISSING
Evelyn Piper

240 pp., $12.95 paperback, ISBN 1-55861-474-5

◆ ◆ ◆

Small-town girls and big-city passions collide on the brink of the
1960s

THE GIRLS IN 3-B
Valerie Taylor

232 pp., $13.95 paperback, ISBN 1-55861-462-1

◆ ◆ ◆

Classic noir—the basis for the 1950 film with Humphrey Bogart

IN A LONELY PLACE
Dorothy B. Hughes

272 pp., $14.95 paperback, ISBN 1-55861-455-9

◆ ◆ ◆

Thrilling WWII espionage with a hard-boiled heroine

THE BLACKBIRDER
Dorothy B. Hughes

288 pp., $12.95, paperback, ISBN 1-55861-568-0